THE MASTERS REIMAGINED 2

A Speculative Fiction Anthology

BLUE BEECH
PRESS

5923 Kingston Pike #161, Knoxville, TN 37919

Front and back cover designs by Charles A Cornell

Cover images licensed from Shutterstock.com

The Masters Reimagined Volume 2: A Speculative Fiction Anthology, Second Edition (PRINT) MAY 2023

ISBN Print (PB): 9781960974020

ISBN Ebook: 9781393251767

BLUE BEECH PRESS

ABOUT THE ALVARIUM
EXPERIMENT

The Alvarium Experiment is a consortium of writers working "independently together" to create short stories based on a central premise. The name comes from the Latin *alvarium*, meaning beehive, a colony working towards a common goal for the benefit of all involved.

The Masters Reimagined 2 is the fifth anthology published by this Hive Mind of award-winning and bestselling authors. Stories from the first, *The Prometheus Saga*, won seven literary awards including five prestigious Royal Palm Literary Awards from the Florida Writers Association. The subsequent anthologies—*Return to Earth, The Masters Reimagined, and The Prometheus Saga 2*—have also garnered multiple awards and critical praise.

Follow The Alvarium Experiment's current and future projects:

Website:
AlvariumExperiment.wixsite.com/prometheussaga/alvarium
Blog:
TheAlvariumExperiment.wordpress
Facebook Page:
@alvariumbooks

ABOUT THE MASTERS REIMAGINED 2

The Masters Reimagined 2 is the fifth project of the Alvarium Experiment, a consortium of accomplished and award-winning authors. Each author was given a central premise of tackling a classic work of art and reimagining it with the elements of speculative fiction, be they fantasy, science fiction, alternative history, or horror.

The stories may be read in any order. *The Masters Reimagined 2* stories and authors are:

"Upon the Styx" by Jade Kerrion. Charon, immortal ferryman of the Underworld, has only one friend—Phaedre, a slave girl stranded on the banks of the Styx, unable to pay for passage across the dark river. To grant her eternal peace, he ventures into the world of mortals to complete her funerary rites. But the seemingly simple task unravels the mystery of a headless, winged sculpture at the Sanctuary of the Great Gods, and pits him against the fury of a vengeful goddess. How many enemies will he make and what terrible price will Charon pay for Phaedre's eternal peace?

Visit Jade at www.jadekerrion.com

"The Scream" by Charles A. Cornell. A man steps into the path of a tram. An art school love affair turns tragic. And the eccentric wanderings of an antiques dealer catches the attention of a detective investigating the theft of Norway's most celebrated work of art, Edvard Munch's The Scream. Haunted by weird dreams and psychic visions, former mental patient Torsten Egland may hold the key in Detective Inspector Henrik Nordkapp's search for the stolen painting. Nordkapp must decide if he should abandon traditional police methods and place his faith in a quirky man whose troubled mind may be communicating with the painting itself.

Visit Charles at www.charlesacornell.com

"The Medusa Jump" by Ken Pelham. A terrified father follows his son, an art historian, from the year 2367 to 1816 to study the real-life tragedy of the French frigate Medusa, only to find themselves both among the subjects of Théodore Géricault's masterpiece.

Visit Ken at www.kenpelham.com

"Soul for a Soul" by John Hope. Before St. Augustine earns his position as bishop, he and his teenage son must save the good name of the early Christian Church and rescue an abused altar boy from the clutches of a soul-capturing daemon. To do so, one of the two must travel to an unknown spiritual realm called the Neither, between Purgatory and Hell, risking his eternal soul in the process.

Visit John at www.johnhopewriting.com

"Oil and Hemlock" by Kristin Durfee. Amita, a young New York philosophy student, is whisked from 1977 to 399 BC Athens, and into the life of one of her heroes, Socrates. Yet her excitement plunges into horror as she realizes she's arrived on the day of his trial and execution.

Visit Kristin at www.kristindurfee.com

"The Eyes of Mona Lisa" by Bria Burton. If the entries in her great-great-great-grandmother's diary are true, twenty-year-old Lanea will see the future if she gazes into the eyes of da Vinci's *Mona Lisa*. When a special exhibit of the famed painting arrives at the National Gallery of Art in D.C., Lanea brings her best friend along on her quest to see if the visions are true, and what they may foretell.

Visit Bria at www.briaburton.com

"Storey's Orphans" by Veronica H. Hart. Grunsberry Murphy, a time traveler, appears as a twelve-year-old in 1878 London just in time to save Winifred and Laurance Allen from death when ships collide on the Thames. After rinsing the stench of the river from them, she leaves them to search for their parents. The children disappear, and she hurries to the Alexandra Orphanage to find them. George Storey has arranged to do one of his London life scenes at the home and captures the arrival of Winifred and Laurance, made famous in Arrival at the Orphanage.

Visit Veronica at www.veronicahhart.com

"Among the Blue Horses" by Elle Andrews Patt. Muriel has a secret she doesn't dare tell anyone for fear of being locked away forever. The she discovers German artist Franz Marc might be the only person in the world who understands her. But he's been dead for over a century. When an art museum director takes notices of her frequent visits and outs her, Muriel finds out more than she ever wanted to know, in a way she never could have imagined. Come trip the light fantastic, spirit-walking with modern artists Franz Marc, Wassily Kandinsky, and bestie August Macke through the years before the Great War....and then beyond.

Visit Elle at www.elleandrewspatt.com

INTRODUCTION

"To my mind one does not put oneself in place of the past, one only adds a new link.   —Paul Cézanne

The ability, the compulsion, to make art is one of the defining hallmarks of the human species. Throughout history, works of art have spoken to the contemporaries of their creators. The greatest works speak to generations long after the moment of creation, moving us emotionally and intellectually, inspiring us to do better, to be better.

We ask that you revisit some of the greatest artworks and artists, to see them anew, or perhaps become intimate with them for the first time. But with an unusual twist.

Reimagine these masterpieces with a touch of the speculative. Reimagine their stories, or the artists' stories, with elements of science fiction, fantasy, or horror. Reimagine Edvard Munch's *The Scream* involved in a mystery story with unexplainable echoes and voices of something outside our normal lives. Reimagine *Winged Victory of Samothrace* as an icon in a conflict between gods and humanity. Reimagine *Mona Lisa*'s beguiling eyes as the catalyst enabling a young woman to see the future. Some of the greatest masterpieces of art across the centuries continue to amaze and inspire. Explore them again with open hearts and minds. And enjoy the fictional "what if" speculations of *The Masters Reimagined 2*.

~The Authors of *The Masters Reimagined 2*

PUBLISHER'S NOTE

Rounding up these anthology stories didn't prove as hard as most daily tasks of life in 2020 have become. Like readers, the authors found escape from the daily doom-scrolling by losing themselves in the creation of imaginary worlds.

And, oh, what worlds! From murder mystery to time travel, demonic possession to art theft, these stories all have one thing in common. From single pieces of art, each author has built an entire world, populated with people who are trying to survive their surprising circumstances. This is speculative fiction at its purest. Every story has realism at its heart, with well-researched settings related to each unique masterwork and a single twist of what-if added.

Some of those twists are broad; what if the Underworld were real? Some narrow; what if a small group of artists shared a psychic ability? But all create strange and engaging journeys for our heroes and heroines, who could be you or me or the neighbor next door.

I hope you'll find this anthology a worthwhile escape from an unrelenting year and end up coming back to it time and again in years to come.

~Laura Andrews, Blue Beech Press

THE MASTERS REIMAGINED 2

UPON THE STYX

JADE KERRION

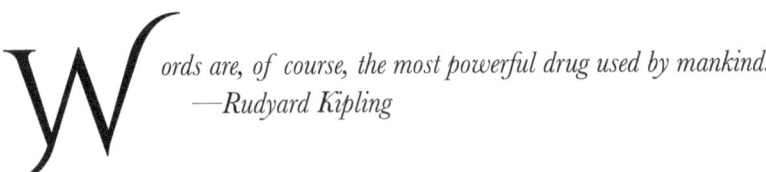

ords are, of course, the most powerful drug used by mankind.
        —Rudyard Kipling

"I DON'T UNDERSTAND why you won't come with me." Thanatos demands. His impatience with me borders on querulous.

And I don't understand why my elder brother is here, asking the same question he's asked for centuries, when he knows nothing has changed. "I have responsibilities here." If I sound equally impatient, it's because even an immortal can get tired of rehashing the same old debate.

His eyes narrow—a prelude to argument—but I'm not cowed. Thanatos is *Death,* and like my other siblings, the children of Nyx, his immortal Titan blood grants him divine perfection. His sculptured symmetry is too precise to be mortal, his swift grace too effortless. It's said that when he arrives to claim a soul, mortals see different things through their dying eyes.

A wizened man.

A flaming skull.

A great horned beast.

They see Death as they imagine him to be.

Yet when their souls arrive here, at the banks of the Styx, their vision is transformed by truth. They see Death as I see him. As he sees himself.

Enchanted by his remote and flawless perfection, they've told me Thanatos's eyes are bluer than a clear summer sky, the light in them sharper than a sword. I understand the words, but still cannot put a color to the name. The skies are always grey here at the borders of the Underworld, as flat and unchanging as a parchment soaked in dye. The vastness here seems endless, the color transforming only when land touches water. The River Styx is black, its surface impossibly smooth, never rippling even when I guide my boat through it. The cloak and hood I wear are as dark as its waters; the many folds of the robe conceal my form and face.

Habit, I suppose.

I've worn them for many millennia, and I know how foolish I must look to my brother. Does he realize how foolish he looks to me? He's wearing clothes he calls a shirt, pants, and jacket. They look too tight, but he says it is what the mortals wear on Earth.

I wouldn't know. The last soul that arrived at the banks of the Styx wore a tunic and mantle, but that was hundreds of years ago.

No one since.

No one believes in the Greek gods anymore.

And I, Charon, the ferryman of the Underworld, have waited for as long, doing absolutely nothing.

"No one else is coming," Thanatos enunciates each word slowly and carefully.

"I know," I freely acknowledge the truth I've realized for a long time. "But someone is still here."

I look over my shoulder.

She stands some distance away, as she does whenever Thanatos visits. Watching and waiting until she can return to my side.

Her name is Phaedre. She arrived almost two thousand years ago, delivered by my sisters, the Keres, the twin goddesses of violent death.

Thanatos shrugs. "That girl's not going anywhere. Just leave her here—"

"I can't," I snap back at him. We've gone through this exact argument so many times. I don't understand why he thinks repeating it changes anything. "As long as anyone is here on this side of the Styx, my work isn't done."

"Your work isn't going to get done. She arrived without payment."

Payment. A Greek *obol.* A coin to pay the ferryman for passage across the Styx. I had offered to ferry Phaedre across the river without payment, but she refused for fear of the judgement that would follow. *It is not right*, she had said. *The rituals must be followed.*

I don't understand her obsession for abiding with the rites of the dead, but then again, I have no fear of the three judges of the Underworld, Minos, Aeacus, and Rhadamanthus. I am the youngest born of Nyx, the goddess of Night, who is herself born of Chaos. My blood runs purest gold, and the three judges were once only mortal men.

Titans fear nothing from mortals, not even those who gain power after death.

But mortals are bones and skin held together by fears. Even dead, their souls are knitted by terrors, more imagined than real. My words have not swayed Phaedre.

Not in the nearly two thousand years she has been here.

Between Phaedre's stubborn insistence on fulfilling the proper rituals, and my stubborn refusal to abandon my duty, it is not impossible to suppose that our impasse will last for all eternity, until the Earth itself has faded from memory.

Thanatos, as immortal as I, however, has no patience for mulishness. "All the other immortals have joined the mortal world. Our brothers and sisters are already there, waiting for you. If you will not join us until Phaedre crosses the Styx, then just find where her body lies and complete the funerary rites. Give her the payment she needs for passage," he says.

My head snaps up, and I stare at my brother. "You will do this for her?"

"No," Thanatos says. "*You* will do this for her."

"But I cannot leave—"

"Don't be ridiculous. There is no law that binds you to the Styx. Nothing that says you cannot leave for a brief moment to solve the very problem that would keep you here forever, doing nothing."

"But to enter the mortal world—"

"It is not the terrifying thing you think it is. Besides, you've spent your life surrounded by mortals."

Yes, but only when the thread of life has been cut from the Great Spindle. When they are mere shades—echoes and memories of the person they had been.

I have never seen them alive. And I have never walked the surface of the Earth. I press my hand against the pitching of my stomach. It cannot possibly be fear. What Titan would fear mortals? "Where will I go?" I ask.

"To where her body lies, of course. Surely she can tell you that." Thanatos shrugged. "Or did the Keres tell you?"

They had not. In those days, they had little interest in pointless chatter. I do not think that even now, they would have developed a taste for it. I recall perfectly, though, the day Phaedre arrived at the banks of the Styx, utterly bewildered, shocked into muteness. It took hundreds of years to win her confidence and coax her story from her; and five times longer for her hesitant trust to settle into friendship. "Phaedra spoke little of her death, and scarcely more of her life," I tell Thanatos. "She lived on Samothrace—a servant at the Sanctuary of the Great Gods."

"Ah," Thanatos says. "*The Mysteries*." He does not bother to hide the scorn in his voice. The Titans have little interest in rituals. Olympians, however, crave them; so much so that they would cavort as mysterious primeval deities in marble sanctuaries set in ancient groves. Gullible mortals are easy prey for the pomp, grandeur, and secrecy of those rituals; Phaedre among them.

Thanatos continues, "Then there you must go to find her body and complete the rites." The brightness in his eyes fades slightly. "Only, be careful."

"Of the mortals?"

He shrugs. "All of those whom the Keres delivered to you received funerary rites in due course. Violent death is no excuse for not tending to the souls of the dead. But Phaedre was never tended to."

"Perhaps she was forgotten."

"More likely, she was remembered."

I glare at Thanatos. What is it about immortals that compel them to speak in incomprehensible sentences twisted to conceal the truth? Isolated from both Titans and Olympians, I have never learned the trick of it. Yet they treat it like currency, using prophecies to bargain, even though they cannot trick fate or destiny.

Mist, summoned by Thanatos's will, rises from the ground, and he departs, leaving my realm to me.

And Phaedre.

She returns to my side. "You were arguing about me again?"

"How much did you hear?"

She shrugs. "Some of it. Death does not speak quietly. He wants you to go with him."

I nod.

"I don't think anyone has said no to Death as many times as you have." She laughs, flashing white teeth. "He's befuddled by your refusal."

I smile with her, and when I extend my hand to her, she takes it, slipping the palm of her hand easily against mine.

"Why won't you go with him?" She questions me freely now, but in truth, it took her hundreds of years to even ask a question. And that first time, she spoke so quietly, I had to strain to hear her voice. *"Why am I here?"*

It is the most piteous question a mortal can ask, and it's the one question I hate hearing most.

It's the question that pours from the depth of a soul that was not ready to depart.

I step into my boat, and she immediately pulls her hand from mine. I deliberately hold my hand out to her. "Will you sit with me?"

Phaedre nods, but sits on the banks of the Styx instead, folding her long legs beneath her pale chiton. She gathers her himation like a shawl around her shoulders. Her color is muted, as faded as her last breath, but her hair hints of once-gleaming copper, and her slim limbs have retained the grace of her truncated youth.

Alive, she must have been beautiful.

And she has been my only companion these hundreds of otherwise silent and empty years.

"I would take you across the Styx," I say again, as I have said every year, every month, every week, indeed, every day since we became friends close enough for such a conversation. "Your journey extends beyond this shore."

"I have no payment," she says. "It is not the right way."

The deity of stubbornness, if there is one, has nothing on Phaedre. I've told her that 'the right way' is an invention of gods, designed to avoid the tedium of answering mortals' questions and making up something new each time, but she will not believe me.

She was, after all, a servant at the Sanctuary of the Great Gods, steeped in the Mysteries, her day structured around rituals, whatever they were.

Phaedre has not revealed them to me.

She was pledged to keep them a secret until death.

Even beyond death.

"Thanatos says that there may be a way for you to cross over the Styx," I tell her. "If I can find your body and complete the funerary rites, you will be able to pay your way."

Her eyes widen. They are as grey as the sky. "You will do that for me?"

I stare at her. She always tilts her head when she smiles. Her voice lilts in happy melodies when she tells me stories of her childhood, and when we walk, side by side along the Styx, I shorten my stride to match her graceful steps.

And yet at the anniversary of her death, she wanders away for weeks, even months at a time, her inexplicable sorrow too deep to share, even with someone who is trying to understand. She flinches when other immortals draw near, even Thanatos, whom she has seen so many times.

She is terrified of gods and Titans even though she cannot explain why.

Whatever *we* did to her has ruined her beyond my ability to fix.

I don't know if crossing over to the Underworld, where Hades rules, will fix what ails her, but it's not about healing what cannot be healed. It's about taking the next step, regardless.

And her next step lies on the far banks of the Styx.

"Phaedre, I need to know what happened to you when you died."

Fear lances into her eyes. "I don't know. I've told you. I don't remember."

"Then tell me what you do remember."

"Hours—long, cold hours of standing in the wind, my garments soaked."

"Were you on a boat?" I ask.

"No, I was at the Sanctuary."

"What were you doing there?"

"I was a servant. I did what I was told," Pheadre says. "To stand, my arms raised. To look into the wind. To endure when other servants drenched my garments with salt water."

It makes no sense. None of the Mysteries make any sense.

But, no... Phaedre had never...would never...share the Sanctuary's secret rituals with me. So, this was something else then.

"What is the last thing you remember?" I ask her.

Her eyes take on a dreamy cast. "Light. So much light. Then terrible pain." She clasps her thin fingers around her neck. "Then nothing else."

"Nothing?"

She frowns, as if trying to remember. "The sound of great wings."

Definitely *not* the Keres. My sisters had eventually carried Phaedre's soul to the Underworld and deposited her at the banks of the Styx, but they didn't have wings.

And they usually wait for the completion of the funerary rites.

Either the Keres didn't wait—which is unlike them—or they knew the rites would not be completed.

Thanatos's warning rings through my mind. *More likely, she was remembered.*

And Phaedre's funerary rites, for whatever reason, had been thwarted.

Who had she offended? Which Olympian? Which Titan?

And if I complete her funerary rites, who would *I* offend?

I have spent all my life at the banks of the Styx, away from the bickering Titans and Olympians, insulated—mostly—from their spite. If I leave the Styx, I would give up the privacy of my sanctuary and my protestations of neutrality.

No longer *just* the ferryman.

No longer just the passive mover of souls across the Styx.

I don't know if I am ready to be more than the person I was born to be.

But I know I cannot extinguish the sudden hope in Phaedre's eyes.

It is time for her to continue her journey.

Even if it means turning aside from my divine destiny as ferryman of the Underworld.

I stare at her, memorizing her faded beauty.

For Phaedre, I will do it.

I stand, gathering my black cloak around me. "Tell me to find you."

She tilts her head, but she's not smiling. Instead her brow furrows. "What?"

"Just tell me to find you."

"But I am right here," she protests.

"Phaedre..."

"Very well. Find me, if you please, great ferryman."

Ferryman.

I am the ferryman, not just of the Underworld, but of all places and all things. I can move *anything* from one place to any another, and it is fated that nothing can stand in my path. All doors open. All obstacles give way. My power lies only between points of origin and destination.

And Phaedre has just given me the destination.

The resting place of her human body.

I step off my boat and into the Styx.

"Charon," she calls out.

I look over my shoulder. I think she will tell me to be careful, but instead she says, "I think you should change."

I look down at my robes.

"Wear what your brother wears," she says. Her advice is both practical and correct.

"What about the rest of me?"

She knows that I'm referring to my form. My face. Like all immortals in whom Chaos's blood runs pure and thick like sinewy ropes of gold, I can take any form I choose. Hooded skeleton. Hunchbacked, gnarled monstrosity.

But Phaedre shrugs. "You're fine as you are."

I stare at her, then concede to her wisdom. If my true form seems acceptable to her, then I would keep it. She was mortal once, right? She should know.

I walk into the Styx until the waters surround me in its unfaltering embrace. I inhale and exhale, mostly out of habit. I need air no more than the gods need mortal food. The Styx, like all waters, flow from Oceanus, the river that encircles the world. As the ferryman, I pass freely through it all. A wish—scarcely more than a whim—and I am flashing from the Styx, through Oceanus, and into the warmth of the Aegean Sea.

I break the surface of the water. White-foamed waves—so different from the unyielding smoothness of the black Styx—flow past me and rise to smash against the basalt and granite rocks on the island of Samothrace.

The sun is but a sliver on the horizon. Helios has scarcely begun his daily journey across the canvas of the sky. Grateful for the cover of near darkness, I wade onshore, but my pants and shirt, perfect replicas of what I had seen Thanatos wear, do not dry instantly the way they would have if I had stepped out of the Styx.

A minor inconvenience, and a timely one.

A reminder that not all my divine powers—and I have few to begin with—work here in the mortal realm.

I squeeze what water I can from my clothes, but still they cling to me. They are far more fitting than my robe, and when wet, infinitely more uncomfortable. Does Thanatos realize the absurdity of modern fashion?

More likely, he doesn't get them wet. Death travels through mists. Unfortunately, I have to make do with water. Squelching with every step, I turn toward the city. Its ancient fortifications have blended with its modern foundations, but it is as pretty as Phaedre's description of the Samothrace she knew—a harmonious blend of white and grey stone houses capped with brown tiled roofs lining cobblestone roads.

The brightening sky splashes color over the city, slathering hues across a blended palette until I can no longer name the dazzling shades before me. A bird's cheery warble lures me into awed silence, as the scents oozing from the earth and the smells spilling from the trappings of humanity blend into a distinctive signature of time and place.

I never realized how beautiful the mortal world is.

And then I see people.

The first is a woman with a stout face and narrow eyes. She almost hits me with the window shutter she flings open. She squawks an impatient apology, which I understand perfectly even though her Greek is different from what Phaedre and I speak to each other. Innate mastery of every mortal tongue is a convenient divine ability, which, of course, we have never permitted to get in the way of our profoundly poor communication skills. Immortals comprehend, but we do not understand.

There are others. A young couple, arguing on the balcony. A middle-aged man creeping along side streets, and looking over his shoulder before slipping in quietly through a door he unlocks with a key.

They are vibrant with color, vivid with life in a way that Phaedre isn't, and can never be.

I have only ever dealt with the souls of deceased mortals.

I have never seen a living mortal.

Until now.

And they are beautiful, *all* of them. The stout woman grumbles, but there's affection in her voice when she swings a crawling child off the floor and sets him in a chair. On the balcony, the man is shouting and the woman is yelling, louder than he. They gesture fast and furious. He hits the balcony and smacks the wall. She pounds her fist on the rail. Yet an unseen bond restrains them to angry finger jabs at each other's chest.

And that man in the shadows. Even in stealth and secrecy, there's an alluring beauty in a mortal's timid glances at moving shadows. Fear trembles in all their hearts. And yet, they keep moving.

It's the most astounding thing of all.

It's the very same thing in Phaedre that takes my breath away.

The thought of Phaedre attunes my awareness to the pulse of something within me, drawing me toward the ruins of the Sanctuary of the Great Gods that straddles two rivers on the western slopes of mount Hagios Georgios.

The destination.

The most direct path is straight up the mountain, but it would draw too much attention from the city that is just waking to the day. Phaedre has told me enough about the Sanctuary that I enter, as most initiates once did, from its eastern gate.

The trail is well-maintained. I don't doubt that the Sanctuary still draws visitors aplenty. When mortals come, do they sense the blood-stained power in the rocks? Do they know that the first thing they see—a paved circular depression—is an altar? The spilled blood has been washed away by rain and time, but it still reeks of sacrifice and loss. Do they sense, as I do, the fluttering threads of life cut from the spindle of life by a sharp dagger's edge?

I do not linger. The path winds down, and I cross the narrow bridge over a fast-flowing river. The wind rustles the sparse olive trees. I pass the large rotunda, a place of gathering and of yet more sacrifice, then turn toward the largest building, the *Temenos.* Even in ruins, it is magnificent, large beyond reckoning.

But I know enough of halls of power—Zeus's palace, Poseidon's palace, and Hades's palace—to know that the largest guard the most sacred. The bulwark of the *Temenos* conceals the graceful ruins of the *Epopteion*. Sunlight slants like gold through the weathered, fractured columns, and reflects off the carved portico. Even though it is scarcely a memory of itself, the unsupported span of its interior stretches beyond mortal ambition, as if held up only by the hand of a god.

The *destination* beckons me toward the southern end of the building. I frown, sensing something else. It's here—concentrated here— the divine power that still resides at Samothrace. I run my fingers over the ancient stones. Here, the priests and priestesses conducted their most sacred, secret rituals.

Rituals involving the Underworld.

Did Phaedre die here?

No, impossible. She had described the wind in her hair, the salt of the sea in her clothes.

She had not died at the blood-soaked altar concealed within cool marble walls.

I raise my gaze, and then I see her.

Phaedre.

On the southernmost point of the plateau.

On the highest and most remote part of the sanctuary.

Immortalized in marble, she braces against the fury of the wind, the wet folds of her tunic and robe cleaving to her body. She is headless and armless, but I recognize, effortlessly, the grace of her limbs. I have lived for nearly two thousand years, watching her step forward, arms extended, to welcome the newly dead to the Underworld.

Yet in this infallible marble vision of Phaedre, two large wings rise from her shoulders to frame the sky.

It is not my Phaedre.

Yet Phaedre had heard the beating of great wings in the final moment when her life cleaved from her body.

Whose wings?

I cross the second river to the third terrace of the Sanctuary and walk past the layered ruins of the theater to the statue of Phaedre.

Her body angles toward the sea. Her eyes would have surveyed the brilliant blue spread of the Aegean Sea

The *destination* pulses. *Just a little further.* On the far edge of the statue, in a rough-hewn niche, I kneel to touch the packed dirt. It is old, thick, and almost immovable.

But my power as the ferryman compels all doors to open, all things to give way. The dirt shifts beneath my fingertips, soil parting like a door opening to reveal its secrets. I reach deep and brush my fingertips against the smoothness of bone. Not one, but many. I draw them out, one after the other. The proportions are slender, the hips wide. *Phaedre's bones.* I know it because the pulse that draws me forward is gone.

I have found my *destination.*

Except that Phaedre's *skull* is missing.

The skull in which I have to place the coin for her passage across the Styx.

I cannot complete Phaedre's funerary rites without it.

Distant footsteps draw close, crunching upon gravel. I replace Phaedre's bones in its grave. Dirt and stones tumble into the crevice, filling it. And just in time. The footsteps pause behind me, and I rise and turn.

He's an elderly man with a shock of white hair beneath a fisherman's cap. He wheezes hard from his long trek across three terraces and two rivers to the southernmost point in the Sanctuary. "You're out and about early," he says. "The sanctuary doesn't open for visitors for another hour." He looks up at the statue and smiles affectionately. "I see that you have come to admire our greatest treasure. Unfortunately, it is just a copy."

"A copy? And the original?"

He spat into his palm. "In a French museum. The Louvre. Thieving bastards. They steal our treasures, then refuse to return them."

"So this statue of Phaedre—"

"What?" He looks confused. "No. This is *Niki tis Samothrakis.*"

I stiffen.

The Nike of Samothrace.

The *winged* goddess of Victory.

Were Nike's wings the last sound Phaedre heard?

I need answers only Nike can give, but Thanatos had said that almost all immortals had joined the mortal world. Nike would surely be among them. How could I possibly find her?

Wait…

I need not find Nike. She is the daughter of the Titan Pallas, by the great river goddess, Styx.

And I know where her mother resides.

I RETURN TO THE UNDERWORLD. When I emerge from the Styx. Phaedre rushes to me. "You have found me?"

"Not yet," I reply. "But I have found something." My clothes dry as soon as I step out of the water. I turn to face its dark depths and raise my voice. "Great river goddess, will you come to me?"

Silence lingers for a moment, then the waters part and she comes forth, her hair as black, lustrous, and smooth as the river that bears her name. Her skin is as pale as crushed coral against her deep blue robe, intricately woven with silver threads. She gleams with her own light in the unending grey of the Underworld.

Phaedre retreats behind me and presses her body so tightly against mine that I can feel her tremble.

Styx and I take each other's measure, but little has physically changed in the many millennia since our last meeting. The immortals do not change; it is what makes us immortal, after all. Reputation, however, does. Homage between immortals is a delicate thing, our genealogies precisely calculated based on our lineage to Chaos, Gaia, and Tartarus—the three great primordial beings—then adjusted for our powers, or lack thereof.

I have little power, but I am Chaos's grandson, and even Zeus fears my mother, Nyx.

And here in the Underworld, as on Olympus and on Earth, power is often less about what you can do and more about who might be angered if something happens to you.

And there is nothing at all that is predictable about Nyx.

On the other hand, Styx is the unchanging river by which the gods and mortals alike pledge unbreakable vows. She is the eternal waters by which mortals can be made immortal, and the boundary that separates the living on Earth from the souls in the Underworld.

And I am the one who needs something from her.

But unexpectedly, Styx concedes first. "Ancient ferryman." Her head dips fractionally.

I don't know if my sharp inhalation conceals my surprise, but I speak, "I seek your daughter, Nike. Do you know where I can find her?"

"It is too late to debate what happened to the slave girl."

The slave girl. *Phaedre.*

So Phaedre's death *did* have something to do with Nike.

"It's not too late," I counter. "Not as long as Phaedre waits to be ferried across your dark waters. Where is your daughter?"

"You are no match for her, Ferryman."

"I'm not going to fight her. I'm trying to talk to her. Tell her I await her at the Garden of the Hesperides."

"I will convey your message to her, but she will not be there."

I shrug. "It's true then, what they say in the mortal world."

Styx's gaze sharpens on me. "What do they say?"

"That victory now exists without honor."

The glassy smooth surface of the river suddenly ripples. Cascades of waves flow from the hem of her garment and surge across the water.

Styx's expression does not change, but the river speaks for her. She is angry. Far worse, afraid.

And not for the first time, I wonder how many enemies I am going to make.

FROM A DISTANCE, the Garden of the Hesperides, on the far western edge of Oceanus, is as luminous as I've always imagined it to be, but when I approach, the path into the grove is almost impassable. The grasses grow knee high and golden apples sag from laden branches. The once-bright gleam of the tree trunk is patchy and tarnished. The garden's mythical beauty is as fragile as peeling plaster.

So this is what an immortal ruin looks like.

"Your sisters abandon their duties," a calm voice carries across the breadth of the grove. "You, Charon, are much more diligent. Or so I've heard."

Nike wears a tunic and mantle, not unlike what Phaedre wears, but this one gleams gold and red. Gold for victory, and red for the blood endlessly shed in its pursuit. She eyes my shirt and pants, and smirks. "It appears the times have finally caught up with you too, Ferryman."

"It seemed necessary to pass through the mortal world without drawing attention."

Nike shrugs, and it occurs to me that it's in her nature to draw attention. Small talk isn't really her style either, and because she is as direct as her gaze is clear, she goes straight to the point. "That waif of a slave girl still lingers at the banks of the Styx."

"She cannot cross without payment, and she will not accept my charity. So, I sought to complete her funerary rites, but found only her headless body."

"At the Sanctuary. You saw then, that headless obscenity the mortals consider art?"

"The Nike of Samothrace? I've heard that it is only a copy, but even so, it is stunning." And it was. The perfection of strength in the face of a storm, the promise of movement in the utter quiet of stillness.

Nike flipped her wrist as if my assessment were inconsequential. "He had the audacity to put *her* face on me."

"Phaedre...she was the model for the statue." Her memory of standing braced against the wind, her clothes soaked with sea water, her arms upraised...

"Someone had to be. I certainly wasn't going to do it," Nike says. "But the sculptor was too bound, too captivated by mortal imperfection. He could not see me. So, it was *her* face he put on *my* statue."

An affront too deep to be borne.

Nike laughs, the sound bitter. Gods have perfect memories. The spite, the anger, the hate is never assuaged. "Those fools think the statue is headless because it was lost somehow to the ravages of time, but no. I cleaved the head from the statue a moment before I cleaved Phaedre's head from her neck."

"The beating of wings. The last sound she heard…it was you. Where is her skull, Nike?"

"Buried, forever."

"The rites must be completed, or she will never be able to cross the Styx into the Underworld. She will never know peace."

"There will be no peace for her. The judges know that she usurped a goddess's glory."

"She was a slave girl who shivered, drenched and cold, in the harsh wind for a sculptor's art. She had no control over what he would sculpt. She's not the reason you're angry."

"You're just the ferryman, Charon. You were never worshipped, never deified. You have no idea what it is like to have these mortals see the divine in other mortals no less frail than they. You have no idea what it is like to see their eyes glaze and drift over you because they have found their pitiful 'perfections' in each other."

"She is not to blame."

"Of course she is!" Nike shouted. "Her shallow pretense of divinity—"

"I will tell you what the sculptor saw. It is the same thing I see in her when Thanatos and Keres arrive at the banks of the Styx. She is terrified of Death in all its forms, yet she steps forward, arms open, to welcome the souls who have newly arrived at the banks of the Styx. She bids them welcome, promises that their long journey is near its end. She is not you—she is not Victory in battle—but she is the promise of rest and peace after the battle. And that was what the statue was, wasn't it? The battle already won, she stands, braced against the furious winds, arms outstretched, wings spread, to welcome the weary warrior home. It was *that* divinity the sculptor saw within her. That divinity he sculpted. That divinity he set her face upon. It's not your statue, Nike. It's Phaedre's."

"It is the Nike of Samothrace, as it was always intended to be." But her voice trembles.

"Headless. Anonymous. Where is her skull, Nike?"

"Her skull will gain you nothing."

"Phaedre's skull will gain her peace. She deserves it. She has spent almost two thousand years at the banks of the Styx, watching with tears in her eyes as souls step into my boat for the final crossing. She raises her arms in farewell, then turns to greet newcomers. She has transformed my river bank into a restful sojourn, but now, it is time for her to move on. No more dead will come to the Styx."

"No…" Nike murmurs. "No one believes in us anymore."

"Then will you release her to her final judgement? She is only a slave girl. She is not worthy of your anger."

The goddess of Victory eyes me, then smiles. "I think she is more than a slave girl to you, Charon. Will you bargain for her, Ferryman?"

"I have nothing to bargain with."

"Oh," she says. "You do. And more than you think. Swear that when I come to you for aid, you will grant it."

I laugh, the sound without humor. "I am not stupid, Nike. I will not bargain without terms."

"But no one yet knows what the prophecy means."

"What prophecy?" I ask. Is she trying to bait me?

"The final prophecy uttered by the last Oracle of Delphi. *An innocent will rise from the Underworld to overthrow Olympus.*"

I shake my head. "Many in the Underworld and Tartarus crave the destruction of Olympus, but no one among them is innocent."

"On that note, all the Gods agree, which is why the prophecy is so puzzling. But I am Zeus's charioteer, and you are of the Underworld. When the war begins, I would have allies there. Even reluctant ones."

I draw my breath in sharply. I have no gift of prophecy, but if —*when*—the next war begins, I know I will no longer find safety in neutrality as I have for these thousands of years though hundreds of wars.

For Nike will have her Victory, whatever it costs.

And she holds hostage the only thing I want—the location of Phaedre's skull.

Phaedre need never know what it costs me.

"I swear it," I murmur my consent to Nike's nearly impossible bargain. "Upon the Styx."

Gracious in victory, she smiles. "The slave girl's skull is hidden within the Altar of Victory."

"Your altar? Where is it?"

She shrugs. "It was in Rome."

"*Was?*" I demand sharply.

"When the city was sacked by the king of the Visigoths, the altar vanished, along with many of the city's rarest treasures. It has not been seen again."

If there were an altar made to me, I would not have been as casually indifferent as to its loss. "And this king...did he take the treasure back to his home?"

"He never made it home. He died on the way. And took the secret of his treasure horde to his grave."

NIKE KNOWS little of the king's story—she pretends the altar had not meant that much to her—but she recalls enough to send me on my way. I travel through Oceanus and the waters of the world to the merging of the Crati and Busanto rivers, in the heart of the town of Cosenza in southern Italy. The warm weather is almost welcomingly Mediterranean, but the red-bricked buildings are taller and sterner than those at Samothrace. I receive only a few odd looks when I step out of the river, and an old woman laughs at me through the gap in her yellowed teeth. "So you're looking for Alaric's treasure too."

"Alaric, the king of the Visigoths?"

"Why else would you be in the river, but to search for his treasure?"

I walk up to her. "Will you tell me about Alaric?"

In a cozy *osteria* by Busanto river, she regales me with the story that apparently every human child within a hundred leagues knows, but I do not. "He sacked the Eternal City, he did." She takes a long drink from a glass of red wine. "Alaric, King of the Visigoths. He and his horde of barbarians drove Rome to its knees. Then he took from the city its most priceless treasures before heading toward the south."

"But he never arrived."

"No." She shakes her head. "He died suddenly. Here. The historians say it was malaria, but perhaps the gods struck him down for his boldness."

"Boldness?"

"The treasures he took from the holy places of Rome. It's said he emptied the city. Not just the treasuries, but also the temples, the churches. All of it."

"So where is his treasure now?"

"Buried with him, they say."

"Where?"

The old woman waves her hand at the river. "According to the old stories, they diverted the river and buried the king together with his most priceless treasures beneath the river bed. Then the river was returned to its course." Her thin lips quirk toward a smile. "Then they were all killed, of course."

"They?"

"The slaves and prisoners who diverted the river and buried the king. They were killed to protect the secret location of Alaric's tomb."

I frown at the flawed logic. "Were the generals who made that decision—who surely knew the location—killed too?"

"Of course not." She shrugs. "Doesn't make much sense, does it?" The old woman smiles again. "But there it is, the story of King Alaric's treasure. No one has ever found it, of course, even though people go diving often in search of it. They even bring out the big machines that can detect metal, but nothing."

"Nothing…?"

"The river conceals all. Alaric's treasure is lost forever."

The river conceals a great deal, but not from me.

I thank the old woman and bid her farewell, and return to the water's edge. I dip my fingers into the water. It would give me passage—anywhere I choose to go—but this time, the water also tells me where it has been.

And it has surged deep.

The Busanto river, unbeknownst to mortals, has diverged. On the surface, it flows, apparently unchanged, but a tributary delved far into the earth, carving caverns through rock and plunging ever farther down. It has grown stronger and larger than even the Busanto that meanders crookedly through Cosenza.

The true Busanto river flows underground.

I step into the river, dive beneath the water, then my powers flash, carrying me to Oceanus before whisking me back to the Busanto hidden from mortal eyes.

My surroundings are pitch black, but Titans do not need light to see. Jagged mounds rise out of the shallow water. Careless tumbles of swords and shields, chalices and statues. Gold coins gleam like pebbles strewn under water. I step back to take in the immensity of Alaric's burial vault. It is at least as long as Athena's great temple, and as wide as Zeus's.

And it is filled with the plunder of Rome.

Somewhere, in here, is Nike's Altar of Victory.

I clamber over the mountains of treasure. The bronze is green-streaked, and the silver tarnished, but the gold still glitters. My gaze moves over the spread of Alaric's treasure, and pauses upon a large altar. Olive leaves, hammered from thin flakes of gold, entwine along its edge. Standing over its smooth, gleaming surface is a golden, winged figure. One leg poised forward, mid-step, her wind-blown clothes draped around her body. In her left hand, she holds her spear; in her right hand, a laurel wreath.

Unlike the Nike of Samothrace, this statue has a head.

And I recognize Phaedre's face.

I approach the Altar of Victory and run my fingers over its surface, probing beneath the rim until I find an uneven notch in its surface. I press against it, and a panel beneath the altar slides apart. I crouch to reach into the darkness, and I draw out a skull.

The neck vertebrate at the base of the skull is shorn smooth, cleaved by a divine weapon.

Phaedre…

Her skull is the only priceless thing here in this treasure vault, the only thing that matters to me.

I will pay dearly for it.

I RETURN to the windblown cliff on the island of Samothrace. Beneath the gilded sheen of moonlight, I reunite Phaedre's skull with the rest of her bones. In her mouth, between her teeth, I set a silver coin. I wrap her bones in spun-gold cloth, and murmur the rites and blessings to speed her soul on its way. Only then do I bury her remains, deep in the earth, directly beneath the headless statue of the Nike of Samothrace.

When I step out of the black water and onto the banks of the river Styx, Phaedre flings herself into my arms. "I knew you'd found me!" She waves a silver coin in my face. "It suddenly appeared in my mouth. I almost swallowed it in shock!"

"I'm glad you didn't, or I would have had to return to the world to give you another." I smile at her in spite of the deep ache that claws through my chest. "Are you ready to depart now?"

"Yes!" She places the coin in my hand and leaps into my boat.

I want to savor every last moment with Phaedre, but the journey across the Styx has never seemed shorter. The Underworld draws closer, and my boat finally bumps against the far shore. The walls of Erebos—my father—stretch in both directions, farther than any eye —mortal or immortal—can see. Phaedre stares at the immensity. "How will I get through?"

"You will know what to do once you step out of my boat. Cerberus awaits you at the gate. He will let you pass."

"And then judgement?"

"You have nothing to fear in judgement, Phaedre."

"I do not wish to wander aimlessly in the Asphodel Meadows forever, or worse, be banished to the Mourning Fields."

"The Mourning Fields are for those who died unloved. You are not unloved, Phaedre."

She stares at me, almost as if she understands. Her lips move. I think she is about to say something that could mean everything to us. Perhaps a plea to return to the side of the Styx that served as her home for almost two thousand years. Perhaps a plea to stay with me for as long as I care to have her.

Even for all eternity.

If she asks, I don't think I can say no.

But she bites her lip and swallows the question. She is stronger than I am. "And...and what if I am ordered to drink from the waters of Lethe? I do not wish to forget...anything."

"We can always choose to remember, Phaedre." I touch her cheek, and she leans into me. "And I will always be grateful for the memory of you, but this is your path forward." I draw strength from knowing that *this* very moment is why I paid Nike's price. "It is time for you to move on."

"Will we meet again?" she asks.

"I don't know," I say, because truly, I do not.

"I choose to remember you, ancient ferryman. Charon. My friend." She presses my hand against her cheek, the closest I have ever known to a caress.

She steps out of my boat.

I wait, watching as she approaches the gate guarded by Hades's fearsome three-headed dog. But she is fearless. Phaedre has waited too long for her path to unfold, and now that it has opened and she has chosen to step forward, she does not hesitate.

She looks back only once before she steps through the gate and into the Underworld. Our eyes meet in perfect understanding. She raises both arms to me, and for an instant, the wind lifts her mantle, and swirls it around her like outstretched wings.

She is—and has always been—Victory.

My Phaedre of Samothrace.

AUTHOR'S NOTES - JADE KERRION

HAVE you ever wondered what became of the Greek gods after their worshipers stopped believing in them? What would they do? Where would they go?

Why not Fort Lauderdale? Sun. Sea. Lots of boats...

In my urban fantasy serial *Underworld Boater*, available exclusively through Patreon, Charon, the Ferryman of the Styx, makes a new life for himself in Fort Lauderdale, Florida. Unfortunately, immortal grudges and eternal enmity follow him into the mortal world, transforming it into the perfect battleground for a long-overdue war between the gods of Olympus and the offspring of the Titans.

If you'd like to follow Charon's adventures, please visit my Patreon page.

~Jade

THE SCREAM

CHARLES A. CORNELL

N*othing ceases to exist—there is no example of this in nature. There is an entire mass of things that cannot rationally be explained. There are newborn thoughts that have not yet found form. How foolish to deny the existence of the soul.*
--Edvard Munch, 1892

I

August 2006

TORSTEN EGLAND, suddenly blind, waved his arms aimlessly in front of him. He reached for something that wasn't there and stumbled into the path of a tram. The massive tramcar braked, its piercing screech shattering the quiet of the plaza in front of Oslo's National Theater. Sparks cascaded from the tram's overhead lines. The shuddering carriage ground to a panic stop, barely two feet in front of Egland's misguided steps. Egland meandered across the tracks, oblivious, and collided with a lamp post. Blood spurted from his nose. He collapsed to the pavement.

The crowd gathered around him. "Are you all right?" someone asked.

"Fog," he replied. He was lifted to his feet. The late summer day was bright and sunny. "All I see is fog."

"FOLLOW MY FINGER," the young doctor said. She was pretty, blond. He couldn't stop staring into her blue eyes. "My finger," she repeated.

"Sorry."

She shined a light into Torsten's eyes and delicately pressed her finger around his eye socket. He winced. "A bad bruise. But no damage to your eyeball." The doctor flipped the light on the X-ray viewer beside the examination table. "And you'll be happy to hear your nose isn't broken either."

Torsten Egland nodded.

"You'll have quite a nasty headache for a while," the doctor said, returning to her desk. "The discomfort will be temporary. If you can live with it, I don't recommend a painkiller. Too addictive. Any over-the-counter headache medication should suffice."

The doctor opened a file. "The paramedics who brought you here said you claimed to have lost your sight. But your eyesight seems quite normal now."

"I couldn't see clearly. A dense fog surrounded me. I could only see the outline of objects, the shapes of people."

"You didn't see the tram coming?"

"I—"

"The police will want to know the results of your blood tests."

"I don't do drugs."

"Then your bloodwork won't show any illegal drugs in your system and the police will be satisfied it was an accident. Ultimately, they will decide that issue."

"I told you. I *don't* do drugs!"

"Alright, Mr. Egland. My main concern is your health. Have you experienced this kind of episode before?"

Torsten hesitated.

The doctor cocked her head, "Well? Don't be afraid to tell me if you have."

He answered, "Umm...no."

"I see. Well, the paramedics said you were upset by the people in the crowd. When they screamed."

"That's not what I said. Yes, I'd heard a scream. But it was a different scream. Not their scream. A very loud scream. And I heard it again. It was inside this...*fog*. I was following these screams. So I didn't see the tram coming. There was this 'fog'..."

"You were following screams? Whose screams?"

"I don't know."

The doctor made some notes and leaned back in her chair. "Mr. Egland, do you have any history of anxiety? Panic attacks?"

"No."

"Depression? Manic episodes?"

"No. I'm quite happy. I'm not mentally ill, if that's what you're implying."

"What about stress? What do you do, Mr. Egland?"

"I'm an antiques dealer. I have my own shop."

"Is business good? Any financial difficulties?"

"I get by. I own the shop. No rent to pay. I live comfortably on what I earn. I can't complain."

"Hm," she said. "Alright. Then I would recommend we schedule an MRI. I don't want to alarm you, Mr. Egland, but these visual anomalies—sensory hallucinations with no apparent cause—could be the result of a brain tumor. In the meantime, as a precaution, I'm going to prescribe you some anti-anxiety medication. It's very mild. We'll see what the scan reveals and then decide what the next course of action might be. All of this could have been due to a physical condition. We need to eliminate that possibility before we pursue the cause as something psycho-logical."

"I'm not crazy."

"I didn't say you were, Mr. Egland. But there must be some explanation behind these strange hallucinations. These tests will help us find out what it is. You don't want something like this to happen again, do you? For your safety. And for the safety of the people around you. The next time, you might not be so lucky."

"I'm not crazy."

The doctor handed him a slip. "Give this to the nurse on the way out and she will schedule your MRI. You can pick up the prescription at the pharmacy next to the clinic."

Torsten Egland—blond, forty-five years old; an avid cross-country skier and cyclist; tall, fit and muscular; and in otherwise perfect health, apart from a bluish bruise on his face—left the doctor's office, passed by the clinic's nursing station without stopping, and dumped the prescription slip in the nearest waste bin.

II

"IT'S BEAUTIFUL, MISS OLSSEN," Egland said as he examined the ring with his jeweler's loupe. "But I can't possibly buy this."

"Why not? You've sold my grandmother's things before."

"Yes, well...," he stumbled. "This ring is different."

"Different? What do you mean? I really need the money. Make an offer. Please?"

"I..." He hesitated. "It's...well...umm...she won't let me buy it."

"*What?* Who?"

"Your grandmother."

"You've never met my grandmother."

"She always wanted you to wear this ring. It was very precious to her. It was given to her by someone she loved. Someone she lost in the war. He was in the Norwegian Resistance."

"How do you know that?"

"She's telling me."

"She's been dead for ten years!"

"I...well, she...I mean..."

Anette Olssen looked at her watch. "I'm late for my art class." She grabbed the ring from the counter. "And this..." She held the ring up to Egland's nose. "This was supposed to help pay for my art supplies."

Anette Olssen turned sharply from the counter and bolted to the door. "You've always been fair with me, Mr. Egland. But you won't buy this ring because my dead grandmother told you not to? I've never heard anything so ridiculous!"

"I'm sorry you feel that way. But I—,"

"There are other antique shops you know. I'm sure they would be more than happy to buy this ring. Don't expect me to come back here again."

Miss Olssen flung the door open and marched into the street.

A man entered behind her. The shop door swung into him as it closed, knocking him off balance. The man shrugged. "Lovers' quarrel?" he asked with a smile.

"A client. Not a very happy one. What can I help you with, Mister...?"

"Detective Inspector Nordkapp."

Nordkapp approached the counter. Sixty-something, black-rimmed glasses, bald with swept-back white hair at the sides. He wore a dark grey overcoat. A rolled-up newspaper was tucked under his arm. He laid the newspaper on the counter's glass top. It was a copy of last week's *Aftenposten*, The Evening Post, Oslo's largest daily. He opened it to page three, to a photograph of a crowded plaza with a stopped tram. The article's headline read, "Do Oslo's Tram Drivers Need Safety Training?".

Nordkapp pointed to a man in the photograph. He was on a gurney and was being lifted into an ambulance. "This is you, isn't it?" He pulled out a small notebook and read from it, "Mr. Torsten Egland?"

Egland picked up the paper and skimmed through the article. "It wasn't the driver's fault. It was mine."

"No doubt it was." Nordkapp produced a small photo from his jacket. "Do you know this man?"

The man in the photograph was young, maybe early thirties, handsome. He had a day-old beard and his hair was expensively coiffed. The photo was a headshot, professionally taken, not just a family photo, like a publicity shot for a model.

"Never seen him before in my life."

"You're sure?"

"I'm positive."

"You don't watch much television?"

"I read a lot."

"Well, two miles further down the same tram line—the one where you stepped in front of a moving tram car—and at roughly the same time as you, this man also stepped in front of a tram. He was not so fortunate. He died at the scene."

"How tragic."

"Hans Jordahl was his name. For soap opera fans, his death was most definitely a tragedy. An unscripted one. And a very real one." Detective Nordkapp took back the photo.

"Every death is a tragedy whether you're a TV star or not."

"True. But in this case, it's also odd that two men should cross in front of the path of a city tram at virtually the same time."

"A coincidence, I guess."

"I would have said the same thing. But is it a coincidence that both men said they were in a 'fog' on a bright sunny day? At least that's what witnesses overheard Jordahl say before several tons of steel and glass smashed into him and ruined his good looks."

"I didn't cause his accident. How could I have? But I take full responsibility for my own negligence."

"Yes, accidents. I see them all the time. With no one to blame? Perhaps. I just want to know if there's a connection between the two incidents. Your eyes suggest there is."

"I...don't think so."

"Really?" Nordkapp's eyebrows raised. "Just a strange coincidence?"

Egland looked down at the counter. He pushed the newspaper back towards Detective Nordkapp. "Just a coincidence."

Nordkapp referred to his notebook. "You're sure you don't know Hans Jordahl?"

"I'm sure."

"Two years ago, you sold stock in his company, avoiding quite a loss."

"I don't know what you're talking about."

"JE Gruppen?"

Egland paused. "I don't remember that."

"Let me refresh your memory. The full name of the company is Jordahl Engineering Gruppen AS. The television star, Hans Jordahl — the man who stepped in front of the tram last week—and his brother, inherited their father's company. But two years ago, his brother made some bad decisions and the company lost some huge contracts, oil drilling rigs. JE Gruppen AS was on the verge of bankruptcy. But you sold your stock before the news of the lost contracts came out. In fact, you dumped it only a few days before the stock dropped seventy percent."

"I got lucky, I guess."

"Very convenient. Who told you to sell? Were you and Jordahl friends? Did he come in here to buy something and tip you off?"

"No, I told you. I've never met him."

"Perhaps you need to come into the station and make a formal statement about that. Maybe a change of scenery might jog your memory."

"I didn't know Hans Jordahl until you showed me his picture and told me who he was. I didn't know JE Gruppen was associated with the Jordahl name until you said so. I'm not a sophisticated investor."

"No? Then who gave you that very timely advice to sell? That was a very astute and profitable decision, wasn't it? For someone who isn't a 'sophisticated' investor?"

Egland hesitated. He wiped the sweat off his forehead with his sleeve. "Things...are *told* to me. But not in the way you're suggesting. Nothing illegal. Most people don't understand. They've never understood. You wouldn't either."

"Try me. Voices in your head, perhaps?"

Egland fidgeted with his ring. "I prefer to call them 'connections' not voices. Sometimes they're verbal, sometimes they're not. Sometimes they're feelings...strong feelings, compulsions. Things that compel me to act on something. Sometimes they're a warning."

"Like sell Jordahl Engineering Gruppen before it tanks?"

"Nothing that specific. It was a dream. A nightmare. I was in a bank. I was holding pieces of paper, engraved paper, certificates of some kind. A pit of fire opened in the floor next to my feet. The pit grew, threatening to swallow me up. I didn't know what to do. The teller gave me a bag of gold coins and took the papers from me. All of a sudden, the pit of fire disappeared. That dream was a warning, symbolic. I decided to sell all of my stocks, not just JE Gruppen."

Nordkapp glanced at his notebook again. "You're familiar with Gaustad Hospital, aren't you?"

Gaustad. Egland stepped back, a sudden pang of dread coursing through him. "What business is that of yours?"

"Everything is my business." Nordkapp checked his notes again. "You were committed to Gaustad State Mental Hospital for seven months in 1997, correct?"

"They changed the law because of that. Because of me."

"Changed what law?"

"The Mental Health Act. Specifically, Chapters 2 and 3, regarding a patient's rights on appeal. The law was changed two years after my release. The investigation into my case said the statutes were inadequate. So because of me, Parliament changed them. Because of how I was treated. I've never been mentally ill. I wasn't then. I'm not now."

"Coincidences pile up, don't they? Two men in a fog. Convenient symbols. Warnings. Voices in your head."

"You need a court order to access my medical records."

"I appreciate the advice. But if you think of any information that might help me understand this 'coincidence' better, please call me. Here's my card."

The detective placed the card on the counter. Egland did not look down.

"Call me?" Nordkapp said.

Egland stood ramrod straight, arms flat by his side.

Nordkapp's eyes locked with the shopkeeper's. "You will call me?"

"I will call you."

The detective bundled the newspaper under his arm, took a cursory look around at the display cabinets, and said in a singsong voice, "Nice shop you have here, Mr. Egland. I may come back. My daughter's birthday is coming up. Maybe I'll buy her a ring."

Inspector Nordkapp left.

Egland stood at the counter, shaking. Sweat beaded on his forehead until it dribbled down his nose. Three minutes of stunned silence passed by without him moving, his eyes focused on a distant point outside the shop's window.

He checked his watch, grabbed his leather jacket, strode to the front door, flipped the sign to 'Closed', and locked up his shop.

It was two o'clock on a Wednesday afternoon.

Egland walked to the nearest tram stop, waited, and boarded the next one that came by.

As the tram pulled away, a man—bald, with glasses, and wearing a dark grey overcoat— slipped out of a nearby alley, sprinted across the street, and got into a black unmarked Volvo. With a screech of tires, it followed the tram.

III

TORSTEN EGLAND WRAPPED his hands around his cup, warming them. Thin wisps rose from the coffee; strands of warm vaporous silk dissolving into the air. A chilly late summer afternoon in Oslo. The street was a colorless collection of faceless buildings with one lone exception: an art school opposite the café. The four-storey building's pale green exterior with white-trimmed windows added a hint of gaiety to an otherwise bland urban canvas.

Egland had alighted from the tram at the Birkelunden Park stop in the heart of Oslo's Art District. Something told him this was where he needed to get off.

He questioned several young people basking on the grass in the park. But no one knew Anette Olssen. *There must be a dozen small art schools in the neighborhood*, they told him. *Which one did she attend?* He hadn't a clue. *Sorry, mister. Can't help.*

He'd wandered away from the park, down one side street then another, with nothing more to guide him than intuition. The studio across from the café had closed at 3:00PM. But rather than return home, something compelled him to sit down, order a cappuccino, and wait. *Wait for what?*

"More coffee?" the pretty waitress asked as Egland sipped the last drop. "Some cake perhaps? Freshly made today."

"Yes, to both. Thank you."

Waiting seemed the right thing to do.

A fresh cup and a thick slice of cake soon arrived.

He picked up the fork just as a flock of wood-pigeons took flight in all directions from the roof of the art school. He jumped up, his hands clasped over his ears. His foot, catching the leg of the table as he rose, tipped the table over. The coffee cup and cake plate slipped off, fell to the concrete, and shattered. The sudden burst of breaking ceramics startled the people in the tables next to him.

He fell to his knees and clasped his throat. His face turned blue.

"Quick!" someone yelled. "He's choking!"

The waitress knelt down and wrapped her arms around Egland from behind. She performed a Heimlich maneuver. Nothing came up. Egland clutched at his neck.

"Do you have allergies?" the waitress asked, her voice frantic. "There are nuts in the cake." Egland continued to struggle for air. "Get the EpiPen!" she yelled to her colleague.

A circle of customers formed around Torsten Egland as an EpiPen arrived. The waitress tore at the package, clasped the pen in her hand, and was just about to stab his thigh, when Egland cried out, "No! No! It's not necessary." He relaxed his hands from around his throat. "I'm fine. I can breathe now. Really. I'm fine. Please. I'm sorry..."

A man pushed his way through the crowd. He flashed a badge. "I'll take it from here," Inspector NordKapp said. "Clear away. Give him some room." Nordkapp lifted Egland up. "Are you sure you're okay? Your throat. It's bright red."

Egland stared past him and pointed across the street. Nordkapp glanced over. A young woman, clearly in a hurry, skipped along the sidewalk in front of the art school. She took a key from her jeans pocket and unlocked the studio's door.

"No," Egland cried out. "She shouldn't go in there!"

"Who?"

"Olssen. Anette Olssen."

Nordkapp waved his hand towards a black Volvo parked down the street. A man jumped out. "Feyerstrom, in there!" he yelled. "Follow her."

"The third floor," Egland said. "It happened on the third floor."

"What happened?"

Egland stared at the pale green building. "Did you hear that scream?"

"What scream?" Nordkapp asked.

"They heard it. The pigeons. They heard it too."

"Pigeons?"

The art school's door flung open. Anette Olssen ran out screaming. The other detective arrived in time to catch her in his arms. She melted to the pavement, crying.

"Stay here," Nordkapp said to Egland.

The inspector dashed across the street and conferred with his assistant. The policemen calmed Anette as she sobbed uncontrollably. Words were exchanged between her gasping breaths. Nordkapp took out his phone, his eyes wide, and barked instructions. The other detective ran into the studio.

"What's happening?" the waitress asked, as she watched the incident from the café.

"The third floor," Egland replied, picking up the shards of broken crockery. "He hung himself on the third floor."

IV

Nordkapp, seated at a grey table, opened the top file from a stack of files, reached to one side, and pressed a button to start recording. "Interview commenced. 20:30 hours. Oslo Police Headquarters, Grønland. Detective Inspector Henrik Nordkapp. Detective Sergeant Bengt Feyerstrom. Interviewing Mr. Torsten Egland."

Egland, fidgeting, turned his head to stare out of the window at the rooftops of Oslo. He rotated the signet ring on his right hand

and winced. He took it off and threw it on the table. It skittered halfway between him and the policemen.

"Problem?" Nordkapp asked.

"It was burning my finger."

"Cheap rings will do that."

"It's twenty-four carat gold."

"Maybe it's radioactive."

"Yes, something like that."

Nordkapp's eyebrows raised. He frowned at Feyerstrom. His colleague shrugged.

"Can we begin now?" Nordkapp asked. He produced a photograph of a man in an art studio. The man was standing behind a woman, pointing, as if instructing her as she painted. He tapped the photo with his finger.

"I don't know him," Egland said. "If that's what you're asking."

"How about this one?" Nordkapp asked. "Same guy. Forensics shot this photo at the scene. Professor Anton Haglund." He spoke with barely any inflection. "The man who hanged himself on the third floor of the Paulus School of Art."

Egland grimaced. He looked away from the dead man's blue face. "I told you, I don't know him."

"But I found you sitting outside his art school in a café, sipping coffee and eating cake, while Professor Haglund was hanging himself inside. A week after another man stepped in front of a tram and died."

"I didn't eat any of the cake. I accidently knocked it off the table before I had a chance to take a bite."

Nordkapp ran his hand across his bald head. "What a pity."

"Are you going to charge me with breaking dishes?"

"We ask the questions, Mr. Egland."

"I didn't know this man. What connection does he have with me?"

"Anette Olssen. She's the connection. She was having an affair with Professor Haglund. At least that's what she told us. That's why she had a key to his studio. But her classmates think the affair was something else. They said she was using sex as payment for her art classes, lessons she couldn't afford. She was always scrounging money, they said. For art supplies. That's why she came to your shop that day, wasn't it? To get some money."

"That's why my finger is burning."

"What?"

"Her grandmother's ring. Anette Olssen wanted me to buy it from her. But I refused. Now her grandmother is trying to tell me something." He pointed to the ring on the table. "The burning. It's a signal."

"Another dream?"

"I'm wide awake."

Nordkapp frowned. "Let's get back to the facts, Egland. You're an antiques dealer. Why didn't you want to buy her ring?"

"Gaustad Hospital. Anette Olssen's grandmother worked there. During the war." Egland closed his eyes. He paused. A deep breath. "Yes, okay," he said to no one. "I understand. Yes, I'll tell them."

"Tell us what?"

He opened his eyes. "She says if you want the real answers to your questions, you'll have to go there. To Gaustad. To visit someone in Ward 18."

"Is that the ward you were in when you were committed to Gaustad?"

"The answer you seek lies in Ward 18, she said. I was never in Ward 18."

"You may need to add Chapter 19, Section 157 of the Penal Code to your reading list very soon, Mr. Egland."

"Which is?"

"Obstruction of justice. Stop wasting our time."

"Justice?" Egland laughed. "You talk of justice? Whose justice? I sensed an infinite scream passing through nature."

Nordkapp leaned back in his chair and exhaled. "You're a very unusual person, Mr. Egland. And very, very annoying."

"I broke a cup and a saucer. And a plate. That's all I did. I offered to pay for it but they said no."

"Let's get back to Anette Olssen."

"All right. One evening I was walking along a path."

"Finally, something concrete."

"The city was on one side and the fjord below. I felt tired and ill. I stopped and looked out over the fjord. The sun was setting, and the clouds had turned blood red. I sensed a scream passing through nature. It seemed to me that I heard this scream. So I painted this picture, and painted the clouds as actual blood."

"What the hell is this drivel?"

"Edvard Munch. 1892. That's what he said. About why he painted *The Scream.*"

"*The Scream*? The painting that was stolen two years ago?"

"He painted injustice. The injustice he saw all around him, that he felt in his heart. Injustice of a kind no penal code can fix."

Nordkapp thrust the photo of the dead art professor towards Egland. "What in God's name, has all *this*...got to do with *that*?"

"*The Scream*. I can help you find the stolen painting before anyone else has to die. But first, you must go to Ward 18."

V

THE RAYS of the setting sun cast a solemn glow across Gaustad State Mental Hospital and its slate-roofed annexes. A clock tower with an onion-dome top loomed in silence over the black Volvo as it passed through a set of iron gates into the hospital's empty court-yard. Inspector Nordkapp got out of the car and marched across the gravel to a red-bricked portico at the tower's base, the entrance where patients were delivered by horse and carriage when the hospital was first opened.

Inside a grand Victorian foyer, a staff nurse approached. She was about fifty, brown hair tied back in a bun, wire-rimmed glasses. She wore a royal blue smock, clipboard in hand. Impatience was written in the creases across her tired face. It was well after visiting hours.

Nordkapp flashed his badge.

"You're late," the nurse grumped. "This way."

The old entrance was austere, its floor tiles and dark brickwork an echo of a troubled past. But the rest of the hospital had thank-fully been refurbished: shiny polished floors down long corridors; white painted French doors, bright and cheerful, leading into the wards.

The nurse set a blistering pace. The pair's quick footsteps resounded down the hallways, around many corners, from one set of wards to another, until they reached a door that led outside. They exited into a desolate courtyard where a cloister-like passageway connected the main building to a smaller neighbour. The wind whis-tled over the hospital's grey roofs.

"This is one of the original wings from the nineteenth century," the nurse said, unlocking the door into the next building. "It's been more than fifty years since the last patients were housed here." She flipped a switch. Dim fluorescent strips flickered on. A grey pallor painted the bare walls of its entrance hall. "The old Ward 18 is down here."

Halfway down the corridor, the nurse's quick gait stopped abruptly. She pointed to an oak door. "We're here. This was Ward 18. It's just a storeroom now. Why on earth do you want to see it?"

"Official inquiries."

"Policemen. Men of few words and big egos."

"An occupational hazard."

"Big egos?"

"Discretion."

"Really? If you worked in a place like this, as long as I have, you would learn the true meaning of the word, discretion, detective." She pulled a set of keys from her apron. "Okay, this is what brought you here. For what it's worth."

She opened the door and a wash of dull light flooded into the room from the corridor. The room was surprisingly large, wide and long, its ceiling cavernous in height. Wooden shelves lined one side, filled with stacked paint cans. But other than a single set of shelves, the room was an empty void. Rusty marks stained the old flagstone floor; marks that outlined where iron beds once rested, announcing the room's former purpose. At the far end of the room, a triangular dormer of bricks gripped a single window in its shadows. The setting sun glowed dimly through the dirty glass to create a dull band of crimson red framed by iron bars.

"His sister was confined in this room until her death," Nordkapp said.

"Who's sister?"

"Edvard Munch." Nordkapp shuffled forward to the edge of the doorway and pointed to the window. "Munch must have seen that very same red sunset, through those very same bars, when he visited his sister. He painted that glow in the sky in *The Scream*."

Nordkapp's breathing deepened as he stepped into the ill-lit room. "Do you feel that?"

"What?"

"That cold draft," Nordkapp muttered.

He took another step inside and then leapt backwards, stumbling into the hallway as if he'd been pushed. He braced himself against a radiator and once steadied, pressed his hands tight to his ears. He slumped to the floor.

The nurse ran to him. "Oh my God, what's wrong?"

"Someone's in there. Inside that room. Screaming."

"I don't hear anything."

"Shut it! Please!"

The nurse quickly closed and re-locked the door. "If you need to see someone, there's a doctor on call."

"I'm sorry." Nordkapp rose to his feet and dusted down his grey overcoat. "I shouldn't have come. But I was told I had to. Now I understand why. Why he painted *The Scream*."

"I've never liked that painting. I hope they never find it again. When you work in a place like this you see so much pain and anguish on people's faces. I know the painting is one of Norway's greatest treasures. But that look on that face...it's not something I want to be reminded of. For many of my patients, there's not much I can do for them but listen."

"Listen to their screams."

"Most of them scream in silence."

"Yes, I know," Nordkapp replied. "I've just heard it."

VI

THE DOOR to Egland's Antiques opened with a tinkle.

"You've installed a bell," Nordkapp noted.

Torsten Egland served an elderly customer at the counter, wrapping an article she'd bought. "It only works when the police arrive." Egland put her purchase in a bag. "Thank you, Mrs. Køpping. Come again."

"He's such a comic," the rotund woman said to Nordkapp as she left.

"Yes, a barrel of laughs," he replied.

"Another satisfied customer," Egland said. "How about you, inspector? How was Ward 18? Did you find what you were looking for?"

Nordkapp flipped the store's sign to 'Closed'.

"I thought your visit to Gaustad might bring you back here sooner rather than later."

"Another one of your premonitions?"

"Not exactly. Just logic." Egland walked around the counter to a display case. He opened its glass door and retrieved a curio, about eight inches tall. It was a chromed-metal model of a propeller plane, held aloft on a curved chrome plinth. "I sell a lot of these. A reproduction of a World War Two British Spitfire. Many of my customers are the children or grandchildren of the generation that flew them. It's a piece of nostalgia. But not antique. Made in China. I sell one, and then get another."

"And you're telling me this because?"

"I dreamt I was in one. A Spitfire. And it crashed. Into a giant sand dune."

"How unfortunate. Lucky it was just a dream."

"There was something strapped to its wing. A painting. *The Scream*."

"Now you have my undivided attention."

"Ah...the skeptic turned convert?"

"The policeman who follows whatever information seems credible at the time."

"That's what I said. Skeptic turned convert."

"So what do you think your dream means? What can I act on? Find an old Spitfire in working order so you can fly it? And where would I find a sand dune in Norway so you can crash into it?"

"Symbolism, inspector. Purely symbolic. The painting is on the move. It's going on a journey. In fact, I believe it's already been moved several times in the past. Whenever it is, that's when the painting acts to free itself. And when it screams. You've heard it, right? So, if my dream is another sign of things to come, we can expect another tragedy. This time involving a plane."

"Okay. I'll tell Sergeant Feyerstrom to keep a watch out for Spitfires over Oslo."

"Symbolism, inspector."

"Got it. But first, I have something to tell you," Nordkapp said. "Something I wanted your opinion on. It might be a piece of the puzzle. Or maybe not."

"Go ahead."

"Hans Jordahl knew Professor Haglund."

"The coincidence you've been looking for?"

"You and your coincidences. This one has a rational explanation. Jordahl was an art collector. He bought paintings from Haglund's gallery at the Paulus School." Nordkapp produced a photo. "This was found during a search of Jordahl's home. In a garden shed."

"*The Scream*? You found it?"

"No, it's just a copy."

"A copy? So what does that mean?"

"I have a hunch. If Hans Jordahl or his brother were involved in the theft of the real painting, they knew it wouldn't be wise to move it out of the country so soon after its theft. Too much police activity. They may have commissioned a copy from Haglund."

"But why?"

"To secure a legitimate bill of sale. You need that to get an export certificate. But in this case, I think it wasn't to ship the copy, but to ship the real thing in its place. A sleight of hand. The question remains, did they steal the real painting 'to order' for a collector? Or did they steal it in hopes of finding a buyer at some point in time? Either way, they'd secured huge loans to save their business by using all of the company's assets as well as their homes as collateral. The Jordahl brothers needed money desperately or they would lose everything."

"Who would buy something so famous that they also knew was stolen?"

"Some of the richest people in the world. They acquire stolen art for their private collections all the time. With no intention of displaying anything to the public. Ever since *The Scream* was stolen, we've been working through Interpol. They have informants in the world of underground art sales. We've been trying to understand who might want to buy *The Scream* if it ever came on the market."

"I need to see that copy of *The Scream*. I need to touch it."

"Why?"

"Perhaps Professor Haglund can tell me something that might help us."

"Haglund's dead."

"Skeptic? Or convert?"

VII

NORDKAPP STOPPED the black Volvo in a restaurant car park near the Jordahl home in Vestre Aker, an affluent suburb tucked in rolling hills between the Holmenkollen ski jump park and the Oslofjord.

"Where are we, Egland?" the detective mused. He rolled down the window and lit a cigarette. "I'll tell you where we are. A person stepped in front of a tram. Another hung himself. And the common denominator in their deaths? A painting. And *you*. Now you've seen Jordahl's copy of *The Scream* and you've said it 'told' you *nothing*. Nothing? You're a total blank? A big zero. Which means I've circled back to nowhere. If my superiors find out I've been basing my investigation on the 'intuitions' of an antiques dealer, I'll be enjoying an early retirement."

"Haglund probably didn't paint that copy himself. He must have had one of his students paint it for him. I can't connect with him. This has happened to me before. Sometimes if an object lacks intimacy, something precious to them personally, I can't see what I'm supposed to see. There are no rules, detective. No instruction manual. It is what it is."

"I can hear my boss now. So, Nordkapp, why aren't you making progress? Well sir, you see, one of my sources couldn't communicate with the dead. He says back to me...good job, Nordkapp. Here's your papers. Please sign them. End of career, time to take up fishing."

"That wouldn't be so bad. It's a relaxing hobby."

"Have you not been listening to a word I've said? This better not be some kind of warped game you're playing, Egland. Because this isn't a game. It's deadly serious. People are dying."

"You turn on a tap and water appears. You shut the tap off and it stops. But next time if no water comes out, blame the source. Maybe the water has run dry. Don't blame the pipe for that."

"Pipes and water? Spitfires and sand? A ring that burns your finger? What next?"

"I know all this doesn't add up to much so far. Not the way you people in the police expect. But I read clues too. It's not always obvious what these clues mean, where they might lead. You know that. There are dead-ends in your line of work, right?"

"All the time."

"The same applies with people like me."

"There's more than one of you? Heaven help us."

"You would be surprised. We just don't put flashing blue lights on our cars to tell people who we are." Egland looked out the window. "A beautiful clear day. I can see the ski jump at Holmenkollen. It has no snow."

"It's summertime. I'd worry if it did."

"And Norway has no sand."

"We're not known for our beaches."

"So why did I dream of crashing into a sand dune and not a snowdrift?"

"Why were you flying a Spitfire and not a jumbo jet?"

"Exactly."

"Oh gee, forget I said anything."

"No, you're right. Both things must mean something. Something very specific. The clues we're looking for. The painting is traveling to somewhere where there's sand."

"Well, that narrows it down."

"I can see it now." Egland closed his eyes. "The person that wants *The Scream* flies a Spitfire."

"Flies a Spitfire? That narrows it down even further. Are you kidding me?"

Egland scowled.

"Don't give me that look. All right. I give up. But this is your last chance, Egland. And I really mean it."

Nordkapp got on his phone. "Feyerstrom, contact Interpol. Ask them if they know of any dubious art collector who lives in a country with a lot of sand. Yes, I know that may be a lot of people." He paused as his assistant replied. "Yes, that's right. From a country in the Middle East, the Gulf States, or the Caribbean, somewhere like that. And then ask them, which of these art collectors might have an interest in owning World War Two aircraft?" Nordkapp paused again. "Don't ask me *why*, damn it. Just ask! We'll figure it out when we get the answer back."

"See, that wasn't so hard, was it?"

"Get out, Egland. I'm hungry. It's lunchtime."

NORDKAPP'S PHONE RANG. "Yes, Feyerstrom? What is it?" He took down some notes. The message was long. Finally, he replied, "Alert the police at Gardermoen. That plane mustn't take off! I don't know, man, make up a damned reason. Yes, use my authority. Have them detain the plane's pilots and anyone else waiting to board it. Get there as soon as you can. We're on our way." Nordkapp pocketed the phone. "Let's go, Egland!"

"But I haven't finished my sandwich."

Nordkapp reached over, grabbed the sandwich, and said, "You can eat on the way."

"Where?"

"Hurry up or I'll leave without you."

Nordkapp whipped several bills out of his wallet and thrust them on the table. He slung his coat over his arm and flew out of the restaurant. As soon as Torsten Egland climbed in the Volvo's passenger seat, Nordkapp plopped the sandwich in Egland's lap and flipped a switch on the dash. The car's siren blared. "Blue light time. Strap in."

The Volvo's tires spun, sending up a pall of smoke as it raced out of the parking lot.

"Where are we going?"

"Gardermoen Airport," Nordkapp replied as he careened past cars. "The Executive Jet Terminal. A plane has been chartered by an offshore company listed in the Cayman Islands. We put a watch on any export documents filed by Jordahl Engineering and...bingo...the company applied to ship a box of spare parts to a pipeline in Dubai. Spare parts? Yeah, right. Interpol says the pipeline company receiving the shipment is owned by a wealthy sheik linked to Russian money laundering. Because of that, they know a lot about him. And guess what? The sheik has a hobby and it's not fishing. He restores vintage aircraft."

"My Spitfire's plunge into the sand?"

"More importantly, he's a known buyer of black market art. He doesn't care how he feeds his obsession. As long as he stays in Dubai, Interpol can't touch him." Nordkapp accelerated onto the expressway's ramp. "Let's hope we get there in time."

VIII

THE BELL to the shop tinkled. A man in a grey overcoat entered—sixty-something, black-rimmed glasses, bald with swept-back white hair at the sides.

"It's been a quiet day so far," Torsten Egland said to him. "But I knew you were coming."

"I have no doubts you did," Nordkapp replied as he turned the shop's sign to 'Closed'. "We missed you yesterday at the Munch Museum. The Prime Minister unveiled *The Scream*. For more than two years, the whole of Norway has waited for that day and you weren't there to see it."

"I don't do glitz and glamour." Egland finished dusting a bronze sculpture of a bear. "What have you got for me this week?"

Nordkapp handed him a small object in a plastic bag. "It's okay, you can touch it. It's been dusted for prints."

The plastic bag contained a silver locket on a chain. Egland opened the locket. There was a photograph of a ginger cat inside. "Is this all I have to work with?"

"It's about as much as you usually get, isn't it?"

"Just checking."

Egland rubbed the smooth metal with his finger. He placed it in his palm, closed his hand, then his eyes. A moment later, he gasped. "Ssh...it will be all right. We're coming."

"And?"

Egland opened his eyes. "You will find her buried in a steep pasture facing the sun. In a tiny village near Bergen. It has a small harbour. There are two fishing boats. One has a blue hull; the other a red one. There's a church next to this pasture with brown wood siding. Its steeple has metal shingles. You'll know the village when you see it. It's a very pretty spot."

"I guess I'm going to spend my weekend visiting fjords around Bergen."

"It's nice this time of year. Few tourists. You could take a fishing rod with you."

Nordkapp smiled. "Call me if you sense anything else?"

"As always. I have your card."

AUTHOR'S NOTES – CHARLES A. CORNELL

One evening I was walking along a path, the city was on one side and the fjord below. I felt tired and ill. I stopped and looked out over the fjord—the sun was setting, and the clouds turning blood red. I sensed a scream passing through nature; it seemed to me that I heard the scream. I painted this picture, painted the clouds as actual blood. The color shrieked. This became The Scream.
~Edvard Munch, January 22, 1892

THIS WAS HOW EDVARD MUNCH, Norway's most famous painter, described the inspiration for painting his masterpiece, *The Scream.*

When an 1895 pastel-on-board version of *The Scream* sold in London in May 2012 for a then-record price for a piece of art of nearly $120 million US, Sotheby's called *The Scream* "one of the greatest icons of art in the world." This 1895 version was the most colorful and vibrant of the four versions painted by Munch and the only one whose frame was hand-painted by the artist to include his note of the work's inspiration.

Iconic indeed. An androgynous figure, hands clasped tightly over his or her cheeks. Anguish written across its face. A blood red sky. If ever a sound could be captured in a painting, *The Scream* must be the epitome of that art form. Even if viewed in a church-quiet gallery—in complete and total silence—one could not fail to hear *The Scream.* And that's exactly what Edvard Munch intended when he painted it.

To be sure, *The Scream* has had a troubled past from the moment Munch applied his first brushstroke. The scenery behind the figure has been attributed to the view from a hillside overlooking a fjord in Oslo's southern suburb of Ekeberg. Nearby was the Gaustad Hospital. Founded in 1855, it is Norway's oldest purpose-built psychiatric hospital and is still in use as a hospital today. Edvard Munch's manic-depressive sister Laura Catherine had been a patient. Clearly, her illness haunted his thoughts. Who knows what he saw and heard when he visited his sister? What we do know is that he painted *The Scream* and as my protagonist Inspector Nordkapp was told about the patients in Gaustad, "Most of them scream in silence."

Munch created four versions of *The Scream*, two in paint and two in pastels. The 1910 version was stolen in August 2004. Masked gunmen entered the Munch Museum in Oslo and stole it along with Munch's *Madonna*. Although the paintings remained missing, six men went on trial in early 2006 charged with planning the robbery. Three of the men were convicted and sentenced to between four and eight years in prison.

On 31 August 2006, Norwegian police announced they had finally recovered both *The Scream* and the *Madonna*, but the police did not reveal the circumstances surrounding the paintings' recovery. To this date, no one knows what clues led them to find the paintings. This story provides a fictional spin on how *The Scream* might have been found. It's pure fantasy, a figment of my overactive imagination. The names, places, and events depicted in my version of *The Scream* are speculative fiction in its purest form. But who knows the truth? Until we have another explanation, my story will have to be an entertaining substitute for the real thing.

~Charles A. Cornell

THE MEDUSA JUMP

KEN PELHAM

With the brush we merely tint, while the imagination alone produces color.
—Théodore Géricault

I

The Louvre, Paris
Present Day

CORINNE DUCHAMP, pragmatic and skeptical, was never one for silly chatter about premonitions. Still, the feeling that she'd reached her own crossroads between past and future electrified her today.

Easy, girl, she told herself. *Be ready*.

She moved through the galleries of the Louvre, drinking in the sights, her life shifting with each moment. She belonged here. Here, in her cathedral of art.

Today made Corinne's fourth visit in four days, and she'd

already been here six hours today. She would immerse herself, know every painting, every nick in their frames, every play of light and shadow on the marble statues. Her job interview loomed, thrilling and terrifying. It would be Friday. *Tomorrow.* She was one of just eleven to be interviewed, a select few pared down from hundreds of applicants. The other finalists boasted more experience than her. Three already sat on staff. Daunting odds, but she would nudge them in the right direction by knowing the museum like an old friend.

It was a chilly offseason day, midweek, the best time to visit the great museum, away from the thronging mobs of summer. She could negotiate the galleries without negotiating hordes of grumbling tourists. She mentally ran through notes on the great paintings all about her, stopping to scroll through her tablet to check this or that, to uncover obscure gems about them. It would be interview suicide to bungle facts about the greatest of the artworks. They must be second nature, recitable as if in casual conversation.

Corinne's feet ached, and she glanced at her watch. The hours had caught up with her. Today she'd limited herself to the Denon Wing, having plowed through Sully and Richelieu the two previous days. But Denon in itself comprised a vast collection. Just one more hour. Or two. The job meant too much to ease up now, but a bit of a rest would help her rally. She entered the Mollien Room, and the blessed, broad, cushioned benches in the center beckoned. She sank onto the end of the empty bench, and exhaled. Mollien's openness, with its blonde parquet floor, its towering rose walls, its vast skylight high above, calmed her. Artists and art lovers would sit in the middle of the bench, the better to appreciate and sketch. Bored teens would sit at the end communing with phones, scarcely noticing the paintings. Her own motive was simple. If she sat at the end of the bench, she cut in half the chances of engaging with someone.

And there was always someone. Usually a middle-aged man who'd eased away from his wife to sit by the young, pretty brunette. Impress her with his worldly knowledge, self-importance, and fake sensuality.

Corinne looked down at her tablet, scrolled through her notes, typed in a few more, and returned her attention to the Mollien Room's glorious French Romanticist paintings, mentally ticking off the artist and title of each. As always when she settled in this gallery, she finished her appraisal with the gigantic Théodore Géricault canvas, *The Raft of the Medusa*.

She studied its careful composition, the arrangement of volume and mass, the sweep of the eye from element to element, crafted for drama and emotion. The vision of death and despair and hope on a tossing ocean dared you not to look. She pitied the paintings near it.

Corinne stirred from her reverie when someone sat upon the other end of the bench. A sideward glance revealed an elderly man.

Corrine continued to admire the Géricault.

After a moment, the man sighed. "Stunning, isn't it?"

Don't engage. "Mm," Corinne said, not turning. She felt a small sharp stab of guilt. Years of self-suppression warred with her compulsion to accommodate, so often to her own detriment. After a moment, she said, "Yes." Perhaps he would take the hint. But they never do.

And he didn't. "What do you suppose Monsieur Géricault missed?"

The question surprised and annoyed her. She glanced at him. He seemed harmless enough; an older man, well-dressed and groomed, wavy gray hair, dark brown eyes. His French was fluent yet tinged with an accent she couldn't place. She looked back to the painting. She knew its details as well as—or better—than anyone she knew. "It's not a photograph, you know. It's an interpretation."

"The men all look a little too robust, don't you think? They're adrift and starving. Sea life in that time was hard enough, and deprivation the norm, even when all is going well."

He made sense; the survivors exuded strength and power, some thin, but all muscular. None emaciated. "Géricault expressed an ideal of the common man," she said defensively, realizing the answer sounded rehearsed. "And besides, they'd only been adrift thirteen days before being rescued."

"Thirteen days starving on a raft. Everyone should try it."

Corinne withdrew pad and pencil from her satchel and began

sketching, a detail of the survivor waving a cloth, hoping the man could take a hint. Several minutes of silence followed, but he remained seated. At last, he turned to her again. "I need to tell you something, Mademoiselle DuChamp."

She spun to him as he spoke her name, fear stabbing her thoughts, her skin tingling. She looked about, searching for a security guard, spotting one standing resolutely in the corner.

"Don't be afraid, Corinne."

"You're spying on me?"

"Only today."

She stuffed her pad and pencil back into the satchel. "Keep away from me, old man."

"I met Théodore Géricault," he said. "Such an intense, engaging young fellow."

At first, she'd imagined herself the object of some elderly man's misguided sexual fantasies. Then the attentions of a stalker. Now it was worse; the man was out of touch with reality.

"You've done your homework, Corinne. You will do well in your interview tomorrow."

She hesitated, her thoughts racing. How could he know about the job? Was he in the employ of the museum? How else could he know of her job interview?

"I no longer want the job," she snapped, gathering her belongings and stuffing them into her bag. "I'd rather sketch caricatures for tourists in the Tuileries."

"I'm not with the Louvre in any capacity."

She stood and took a step towards the security guard, but stopped. The guard glanced at her, his eyebrows arching with concern and questions.

"My son studied you at great length," the old man said. "It's because of you that he could study Géricault and all these others. And the reason I'm here."

"I'm going now."

"This is your cathedral, is it not?"

She stopped.

"Your cathedral of art."

She tensed. She had never shared her secret name for the Louvre. With anyone. Not her father, who cared little for art, nor her mother, a talented, shy watercolorist who had succumbed to breast cancer when Corinne was eleven. Not her little brother. Not to friends. She had never even committed the phrase to her notes or diary, fearing she may sound sentimental.

"How... why do you say that? Guess that?"

"It's in my son's book. Please, Corinne, sit a moment. Hear my story. My son's story. It will help you tomorrow."

Against her better judgment, she sat. "Two minutes," she said. He smiled gently. "Thank you for your moment's trust and I—"

"Your name?"

The man hesitated, as if debating the wisdom of divulging. "Ah, well. It's the least of my worries at this point. My name is Henri Komarov-Banks."

"Sounds made up."

"May I begin? My two minutes will be up soon."

"Speak."

"My son, Marcel, has made a name for himself as an art historian. Not to be too boastful a father, I daresay he has become one of the four or five best in the world. He did so by focusing his expertise. Like the best, he concentrated and specialized." The man gestured toward *The Raft of the Medusa*, and swept his arm around the room. "French Romanticism. Your favorite as well."

"Hm."

"Marcel has made the Romantic movement his life's work, immersing himself in it, experiencing the art first hand, not just brooding over moldy treatises."

"So he visits museums and private collections. Good for him."

"More than that. He's dived headfirst into inspiration, environment, and context. What fuels the artist's passion? What makes a painting *live*?"

Something buzzed in Corinne's mind. She'd often felt the same desire to know.

"Are my two minutes up?"

She studied the man. Something so familiar about him. "Do I know you?"

"We've never met."

She wasn't so sure. Something bothered her, coiled below the surface. Alarms had gone off in her mind, but his calmness dulled them. "I don't know any art historians named Marcel, top ones or otherwise."

"He isn't well known yet."

"But you said—"

"He'll be world-renowned in three hundred years."

"Ah, a misunderstood genius, years ahead of his time. Marcel keeps good company."

Komarov-Banks nodded toward *The Raft of the Medusa*. "You understand, of course, why this subject became the fevered project of a Romantic idealist?"

"Out of frustration with the restored monarchy."

"Corinne, stop. Stop reciting history, and *feel* it. When the loss of the *Medusa* struck, it tore at the French conscience. You can see from Géricault's sketches how he struggled to find the exact moment to capture, to tell the story as if he'd witnessed it himself. Most casual viewers today see an exciting shipwreck and survival, but without context. Géricault knew his fellow citizens and the feelings burning in them. This was his clarion call to them. Centuries later, the painting survives. It survived even the second world war, spirited away from this museum disguised as theatrical scenery to keep it out of Nazi hands. And here it is, the passion still bursting off the canvas, even though most viewers have no idea of its context. My son has been writing a book about it. He wanted to experience its origins firsthand."

"Rather impossible," she said reflexively.

"From your perspective. Listen. My son has written and published seven books on Romanticist art and the Louvre's collection."

"I would know of such books, but I don't. What's your game?"

"Ah! I use the wrong tense, a frequent mistake. I said Marcel has written and published these books. What I meant is that he *will*."

"You seem pretty sure. You must be the one who'll publish Junior's books."

"He was writing the new book."

"Was? Changing tense again?"

"It's a matter of perspective. He both *will* write these books and he *has* written them. I have a story to tell you."

II

New Stockholm, 2367 AD

I LEANED FORWARD in my apartment, staring at my son in disbelief. My boy—Marcel was thirty-two, but still a boy to me—had that earnest, passionate look on his face that told me all I needed to know. "Marcel, listen to me. It's still a bad idea. A terrible idea."

"Dad, I need to see the *Medusa* to understand it. To experience it. I need you to make it happen. No one else can."

"And I won't."

"This book will be my crowning achievement. I can feel it. It just needs authenticity. Truth."

"Time travel seduces us, Marcel, but things can go wrong and they do."

"Dad! Five decades of temporal expeditions have not once changed the world. Not in the slightest. In spite of accidents, in spite of overshoots, our world is unchanging. What difference does it make if an expedition flops?" He threw up his hands. "You and I will still be here in this moment having this same damned conversation."

"That's what we think, not what we know. So we try to manufacture a little insurance. Temp jumpers are carefully screened and trained, and then we monitor and regulate the hell out of them."

"So regulate the hell out of me. But send me. Please, Dad, I'm begging you."

I sighed and leaned back. I could make it happen. I'd clawed my way up the stifling ranks of the Temporal Manipulation Congress to earn a seat on the Expeditionary Council, one of only seven persons in the five worlds that could authorize a temporal jump. Once there, I earned a reputation for uncompromising adherence to protocol and safety. I simply refused to let anyone bend jump rules. Only ninety applicants had ever been approved for a jump, each strictly monitored and accompanied by a Council member.

"Marcel," I said at last. "It's not as simple as you think. There are politics and this will certainly be cast as nepotism."

"Fine. Put family aside. You've studied my proposal. You know my credentials. Do they come up short or not? Be honest, Dad."

I wanted to lie, to put an end to this nonsense. But when he was a little boy, I promised him I would never lie to him. "No," I said. "In fact, I've already taken it to Council. Your credentials are the best we've seen. Ever."

Marcel's eyes widened and he leaned closer. "And?"

"The vote was four to three to approve the jump."

He gasped, and struggled for words. "By one vote? Dad—thank you! With all my heart, thank you. You don't know how much this means to me."

I nodded, my eyes moistening. "Council requires me to accompany you. Nguyen-Ramos led that charge; she hates my guts, you know."

Marcel hugged me, squeezing tightly.

He didn't need the whole truth. That's not a lie, is it? I voted against approval, in a loud, fist-pounding dissent. But once the vote was made and the *Medusa* jump approved, I demanded that I be the Council member to accompany him.

JUMP CALIBRATIONS WENT SMOOTHLY, the working out of an exact 4D point in space-time so that we would not materialize within the void of space, within a hill, a wall, underwater, or in a tree. As it was, the open countryside near Rochefort, France in 1816 offered simple negotiation. We materialized a meter above a wheat field, and tumbled in a heap onto the ground, laughing. Marcel turned an ankle, and bruised and scraped my palms. They train you for spills but I'm too damned unathletic to learn. But we held up, more or less intact.

The engineers pinpointed that exact same location for our temporal exit and return. We would need to be back in the wheat field at noon in three years and ninety-five days, with organic temp marker implants intact, to be whisked back to 2367, back to the New Stockholm jump chamber, exactly ten seconds after we'd left.

We made our way to Rochefort, three kilometers west, and caught a ferry to Ile-d'Aix, in the mouth of the River Charente, where we found lodging in a weathered inn. *Medusa* rested at anchor in the snug harbor, a fine, trim ship, its gleaming hull freshly painted white and black. Our plan had been worked out in minute detail, following the strictest protocols. *Medusa* was a warship, a frigate, under the command of Captain Chaumareys. The French Revolution had been undone by the defeat of Napoleon in the War of the Sixth Coalition in 1814 and the monarchy restored. The Bourbons raced to solidify power, appointing old royalists to positions of rank in the military, a hedge against new revolts. They gift-wrapped and handed Chaumareys command of the *Medusa* even though he'd barely been to sea in twenty years.

Medusa was to take on passengers and leave for France's colony in Senegal. Important passengers. The voyage would deliver the new governor, Colonel Julien-Desire Schmaltz, and his wife and daughter, along with two-hundred and fifty soldiers to restore French rule over Senegal.

Over the next few days, Marcel and I wandered the town, bantering with shopkeepers and fishermen and maids; chatting up whores and the sailors and drunks they clung to; and arguing politics and the price of ale with bureaucrats and gadflies alike. Marcel even wrangled a laugh or two over a beer with Governor Schmaltz.

We knew *Medusa*'s departure would be delayed two days by blustering headwinds, and once it left would never reach Senegal. The

Council had approved expeditionary time before and after the tragedy, but had laid down strict prohibitions against boarding the doomed ship. Any positions taken by ourselves aboard ship affects things. The plan allowed us to observe the workings, the loading, and the staffing of the ship and her companion vessels, and to get to know the temperaments and talents of those to sail upon them. After the ship's disembarkation, we would make our way to Lisbon, book passage to the Portuguese colony in the Cape Verde islands, bribe our way to Saint-Louis in Senegal, and interview survivors as we could. Then we would buy passage back to France, where Marcel would observe Géricault at work and interview those near him, but never approach him. We would attend the unveiling of his masterpiece at the Paris Salon on August 25, 1819. At noon on the fifth of September, from the field outside Rochefort, we would be jumped back to 2367. It was a good plan, a meticulous, robust plan.

But Marcel had other ideas.

June 17th arrived, and *Medusa* would sail at seven that morning. We would be at the dock two hours prior to witness the final preparations and boarding. But when I awakened at four-thirty, Marcel was nowhere to be seen. I dressed and searched our neighborhood, thinking him out on one of his restless walks, or a breakfast. Again, there was no sign of him. On a sudden, uneasy feeling, I returned to the inn and sorted through his belongings. Most were there, but a change of clothes and a few essentials were missing. I counted out our money; most remained but a sizable amount—more than enough to secure passage on a ship—was missing.

My pulse quickening, I stuffed the remaining money into my pocket and hurried down to the dock.

MARCEL STOOD on the aftercastle deck of *Medusa*. He saw me but pretended not to, and drifted away from the railing. "My son," I called. "What are you doing? Come down at once!"

He glared at me and shook his head. "Dad, stop. Please. I won't miss this opportunity and. I'll see you in Saint-Louis." He dismissed me with a wave and disappeared below the aftercastle.

I shouted again, earning scowls and suspicious looks from the crew. I ignored them and approached the foot of the gangway. Three officers, seated at a small table, stared at me. One raised an abrupt, cautionary hand. "Name?"

We were using false names, of course. "Jean-Luc Rousseau," I said. "I wish to come aboard."

He scanned a list of names, and then a second list. "You are among neither crew nor passengers, Monsieur Rousseau."

"I could have told you that. My son has boarded and I wish to remove him."

"And does he have a name? That might prove useful."

"Algernon Rousseau."

"He is listed. A late addition."

"Let me speak to him."

"He appears disinclined to listen."

"I need to talk him off this ship. We have…urgent family business that needs attending."

"If I had a centime for every young man that went to sea to escape urgent family business, I would buy the damned ship and sail to Martinique. Now if you will please be on your way, Monsieur, we have a schedule and more pressing matters that need attending."

"Ten minutes is all I ask."

He shook his head. "All passengers have boarded."

A sudden, chilling thought occurred to me. I already knew how many that would sail aboard *Medusa*. Four-hundred, precisely. "How many are sailing today? Total number?"

"Why?"

I slipped the three men each a silver franc, a considerable value in 1816. "Simply a request from a superstitious old man."

The officer's eyes widened. He studied me for a moment, glanced about, and stealthily pocketed the coin. His compatriots followed his cue. "Louis, give him the number of passengers."

"No!" I slapped the table. "Tell me the total, passengers and crew."

"Three hundred and ninety-nine."

I felt the blood drain from my face, and a cold shiver raced through me. There was no escaping history, the fact of the four-hundred. With trembling hand, I withdrew my billfold. "Name your price. I wish to book passage aboard *Medusa*."

MARCEL LEANED with his hands upon the railing, gazing down at the placid brown harbor water.

"Marcel," I said softly.

He startled, and surprise colored his face. "Dad! What are you doing? Get off the ship."

"It's done. The future doesn't change. Fifty years of expeditions have proved that. I was last in the queue to board and the gangway was hauled right after me. *Medusa* carried four-hundred on this voyage. With my boarding, I complete the four-hundred. The officers confirmed it. It seems that joining you on this doomed ship is not a violation of space-time, but in fact a requirement."

"You don't know that! Someone may buy a passage at the last moment, or there may be a stowaway. Or a simple miscount."

"If that were the case, I, or someone else, will be removed from the ship."

He struggled for words. "I—I'll speak with the Captain."

"You're tilting at windmills. I'm here. But damn it, why did you do this?"

"You've never really gotten me, Dad. Half-measures don't bring understanding. This will be my greatest work, and just interviewing sailors and survivors won't capture the entire scene. If I'm going to write it honestly, I need to experience it, to live it."

"You know I can't protect you when we return. I can't even protect myself. This is the severest breach ever of the protocols and the Council will demand full accounting. I'll lose my job and we'll both go to prison. You get *that*?"

"Dad—I'm prepared to suffer consequences for my life's work. But not to harm you. We can stop, get you off—"

"No! I'm here with you."

The *Medusa* shifted gently underfoot. Sailors and longshoremen cast off lines and the frigate edged from the mooring. Men shouted and scurried; men in tender boats leaned into their oars, their lines to the ship tightening and creaking. *Medusa*, accompanied by our companion ships, the slow, clumsy *Argus* and *Loire*, and the sleek, speedy *Echo*, eased out of the unworried waters of the harbor and entered the restless, flexing Atlantic.

WHAT A FEAST for the senses is a grand sailing ship of old! *Medusa*, less than ten years in age, breathed power and grace, and heeled sharply in a brisk beam wind, groaning with the swells of the ocean, its great clouds of sails flapping and thundering as they unfurled. Men clambered like monkeys high into the rigging and onto the yardarms. We plowed the sea southward at a good nine knots, foam arcing from the bow, glowing white in the sunshine.

Marcel made friends with many of the crew and passengers, recording every moment with the multiple, organic nano-computers hidden on him. Nano, designed to dissolve in four years, is the only future tech allowed to be carried into the past. Leave only footprints, we say.

While preparing for the journey in our home-time, Marcel had pored over the details of the *Medusa*, and even designed a holo of the vessel at full size. The dimensions of *Medusa* made it sound like a large ship, one-hundred fifty-four feet in length, thirty-nine in the beam. In reality, it was shocking to see the cramped conditions of such a vessel with four-hundred aboard.

On June 22nd, we lost sight of the sluggish *Argus* and *Loire*, making haste at the insistence of the Governor. All went well, the officers, crew, and passengers brimming with good spirits. But shouts of alarm raised when a lad of only fifteen fell overboard. Crewmen reacted as one and brought the ship about. But even with haste and skill, such a maneuver devours precious minutes. The boy screamed and flailed, and it became obvious that he could not swim. We watched, helpless, horrified, as he disappeared under the waves before we drew within fifty yards. Marcel impressed me with his resolve not to prevent the tragedy, but his silence the rest of the day told me it had struck him in the face. And the incident stabbed me inside; like Marcel, that boy was someone's son. The trip changed in a heartbeat from an engrossing academic exercise to a reality of pain and tears. A pall hung over the ship, an ominous note of sidelong glances and reddened eyes.

Marcel befriended another boy, Léon, a twelve-year-old. Léon shied from others, friendless, bullied by a few bored soldiers. He seemed alone on the voyage, drifting away from attention, making himself invisible. Fitting in with neither his own class nor the aristocratic class. He needed relief from his wrenching unhappiness, and Marcel convinced a kind young officer, Midshipman Coudein, to take the boy under his wing and teach him ship life.

We both knew Léon would be dead within three weeks.

As for myself, I sought out the acquaintances of Monsieurs Henri Savigny, the ship's surgeon, and Alexandre Corréard, a rather excitable engineer and explorer, both fine gentlemen, well-spoken and thoughtful. I ascertained they deftly straddled the chasm between the republicans and the loyalists. But I knew the incendiary nature of their coming account of the voyage, a tome that would inflame anti-royalist rage in the aftermath of the tragedy, blistering the monarchy and the system that allowed such a thing to happen.

Their gentlemanly demeanors made me wonder what agendas they harbored.

We passed Madeira, far off Morocco, on June 27th, and crossed the Tropic of Cancer on July 1st. We enjoyed a day of celebration, a mock ceremony with a sailor playing the Lord of the Tropic, who granted us passage into his realm.

Though we made good time, the Governor grew impatient, and cajoled Captain Chaumareys into speed and haste, a shortening of the route. Chaumareys dithered but finally acquiesced and sailed us southeast, defying orders and common sense, close in to Africa, into the treacherous Arguin Banks off Mauritania, which had earned a reputation as a graveyard of ships. The *Argus* and *Loire* refused to follow and stayed far out to sea. The *Echo* stayed with us for a while, with lanterns hung from the rigging for us to see in the dark, before giving up and moving out. We lost contact with all.

Discontent among the sailors brewed. These may have largely

been uneducated men, but they were far from stupid. They knew the sea and they knew sailing. They knew the murderous reputation of the Arguin Banks.

Chaumareys knew too but ordered his men to bother him only if soundings read less than eighteen fathoms, at which point he would calmly guide the ship into deeper water.

I watched Ensign Maudet, whom I'd befriended, at the bow casting the sounding lead out and hurriedly hauling it back in, time after time. I eased near. He shot me an angry glance, huffed, shook his head, and cast the line again.

"Maudet," I said. "Are we in good shape?"

He swept his arm all about. "The color of the sea changes."

"It's beautiful, the color."

"One man's beauty is another's horror. And see, the fish swarm all about. Any fool, even a landsman, can read the signs of shallow water."

I stayed with him for some time, chatting. His demeanor became one of increasing worry. At last, with one cast, he drew eighteen fathoms. "God damn him," he growled. He shoved me aside and shouted for the captain. Chaumareys strolled to him.

"Eighteen fathoms, Captain!" Maudet cried. A hundred men stopped work and turned. "We're upon the Arguin!"

Chaumareys nodded calmly. "Take care, Maudet. Take care." He ordered the lowering of the studding sails on the port side, and the bringing of the ship about one-quarter to starboard and into the wind. It was the afternoon of July 2nd.

Maudet cast his line, drew it in. The sounding came back with a reading of ten fathoms.

Chaumareys paled. He stammered a moment and shrieked for two quarters more to starboard.

More hurried soundings.

Six fathoms. A mere thirty-six feet.

The sailors knew what this meant but said nothing. *Medusa* itself had a draft of just thirty feet. Silence and terror filled their faces.

A crunching scrape. A shudder ran through the deck below our feet. *Medusa* heeled and lurched to a stop, sending men and women stumbling to the deck. I fell hard, and Marcel crashed into a mast. A cut opened in his scalp, and blood streamed down his face. Cold fear ran through me, knowing the fate of so many aboard. The ship seemed to feel a bit more life and moved again, but twice more ground to a stop.

I examined Marcel. His wound was superficial, and we stanched the bleeding with a bit of cloth torn from my sleeve. Still, in the age before antibiotics, any wound could be life-ending.

The sails were quickly lowered. But bad decisions have a bad habit of piling one onto another. At high tide, we were at that very moment in the best opportunity we would get to refloat off the reef. But Chaumareys shouted down his officers' pleas to jettison the fourteen valuable three-ton cannons, and *Medusa* settled deeper into the sands of the bank.

The crew worked furiously, the long hours of afternoon stretching into evening. As darkness descended, fear and anxiety simmered, reflected in the eyes of crew and passengers alike. The fate of the *Medusa* rested with the power of the tides and the unpredictable, shifting winds.

The next day, the officers attempted one measure after another to lighten and refloat the ship. Top-masts and spars were taken down and thrown overboard. Water butts were pumped empty. Anchors were hauled and sunk in deeper water to drag the *Medusa* free. Nothing worked. The *Medusa* would never leave.

We had just six small boats. For four-hundred people.

After heated debate, Schmaltz and Chaumareys decided to ferry groups in turns to the coast, some fifty miles east. The important people would be the first to leave. There was never any consideration for something as simple and just as who was most fit or suited.

France being a divided, broken nation, its tensions had sailed aboard the *Medusa* from the moment it had put to sea. Among our number, there were many royalists and many Bonapartists, revolutionaries. Marcel had spent the voyage engaging both sides, as best he could. But the Captain and Governor saw only his fraternization with the Bonapartists.

Governor Schmaltz, largely responsible for the calamity, earned some small redemption by drawing up plans for an enormous raft, onto which a great deal of the cargo could be loaded. The men fell to feverish work on its construction, stripping the *Medusa* of spars and planks, lashing them together, and soon had built the thing, which stretched sixty-six feet in length and twenty-three in width. A great, groaning beast, in sheer size almost a ship in itself. The seamen dubbed it *"la Machine."* A small makeshift mast and sail were tacked on, not a worthless gesture but pitifully inadequate for steering.

The plan was to have the raft towed by the boats, but human nature and the elements soon destroyed that plan. The next night, heavy drinking swept through the soldiers and discipline broke down. A gale whipped up the sea's fury as midnight approached on the 4th, pounding the stranded ship with wave after wave, threatening to tear it apart. A ship stuck in one place has no defense against storms. With a loud splintering creak and a crack, the keel broke in two. Waves crashed over the deck, tearing loose the helm and whipping it about like a toy. Water poured into the aft cabins. Panic gripped the ship. Chaumareys abandoned the ferrying plan and decreed that the longboats would tow the raft, with people rather than cargo, to shore. Accompanied by two officers brandishing clubs, he hurried through the four-hundred, singling out those chosen to board the boats by tapping them on their chests and motioning them towards the craft. He paused at me, scowled, and moved on.

Sailors and soldiers, officers who'd fallen out of Chaumareys' favor, and suspicious Bonapartists were consigned to the raft.

I grabbed his sleeve, unable to take it any longer. "Captain! We are gentlemen, our passage paid in full."

He shook me loose, glaring. *"Je m'en fou!* Gentlemen you may be, but also revolutionaries and not even true Frenchmen. You'll not cut my legs out from under me. Onto the raft with you."

"But, Captain—"

Chaumareys nodded to his officers, jerked a thumb at me. One of the men struck me with his club, knocking me to the deck. "Get on the raft!"

I struggled to my feet and took a step toward the officer, who raised his club for a second blow. An arm encircled me, restraining me.

Marcel.

"Dad, stop. You can't win this fight but you can get yourself beaten senseless. We have to get on the raft."

"That raft will be the gate to hell," I whispered.

"But we will survive it. You know the numbers better than anyone else in the world. In hundreds of temporal jumps, not one jumper has died or even been seriously injured. A few scrapes and scratches. And the future was not changed one iota. Nothing can happen to us because the future is set. The statistics prove it."

"Statistics prove *probabilities*. Not *possibilities*."

"Dad, we have no choice! We will survive, and as men not even of this time, we cannot—I will not—take the place of any other who might enter the boats."

I knew he was right, although the horror of what lay ahead tempted my refusal. My son was a better man than me.

We boarded the raft.

THE GOVERNOR'S BOAT, a fourteen-oared vessel, took on thirty-five persons. It could have carried more, but his belongings were judged more valuable than people, and took up space in three massive trunks.

Overloaded with men and a single woman, our raft settled low into the water, its deck below the surface. One hundred and forty-seven souls had been crowded aboard it.

We hitched *la Machine* by ropes to three of the boats, and all six boats began to pull east for the desert coast of Africa.

Seventeen men chose to stay with the *Medusa*, some too frightened to set foot on the overcrowded boats, some too drunk to care.

We made slow progress that first day, six or seven kilometers, our officers estimated. At that rate, we would make the coast within a couple of days.

I knew better.

Strange, how stress and danger twist manageable situations inward upon themselves. Frictions soon erupted aboard the boats. Shouting, arguing, shoving. One boat, its helmsman glaring, veered sharply toward one of our tow boats. Perhaps fearing he was to be rammed and capsized, the tow boat's officer drew his saber and with three blows severed our line. The other towing boats followed suit, hacking their lines and leaning into their oars. One circled back, its young officer pleading with the other boats to help us to shore. His own crewmen spat curses and threats at him. One sprang to his feet and took a wild swing at him, missing. On the brink of mutiny, the officer sank into his seat and gave up, weeping, his eyes fixed upon us.

The men of our raft shouted pleas at the boats. A gray-haired sergeant shoved me aside and stared at them. "Heartless bastards, pigs all," he growled, and leapt into the sea and swam after them. A wave rolled over him and shoved him under. He surfaced, sputtering, and returned to the raft. Our pleading boiled into shaking of fists and hurling of obscene curses and threats of revenge, anguished begging and tears and, at last, stunned silence, the only sounds remaining being the splash of sea and the whispering of the wind.

The boats receded into the distance and vanished below the horizon.

La Machine drifted, abandoned and alone.

THAT FIRST DAY on *la Machine* slid into a morass of minutes and hours as we drifted between endless sky and ocean. The sun beat down, and our hunger and thirst grew. In the confusion of the panicked abandonment of the *Medusa*, the promised stocking of our raft with provisions had gone undone, other than a woefully inadequate store of water, biscuit paste, and wine. The officers portioned and passed a bit of each to each of us.

Anger at our abandonment simmered and grew, hostile glances and whispers becoming ever more frequent. Men in authority had left us to die. And now new men in authority commanded the raft.

With the night came growing wind and waves.

We strung a rope in haste about the perimeter of the raft, a desperate and pitiful excuse for a railing. The seas rose and pitched us about as twilight gathered. Terror gripped us and the officers aboard commanded the center of the raft, the safest spot, away from the dangerous edge. Already partially submerged, waves swept into us and over us in the darkness, hour after hour.

A raft of such size, built of timber and masts that once were tree trunks, might make you think such a craft is sturdy. But the massiveness of the timbers created a new menace. Bound together by rope, and flexing and moving with the sea, they were as nothing against the power of surging mountains of water. Men slipped between the gaps in the shifting timbers and were mangled and crushed, or fell through them into the sea. Screams of agony, cries for help, and the sharp crack and dull crunch of breaking bones punctuated the long night.

Pitch blackness and blind terror engulfed us. I clung to Marcel and he to me, entwining ropes about our arms and hanging on with fists clenched. Midshipman Coudein, next to us, held Léon tightly, knowing the boy could not swim. With each wave, I believed I would be torn and swept into the pitching ocean. I told myself that Marcel was right, that we could not die in that time, that the future was written and unchangeable. But fear smothers reason.

The gray of morning came at last and the sea eased its assault. The raft rode a few inches higher, and I knew the reason; in the night, twenty of us were dead or gone. One hundred twenty-seven remained.

On the second day, the seas and temperaments calmed. Those about us mustered a hopeful dialogue of reaching the coast in short order, many convinced the boats would return that day and deliver us to salvation. Marcel and I said nothing about this, and just as we knew it would, the ferocious waves returned and slammed into us that second night.

Despite the pummeling of the Atlantic, the night sky remained clear and moonlight glittered like diamonds on the waves. Fear and discontent drove the soldiers to drinking, whispers became grumbles, and grumbles became shouts of rage at the officers and passengers. And at us. A soldier grabbed an officer by the lapels and shook him, and the officer landed a blow in the man's face. A melee exploded. Mutiny and fighting raged throughout the night. Screams pealed in the dark. Fists thrown, eyes gouged, men hurled overboard. We held our own amidst the melee until dawn, exhausted, bleeding, and battered. My son and I were no longer enlightened men from a gentle future; we were cornered animals bent on survival, and the rules of temporal expedition, of non-engagement, meant nothing now.

Sixty-five men were killed that second night. Sixty-two of us still lived.

I examined my bruises and cuts and found nothing serious. Marcel had a broken finger, an eye swollen shut, and a cut across his chest that dripped red into the sea. I tore a bit of cloth from my shirt and pressed it against his wound, managing to stop the bleeding.

There were no medical supplies amongst us.

Worse, our only cask of water had been lost overboard.

A semblance of order returned, the fury of the night subdued by the stark realities of survival. No boats or ships appeared. Only an empty horizon of ocean stretched in all directions. Pushed about by current and wind, we made scant progress east toward Africa. Sharks now circled and haunted us. We tried catching the smaller of them for food, without success. A few of us ate belt leather or linen. Without food now, the realization dawned that we had but one resource in ample supply. Human flesh.

That third day, some gave in to hunger. The nightmare faced us. They drew knives and cut flesh from the dead—the meat coming away in brownish, purple chunks—and ate it raw. Some cut the flesh into strips and hung it from the little mast to dry.

Marcel and I, and the majority of the survivors, turned away in revulsion, unable to watch. My stomach heaved, but there was nothing inside me to vomit.

On the morning of the fourth day, we found ten more dead, and let all but one slip into the sea. That poor man would be saved for food.

Blisters and ulcers scarred our bodies. Our lips cracked, our tongues grew swollen. Our feet and lower legs, immersed in salt water, deteriorated into masses of red sloughing skin, the pain making it impossible to stand and rest out of the water. Saltwater stung our wounds without cease.

Suspicion and delirium swam through me, and I suppose, through everyone. We had reduced to a crawling, numbed, weak mass of humanity. Despite that, anger at the officers welled up once more, and fighting erupted yet again, an animal snarl of clawing and wrestling. By dawn, there remained only thirty alive on *la Machine*, down from the hundred and forty-seven that had boarded it. The lone woman amongst us had twice been thrown overboard by mutineers, but rescued both times.

On the sixth day, trembling and mad with hunger, I took a dried strip of human flesh, tore a bit free with my teeth, and ate it. I handed a strip to Marcel. He took it without a word. Neither of us spoke or looked at each other.

Though most of the wine had been lost in the fighting, we still possessed some, and some tiny flying fish that had been caught in the timbers of the raft. Strict rations were agreed to. But on the seventh day, we caught two men stealing wine, passed a quick judgement, and threw them overboard. I smiled as the thieves died.

Léon, who had gone to sea on his life's first great adventure, fell ill, and sank into a fevered delirium. He drifted for hours, by turns whimpering or crying out for his mother, at last quietly dying in the arms of Coudein. Marcel and Coudein wept tearlessly for the lad, while starving soldiers watched in sullen silence. One soldier glanced at his compatriots, and crept closer. Marcel kicked him, knocking him back, and nodded to Coudein. Together they committed the boy to the depths of the uncaring Atlantic.

Just twenty-seven of us still lived.

Marcel's certainty that we could not die in that time seemed to be holding true.

You read the accounts of such disasters. You think you

understand. You are bigger, stronger, than the victims. You aren't. You fail to understand how the human mind works, or doesn't work. I found myself confusing faces, hallucinating. I strolled with my dead wife among the towering redwoods of California, dreaming of our unborn child. Under such extreme deprivation and terror, the mind tries to construct a safer reality. It wants to stave off its own gathering whispers and darkness.

A dozen of our number lingered near death, too weak and sick to move, and drew ragged breaths, their eyes glazed. And yet they clung to life, and we faced a desperate decision. Should the doomed live and endanger the whole of us? By our calculation or wishful thinking, their absence granted the remaining of us an additional six days of life. The debate raged, in the presence of those whose fates we were deciding.

I had journeyed to that wrenching moment and place from my pampered 24th century existence, with strict orders not to affect outcomes. I wish I could tell you I followed that rule, a rule I myself had crafted. But thirst, hunger, and fear ruled my every thought, and I cast my vote. We sent the twelve overboard to their deaths, convincing ourselves we acted out of need and mercy.

The lone woman, her thigh having been snapped in the shifting timbers, and whom had twice been saved after being thrown into the water during the riots, was among those we now sacrificed, along with her husband. The terror, the pleading in her eyes, will haunt me the rest of my life.

Marcel's condition deteriorated, his face turning pale and gaunt. What sleep he could get was wracked by cries of terror, and his waking moments were fraught with spells of hallucination and shivering. He grew weaker by the hour.

A hasty conference was called, and in one of the few moments of reason aboard the raft, it was agreed the violence must end. We threw all sidearms and weapons into the ocean, with the exception of one saber and a few tools.

Yet the next day, one soldier eyed Marcel, and claimed he'd fought alongside Napoleon at Waterloo and knew a dying man when he saw one, and he saw one in Marcel. My son should be tossed, he growled. Or killed and eaten.

I shouted him down. Marcel remained healthy, I argued, his wounds superficial, and he would recover. Savigny, the surgeon, examined him and agreed, giving me a concerned, unconvinced look. But his opinion carried the moment.

The blistering sun of the tropics worsened our condition by the day, by the hour. On the tenth day, the sodden timbers of the raft drifted into swarms of giant jellyfish and Portuguese men-of-war, and we endured painful, debilitating stings.

Every man on *la Machine* lingered near that fragile boundary between life and death, inching closer by the minute.

MARCEL WORSENED, and fell into delirium on the morning of July 17th, our thirteenth day aboard *la Machine*, the raft of death. He awakened sporadically, lucid and fearful. I cradled and rocked him in my arms, lest he be swept overboard by the waves. Upon his third awakening that morning, he gripped my forearm, weakly.

"Dad. What day?" His voice cracked, barely more than a whisper. "What day is this? The 17th? It's today, isn't it?"

I shushed him. "Yes, son," I whispered. "And there are fifteen of us. We've made it. The *Argus* will save us today. We've survived!"

He coughed and smiled. "The future is set, Dad. It's set. We would always survive." He paused, drew a deep, dry breath. "Fifteen survivors. There would always be fifteen. That couldn't change."

And he was right. The fifteen survivors comprised an unchangeable fact. Fifteen of us *would* be rescued by the *Argus*.

And to comfort him in his last hours, I lied to my only son.

Sixteen still lived. One of us would die before the *Argus* saved us.

"Yes, Marcel, beautiful boy." I drew him close against me and stroked his hair. "We've come through hell. We will be off this raft in a few hours, fed and clothed, and taken to luxurious homes to recuperate. We'll see Paris, the City of Light. We'll meet Monsieur Géricault and drink coffee and wine, and talk of tragedy and art, and witness the creation of one of the greatest paintings the world has known. Your book will be completed, and the 24th century will read it in awe. Be still now, and rest, and know it's coming to pass." My eyes clouded and I swiped at them with my arm. "Rest now. Rest."

Marcel smiled and closed his eyes. His breath came long and slow and labored for some time, and minutes stretched into hours.

He shuddered in my arms. His grip tightened on my arm, then relaxed.

His breathing stopped, and his body sagged.

I had lost him. My whole body shook with anguish and sobs.

A shout. One of the men pointed, his hand trembling, at the northern horizon. "Sail," he cried in a voice like wind through brittle, dead leaves, and louder, "A sail!"

Men scrambled and shoved and clawed to see.

A tip of white sail peeked above the edge of ocean far away, its hull hidden below the curvature of the earth. Men waved rags, screamed, begged the ship to come nearer.

And yet it receded and disappeared from sight. The men collapsed in despair, weeping.

But within a few hours more, the shout went up again. Nearer, much nearer, the *Argus*, with its sails full, bore down upon us.

We were saved. The fifteen were saved.

I eased Marcel to the edge of the raft and released him to the sea.

III

The Louvre, Present Day

CORINNE STARED AT KOMAROV-BANKS, her mind reeling.

He sat silent now, looking down at his folded hands. His eyes glistened, and he shook with sobs.

He had told his story in barely more than a whisper, sometimes

looking deep into her eyes, sometimes at the great painting, sometimes staring at some unseen world.

The tale was too fantastic to be believed, yet told with such
depth and anguish it had to be true, at least to this poor old man.
Delusion is truth to the mentally ill. Whole worlds and realities can
be constructed within the mind and believed with certainty. Her
apprehension of this man had morphed into pity during his tale,
and she felt it her duty, the right thing for any person of compas-
sion, to hear him out and to comfort him.

"So you see, Corinne," he began again, looking up at her, "I
survived what few of those that boarded the raft did. Nothing of my
world varied from when I had left, except that I now had no son. I
languished in a quiet, shaded hospital, recuperating, regaining my
strength. Or what of it I could; I've never returned to my old self.
But I got better and traveled to Paris. I met young Monsieur Géricault in a café and told him my story. Everything except my journey
across time. He watched me with wide eyes, questioning often,
capturing every detail. And he drew me, dashing off sketch after
sketch. Never have I seen such magic, such genius, at work. Look at
his greatest work, Corinne. *The Raft of the Medusa.* Look closely. Tell
me what you see."

Corinne turned to the painting. Géricault had captured the
moment of hope, the swirl and movement of the living, the stillness
of the dead, the moment the sail of the *Argus* appeared on the
horizon.

And a pale old man in the painting, turning away from the joy,
the hope; uncaring, as if he knew what would happen. An old man
clutching the body of a young man. A pale man, bearded.

The man, now clean-shaven, sat next to her.

The blood drained from her face, and she shivered.

She touched his arm. "You're the old man on the raft."

His eyes shone with tears. "I lost my son and my soul on that
expedition. Géricault captured that. He captured me and the entire
nightmare in a single canvas, and with it, shook France to its core.
The Bourbons never recovered from the fallout. France righted and
set itself again on a course towards democracy."

The museum guard gave them a phony cough and arched his eyebrows in both a frown and a question. Corinne glanced about to see the gallery had emptied. Down the corridor, the remaining few headed for the exit.

Komarov-Banks touched her arm. "We've overstayed. Apologies." They stood and he gave a slight bow. "And I've broken a half-dozen laws by telling you what I have. I trust you'll never mention a word of your talk with the crazy old man, ever? Not in confidence, and certainly not in writing?"

She nodded.

"Adieu then, Corinne. I'm completing Marcel's book for him. His way. He'd have loved to meet you because you have a hand in the future of this painting. But meeting you meant more than I thought. This has been cathartic. Healing."

"Mr. Komarov-Banks."

"Call me Henri."

"Will I—my interview is tomorrow. Will I get the job?"

He smiled. "Corinne, you know the answer. This is much too political a hire for such a young, unconnected person, even one of brilliance. No, the job will be awarded to an elderly gentleman on staff, who has put in years of work and obsequiousness. That's the way of the world. Hasn't changed, even in the 24th century."

She sagged. Why then even bother?

"A minor setback, dear. You will interview, be passed over. But in eleven days, you'll get a call from the retiring director, offering a lesser job, that of an entry-level curator. You'll be working here within the month, and in seven years you will be the new director of the Louvre. The youngest ever. The greatest ever. You'll design the plan that will preserve the world's greatest art from the destruction of the next great war, twenty-three years from now."

Corinne gasped. Her skin prickled, and her legs grew weak. She sat down, trembling.

Henri smiled sadly. "Go now, Corinne. Rest. As I said, you will assume a great responsibility for this painting." He swept his hand across the gallery. "For all these paintings. You have a world to save."

He bowed and was gone.

Corinne drew a deep breath, and stared at *The Raft of the Medusa*, and Henri clinging to the body of his beloved Marcel. Her eye moved to the nameless dead, and to the saved men, and found the last gathering of will within them, focused on the moment of hope, on salvation, on the ship on the horizon.

Salvation.

All these works of brilliance, the world's treasures. Humanity's legacy. The world's art would soon need a hero. A savior. The seeds of a plan to save them took root.

Marcel knew his life's work, his purpose.

She now knew her own.

It stretched before her, a great unfinished canvas, defined yet unbounded, a canvas of strife and struggle, but also one of hope and promise, like a sail beckoning from a far horizon.

AUTHOR'S NOTES - KEN PELHAM

Théodore Géricault was driven to create his masterpiece after reading *The Shipwreck of the Medusa*, by Corréard and Savigny, the only account written by survivors of the raft. Other eyewitness accounts were written by survivors of the wreck of the ship and of the trek through the African desert to Senegal. As one would expect, not all accounts matched on all points. Views and agendas differed, CYA efforts appeared, and biases bubbled up. I found the source that best sifts through the available information is *The Wreck of the Medusa: The Most Famous Sea Disaster of the Nineteenth Century* (2007), by Jonathan Miles.

The tragedy marked a turning point for France. The Revolution had come apart, the monarchy returning to power in the Restoration. But France simmered, embracing anything but unity. When the Crown began appointing favorites to positions of power more for loyalty than competence, something was bound to explode. And then *Medusa* ran aground off the coast of Africa. The details of bad decisions and gross incompetence are too many to corral within a short story, but they were all too real.

The reception upon the unveiling of Géricault's *The Raft of the Medusa* came swift and loud and mixed, falling along predictable lines of allegiance.

The notion of Corinne saving the great works of art from a future war is rooted in World War II. In August of 1939, with conflict with Germany just days away, the Louvre suddenly shut its doors for three days of "repairs," during which the greatest artworks were secured and secreted away to other locations. *The Raft of the Medusa* was hastily trucked to Versailles, and later to Chateau de Chambord. In 1940, the French army collapsed under the onslaught of German blitzkrieg but dedicated saviors of art, led by Jacques Joujard, risked their lives in a dangerous shell game with the Nazis, who looted the cultural treasures of conquered lands wherever they went. Shifting the art around, stalling with endless letters and red tape, and pitting German officers and bureaucrats against each other, Joujard and others managed to delay surrendering the art. An engrossing look at the rescuing of the world's art from Hitler's plunderers is Robert M. Edsel's *The Monuments Men* (2009). Louvre masterpieces similarly saved include *The Mona Lisa* and *Winged Victory of Samothrace*, the subjects of other stories in *The Masters Reimagined 2*.

Hope you enjoyed this little tale of art, survival, and the sea.

~KP

OIL AND HEMLOCK

KRISTIN DURFEE

"The hour of departure has arrived, and we go our separate ways, I to die and you to live. Which of these two is better only God knows."
--Socrates

I

"SOPHIA," Amita called to her granddaughter, her voice high and stressed. "No, not that way."

Amita picked up her pace, panic rising in the back of her throat as Sophia skipped across the hall from the special exhibition rooms toward the European Paintings wing.

Taking her granddaughter into the city for the day seemed like a great idea the week prior. The weather was supposed to be beautiful and there was a special event at the Metropolitan Museum of Art on comic books, Sophia's latest obsession.

When Amita brought it up to her youngest daughter, Ophelia readily agreed. The boys had an away game that weekend and Ophelia was trying to figure out what to do with her youngest, Sophia. The girl kept her nose buried in books and comics—

graphic novels, Amita had been corrected more than once—and had little interest in following her older brothers to yet another soccer game.

At eleven years, Sophia was old enough to be relatively self-sufficient, but not quite old enough to be left by herself for an entire day. Amita, retired and widowed, was the natural—albeit at times reluctant—choice to watch the girl.

Of her four children, only Ophelia still lived nearby. Amita both loved and loathed the closeness. It enabled her to see her daughter, but also meant Ophelia felt like she had jurisdiction over her life.

Since Nico passed away six years ago, their children were under the impression Amita could no longer be trusted to be alone for too long. Even though Amita had been alone for years, many years, and survived perfectly well.

But she humored them. Allowed Ophelia to take her to doctors and out to lunch once a week. Let her daughter refill any prescriptions and occasionally pick something up for her at the grocery store. She flat-out refused to relent the holidays to Ophelia, insisting on still hosting Thanksgiving and Christmas, but she knew those would be taken away one day as well.

So here she was, in her mid-seventies and put out to pasture, chasing after a pre-teen through the marble halls of one of the most beautiful buildings in the world, desperate to coral her.

Not in there, she repeated in her head. Begged, really. She wasn't ready. Even after all these years and countless trips to the museum, she avoided this wing entirely. She hadn't seen the painting in years, and wasn't prepared to now.

"Giagià, the exhibit goes into here, too," Sophia called back.

Amita noticed the stand to the left of the entrance and quickly read the words.

Due to the Skylights Project as well as the expansive nature of Comics: A History, *Portions of the Department of European Paintings have been temporarily closed. Select paintings have been relocated throughout the museum. We are sorry for any inconvenience.*

Amita let go of the breath she'd been holding in a steady stream, willing her heart rate to return to normal and her fingers to stop trembling.

Sophia talked on and on about the pictures they looked at, as well as 3D-printed sculptures of characters Amita didn't recognize, but which thrilled Sophia. When another hour passed and Amita suggested they go upstairs to the Balcony Lounge for a drink and afternoon snack, she'd completely forgotten her earlier panic attack.

Sophia took the marble stairs two at a time, chatting equally about being starved and all the other things she wanted to see. Amita's foot hit the top step when she saw it. The painting was large, over six feet wide and surrounded by a simple gilded frame with ornate details in each corner. Seeing it disoriented her, as if time pulled her back into its grasp like all those years ago. Her heart quickened again, and her hands turned slick with sweat as they clutched her leather handbag.

A couple behind her brushed into her. "Excuse me," the man said, sneering as if her stopping had ruined his entire day. Amita said nothing.

In the distance Sophia called to her, then her loud, smacking footsteps echoed back toward her. Part of Amita's brain admonished the child and she almost yelled at her to pick up her feet, but Amita found herself without words.

"Giagià, do you want to sit down?" Sophia asked, her little voice laced with worry. A small hand wove into Amita's, snapping her out of her daze.

Amita looked down and around. They were standing on a small landing which split the staircase, the frame the only one on the wall. Evidently this was one of the rehomed works, deemed important enough to not be packed away during the renovations. A bench sat in front of it and a small light illuminated a plaque on the wall, presumably giving information about the painting, but she didn't need to read it.

"Yes, yes, let's sit," Amita was able to get out. Her throat suddenly felt dry and she found it difficult to swallow. Her previous hunger pains vanished.

Sophia tugged on her softly and sat beside her on the bench.

"*The Death of Socrates,*" she said, leaning forward and reading the plaque. She stared up at the dark colors and robed figures. "Well, that's creepy."

"Creepy?" Amita asked.

"A bunch of super-muscled old dudes crying while one is yelling at them."

Amita looked up at the painting. Yes. She supposed it could be interpreted that way. She searched the upper left-hand corner, a smile tugging on her lips.

She breathed a laugh. "Not a bunch of old dudes crying. Just one." She gave another small chuckle. Apollodorus, leaning against the wall, visibly crying, turned away so the man sitting on the bed couldn't see him. "That's not what it was like at all," Amita said. Her voice sounded far away as her eyes focused on the Jacques-Louis David oil painting. "Apollodorus wasn't even there. Well, not *then*." The memory came flooding back to her with such vividness, she could almost hear the sobbing down the hall. "Socrates had sent him away."

Sophia turned to her grandmother. "Giagià, what are you talking about?"

"It was a long time ago. A *lifetime* ago," she said.

She'd never told anyone. Not even Nico. Certainly none of her children. It wasn't that she was planning to take it to her grave, but she never saw a moment to bring it up. Never really acknowledged an opportunity. Maybe now. Maybe it was time.

She took a deep breath and pointed to the corner of the painting. "You see those three figures there? Walking up the stairs."

Sophia squinted before nodding.

"The one waving," Amita said, her pointed hand still hovering in the air. "That's me."

II

AMITA WAS LOST.

She'd turned down a road not paying attention, engrossed in the assigned reading from her professor, desperate to not screw up another assignment. When she looked up, she didn't recognize the street. The houses touched on each side with small yards in front, each surrounded by a wrought iron fence. Each were in various degrees of holiday decorations. One yard had lights covering each inch of available space. One with a single string of large, colored bulbs haphazardly wrapped around a tree.

The farthest house was dark, not a single window illuminated. Amita found herself walking toward the structure without even thinking, unsure of what unseen force propelled her forward.

The structure was brick like the rest, but the windows were covered in plywood, explaining its darkness. Black discolorations could just be made out under the wood. The roof had a small hole in the top. Soot stained the remaining gray shingles.

Amita looked back the way she came. No one else was on the sidewalk or street. Some cars were parked on the road, but other than that, no signs of life were apparent. She pulled her coat tighter, puffs of her breath floated away into the growing darkness.

She could go inside.

The thought entered her mind without prompting, as if whispered into her ear.

The front door was partially askew, like a man's tie not quite straight in the middle of his shirt. Amita pushed open the small gate and was surprised when it didn't make a sound or fall off the hinges, knowing her luck.

Her grandfather called her *átychos* all the time instead of Amita. Unlucky.

It was true. She had a knack for ruining a situation or causing problems when none seemed to be on the horizon. Her father would laugh, tell his father to stop, that she would bring bad luck upon herself with that thought process. True or not, it still followed her wherever she went.

She knew walking up to the house was stupid, risking an already jinxed evening which included misplacing her bus token and getting lost. Even as she walked up the cracked concrete pathway, no alarm bells went off in her head. The normal voice deep in her gut stayed silent. The only thing she heard was the whisper to keep going.

Her feet barely made a noise on the three steps up to the small stoop. Rotted leaves blanketed the concrete, pillow-soft beneath her. The door loomed. She touched it, and peeled off a fleck of faded blue paint with her nail before knocking.

She hadn't pressed hard against the door, half expecting it to clatter off its hinges and fall to the ground, but at her touch, it moved forward, exposing darkness beyond it. Once again, she looked behind her, but the street remained empty.

Amita placed her book in her backpack, a primal want to have her hands free. She wasn't a risk taker. Hell, she'd never even had a drink, tried any of the drugs her fellow psychology majors swore by, or rolled through a stop sign. She was a rule follower. Countless lectures from her father to be a "good girl" to do nothing to "ruin her reputation" ran through her head. Her heart pounded in her chest, screaming for her brain to pay attention, to use logic and turn back, but her mind didn't listen.

She stepped forward.

The air shifted and had a different weight. It was strange to think of it that way. It felt soupy, but didn't have the same humidity she'd expect with the oppressive air.

The same carpet of rotting vegetation littered the floor inside and tinged the air with its pungency. But beyond the sickly scent, there was the faint smell of salt.

No, not salt. *Salt water.*

Amita took deep breaths with each step further into the house. What little light the moon and streetlamps provided fell away and her eyes struggled to adjust. She could just make out a staircase to her left as she moved through a narrow hall, instinctively putting her hand out to touch each of the walls as she moved. Vines and leaves snaked over them.

She entered a large space that must once have been a dining room, though any furniture had long since crumbled and decayed into heaps of debris. She stepped gingerly, unable to avoid crushing objects beneath her feet, creating such a ruckus she was sure someone would burst through and catch her any second.

Faint light poked through what must be floor-to-ceiling windows beneath the vegetation on left side of the room, enabling her to see an immaculate white wall straight ahead with a door. Not a single vine or weed traversed its entire surface. A ghostly halo of light glowed around the door frame.

She picked her way over the littered floor and paused, her hand hovering over the handle, and opened. Like the front door, it gave way without protest. But unlike the other door, instead of depositing her in a dark, crumbling house, sunlight and warmth met her.

Then a hand reached out and pulled her through.

III

AMITA WANTED TO SCREAM, but the sound trapped in her throat as she catapulted through the doorway. She landed in a painful heap, expecting to find more rotting plants and wood under her hands, but instead, hard stone covered the ground.

The hand that pulled her through now helped her to her feet and shoved a pile of dark blue cloth in her hands.

"Quickly, quickly, put these on," a man's voice said, a heavy accent tinting his words.

Amita tried to make out his face, but the sun was so bright bouncing off the white stones around her, she was momentarily blinded.

"*Quickly!*" He mimed putting the clothes on.

She obeyed, catching the strong scent of straw and horse as she pulled the fabric over her head. The added layers, along with her heavy book-bag, made Amita break out into an instant sweat.

He furrowed his brow. "I assumed, as those who came before you..." he trailed. "Do you speak English?" he asked. "*Ellinikā?*"

Amita nodded. "I speak English."

He clapped his hands, his bearded face looking vaguely familiar. "Wonderful. I was worried maybe you spoke yet another language and I'd have to spend a few years learning that one as well. English is good."

She nodded, having no idea what he was talking about.

"Follow me," the man said as he strode away from her.

She half-ran-half-tripped as she pulled the garment down and sprinted to catch up. The sunlight made it difficult to see where they were going, but the urgency of his voice made her follow without question.

If he tries to take me into a building, I can always scream. I can always run away, she repeated in her mind.

Amita kept her eyes fixed on the man's billowing red robes as he dodged people on the now-busy street. She stole glances, afraid to lose him, but more frightened by what she saw.

People, mostly men, bustled around her dressed in similar woolen garb. They spoke in animated tones, the words vaguely familiar as they rushed by, barely looking where they were going and several times she came to an abrupt halt to prevent from crashing into someone.

Once, someone from the crowd called out to the man, but he didn't slow down so she obediently followed.

He darted into a dim, empty alley. She was a half-step past him before she realized he'd changed directions. With a glance behind to make sure she wouldn't barrel into someone, she entered the silent side street.

Tall stone walls, the color of sand, surrounded them. Her heart pounded in her chest. Lost amid the din and clatter behind her in such a roar, she hadn't realized the man was speaking.

"I'm sorry," she said, the words slipping out of her mouth in the automatic way she'd been raised to always apologize.

The man shook his head, as if dealing with people who couldn't keep up with him was a constant occurrence, and annoyance.

"I said, in here." He gestured to a small wooden door to his right.

If he tries to take me into a building...

Amita stayed rooted in place, desperately unsure. It was clear she was no longer in New York, but then, where *was* she? This man seemed to want to help her, but she couldn't be sure. With nowhere else to go, and no clear path back to the door she'd fallen through, that voice in her head, the one she did trust, urged her to keep going, to see where all this was leading.

He motioned again, the same impatience of his tone now showing up in his gestures. She followed.

IV

THE ROOM, with its stone walls, floor, and ceiling, chilled her. Amita pulled the robe around her more tightly, shivering from her cooling sweat and lowering adrenaline. The man gestured to the wooden stool by the door. She took it without protest, a wave of exhaustion pulling her onto its seat.

"When are you from?" the man asked. He sat in an identical stool across from her. His posture was relaxed, his hands palms-up on his lap but his words made the hairs on her neck stand again.

Not *where* are you from. *When.*

She opened her mouth to answer, but closed it wordlessly.

"So," he started again, but his words were slower and more pronounced this time. "When are you from?"

"Nineteen-seventy-seven," she said, trying to keep the question mark off the end of her words. It sounded so ridiculous. The whole thing was almost laughable.

Almost.

He clapped and looked up for a few moments, fingers twitching, before looking back at her. "Two-thousand three-hundred-and-seventy-six years from now. Oh, wonderful. I do not believe I've had someone from that exact time before. Tell me, what are your thoughts of your place in the world as it relates to the age you live in?"

Pure joy washed over his eager face. He leaned slightly forward, allowing the dim light in the room to illuminate his features. Amita got a good look at him for the first time and realized with a shock who he was, the previous faint recognition falling into place. There had been debates for hundreds of years regarding the accuracy of his portrait. Amita could say without hesitation it was pretty spot-on.

She stuttered, unsure of how to address him.

"M...Mr...Socrates?" The words felt thick on her tongue. She took slow, steadying breaths, fighting the feeling of her throat tightening.

"Brilliant!" he exclaimed, clapping his hands again. His excitement was causing more alarm in her.

What in the hell was going on?

"I need you to explain," Amita said, taking care to speak clearly and slowly.

He sighed. "This part is always so tedious." He leaned back and crossed his arms.

Amita felt like she was supposed to apologize.

She didn't.

The silence swirled along with the dust in the room, settling around them like snow.

After what felt like an eternity, Socrates sighed. "Well, all right then. For the last forty years, at random time intervals, someone comes through that portal. As far as I know, I'm the only one who finds them, at least at first. They stay for a short while, then one day, some door has a faint glow on it. That is when I know it's time. I open it, the person walks through, and..." He clapped his hands, making Amita jump. "Gone."

Amita found it difficult to take a deep breath. "And how long are people usually here?" Her voice sounded far away and foreign, as if someone else spoke the words.

He shrugged. "Days. Sometimes a few months. One fellow was here for almost two years."

The sound of wood slamming against stone made Amita jump again. It wasn't until she looked around and noticed she was standing that it registered her stool broke from the force of her moving so abruptly. She closed her eyes and picked up the shards of wood, afraid to look at Socrates. When she dared a glance, she saw he hadn't even flinched.

His calm had the opposite effect on her, and Amita found herself spinning in circles, debating if she should make a run for it or stay put. She felt like a cornered animal, gasping for breath.

Socrates got up and brought over a new chair, gesturing her to sit back down. She complied, gingerly.

He opened his mouth to speak again, when another man burst through the room. The new arrival glanced at Amita, gave a quizzical look, and turned back to Socrates.

He spoke quick words in a foreign language before Socrates lifted a hand.

"English," he said. "This will be good practice."

The man sighed before relenting. "You are going to be late," he admonished. "You cannot be late."

Socrates waved his hand. "They will have to wait for me."

"Teacher," the man said, his voice quieter now. He also relaxed his rigid posture, as if to seem less threatening. He spoke again in the same quiet tongue and Amita realized with a jolt she recognized the language. The shock of their meeting made it difficult for her brain to place at first. *Greek*.

"And her?" Socrates responded in English, gesturing to Amita.

The new man's face flashed with exasperation. "How attached are you to your hair?"

Amita instinctively touched a stray black lock and tucked it back behind her ear. Hair her mother and grandmother were so proud of. Hair she spent Sunday nights conditioning with olive oil as she listened to her grandmother's stories of what it was like growing up in Greece. How it was to move to America. Raising a family away from the only home she'd ever known. How important maintaining culture was.

Socrates moved across the room and picked up a knife from the wooden counter. "You must cut it very short," he said. "It is the only way you can move freely through this town with me."

She took a deep breath, nodded, and took the knife from his hand. Amita understood, she needed to pretend to be a boy. She wondered when—if—she traveled back home, her grandmother would ever forgive her. Her hands shook as she took a fistful of hair.

Amita took another lung-filling breath, and cut.

V

THE WOOLEN HOOD scratched the naked nape of Amita's neck as she hurried to follow the two men. She'd shed her coat and bag, feeling vulnerable now, but glad to have less items on her as they moved back through the heat of the city. The men spoke in clipped sentences, so she still had no idea where they were going, but she could tell they were running late.

The cramped, narrow streets fell away, and the group spilled into a vast square. At one end, a grand columned building stood with six stone steps Amita had to take two at a time to keep up with the men. She pulled her cloak tighter, glad for the first time in her life her chest was boyish-flat.

As they'd moved through the town and now as they burst through the gilded doors of the building, Amita noticed no women loitered around speaking with the men. A few passed them, laden with baskets or babies, but they were always on the move. No time to stop and chat.

They pushed through more doors into a large, rectangular room with hundreds of chairs. In one corner stood a small platform surrounded on three sides by a wooden railing. The room was filled with standing men shouting at one another.

"You stay here," the young man ordered Amita as he pulled Socrates forward and through the crowd.

Amita pressed herself against the wall, desperate to sit, her shaking legs needing respite. Not wanting to draw attention, she continued to stand. The crowd of men grew and she felt the press of bodies against her.

The smell of damp wool and body odor made her stomach churn. She tried to bury her head in her own clothing, taking slow breaths in through her mouth, but she realized she didn't smell much better.

A pounding broke through the din, cracking like thunder. Those around her began to sit and she quickly joined them. Without an obstructed view, she was able to see Socrates in the small box, the younger man sat in the chair closest to him. Three men burst through the open door and strode through the room in sweeping steps. The whole thing looked like a cheap high-school production of a trial.

A trial.

The words spun in Amita's head and she fought the urge to ask the man next to her what they were there for. Though part of her knew. Of all days, of all doors to travel through and all time to be brought into.

It was the trial of Socrates.

VI

IT WAS the first semester of her college philosophy class she'd learned about the trial. Amita sat, wide-eyed and anticipating learning all the worlds secrets. She'd been so naive, a mere four years ago, about what college meant.

She pictured laying on green grass while groups of students debated the ethics of their times. That happened sometimes, but they were just kids smoking pot and yelling at each other about things that didn't matter. Who were they to stop a war? Why did anyone care about their rights as minorities?

Amita had come to college—the first in her family to attend—to be enlightened. She wanted to know why her parents were the way they were. Gain insight into how the "old country" shaped their rigid views of the world. How she could help them see a better way.

When she stated she wanted to study psychology and philosophy, and not a more "useful"—in her father's words—degree like secretarial skills, she knew it would be an uphill battle. But she was up for the challenge. Her first year, though, consisted mostly of classes that felt more like a continuation of high school than the springboard into her adult future.

Finally, in second semester of sophomore year she got to take an applied philosophy class. One in which they had topics to debate, ideas to form opinions on, and where, in a large lecture hall, she fell in love with a man named Socrates.

They began at the end, well, at *his* end. With the trial. Her professor, a dashingly handsome man Amita found difficult to be in the same room with and still pay attention, spoke of how Socrates found himself on trial for his teachings.

Socrates felt so strongly one should pursue self-understanding above all else, he came into trouble with the Athenian authorities for "corrupting the youth". Sitting in class, the whole thing seemed quaint to Amita. How a new form of thought could be so threatening to a government, they'd kill over it.

But they had.

And this was it.

Amita listened in rapturous silence, hungering to understand every word, but the Greek eluded her and, save for a few words her Grandmother said, found herself lost. Bursts of emotion rippled through the crowd. Men yelled and jeered—a few choice words Amita did recognize—while others cried out in protest to what was being said. A few times, those around her stood and shook their fists, and Amita rose along with them, but kept her hands at her sides.

The spectacle had gone on for hours when the pounding noise returned. A man banged two objects together and she craned her head around those in front of her to see what made the noise. She was expecting a modern-day gavel, saw the image of it in her mind, but it appeared the man simply held two small blocks of wood, clapping them together. It made her feel very far away from home.

The three men spoke in succession while passing out disks to the room. Amita took one, making a concerted effort to not allow her hand to shake as she took it. Praying the man who handed it to her wouldn't notice her feminine-looking fingers.

Amita tried to read Socrates' expression, but he remained blank and stoic. One by one, the crowd approached one of two boxes and dropped their coins in. A few bit their thumbs in the direction of who Amita assumed were the prosecutors. When it was her turn, she dropped her disk into that same box.

A period of rapid counting happened and an announcement was made. Gasps and murmurs rippled through the crowd.

Her heart raced. She knew what was going to happen, what *did* happen. The last man spoke, and the banging returned, and people in the room began to weep.

Socrates nodded, stood, and walked up the stairs, motioning her to follow as he passed.

She obeyed, head hung low as she followed him out, part of her wishing her vote could have made all the difference.

VII

AS THEY WOVE BACK through the crowds in the streets, several men and even a few women rushed to embrace Socrates. He shook their hands, spoke a few words, then extracted himself and kept walking. One man embraced Socrates and kissed him straight on the mouth, shocking Amita.

Then a young woman approached Socrates and started yelling, smacking him with fists as those around her attempted to pull her away. Her cries melded into a mix of screams and sobs.

"Xanthippe," the young man said in Amita's ear, making her jump. "His wife," the man explained, in very slow, purposeful English.

"Yes, yes I know," Amita said, finding herself speaking in the same halting manner and hoping it didn't offend the man.

He nodded. "I am Plato."

Amita gasped, and she reached to steady herself on his arm. *On Plato's arm.*

"I..." he trailed off, a look of panic in his expression.

"Come," Socrates barked ahead of them, Xanthippe finally subdued enough to allow them to pass. "There is no woman harder to get along with than that one," he said when they'd caught up.

"Teacher," Plato whispered.

Socrates waved at the air as if batting the words down. "Come, we will talk."

They walked for some time, but Amita couldn't find any familiar landmarks and was unsure if they were in a new part of town. They still got stopped by people—evidently word spread about the great philosopher's fate—but the exchanges were quicker. A hand-hold here, a face touch there, and then both sides parted ways. Amita wished she'd taken ancient Greek in school, it was frustrating to only understand snippets of what was happening.

A few more turns, a few more streets, and they came upon a small dwelling with a gated courtyard. Socrates pushed through and Amita and Plato followed inside the small house at the other end of the yard. It was all too weird. Being here with these two men, these men she knew so much and yet so little about. She wanted to hit pause and ask them a million questions, but knew there wasn't time for that. She knew what was coming.

"I am sorry you came today of all days," Socrates said. "I would have liked to speak with you more, to question you more."

Amita opened and shut her mouth before just nodding.

"I'm sorry, this is just all so, so surreal," she finally mustered. "I've studied your teachings and—"

"You have what?" Plato asked, cutting her off and leaning toward her as if he couldn't hear her properly.

"I have studied, I *am* studying, I should say."

"Where? How?" Plato asked.

She looked between the two men, unsure how to read their shift in reaction toward her. "At my school, at my University."

"University," Socrates breathed the word out. "You attend University?"

Amita nodded. "I am studying philosophy and psychology."

The joy on the two men was instantaneous. They began speaking feverishly to each other in Greek.

Amita held up her hand. "Slow, slow please, I know very little Greek, but I certainly can't follow with how fast you are speaking."

"We have not had a student come to us before," Socrates said, mercifully switching back to English. "Yes, we have had people who have known us, but never a student. And never a *female* student."

"Well, I'm afraid that is both a good and bad thing," she said, a bubble forming in the back of her throat. "Because I know what happens to you. I know what happens today."

Socrates nodded. "Yes. But that is no matter. You are not causing it, so there is no need for you to feel badly about it."

"We must leave," Plato said, reaching forward to touch the older man's arm. "There is time to go. Your sons would understand. I could get word to them. We could find safe passage for you."

Socrates shook his head and turned back to Amita. "You already know. You know that isn't going to happen."

"But it could. You could change it if you want, I'm sure," she said with authority, although she had no idea. This was time-travel, for Christ's sake. She had no Earthly clue how it worked.

Hell, maybe Socrates *did* try to escape all those years ago and that's what quickened his death sentence. No one knew for sure. People only knew what Plato told them.

Amita crossed her arms and gripped her opposing elbows to try to ground herself.

It didn't work.

"No," Socrates said, his voice lacking the gravity Amita expected. "Death is not something to be feared. If that is what is decided for me, that is my fate. It is out of my hands."

Plato slammed his fist on the table. "It doesn't have to be."

At that moment the door burst open and a man rushed through. Amita jumped back, unsure if the man was going to attack them. The stranger widened his arms and threw himself into Socrates' arms, sobbing. Amita was glad they weren't in peril, but the outburst of emotion shook her even more.

"Apollodorus," Socrates said, embracing the man and speaking a few quiet words in Greek.

Plato placed his hands on the man and pulled him out to the courtyard. Amita heard their muffled voices, but couldn't make out any words.

"I don't think I should be here," Amita said.

Socrates waved her off for the umpteenth time. "Nonsense. How does anyone know where they should be? You are here, thus, this is where you should be."

"I don't mean to be selfish, but what is going to happen to me? I need to get out of here, and, correct me if I am wrong, but you are the only one who knows about the doors and how to get back, and if something happens to you." She couldn't finish the sentence, regretting the *if* as soon as it was out of her mouth.

"Plato will be able to help you if needed."

Amita rubbed her forehead to ebb the growing tension headache. "Am I here for a reason?"

His face lit up. "Oh, yes! Yes, of course you are. Isn't that the fun in all of this, to determine *why we are here*?"

The fun? The *fun*? She stifled a bitter laugh. "I do not mean existentially."

"Oh, but why not? This can be a good discussion."

"But you are going to die," Amita said as Plato re-entered the room, alone. As much as she longed for a deep discussion of life's meaning, this hardly seemed the time.

"All of philosophy is training for death," he said.

From a desk, Plato brought out a small square of what looked like paper and jotted something down using a thin reed.

"Well, I am less interested in philosophy in this moment, and more concerned with how the hell I am going to get out of here." Her words and tone made both men freeze and look at her. She wasn't sure if it was the language or the speaker that gave them such pause, but they looked legitimately shocked.

"I apologize," she said, reading the room and realizing she couldn't alienate her only allies. "I am scared and under a lot of stress and unsure how to process it all."

"And I am dying today," Socrates said, and Amita wasn't sure if this was meant as a joke.

"People who travel here do not stay forever," Plato said. "If, like you say, Socrates does not live long enough to see you leave…" His voice caught for a moment. "I will look out for you."

She nodded. "Thank you."

A loud knock came at the door. Both men glanced at Amita and she put her hood on before moving around a small desk and chair to a darkened corner of the room. The door opened and several words were exchanged, Amita steadied her breathing and resisted the urge to look up. Soon the space was quiet and Socrates and Plato rejoined her.

"What happened?" she asked. She felt both a part of what was going on and a voyeur, but decided she wanted to know.

"I am to report this afternoon for the administration of my sentence. They are allowing me to manage it myself, which is most kind. Plato, please let the others know this will happen at the prison, where I will report to with haste."

He turned to Amita, who was speechless. Even though she'd studied it, *knew* all about it, this couldn't be how it ended, right? She couldn't have found herself in 399 BC to meet Socrates and Plato only to witness the former dying that very evening without her getting the chance to ask him a million questions and learn a life-time of education from him? What cruel prank was this?

"I..." she began, lost for words for so many reasons.

"You will travel with Plato," he said, cutting her off. "He will bring you to the prison tonight, and we can talk freely one last time. I wish I had more opportunity to speak with you, to learn from you, but alas, that is life. Or death, as it were." He shrugged, as if it all was a minor inconvenience.

"Thank you," she finally managed.

"Now, I really must be going," Socrates said. He gave Amita's shoulder a squeeze before he and Plato faced each other, gripping one another's forearms before parting.

"Now what?" Amita asked as they were left behind.

"Now, we inform the others."

VIII

AMITA LOST TRACK OF TIME, but she guessed about an hour passed since her and Plato left Socrates. They wandered the streets of Athens, various statues dotting the roads and structures around them. The buildings were magnificent, white facades gleaming in the sun. Amita wished for the millionth time she could hit pause to take it all in. To catalogue every detail of this place to her memory so when she returned home, she could fill in the architectural gaps.

No, she decided as Plato knocked on yet another door. A man came out and after a few exchanged words, held Plato tightly, kissing him before parting ways. No. Somehow, she knew this part of her past would probably die with her. How would she even begin? She'd be thrown into a mental institution faster than she could describe the layout of the room Socrates trial took place in. She'd bring shame on her family. It was gong to be bad enough she'd be returning with cut hair, if she also started gabbing about visiting the real ancient Greece, they'd lock her up and try to forget all about her.

After the first few houses, Plato filled her in on who all the men were and what their conversations consisted of, but after the sixth dwelling, he stopped. Amita could see how difficult this was for him. The reactions of the visited ranged from gut-wrenching sorrow, to anger, to surprisingly happiness to some. Men laughed and pushed Plato out of the way. Some were already crying when they arrived, evident they'd already heard. Even though through gestures she could mostly figure out what transpired, she wished whatever magic pulled her into this time also gave her the ability to speak Greek, even if just to give Plato a better level of much-needed comfort.

When they'd visited the last place, Plato told her he would drop her off at the prison, where Crito, the first man they had visited, would meet her and take her to Socrates.

For the first time she wondered about those who traveled here before her. Were they now the scholars of her time? Did they hide the fact they had inside knowledge and somehow present the world with "new" information? Did she have an obligation to try to seek them out and do the same?

Amita grabbed Plato's arm, stopping him. "You aren't going to come with me? You aren't going to see him?"

Plato lowered his eyes and shook his head. "I am sorry to say I will not be able to be there."

"Why?"

"I wish I was as brave as my teacher, but alas, I am not."

Amita let go of his arm. She'd learned so much about these two men, but never really stopped to think they were actual people who lived real lives. That they were mortal and subject to the same human condition she was.

Plato would go on to become one of the greatest scholars ever, and yet, he was still a man. A man who was sad to be losing his mentor and friend.

"I understand," she said.

When they arrived at the prison, Crito wasn't there. For several anxious moments, Plato left her to speak with the guards at the doors.

Plato returned. "They agree to allow you to speak with him alone before the others arrive."

Amita nodded. "Or I can stay with you."

He shook his head. "Socrates will want to speak with you." He breathed out a short laugh. "He will want to ask you questions before he is unable."

She wondered if Plato meant before others arrived and their secret could no longer be shared, or because he would soon perish. She did not ask.

He pointed to a pair of guards. "I have told them you are from Latium and do not speak Greek."

Amita was touched at this simple kindness. "Thank you."

"I will meet you back here."

She nodded and touched his arm. His smile made her think he appreciated the gesture.

Amita followed the two guards up the prison steps and through the stone building. It smelled of bodily fluids and sweat and she found even breathing through her mouth troublesome. The guards laughed at her discomfort and spoke some words in Greek.

They traveled down a series of stone steps, the last spilling them to a landing. Through an archway and a single step down, a platform stood against one wall. Socrates sat leisurely upon it as if in a room at a hotel. No bars were on the doors or windows as far as Amita could see.

She was shocked to realize she recognized the scene.

It was as if the painting, *The Death of Socrates*, had come to life.

The space was smaller than depicted in the painting, but surprisingly accurate. Amita wondered if this meant Plato did in fact come to the execution after all, or if he just got a description of the place from the other occupants.

She felt like she was stepping through time all over again.

Socrates addressed her guards, who nodded and left. Amita counted to ten just to be safe, then lowered her hood.

He smiled at her, without the same brightness as before. Maybe the reality of his situation was finally settling in.

"Plato thought you would want to see me before the others get here," she said.

"As is typical with him, his instincts are correct."

"You are very calm," she said, unable to keep her curiosity at bay any longer.

"Can I tell you a secret?" he asked.

The question took her so off guard, she nodded without thinking.

"I am curious to see what is *next*, if you know what I mean."

"I do. I wish you could report back."

His barking laugh bounced off the hard walls and echoed before dying away. "As do I. As do I."

She could hear distant commotion and knew she didn't have much time alone with the man. "You asked me what I thought my place was in the world, in my world."

His face regained some of its brightness. "Oh, yes. I was hoping you'd have an answer for me."

"I am a destroyer. That is my place."

He cocked his head to one side.

"I guess it doesn't even matter what world I am in," she continued, gesturing around her. "I have the luck of a front-row seat to downfall. The downfall of my parents' culture. Of my own generation's view of the government. My own direction in life. Everything I touch or that touches me, seems to get an expiration date on it. I'm a human stick of dynamite."

"I am not sure what an 'expiration date' or 'dynamite' is." He sounded out each word like he was trying it on for size.

"An expiration date is when something isn't good anymore, like spoiled food. Dynamite is like a bomb in a stick, an explosive? Like gun powder?" she blabbed on, hoping he would understand one of these references.

"Oh, like the Chinese use. Yes, yes, I understand now," he said, his eyes glistening with the simple joy of learning a new thing.

"Yes," she said. "Like that."

"Oh, if we could only influence like that," he said, a seriousness to his voice. "If only we could be so powerful, imagine the *good* we can do. But alas, we aren't. We are mere cogs and our job is to turn those wheels and try to figure out what small part we play. This," he said, opening his arms to indicate the place they were in. "I hate to disappoint you, but it has nothing to do with you. This day was set into motion the day *I* was born, not you. It may seem like you are the center of the universe, and believe me, I say this with as much kindness as I can, but you aren't. As Plato often tells me, the universe is the center of the universe. We are merely planets spinning about trying to figure out what our path should be and occasionally knocking into one another."

She nodded and brushed a tear off her cheek.

The door opened above them and a sunbeam lit Socrates's face, making him look angelic. Amita decided that was the way she wanted to remember him.

She pulled her hood back up over her head and leaned over and kissed his cheek. He didn't flinch, but even if she'd broken some sort of social norm, no one was there to see it, and she doubted he cared.

"I only wish we'd had more time," Amita said, although not wanting to take away from the others who were coming to learn from him one last time.

"The plight of man," Socrates retorted.

She nodded and turned back toward the stairs. Several men in robes, including Crito, clattered into the room, one holding a small red bowl. She caught eyes with one of the guards, who nodded. A young man made it to the bottom of the stairs, but started crying and turned right back around to leave.

Amita turned and raised her hand in a small wave, but Socrates was already busy giving a speech to the new arrivals, a teacher to the very end.

IX

AS SHE MOVED BACK through the stone halls following the guard and now the sobbing man, Amita's mind was lost in panicked thought.

What was she going to do?

She hoped Socrates was right, that a portal would still open and Plato would see it. Sure, he'd mentioned a glowing door, but she'd forgotten to ask Socrates if the door itself glowed? Of if it looked more like the perimeter was illuminated?

Her heartbeat felt rabbit quick as she fought the urge to sprint back into the bowels of the prison to throw herself at Socrates. To beg him to avoid execution and keep her safe.

But she knew doing that would likely doom them both.

She was trapped in so many ways, her only option to stay with Plato and hope it all worked out.

Outside, Plato embraced the crying man and kissed the top of his head. When the man nodded and walked away, Amita approached Plato and tripped on the last step out of the prison. A gust of wind picked up, blowing her hood back. She stood frozen for a moment and locked eyes with Plato a second before she heard yelling behind them. The guard, now joined by three more, came rushing down the steps toward them, shouting something Amita couldn't decipher.

"Run," Plato called out, reaching toward her. She took his hand and the two began weaving through the crowd, Amita fumbling with one hand to pull her hood back up.

The shouting behind them increased, but the townspeople

around them seem unbothered by the commotion, none turning to look in their direction or to help intervene for the authorities.

"I'm sorry," Amita gasped between breaths. The stress and lack of sleep caught up with her, making her legs feel leaden and difficult to lift.

"Keep moving," Plato called back to her. His grip was firm and tugged her into a quicker pace.

Amita had no idea where they were going and cursed herself for leaving her bag. She wondered if she'd ever be able to retrieve it. All her books. Her ID. Her schoolwork. Possibly gone to history.

For a hysterical moment, she pictured an archeologist digging it up thousands of years in the future, trying to make sense of a modern object amongst ancient ruins.

Amita's legs tangled and she felt herself pitch forward in the exact moment Plato yanked her down a side street. She righted herself and was about to ask him where they were going when she saw the expression on his face.

"Quickly," he said, his voice clipped with urgency.

She followed his gaze over her shoulder and saw it.

About halfway down the alley stood a door.

A door with a faint glow around it.

X

ALL SOUND except for her ragged breathing vanished. Plato's firm grip both figuratively and literally pulled her back to reality.

"Amita, we must go," he said.

For a moment she wondered if he wanted to travel with her. The extra credit for showing up to class with the actual Plato surely would help negate all her lost books and assignments...

Noise flooded back into her head as the calls of their pursuers crept closer. She ran forward, coming to an abrupt halt before the glowing door.

"What do I do?" she whispered.

"Go through, I suppose," Plato said.

She turned to him, a man who was losing his beloved mentor, yet still helped her without question. How could she thank him for such a selfless act?

"History is kindest to you," she said, and he smiled.

"Go."

She nodded, dropped his hand, and reached for the doorknob. The room beyond was black, but there was no time to hesitate. With the warm air on her back, she stepped through and shut the door behind her.

The smell of dirt and decay let Amita know, even in the dark, she'd returned to the dilapidated house.

She placed her open palm to her chest and said a silent prayer of thanks to her safe return, then picked her way outside.

The night air was crisp, a welcome change to the dusty heat she'd been in for the last day. *Only a day?* It felt like an eternity since she'd touched these half-rotten steps.

Back on the sidewalk, she made a mental note of the house number and the street. Somehow, she needed to find a way to tear the place down. With Socrates gone, Amita couldn't risk someone else stumbling on the portal and finding themselves trapped in Greece.

She had no idea what time it was, and hoped it was even the same day she left, but what was done was done. Everything and nothing had changed for her. She'd return to her classes, somehow explain to her parents and teachers all her things were gone. But she'd have a deeper understanding of the founding fathers of philosophy, a worthy exchange for some added scrutiny. But she knew she couldn't speak the truth of what she experienced here. They'd lock her up for sure.

She pulled her hood tighter and cursed to herself. How the hell was she supposed to explain her clothes and her hair? Oh, her hair! Forget the books, her mother would yank her out of school for sure after she took one look at her, convinced the city corrupted her only daughter.

She'd had a perfectly fine thing going, and here she was

destroying it yet again. A door had presented itself, and she hadn't been able to help but walk through it.

She was sure that said something about her character, but wasn't exactly sure what that was. Head low against the increasing wind, wind, she picked her way back down the street and toward her fate.

SITTING across from the painting with her granddaughter, the memories she spent a lifetime trying to forget flooded back.

"Giagià, what are you talking about? Are you feeling okay?"

"It was a long time ago," Amita said. "Do you remember visiting my old house? The one your mother grew up in?"

"I loved that house."

"I loved it, too. I bought that property when I was still in college."

Her eyes widened. "You bought a house when you were, like, twenty?"

"Twenty-one," Amita said. "There was an old house about to fall down on the property, so I got a good deal even for that time. I tore that house down and built the one I raised my family in. Your grandfather was progressive for his time, not minding moving into a house his wife purchased."

"The house you still live in?"

Amita nodded. "I've had many offers over the years, but I could never let that place go. I couldn't trust anyone else with it…" she let her voice trail.

"I sort of remember staying in that house when I was very little."

Amita smiled, having forgotten that piece of its history. "Yes, when you first moved to the neighborhood, your house needed some work, so you all lived with us for a few weeks. How do you remember that? You were so little?"

"It's strange, I remember pieces, but some don't make any sense," Sophia said, eyes fixed straight ahead at the painting.

"Like what?" Amita asked.

"I must have been dreaming, but I *swear* I woke up one night and the closet door was glowing."

Amita's heart stopped in her chest for a moment and she had to clutch her hand to it to stop from passing out. "What do you mean?"

Sophia waved her hand. "Like I said, it must have been a dream, but it was so vivid, I'll never forget. It never happened again. Sometimes I would even sneak to that room when we were over and sit in front of the door, but it was just a door," she laughed. "I guess I had a good imagination."

"I guess you did," Amita said.

They sat quietly again. Could it have been possible? Could it *still* be possible?

She thought back to buying that house, hiring the crew to tear it down, terrified the whole time its secret would be discovered. There was some good wood in the place, they'd told her. Maybe some flooring she wanted? Surely, the cabinets could be reused. Maybe even this door without any vines on it?

No. She'd been emphatic. Every piece needed to be hauled away. Nothing could remain. She'd destroy every bit of it.

Socrates's question flooded back to her just then.

"What is your place in the world?"

"I am a destroyer. That is my place."

She'd lived her whole life believing that. Terrified that what she'd touched would disintegrate or fall into oblivion, but in that moment, she realized it wasn't true. As she saw her granddaughter look up at her with ink-colored eyes, this life sitting next to her existed because of *her*. She may not have done everything she wanted to in life, might not have made all the right choices, but Socrates's response to her came to her as well. She may be the center of *her* universe, but that was only a small part of it. She may be the seed, but she couldn't blame herself for everything terrible thing that had ever happened in her wake.

But to boil her entire existence into being a destructive force? No. She was a *creator*. She'd made an entire universe herself. She laughed under her breath. Glad to have finally figured it out, but wished it hadn't taken her so damn long.

"Are you okay to keep walking?" Sophia asked, shifting from side to side. The pull of youth to keep moving too strong.

Amita looked at the painting one more time. Some secrets were worth holding on to.

"Yes, I believe I am," she said.

XI

EMIL WIPED the sweat from his brow, tipping his hat up and allowing a forceful beam of sunlight to sting his eyes. He knew entering the graduate archeology program wouldn't be glamorous, per se. He wasn't one of those who thought it was all Indiana Jones-style chases and monumental finds every day, but he also hadn't expected the oppressive heat. The seemingly pointless task of using a paintbrush to clear sand away to reveal…more sand.

He was wrapping up his last week and couldn't wait to get back home to New York, and to reevaluate his life choices. His already brown skin was tanned to a deep tobacco color no matter how much Banana Boat he sprayed on it in three-minute increments.

The other students were scattered upon the dig site, each residing in their own three-foot-by-three-foot stringed off box. The same box he'd practically lived in for the last four weeks. Their professor walked between them all, making small comments about nothing in particular because there was nothing in particular to comment on.

She shared the same look of disappointment as her students. Emil heard her speaking in a strained voice the night before. Practically yelling at someone for the "piece of shit" assignment she'd been given for her class and wondering if her being a woman had anything to do with it.

No matter the reason, Emil was done. Well, almost. He still had five more hours. Then he could pack up his small kit, pretending that taking a shower actually got all the sand out of every crevice in his body, and get ready in time to attend the send-off dinner the University of Greece held for all the summer residents. Emil dreaded going to this dinner. Two other people from his school were at different dig sites from his, and he knew they'd discovered interesting things.

It made Emil burn with jealousy. Plus, their team leaders had the good sense to purchase tents so everyone didn't get fried.

Emil was just about to get up to take a break and stretch his legs when the sun glinted upon something small and metal. He brushed carefully at the area, heart racing, hoping beyond hope it wasn't some sort of mirage, or a gum wrapper.

The metal was tear-dropped shaped with a small hole at the bottom. Emil could just make out some writing along the edge.

YKK.

Forty minutes later, and there it stood, exposed to the sun for the first time in who knows how many years.

"I don't understand," his professor said. "I was assured this was a pristine dig site. This area of Athens was just released by the World Historical Society as an approved area. There are no records of previous teams here."

"What do we do?" Emil asked.

"Take a million photographs, make sure you get a ruler in the picture, then pick it up and carry it over to this table. I can't wait to open this up."

"There's no way it's that old," someone called over Emil's shoulder. "It looks in too good of shape."

"Plus, they've only been around for like fifty years or something," another voice said.

"Lalani, fetch some specimen jars so we can collect soil samples. I want to see about dating this thing," the professor said.

Another thirty minutes, and it was extracted and on the table.

"You found it," the professor said. "You may do the honors, Emil."

With a shaky hand, he pulled back the zipper of the backpack. The inside held several books and notebooks in various stages of disrepair and rot. The pages began to crumble as soon as he touched them, which caused his instructor to step in.

There was also a wallet, or what little was left of it, but the plastic student ID it held looked like it was just printed, the face of a beautiful smiling girl looking back at them.

Amita Hatzi in black ink below it.

AUTHOR'S NOTES - KRISTIN DURFEE

WHEN DISCUSSION first started around the premise of this newest project, I immediately knew what painting I wanted to use: *The Death of Socrates*. I saw it many years ago and it has stayed one of my favorite works of art. The movement of light from one side of the painting to the other as well as the pure emotion captures grabbed my attention and has kept it all these years.

The thought of suddenly being able to travel back in time to meet a hero, only to have that be the day of that person's demise, was an intriguing concept for me. The panic of the moment coupled with wanting to pick that person's brain is a conundrum I hope never to be in.

~KAD

SOUL FOR A SOUL

JOHN HOPE

"*Since love grows within you, so beauty grows. For love is the beauty of the soul.*"
—*Augustine of Hippo*

I — Brother Fides' Sin
Milan, Italy, A.D. 388

"SHHHH..." Brother Fides Alberello's moist voice echoed through the dank barn as he slid his fat finger over Olmo's quivering mouth. The raw stench of manure hung strong among the urine-damped hay. A burning oil lamp lit the blackness. Olmo wriggled his bare back against the dirt, his teary eyes staring up at the rotting barn's wooden rafters. The lamp's wavering light cast ghostly shadows that jerked and flicked as erratically as Olmo's shaky heartbeat.

Brother Fides lurched over the prepubescent boy like a wolf salivating over a hunk of meat. He slid a hand down his prey's smooth, naked body.

Olmo's peach-fuzz hairs stood upright, tremoring in the night's stillness.

"Shhhh…" Brother Fides repeated, his caterpillar-like mustache twitching. His head sank toward the boy's lower torso.

Olmo clenched his jaw. He focused on the barn's upper loft, watching puffs of dust cough from the planks of wood whenever the goats bleated and kicked. Chills spasmed Olmo's narrow frame, climaxing him into shame. Like a rip at his soul, he knew this was wrong.

The distant laughter of men and the occasional playful scream of children carried through the walls. The village's festivities lay so close, yet far out of Olmo's reach. He closed his eyes, trying to wish away the horrific tickle of Brother Fides' mustache on his skin.

Goats. Laughter. Cheers.

Olmo cried.

"Shhhh…" Brother Fides tapped Olmo's shaking mouth. "There, there."

Olmo opened his eyes.

"Let's wash those tears away." He sat the boy up and caressed the youth's face. "There's nothing to be sad about," he said. "See? Look. You're okay. You're all right."

Olmo shivered. The goats complained, knocking loose more dust from above, which landed on Olmo's damp face. He wiped at it, smudging it into streaks of mud.

Brother Fides tossed Olmo's robe over the boy's head and helped him thread his arms through. Then he helped him to his feet.

Olmo wobbled. New tears mixed in.

Brother Fides tussled his hair. "You're welcome, boy. Now, remember: you need not tell of this to anyone."

Olmo's lips retracted. "B-b-brother…Fides…" He folded himself into the giant man, wrapping his arms around him. "Why?"

Brother Fides patted the frail boy. "There, there. Everything's okay. Sin will not take you. I will be sure of it."

Olmo pulled away and looked up. "Take me?"

"This is your sin of the flesh, boy," he said. "Your pleasure."

"B-but Brother Fides. I…I didn't want—"

"Boy." Fides gripped Olmo's arm, his fingers like talons scraping and compressing bone. The lad gasped. "This is your sin." Fides shook the boy. "Your sin. But you need not fret. I will protect you." He lowered his head, his eyes darkening. "Provided you keep this close to your heart. Do you hear me, boy?"

More tears beaded on Olmo's cheeks. He nodded slowly.

A satisfied grin flashed across Fides' face. Then his jaw tightened. "Tell no one. No one. Understand?"

The boy nodded again.

"Good." Brother Fides leaned in and squeezed, the pinch of his nails drawing blood. "Because if you do tell, my boy." His voice grew dark. "I'll make sure you never talk again." He released his grip and patted Olmo's head.

"You'll be fine," he assured a final time, his tone suddenly light.

A flash of light struck Olmo's face, followed by the sharp, nauseous scent of sulfur. He gasped and stepped back from a ferocious attack sure to occur.

Brother Fides spun toward the glow and sucked in his breath. "What the…?"

A green creature, thin and tall, stepped forward, its grotesque appearance prompting another ocular assault. It lifted a lantern, revealing its grotesque appearance. A double-pair of goat horns extended from its head, slick yet bristling with sharp spiraling blades. Scaly, bat-like wings unfurled over each shoulder as its two arms, slender and long, seemed to float on an invisible breeze, causing the lantern to sway. Fangs glistened white on a smooth green face, curving downward to line bloated red lips. Yellow eyes framed narrow, snake-like pupils.

Olmo pressed himself stiffly against the wall, his mouth agape.

Brother Fides shuffled backward. "W-w-w-what are you?"

The creature hissed, sending steam dancing from the edges of its mouth. "What I am is of no concern to you, mortal." It transferred the lantern from its hand to the tip of one wing. "But this is." With a swing of both bony green arms, a giant book materialized amidst a sparkle of light. The creature opened it. "Your name appears in bright letters here," he told the clergyman, bending a long finger and tapping the exposed page.

Even from a few feet away, Olmo could see Brother Fides' name glowing red on the page, like fiery embers.

Brother Fides narrowed his eyes. "M-my name?"

"Yes, mortal," the creature said. "You're mine now."

With a spin of its long green arms, the book disappeared. Then the creature lunged forward, its open mouth unnaturally wide.

Brother Fides cried out. Olmo slapped his hands over his eyes and held his breath.

Olmo turned away. He bit his knuckles and held his breath.

A thunderous crunch chased the goats to one corner of the loft. Then Brother Fides' yelp yielded to an eerie silence.

Trembling, Olmo peered back over his shoulder.

The creature slurped loudly but then twisted its wettened lips, as though sickened by the taste. A bulge writhed inside its once-slender belly.

Olmo quivered in ball. "Y-y-you... you are a daemon. Aren't you?"

"Yesss," it hissed as it straightened upright. "Few of your kind even knows of our existence."

"I've heard stories."

"Ghost stories, my guess. Things to scare little children. I'm no story, child."

Olmo sunk.

"Do your stories tell how I must to quench my appetite to avoid my own eternal damnation?" A glistening, forked tongue slid from its mouth and slivered across its lips.

Still shaking, Olmo forced himself to speak. "You only take bad people?"

"I take those who drown in their personal pool of sin. And in this self-indulgent season of mankind, I am well-fed. I don't often consume mortals as young as you, child, but if your name appears in the ledger, I will not turn away." It patted its belly. "Follow the path of this mortal…" It leaned in uncomfortably close to the boy and licked its fat lips. "…and I will taste your sweet soul on my lips."

The daemon spun away, laughing. The entire barn quaked. As it disappeared into the night, its lantern extinguished, and darkness returned.

Olmo's entire body convulsed. Still pressed against the wooden back wall of the empty stable, he wheezed and struggled for oxygen, steam puffing from his panting mouth. Goats whimpered in the loft above.

As Olmo's darting eyes adjusted to the dim light of Brother Fides' lamp, still perched on a nail protruding from a wooden support, the barn door opened with a whine, breaking the stillness.

Men raced in from outside, Brother Marcus in the lead. "Olmo, what was that noise?"

Olmo hesitated.

The men stepped closer, their faces bathed in confusion, their eyes searching for clues.

Olmo hung his head and cried.

II — Augustine's Commission

A RUSH of air and light flooded the bishop's office as Augustine approached. He eyed the aged clergyman bent over an ornate table in the corner of the tight room, examining a scrolled copy of one of Apostle Paul's letters.

"Bishop Loffredo?" Augustine ventured.

The bishop raised his head from his intense study.

"Ah, Brother Augustine." The bishop smiled and approached the younger man, embracing him in a warm hug. "Please, close the door and sit." He motioned toward a pair of curule seats across the room. Backless, with curved legs forming a wide X and rising into low armrests, the cushioned chairs were aged relics of the Roman Empire.

Augustine closed the door and joined Loffredo, their seats so close the two men's knees nearly touched. His posture and eyes alert, Augustine anxiously awaited what was sure to be a special request from his superior. For, it wasn't often that he, or anyone, was summoned to the bishop's chambers.

The drab, crowded room seemed like it should've been larger, considering the history of St. Thecla's Cathedral. Located in the heart of the ancient city of Mediolanum, the building had once been a Roman basilica used for public functions. A little over thirty years ago, in the mid-fourth century, the Milanese had converted it into a cathedral. The bishop's quaint office used to be a governor's quarters. While the structure now occupied a grand position of leadership, it had been built for function, not extravagance. Even newly refurbished, the well-maintained space felt cold and uninviting.

Loffredo started, "Thank you for coming so quickly. I understand I pulled you away from other commitments."

"Well, yes." Augustine shifted in his chair, bearing a worried frown. "My son and I were about to leave for Hippo Regius."

Located on the North African coastline in present-day Algeria, the growing maritime city had seen a sudden baby boom. Young families now yearned for a dynamic Christian Church in which to raise their children—steering them away from the godless sailors who frequented the ports. As such, the remote community had begged for Augustine to come guide them in the building of a new worship site that would appeal to these families and expand the Church's influence.

"Yes, I know." Loffredo folded his hands. A small man, his weathered olive skin showed his years, although his bright eyes held a youthful sharpness. "But I must ask you to delay your travels."

"Why?" Augustine paused. "Uh, begging your pardon of course, Bishop Loffredo."

"We have a messy situation that needs to be cleaned up."

"You mean the boy?"

Loffredo nodded. "Such news spreads quickly. We can't have Brother Fides Alberello's sins destroy the reputation the Church has worked so hard to build in Milan. Especially not now, with Manichaeism biding for a rebound in Milan."

Augustine nodded, fully cognizant of the religion's rise in popularity throughout Italy.

Having originated in modern-day Iran, Manichaeism attempted to fill in the holes in other religions including Christianity. Its theories expanded Jesus Christ's teachings and the writings of Enoch, whose writings had been rejected by Christian scholars. This rejection had fascinated Augustine for years and he'd gravitated toward Enoch in his own studies, partly to satisfy his curiosity and partly to understand why scholars rejected Enoch's theories.

Augustine was once a proclaimed Manichaean himself, until six years ago. Rome's emperor, Theodosius I, feared the faith would overtake Christianity so he ordered the killing of all Manichaean monks. To avoid harm to himself and his son, Augustine had publicly converted both of them to Christianity.

Augustine leaned in toward the bishop. "So the boy's allegations are confirmed?"

"Confirmed?" Loffredo sat upright. "You have a lot to learn about politics, Augustine. The populous believes the boy—that's all the confirmation they need."

"Is Brother Fides…?"

Loffredo nodded. "Yes, he's still missing. Likely in hiding. Which is exactly why I called for you."

Augustine shifted. "I had nothing to do with him."

"Yes, yes. I know." Loffredo crossed his arms. "However, Brother Fides was once your pupil."

"That was over thirteen years ago," Augustine urged. "Fourteen, actually."

"But you knew his friends. And you still have your own Manichaean contacts, yes?"

Augustine shook his head sharply. "We're Christian, Bishop Loffredo. You baptized me and my son yourself."

"Yes, yes." Loffredo patted Augustine's knees again. "And you've been a devout man of faith. But friendships are the binding ties of men. I recognize we all have friends who may not be as strong in faith than what's in our own hearts."

Augustine looked away.

"Please," the bishop entreated him, "I ask of you to use your resources. Bring quick resolution to this issue before it's too late."

"But how?"

"Find Brother Fides. Return him to the Church so we might pray over his soul. Give him an opportunity to confess and—"

"Dissolve him from the Church?"

Loffredo leaned back and exhaled. "I should never have accepted him."

"Why do you say that?"

Loffredo tilted his head. "Following his studies with you, Brother Fides' first position was with the Archbasilica of Saint John Lateran in Rome. He came to us under somewhat mysterious circumstances: a number of his peer deacons had been found dead—killed in their living quarters. Brother Fides confided that he wished to relocate to Milan out of fear for his life. However, when I later learned that a few altar boys had also been killed with no clear explanation, something didn't sit right with me."

"Then it's possible Olmo wasn't his first?"

Loffredo shook an aged finger at Augustine. "It's not our role to judge the hearts of man. As such, although I don't regret reaching out my heart to Fides, I see now welcoming him into our family was unwise."

Augustine inhaled deeply. "I never knew Fides committed such terrible sins."

"Olmo is the only boy who has come forward, so I believe Brother Fides joined us and kept his soul pure for some time," Loffredo offered. "But the Devil is persistent."

Augustine nodded.

"So now that we have these issues at hand, you must recognize that the Church cannot afford this blight. If nothing else, we must stop Fides. His suspected sins in both Rome and Milan may soon infect other cities."

Augustine stared down at the floor. "I understand."

"Do you, Augustine? I fully realize your relocation to Hippo Regius is not only to reconnect to family. Your potential appointment as bishop there is no secret. And as a bishop, you must learn to make these difficult decisions." He paused, then added, "For the sake of the Church and for the sake of others whom Brother Fides may have wronged—or might wrong in the future."

Augustine nodded again. "I understand." He swallowed. "I'll inform my son that we must delay our trip. And...there are some old friends I'll need to get in touch with."

Loffredo placed a hand on Augustine's shoulder. "God be with you"

III — The Return

AUGUSTINE SLOGGED down the dirt streets of Milan, the barking of vendors and banging hammer of a nearby carpenter offset by church bells ringing out a charming song. He jittered with concern over Bishop Loffredo's commission.

Early spring's northerly breezes chilled Augustine's face and body. He hugged himself for warmth. He'd just canceled the hired wagon that was supposed to take him and his son to Genoa, where they planned to board a ship to Hippo Regius. There, Augustine was promised a prominent position in the church. The prospect of being instrumental in growing a new church had been enticing. In addition, the more space he could have placed between him and his Manichaean past, the better off he would have been; Theodosius' decree was still in effect, which meant the threat of Manichaeans being hung for heresy still loomed.

But now Augustine needed to reverse his plan and possibly lose his window of opportunity. And for what?

Augustine had expected to see Deodatus—the affectionate nickname he'd given his son, Adeodotus—waiting for him at the wagon, but the driver told him his son had gone into the city gardens. It wasn't unusual for the eighteen-year-old to spend hours reading there. An intellectual boy, Deodatus was patient and thoughtful, nothing like Augustine had been at his age. In fact, Augustine was only seventeen when he followed his physical desires and impregnated a married woman in Carthage, resulting in Deodatus' birth.

The woman's husband, a Carthage aristocrat, wouldn't tolerate raising an illegitimate child, so he forced his wife to move out to the country and have the pregnancy aborted while he told his elite circle she had miscarried. In truth, she had the baby and passed him on to Augustine, sending him and their love child off with a kiss and a satchel of gold coins. Augustine used the money to pay for both Deodatus' and Augustine's elite schooling, which found them at the center of Milan's upper class and on a first-name basis with the head bishop.

Unfortunately, Augustine's indiscretions as a younger man meant he was Bishop Loffredo's go-to layman for tasks such as the one he'd been assigned today.

Augustine turned the corner and headed down a path of relatively new woods. The city gardens used to be the site of Roman archery training. Now overgrown with vegetation, its various paths were still littered with broken arrows and cracked, discarded targets.

"Augustine!" the outcry of a female voice broke the gardens' serenity.

Augustine spun around. A beautiful woman appeared from behind a bush, clad in a simple but colorful dress. She carried a woven basket.

"Bellafore," he greeted one of his formal Manichaean lovers.

She stepped toward him, her dress sweeping from side to side as she approached. "I thought you already left for Africa," she said, leaning in to give Augustine a light peck on his cheek.

"Our trip has been delayed."

"It doesn't have to do with that man and the boy, does it?" she asked.

"You mean Brother Fides Alberello?" Augustine hung his head. "I'm afraid it has everything to do with that."

"Oh…" She swept a hand in the air as if swatting a fly. "Don't get mixed up in all that, Augustine. You'll risk your position in Hippo Regius."

Augustine sighed. "Bishop Loffredo asked for my help directly."

Bellafore's eyes widened. "Really? Why you?"

Augustine lowered his brow. "You know why."

She placed a hand on her bosom. "Because…because of us?"

He held her gaze. "Not just us. Because of all the Manichaeans I used to…" He swallowed.

She stepped back. "You say that like we're some undesirables with whom you had unspeakable orgies."

He barked out a hollow laugh. "It was never *that* bad."

"Neither are we." She pulled out a handkerchief and flicked it at him. "Yet you dropped us like we were barbaric nomads. Why?"

Augustine recoiled, unsure how to answer.

He and his son had continued to practice Manichaean behind closed doors even after they publicly declared themselves to be Christian. All while Augustine grew in prominence among Milan's Christian elite. But when Augustine heard talk of Roman officials traveling the greater empire to conduct another mass killing of Manichaeans, he cut ties completely with his Manichaean friends and committed his life to Christianity.

Augustine's bold turnaround infuriated his fellow Manichaeans. Some even used his traitorous actions as reason to renew the strength of an underground resurgence—one that still threatened to topple the Christian Church.

A man emerged from the bushes behind Bellafore. "Isn't it obvious why?"

Augustine knew his conversation with Bellafore was at an end the second he saw Galasso, Bellafore's brother. The muscular ironsmith pounded metal ten hours a day, and his body showed it.

Galasso crossed his huge arms. "You ran out to save yourself from the emperor's decree."

Augustine straightened his back. "I've had great opportunities in the Christian Church, opportunities that are better served without my head on a platter."

Galasso grunted and moved toward him.

Augustine backed away.

Galasso sidled beside his sister. "Come, Bellafore. We've wasted enough time on this hypocrite."

"Wait—" Augustine pleaded with a raised finger. "Please. Our conflicts aside, there's still a man missing, and an atrocious crime—"

"That's nothing of our concern." Galasso cut him off. "This is the Christian's black eye, not ours." He tugged at his sister's arms.

Bellafore gave Augustine a wary glance as Galasso marched her up the path.

Augustine remained rooted in place until the two had disappeared around a thicket of bushes. Finally, he resumed his search for Deodatus.

Augustine rounded a large tree into a clearing where he spotted his son perched on a log next to a much younger boy. Nearing them, Augustine balked when he realized that the boy was Olmo—the one who'd accused Brother Fides of abusing him.

"Deodatus?"

The two turned to Augustine, looking like they'd been caught doing something they shouldn't have.

"Father?" Deodatus rose with Olmo at his side. "I...I assumed your meeting with Bishop Loffredo would've gone longer."

Olmo eased around Deodatus, shielding himself from Augustine. He gripped the back of Deodatus' cloak.

Augustine frowned. "What are you doing with the boy?"

Deodatus swallowed and shot a quick glance at the younger charge. Then he patted Olmo's hand. "Stay here. I need to speak with my father for a moment. I promise to return."

Olmo glanced up at Augustine and nodded.

Deodatus walked back up the trail from which Augustine had come. Augustine followed.

From behind, Augustine marveled over how tall his son had grown. No longer a child, his sharp, narrow frame evoked signs of manhood. His beautiful face was his mother's, soft and supple.

Once a safe distance from Olmo, Augustine asked, "Tell me what this is all about."

"Look. I'd already said farewell to him and I was going to tell you once we left for Hippo Regius. But after you told me Bishop Loffredo wanted to speak with you, I realized I'd better see Olmo right away, since it was going to take some persuasion to get anything out of him."

Augustine waved his hands in front of him. "Hold on. You're getting too far ahead of yourself. Why were you with the boy to begin with?"

"To console him, of course," said Deodatus. "Is it not our mission as Christians to help those in need? Olmo suffered a horrible trauma. He's terrified of all men now. He hasn't returned to services or his church duties since—"

Augustine nodded.

"So now his family's worried they'll expel him from his position."

Augustine knew Deodatus meant the position of altar boy, a coveted job for a son's prospects and for his family's prestige among the city's elite.

"He even tended the church's goats," Deodatus said. "Such duties are a great honor for a boy his age. It was, when I was ten."

"So Olmo's terrified of men," Augustine probed. "But he talks to you?"

"Yes," Deodatus affirmed. "Don't forget I've been training altar boys for the past couple of years. I'm often a big brother to them. When I heard what happened to Olmo, I knew I had to…save him, heal him."

Augustine took a deep breath. He himself had been rebellious throughout his youth, and this wasn't the first time his son had followed in his footsteps, acting of his own accord without asking anyone's permission.

Thankfully, although only eight years older than Olmo, Deodatus had wisdom beyond his age. He spent hours every week assisting Milan's diocesan bishops. Over time, he'd assumed their mannerisms and fed off their patient understanding of life. When Deodatus was a mere eight years old, Augustine recalled him bouncing through the church the day he heard he was accepted as altar boy, the youngest the church ever accepted. Before Deodatus, the minimum age was roughly eleven or twelve. Deodatus' serious commitment even at such a young age convinced the bishops to change the Church's policies.

As proud of Deodatus as he was, Augustine occasionally caught glimpses of other fathers teaching their boys Ruzzola—an ancient game involving racing a rolling a disc using twine—and swinging their boys above their heads and knocking them around in playful roughhousing. Augustine couldn't help but feel a twinge of jealousy. Deodatus never liked such activities and opted for strangely precocious commitments to the church. Deodatus was the only real family Augustine had and the fact that his son preferred the church over him hurt a little. Though Augustine knew he should feel the same joy Deodatus had, such joy couldn't be forced. Nevertheless, every aspect of his son humbled Augustine.

"How'd I get so blessed with a son like you?" he wanted to ask, but such open honesty was hard for Augustine to muster. He struggled with a smile and hoped Deodatus could read his mind.

Deodatus stared back.

Augustine sighed. "You guessed right about Bishop Loffredo. He wants me to investigate what happened to Brother Fides."

Deodatus nodded. "I assumed as much. But do we *have* to?"

"Of course. At least, someone does."

"Look what he did to Olmo. Have you considered it's best *not* to locate a man of such sin?"

Augustine shook his head. "Deodatus, it's not our place to judge the sins of man. However, for the sake of the Church, Brother Fides needs to be found. If for no other reason than to exonerate the Christian faith to the masses. You must understand the times, my son."

Deodatus kicked the dirt and crossed his arms like a grumpy child. "I hate politics."

"As do we all." Augustine patted his son's back. "What has Olmo told you so far?"

Deodatus bit the side of his lip. "That's the problem. He just keeps talking about a daemon. I suspect it's a metaphor, or something he made up to mask what happened to him."

Augustine stepped back. "A daemon? What sort of daemon?"

"He said it was tall, thin, green, and scary-looking."

Augustine tapped his chin. "What features? Did he mention anything specific?"

Deodatus looked at his father strangely. "Uh, I think he said it had goat horns—oh, and slick skin and wings." Deodatus shuddered at the image. "Unbelievable."

Augustine hesitated.

"Are you thinking it's *not* unbelievable?" Deodatus' brow tightened.

Augustine clucked his teeth. "I'm just warning you not to rush to conclusions too quickly, my son. There are beings in this world and beyond that we are but on the cusp of understanding."

Deodatus frowned. "But h-how…" he stammered, searching for the words. "How can a boy see a daemon? I thought such things are only visible through God's eyes."

Augustine shook his head. "You're thinking of this through only a Christian perspective. Other religions have had answers to these questions for centuries."

"But…they're wrong, aren't they? If the ancient scriptures omit the type of creature he's describing…"

"Doesn't mean it can't exist," Augustine finished. "Nor does it mean the daemon's purpose or possibly of coming here is something other than what the Revelation to John describes."

Deodatus' eyes grew huge.

"I know you think this talk to be heresy," said Augustine. "The Christian Church is solid in its beliefs: One God. One Heaven. One Hell. And clearly-defined roles of all spiritual entities. But the more you learn about other beliefs, the more you realize how potentially incomplete existing Christian doctrine is. If my years of teaching religious studies have taught me anything, it's to keep an open mind."

Deodatus continued to gape at his father. "So, you think Olmo is telling the truth? That he witnessed a daemon?"

"I don't know. However, it *would* explain a few things."

"Really?" Deodatus' face quirked in confusion. "What things?"

A child's scream pierced the woods, followed by a muffled grunt.

Augustine and Deodatus dashed down the path, into the clearing where they'd left Olmo. They skidded to a halt in the damp grass.

The boy was gone.

Beside the log where Olmo and Deodatus had sat was a naked man curled in a fetal position, skin slick with a greenish slime. He looked like an aged newborn, trembling and vulnerable.

Augustine and Deodatus shared shocked expressions.

The naked man jerked and moaned. He turned his head and squinted up at the pair staring down on him.

Augustine gasped. "Brother Fides?"

IV — A Twisted Truth

BROTHER FIDES HUDDLED beneath a wolf fur blanket on one of Bishop Loffredo's curule seats facing the office stove, a wood fire snapping in front of him. His face still glistened with greenish specks of the slime that had encased his body when Augustine and Deodatus found him. Bishop Loffredo paced nervously, muttering words only he understood, while Augustine stood, arms crossed, and Deodatus leaned against the doorframe, his bottom lip twisted, his mind in deep thought.

Loffredo broke the silence. "Brother Fides Alberello, you claim you have no recollection of the men who robbed you?"

"What I *claim* is the truth." Brother Fides' darting eyes belied his hardened voice. "The attack was swift and sudden. I have no doubt they must have forced some foreign concoction into me."

"*Into* you?" Augustine asked. "You're covered in slime. Did they not pour something over you, instead?"

"Into me...over me. The point is, they attacked me. That's what's important."

Loffredo exhaled loudly. "Such violence is appalling, to be sure."

Tapping his chin, he said to Augustine, "You must admit, this shines a much kinder light on the Church."

"Kinder?" Augustine asked. "How?"

"The men who attacked and abducted Brother Fides couldn't possibly be connected to the Church. At least, not the Christian Church. The Manichaeans have been trying to use recent events to their advantage, but if we can prove the culprit against Brother Fides is Manichaean, we can divert fault."

"You don't believe his story, do you?" Augustine whispered.

"Augustine," Loffredo counseled, "truth is what we see. And here is an opportunity to change the view of others."

"I trust you're making the best decision for the Church." As these words left his lips, Augustine feared strongly that Loffredo's political concerns were outweighing his core Christian beliefs. Especially considering his prior discussion with the bishop regarding Brother Fides' possible web of lies and a connection to murders in Rome, going along with Brother Fides' version of the "truth" felt like making a deal with the Devil.

"But what of Olmo's disappearance?" asked Deodatus. "And what he said about Brother Fides?"

Fides' dark, bearded face glared. "Boys and their fantasies."

Deodatus stomped his foot. "He didn't hallucinate what you did to him!"

"Every evil heart wants to taint the good name of others," Brother Fides snapped back.

"*You* should know how to taint the lives of others."

Brother Fides growled as he tightened his blanket. "Bite your tongue, boy."

Loffredo stepped between the two. "Please, please. Stop this bickering." He faced Deodatus. "True, we cannot disregard Olmo's disappearance. But we must be realistic. The boy did defile Brother Fides' good name, regardless of the degree of truth. When Brother Fides' captors dumped him, there's little doubt that if Olmo was not kidnapped himself, he certainly would have run off, probably frightened at seeing Brother Fides. So, would you concede the *possibility* that the boy is simply in hiding, rather than in some dire situation?"

Deodatus shifted uncomfortably. "Um. Perhaps."

Loffredo nodded. "Under the circumstances, I feel it wise not to alert anyone to his absence. Especially not his parents. I can inform them he is needed to tend the goats for the next few days, while I work in the meantime with Brother Fides to set the record straight with the counsel and other key officials to clear the Church's name of Olmo's allegations. And possibly refocus their energies toward finding Brother Fides' captors."

"Do you need anything from me, Bishop Loffredo?" asked Augustine. "In respect to speaking to counsel about, um, Brother Fides, I mean." A sinking feeling pulled at Augustine. He knew what Loffredo had in mind, and it was a mistake to partner with Fides. The bishop had himself admitted that he should have never accepted Fides' move to Milan.

Loffredo straightened his robe. "Leave that to me."

"But what about Olmo?" pressed Deodatus. "Even if he's in hiding, he should be found."

"Yes." Loffredo smiled. "Augustine, you and your son need to refocus your efforts and search for the boy."

Augustine glared at Brother Fides. "Before we start off, I have to ask..."

Brother Fides stiffened his lips and repositioned his blanket. "What?"

"Olmo shared with Deodatus a most terrifying, macabre story."

"I've already explained," Brother Fides snapped. "The boy made it up. He was obviously ashamed of his own transgression, so he tried to sour my name after I caught him...defiling himself. I tried to get him to repent for his sins. Instead, he *lied*."

Augustine shook his head. "That's not what I meant."

"What do you mean, Augustine?" asked Loffredo.

"Olmo mentioned a daemon."

Loffredo fell silent.

"More lies," Brother Fides hissed.

Augustine spoke pleadingly. "But he provided a quite detailed and accurate description of—"

"How would you know what's an accurate description of a daemon?" spat Brother Fides.

"The texts I've studied—"

"Any rubbish you garnered in your days as a…a Manichaean…" Fides grimaced. "Those Arabian texts are filled with absurdity. Venturing into such things is dangerous."

"The texts I'm referencing are definitely not Manichaean," said Augustine. "And they describe the same details Olmo recounted: Goat horns. Wings. A *green* complexion." Augustine tugged Brother Fides' blanket from his shoulder, revealing the light-green film that still glistened on the man's skin.

Brother Fides jerked the blanket back and glared at Augustine. "This is preposterous. Horned daemons with wings and a *Book of Vices*? All a child's fantasy, nothing more."

Augustine stepped back. "A *Book of Vices*, you say?"

"Lies! It's all lies!"

"Please, please." Loffredo inserted himself between Brother Fides and Augustine. "There are many truths that need to be explored. Until then, Augustine," he urged, "make the boy your priority. I will deal with the repercussions of Brother Fides' return." He paused. "I know I can count on you."

V — An Unorthodox Avenue

DEODATUS FOLLOWED his father down the crooked cobblestone streets of Milan. Choking on the smell of rot and feces, he covered his mouth to cough as he carefully side-stepped a messy heap of rags. The pile moved, revealing a gnarled beggar. Around them, the hoarse calls of scratch-throated women and chaotic yells of stray children bounced from one dilapidated stone dwelling to the next.

A screech sounded above them, and a rat fell from a tattered cloth overhang onto Deodatus' head.

"Ah!" he cried, slapping at his hair.

The rodent hit the ground next to him and zigzagged off into a darkened building crevice.

Now five steps ahead of his son, Augustine angled back. "You okay?"

Deodatus trotted to catch up, wincing at yet another foul stench. "You sure we need to come...*here*?"

He looked around to find the dark eyes of a little girl staring at him through an opened window. She didn't move and appeared half-dead.

"Yes." Augustine resumed his pace down the alleyway. "We must first bear through Esmerelda's smoke and mirrors so she will eventually take us to Samo."

"Esmerelda? And who's Samo?"

"Samo is a Judaic scribe. Or at least he used to be." He stopped at a closed door and knocked. "Don't worry. Follow my lead."

The two stood, waiting. But they heard no response beyond distant chatter echoing down the alley and the mysterious scampering of yet another rodent.

Augustine pounded the door again.

A muffled female voice spoke from the other side. "Yes, yes. I'm coming."

Moments later, the door scraped open. Deodatus held his breath, apprehensive of what would be revealed. The face of an old wrinkled woman, head draped in a cloth, emerged through the cracked opening.

"What?" she demanded.

"Esmerelda," Augustine said with solid confidence, "we're here to see—"

"Augustine!" The old woman broke into a smile, revealing two solitary rotten teeth. She shoved the door open further. "How long has it been?"

"Too long." Augustine said. "This is my son, Deodatus."

The sagging skin on Esmerelda's face stretched even wider. "My, my. I remember when you were just a small child."

Deodatus swallowed hard and tried to smile back.

She looked to Augustine. "I remember when *you* were a child, too."

Augustine faked the same smile as his son's. "Yes. Is Samo available?"

She waved a wrinkled hand in the air. "Ah, you speak too quick. Come. Come inside."

Once in the cramped dwelling, Deodatus blinked to adjust his eyes to the dimness. A fire crackling in the corner provided the only light. Rope crisscrossed the room in a dizzying array of lines, supporting fragments of cloth. Deodatus couldn't decide if the cloth was laundry drying or a strange décor. Hanging strings of beads covered the walls. As Esmerelda walked through a bead barrier into the next room, the glossy orbs danced.

"Is Samo still here?" Augustine asked as he and Deodatus swept the clinking strands aside to follow her into the next room.

"All in due time," Esmerelda replied. "Now, sit. Sit."

Rows of sputtering candles offered little in the way of light. The old woman lowered herself into the center of a ring of rolled blankets patterned in red and gold.

"Sit. Sit," she repeated, shaking her bony arms.

Augustine and Deodatus sat down together.

"Samo?" Augustine asked. "Is he——"

Esmerelda snatched Augustine's hand. "First. Your palm." She caressed his firm hand with hers. Darkened tracks of veins traversed her crooked fingers, her knuckles swollen and distorted. She flipped Augustine's hand so his palm faced up and traced a wavy line. "Ah, I see, Augustine. You're in a lot of trouble. You wouldn't be visiting your favorite Esmerelda if you weren't, eh?" She cackled, her laughter slipping into a phlegmy cough.

Augustine and Deodatus exchanged a look.

"Let's see, now…" the old woman continued examining Augustine's palm. "You wish to leave all this behind. But you can't. You're trapped, I see. You think Samo will set you free, do you?"

"If you don't *mind*," Augustine said. "We'd love to speak with him for a few minutes."

"Patience, young Augustine." She tugged at his hand. "Always the impatient one."

He slipped his hand away. "We haven't time for this."

She huffed. "I must read the boy, first." She snatched Deodatus' hand as sharply as she had his father's. Deodatus tried to pull away, but the old woman had a grip of iron. She flipped his hand upright. "Ah, such young flesh." She licked her lips. "So tender and salacious." She cackled again.

Deodatus stiffened.

She traced lines down and up his palm. The boy shivered. Then she stopped. Her smile snapped into a firm glare. "You are not without sin, my boy."

Deodatus yanked his hand away and shot to his feet. "What is all this? Witchcraft?"

Augustine grabbed the boy's robe and pulled him back down. "Deodatus, it's okay. She doesn't mean anything by it."

Esmerelda threshed a disciplinary finger in the air. "Never underestimate the fortunes."

The voice of an old man spoke from a distance. "Esmerelda? Who's there?"

"Some old friends," she answered the darkness.

The man grunted as if struggling.

"Stay there," Esmerelda commanded, rolling her eyes. "I'll help you." She stood and disappeared behind another wall of beads.

Deodatus leaned into his father and in a rapid-fire whisper asked, *"What are we doing here? Can we leave?"*

"Please, son, have patience. Samo is why we're here."

"What does he possess that's so valuable?"

"Experience. Wisdom. Namely, regarding a detail that Olmo shared."

Deodatus balked. "The daemon? You mean he's some sort of daemon expert?"

Augustine nodded.

"But...he..." Deodatus' gaze darted around the small room as he tried to think of a response. "You can't be serious."

"Very serious," said Augustine. "Samo is just the man who would have some insight."

"Olmo didn't mean…you don't believe…"

"Yes. I do. Don't you believe the boy?"

Deodatus looked down at his hands. "I mean, of course I do. We trust each other. But—"

"So, it's worth investigating," Augustine cut in.

Deodatus tightened his lips, struggling how to respond. Before he could, the beads parted, and an old man shuffled forward with Esmerelda guiding him from behind.

"Careful…careful…" Esmerelda coaxed as a hunched Samo hobbled forward on unsteady legs. His skin was aged and patchy, his long, white beard frayed and matted, and his eyebrows so bushy they hid his eyes.

Esmerelda led him to a set of pillows in front of Augustine and Deodatus. Samo's bones rattled as she lowered him to the floor.

He gazed up at them, his dark eyes at last visible beneath his shaggy brows. He focused on Deodatus.

"Ah…" his voice crackled. "Augustine."

"That's my son." Augustine spoke up.

"Ah…" Samo repeated with a nod. "Deodatus."

"You remembered," Augustine said.

"I may wet myself from time to time, but the brain keeps workin'." Samo let out a high-pitched snigger.

Deodatus couldn't help but smile.

"Now, why have you come? You wish to tap into old Samo's memory, eh? Another Christian text, perhaps?"

"Sort of," Augustine replied. "We wanted to ask what you know about…daemons."

Samo's eyebrows rose. "Daemons?"

"Yes." Augustine coughed. "There's a chance that someone Deodatus knows, a young boy, may have witnessed one."

Samo didn't recoil. Nor did he exhibit any sign of disbelief. Instead, he leaned back and breathed a heavy sigh.

Esmerelda hovered behind the old man, taking the news with solemn quiet.

"And what were the circumstances?" inquired Samo.

Augustine swallowed. "The details are still in question. But there's a good chance he may have been caught in an act of sin."

"A boy?" Samo asked. "What degree of sin could a boy commit?"

"He was with a man," Deodatus clarified. "A man of the Church."

Augustine straightened at his son's response.

Deodatus continued, "The boy said he…he was…violated."

Samo's eyebrows angled. "I see. The emergence targeted the man while the boy was of witness?"

Augustine coughed. "That was my theory."

Samo rubbed his chin thoughtfully. "Was the man taken?"

"Initially," Augustine said. "But then he returned."

Samo's head jerked up. "Returned?" he shrieked. "Are you certain he was taken?"

"Fairly confident," said Augustine. "He claims he was grabbed by robbers. But his story sounded thin. Also, when he returned, he was…"

"Naked and covered in a green slime?"

Augustine and Deodatus flinched.

Samo displayed his blackened, crooked teeth. "I've struck a chord?"

"Yes," said Augustine. "So, you understand?"

Samo exhaled heavily, his nostrils compressed and flared. "I've read of a similar act that occurred long, long ago."

"What happened?" Deodatus asked.

"From the ancient scrolls of Enoch, son of Jared and father of Methuselah." Samo pulled at his long beard and leaned in, as if preparing to share a deep secret with the pair. "Enoch once learned of a great man, a king of a distant land, who led his people to a victory over a tribe that had oppressed them for generations. During the rumpus bacchanalia that followed, enslaved women from the conquered tribe were given to the king as a prize. He ravished these women throughout the night, torturing them to satisfy his perversions and vile pleasures, and to placate his sense of revenge on the tribe. By the following morning, the king was nowhere to be found. The leading generals searched the area and interrogated people of the conquered tribe but couldn't find a trace of the king. That is, until the next day. His people found the king at the center of their village, balled up on the ground, naked and covered in an unearthly green gelatinous substance. After the king regained his senses, he claimed he'd been taken by a green-skinned daemon."

"Daemons," Augustine ventured. "I've read what the scriptures say about Christ casting out daemons, but so little is understood about the nature of the spiritual realm. I understand Enoch studied this area. What are these green-skinned creatures?"

"Even Enoch didn't know much," replied Samo. "He believed they are lesser deities who play a role in transporting souls to and from spiritual realms. But it wasn't the creatures themselves that fascinated Enoch. Rather, it was what this king did with the daemon."

Deodatus sat forward. "What did he do?"

"Once recovered from his daemonic encounter, the king bragged to his men that he'd cheated death by deceiving the daemon, allowing his return."

"He deceived the daemon?" Deodatus wondered. "How?"

Samo raised a finger. "*That* is the very question Enoch wrestled with. He spent much of his years searching, praying, trying to discover how this king cheated a daemon out of death. Some say it was this pursuit that led Enoch to ascend straight to Heaven without suffering the noose of death himself."

"So," Augustine started slowly, "could it be that Brother Fides— uh, the man of the Church we mentioned—could it be that he, too, deceived the daemon that took him?"

Samo's left eyebrow rose. "Beyond trusting the words of this Brother Fides, there's only one way to find out."

"How?" Deodatus asked.

Esmerelda shifted in the corner of the room.

Samo smiled wide, his narrow teeth glistening in the dim light. "We ask the daemon."

VI — The Séance

AUGUSTINE SWUNG the heavy door open with a loud creak as Deodatus led Samo by the arm. The barn of St. Thecla's Cathedral stood as it had on the evening of Brother Fides' disappearance, the only light coming from the two lamps Augustine and Deodatus carried. Slung over Augustine's shoulder was a bag filled with supplies Samo had gathered before they'd headed here.

Upon strangers entering their home, the goats in the upper loft bleated their warning, kicking straw and dust into the air. Samo stopped when he reached the center of the barn, panting. Augustine had borrowed a donkey to transport the old man to the Cathedral, and the frail old man had then shuffled slowly through the church grounds.

"Do you need to rest?" asked Augustine.

"No, no," Samo insisted between huffs. His bushy eyebrows furled as he took in the scene. "Such a humble place for a miraculous emergence, isn't it?"

"Any less humble than where Christ was born?" Deodatus asked.

"Ah-ah," Samo said, waggling his crooked finger at Deodatus. "This one has wit."

Augustine placed the bag on the straw-covered ground and opened it. "What do you need from in here, Samo?"

"First, close the door. Then take out the furs. Deodatus, you can help me with my clothes."

Following Samo's instructions, Augustine closed the door and placed the furs from the bag in front of the old man. Deodatus stripped the old man down to his bare wrinkled skin. One at a time, Samo wrapped himself in the furs, completing the ensemble with a jackal's skull that he mounted on his head.

"Sweep away the straw," he ordered.

Augustine and Deodatus grabbed brooms from the far wall and cleared the ground at the barn's center. As they did so, Samo removed candles from his bag and positioned them around the open area. He nudged each candle left and right to get them perfectly arranged.

"Should we light them?" Augustine offered.

"No!" Samo snapped.

Augustine stepped back, joining his son along the wall.

As the goats above them kicked up more dust, Deodatus whispered to his father, "Do you recognize this ceremony?"

Augustine shook his head.

The arrangement of candles complete, Samo returned to the bag one last time and removed a pair of strangely shaped scepters. They appeared to be human femurs with an array of smaller bones fused to one end, forming an intricately spiked arrangement that looked part art and part brutal weaponry.

"Augustine, Deodatus," Samo commanded. "Keep your distance."

The pair backed as far from the ring of unlit candles as possible, until they were crowded into a small corner of the barn.

Samo stepped into the center of the candles, lifted the scepters, and rapped them together. The sharp noise silenced the goats.

"*O mentem noctis, venit praecipimus!*" he called into the darkness.

He slammed the scepters together again. This time, the candles illuminated with blue flickering flames.

Augustine and Deodatus glanced at each other in shock, but immediately returned their focus to Samo's strange séance.

The old man went into a dance, hopping from foot to foot, chanting something indiscernible as he dipped and rocked his head, looking unbelievably nimble for a man who could barely make it to the barn a moment ago.

A wind arose from nowhere, swirling hay and dirt into the air. Coughing and blinking, Augustine and Deodatus tried unsuccessfully to swat away the flying debris. The flames in their lamps blew out, although the barn remained well-lit.

As the wind settled slightly, Augustine and Deodatus could see the ring of candles burning blue despite the breeze.

"Copias in tenebris," Samo yelled. *"Ut vos iubes!"* He slammed the scepters to the ground.

Sparks flew upon the scepters' impact. The scepters leapt into the air, swirling around a metaphysical orb that sparkled like a globe of fireflies. Then the scepters joined, and additional bones grew out of the fusion, piece-by-piece, until a complete skeleton formed. From bottom to top, the skeleton morphed into a tall two-legged creature.

The creature formed hooves for feet, a complete spine and rib cage, a pair of bat-like wings extending outward, a pair of arms curled inward, and finally, a deformed skull emerged with a double-pair of goat horns.

With another gust of wind, a swirl of sparks engulfed the skeleton, layering the bones with shiny green skin.

The wind subsided and there stood the most gruesome creature Augustine and Deodatus had ever seen. It was completely green except for its fat red lips, brown horns, and serpent-like yellow eyes. White fangs curved upward from the sides of his mouth.

"Foolish mortals," the creature said, its voice smooth and hollow. "How dare you conjure me to this wretched dominion!"

"Daemon," Samo replied confidently, "we've requested your presence to determine the fate of one Brother Fides Alberello, whom we believe you held for a brief time."

The daemon spat. "I still have his awful taste in my mouth."

Samo squinted. "So, you did take this man?"

"Yesss…" the daemon hissed. "You waste my time, mortal. Return me, or I will take you as well!"

"Please." Samo raised his hands. "We request an answer. Why did you return Brother Fides?"

The creature crept toward Samo. "I wish not to say. Now, return me, or suffer a death worse than life. You know well, Samo, how deep pain can feel."

"Um…uh…" Samo stammered, his confidence rattled.

Augustine approached from out of the shadows. "We ask because we believe you may have been lied to."

The daemon turned toward Augustine. "Lied? Who would dare lie to *me*?"

"Brother Fides might have, um, convinced you of something that was, let's say, *cloaked* in a lie."

"No. No!" the daemon seethed. "There was no lie. There was simply a mistake of interpreting the ledger."

"The ledger?" Augustine asked.

The daemon rotated his hands and a giant book materialized in it. "*The Book of Vices,*" the daemon replied, opening the book. "Look here. The ledger lists 'Fides Alberello.' His name once glowed red, so I seized the mortal from this very place. However, the creature flattered me, so I listened. The mortal noted that *fides* means truth, or deliverer of truth. And that he was only listed herein to convey the truth of a young sapling—or, as translated into your tongue, an *alberello*."

"An alberello?" Augustine echoed.

"Yesss," the daemon hissed. "The mortal fulfilled his role. This deliverer of truth, Fides, called out an 'alberello,' Olmo, and shared with me the boy's sins of self-gratification."

Augustine gasped at Brother Fides' evil cleverness—twisting both of his names to create an illusion of innocence. He recalled when Bishop Loffredo introduced Fides to Augustine, Loffredo had insisted they'd have a lot to talk about since both used to be teachers. Throughout his career, Augustine had picked up on nuggets of information, which he enjoyed sharing with his pupils. Conversely, Fides had used *his* own experience to outwit a daemon and sacrifice a young boy in the process.

"That's a lie!" Deodatus yelled from behind Augustine.

Augustine waved his hand to hush his son.

But Deodatus ignored him. "That bastard practically destroyed Olmo," he said, marching forward. "Do you know how long it'll take for him to get over what happened? *Never.* That's how long." He stared the daemon in the eye. "Just *how many* children does Brother Fides have to molest?"

"How *many*?" Augustine asked. "Who else do you—"

Deodatus stared at him. "Me!"

Silence fell over the barn.

Augustine gaped at his son, who seemed shocked at his own admission.

"He...he went at me first." Deodatus rubbed his face. "And, as Olmo likely did, I begged him not to. But he convinced me that it was God's will that he cleanse me of my sinful desires. Then he told me it was all *my* fault. And I believed him. I never considered that a man of God would lie." He took a breath. "After about the third time, I tried to convince myself it was what I wanted. It was who I was. So, I let it happen. For weeks, then months." He shivered.

"Oh, dear Lord." Swiping at tears, Augustine pulled his son into an embrace. "My poor, poor child," he said, rubbing Deodatus' back.

The daemon hissed. "This is disgusting."

Augustine looked over Deodatus' shoulder at the creature. "You wouldn't understand the love of a father."

"I haven't any need for it." The daemon spun toward Samo. "Now, return me to my dominion or I will consume you all."

"But daemon," Augustine said, easing from his son. "You have heard the lies Brother Fides has conveyed. You should seize *his* soul, not Olmo's."

The daemon's beady eyes gazed down on Augustine. "And I *shall* retake Fides Alberello," the being concurred. "You needn't fear of that. However, Olmo's fate is sealed. His soul is no longer within my control."

"What do you mean?" asked Augustine.

"When I consume a mortal's soul, he remains in Purgatory until such time that he descends to Hell. But, alternatively, I may choose to send him to The Neither."

"The what?" Augustine asked.

"The Neither," Samo said. "It's a secondary place, cold and friendless—devoid of all life, of all hope. It's neither Purgatory nor Hell. The Neither."

"Correct, mortal," hissed the daemon. "I was so annoyed at having to revisit this dominion that when I vomited Fides Alberello and consumed the boy, I sent him directly to The Neither. Once a soul is there, I have no recourse to reacquire it. All I have left of your friend is his face." The daemon angled its narrow frame and pointed its hind end toward Augustine and Deodatus. Its butt twisted and morphed itself into the likeness of Olmo's soft face, eyes closed, mouth open.

"Olmo?" Deodatus gasped.

"It is only an impression of the young mortal," the daemon replied. "Once I transcend a soul, I'm indelibly scarred by its revolting inner beauty—a personal reminder to me of the life I've purloined."

"But you are forced to do this?" Augustine asked. "Who is your master?"

The daemon narrowed its yellow eyes. "Who else?"

Augustine stiffened his lip, needing not say the name of Satan.

"But for this child," the daemon continued, "his soul is forever in The Neither."

"That is not true," Samo said with regained confidence.

"Do you defy me, mortal?" challenged the daemon.

"According to Enoch's writings, travel to and from The Neither can be done by a willing soul if he is not yet carved in red within the Book of Vices."

The daemon smiled. "There has never been a soul willing—and I doubt there ever shall be. Besides, it's beyond a soul's fortitude to resist the eternal pull of The Neither. There, a soul resides in its personal Hell. The Neither's force will never allow a return. Certainly not the return of two souls."

"I'll go," Deodatus said.

The daemon spun around. "What?"

"Take me."

Augustine grabbed his son's arm. "No, Deodatus. You don't know what you're saying."

"Listen to your father, boy," the daemon said. "No one ever returns from The Neither."

"I will."

Augustine yanked Deodatus' arm. "Don't, Deodatus. You're too young. You have no experience."

Deodatus hesitated, and the daemon's mouth drew into a smile. Augustine looked quizzically between the two of them.

"Ah, yes, boy," the daemon flipped through several pages in the book. "Perhaps you do know about such transgressions." He pointed to a name, this one in dark maroon. "Your name, Adeodatus, had nearly changed to fiery red. You were almost mine."

"What such 'transgressions'?" Augustine demanded. He grabbed his son's shoulder. "What is he talking about?"

Deodatus' lowered his head in shame. "It was in the past. I...I..."

"Deodatus," Augustine pleaded. "What did you do?"

Deodatus tensed, his body like a pot on a stove ready to boil over. "I did it, too!" he burst out.

He backed away from his father, shaking his head violently to deny the memory. "*I* became the hunter. I lured other boys to private places around the Cathedral. I went from altar boy to altar boy, consuming them." He raised a tear-streaked face to his father. "I hated myself, but I couldn't stop. *I couldn't stop.*" Tears flowed down his chin.

Augustine's face was frozen in horror. "But you *did* stop?" he ventured cautiously. "Didn't you?"

Deodatus wiped his face and nodded. "It was Emilio, a curly-haired child who'd been an altar boy for only a couple months. He whimpered the entire time. And afterwards, he asked me, Why? Why did I do it? I..." Deodatus shook his head. "I didn't have an answer."

Augustine stared, speechless. The innocence of his son, the child he used to know, was gone. He still loved the boy with all of his heart, but no matter how much he tried to ignore the feeling, he knew he could never look at Deodatus the same way again.

"Oh, Deodatus..." he muttered at last.

Augustine spun to Samo, his eyes pleading.

The old man shrugged. "I may be able to summon a portal. But not knowing where Olmo is, I wouldn't know how to focus the opening."

"So..." Augustine began.

"Someone would need to go," affirmed Samo.

"But...his...name," Augustine struggled to piece his words together. "It's already in the Book of Vices. Doesn't that disqualify him?"

The daemon said, "His name has not yet glowed red. He qualifies."

"Father," Deodatus said, "you made a promise to give your life to the Lord. So have I. And saving Olmo will allow me to fulfill that promise."

Augustine cupped his mouth. "Oh, dear Lord."

"You know I'm right." Deodatus awaited his father, his eyes glassy and red.

A million thoughts and emotions rushed through Augustine: The tiny infant placed in Augustine's arms the first time he held his son; the nights the young boy lay beside him as Augustine shared stories of gallant warriors slaying sea creatures to get him to sleep; the bruised knees and scuffles with other children and the days they worked in the garden together; the hours of prayer; Deodatus' commitment to God and the Church; and now, Deodatus' willingness to sacrifice himself for another.

"Yes. Yes, you are." Augustine inhaled deeply. "We all fall short in the eyes of God. I'm certainly no exception. It's our sins that carve the scars that we learn to navigate."

"And with God's love," Deodatus urged, "how can I fail?"

VII — The Neither

"MY PATIENCE GROWS THINNER YET," the daemon hissed. "Are you volunteering your soul for The Neither?"

Deodatus and his father hugged tightly, and Augustine gave his son a final blessing, then Deodatus stepped into the circle of blue candles. "Yes. Please take me."

"As you wish."

With no further hesitation, the creature lunged forward, opened its mouth to Deodatus' full height, and swallowed him whole.

"Deodatus!" Augustine gasped.

A crunch was followed by a slap of wettened lips and "He is gone."

Then the daemon confronted Samo: "Now, send me back; I have an appetite for another mortal of this community. And this time, he will *not* return."

DEODATUS COLLAPSED ONTO A SOLID FLOOR, as if discarded from above. He landed in an unfamiliar empty gray room, its plain walls adorned with a single mirror. As he slowly rose and dusted himself off, he balked at the sight of his hands and arms. He dashed to the mirror and gasped.

Staring back at him was his ten-year-old self, eyes bright, with an altar boy robe draped over his skinny body. He touched his face, scarcely able to recall ever appearing so young, so innocent.

"*Boy…*" A deep, creepy voice echoed through the empty room. "*Where are you, boy?*"

Deodatus dashed to the room's open doorway and peeked out into a long, empty hallway. He saw a single open door at the opposite end.

"*Boy…*" the voice repeated, emanating from the distant doorway. "*Where are you, boy?*" it sang.

The hallway—its ceiling, floor, and walls—was the same dull gray as the room. Deodatus spotted a staircase about halfway down it, which led upwards. He ran to the stairs and climbed, taking two steps at a time. The stairs switched back. The top led to another gray hallway, as drab as the one downstairs. This hall, however, had two doors at either end that were closed. He ran to the nearest door. Locked. He ran to the other. Locked.

"*Boy…oh, boy…*"

He returned to the stairs he'd climbed a moment ago. To his surprise, the stairs had transformed. He was no longer at the top of the stairs, but at the bottom. The stairs led up.

"Where are you, boy?"

Deodatus spun around. The doors that were closed a moment ago were now open. He took a deep breath and dashed up the stairs. They led him to another gray hallway with a pair of closed doors.

"Oh, boy. Boy…"

He spun back to the stairs, and again the stairs led up.

"Boy…" The voice came from the door at the end of the hall. It was now open.

He ran up the stairs to another gray hallway and kept running to the closed doors. He pounded, but the doors wouldn't budge. He returned to the stairs, which led up.

"I'm waiting, boy. Where are you?"

Rather than running upstairs, he returned to the room, now open; the room opposite from where he'd heard the voice. Once inside, he slammed the door shut. Like the original room he'd dropped into, this room was plain with a single mirror on the wall.

"Oh, boy…" The voice spoke from behind the closed door. *"Where are you, boy?"*

Deodatus leapt to the corner of the room furthest from the door. He sat, legs folded up against his chest, arms wrapped around his legs. Tense, his heart racing, he stared at the closed door.

"I'm coming for you, boy. I'm coming…"

He closed his eyes tightly and shuddered, feeling the abrasive touch of a man's hand running up and down his soft skin.

"Go away…go away…" he said.

"Oh, boy…"

Pressure built throughout his body, as if his blood was bubbling up inside him. No matter how hard he squeezed his legs or how tightly he held his breath, the acute pressure continued to invade his small frame. It crept inside, deeper and deeper, the pressure building and building.

"I'm coming…I'm coming…"

Deodatus leapt to his feet. "Stop! Stop!" he cried, attacking the door until it opened. He dove out into the hallway but landed on a polished stone floor.

Confused, he scrambled across the floor and sat up. The gray world that had surrounded him was now a brilliant white in every direction. Squinting, he shaded his eyes with his hand, but the whiteness penetrated, seeping into his head. He stood up and walked blindly.

With each footstep and teary-eyed blink, objects around him began taking shape. An altar. Dark wooden pews. Stained-glass windows. Stone floors. Angled ceiling.

His tense body relaxed at the familiar sights and damp, welcoming scents of St. Thecla's Cathedral. He stepped across the raised platform of the church's bema that led to the altar. The church's ceiling towered above him. This couldn't be real, yet everything about it was. The redwood pews. The lingering aromas of burning wax and communion wine. The rainbow effect of light beaming through the tall multicolored windows.

"Deodatus!" A pair of altar boys scrambled up to next to him, their eyes lit with excitement.

Right away, Deodatus noticed he was a good few inches taller than they were. He touched his face, realizing he was no longer the ten-year-old boy he'd been in the gray rooms, but probably fourteen or fifteen.

"We've finished our duties," one of the boys said with a smile.

"Yes," the second chimed. "You said you'd show us the secret room."

"Yes, I did." Deodatus' voice sounded youthful yet confident. He took the boys by their hands. "Come." He felt their energy surging through their fingers as they wiggled in his grip.

No. Don't go! Stop! Deodatus pleaded in the back of his mind. *Stop! Don't take them there.* Yet his legs didn't stop as he led them down the aisle to the narthex and then down a dark, narrow corridor. He stopped at a table that lined the wall. *Don't go! Don't go!* He let go of the boys' hands and gripped the side of the table. "Help me move this."

The boys hopped to it, bracing themselves against one side.

Together, the three shoved. The table moaned against the stone floor, revealing a hinged wooden trap door.

"Wow!" the first boy gasped.

Deodatus squatted, blew the dirt off the cast-iron handle, and pulled. The door whined as it opened. With a puff of stale air, a dark staircase was revealed, leading down into the unknown. Deodatus grabbed a lit candle from a small shelf on the opposite side of the corridor and started down the steep steps. His heart raced.

Don't go down there, his mind nagged. *Stop, stop*

The boys followed closely behind.

The steps squeaked. Deodatus stopped after a few steps. He motioned with his finger to the boys to go down ahead of him. They happily complied. Deodatus reached up and closed the trapdoor above him.

The boys' bare feet tapped against the dusty stone floor. Deodatus grabbed a pair of candles set upon a crooked chair, tipped each against the lit candle in his hand, and shared them with the boys.

The flickering light of the three flames dimly illuminated the tiny room, filled with broken tables, chairs, broom handles, and dust piles.

"It stinks!" one boy said, pinching his nose.

"It's the mold." Deodatus pointed to a broken pipe that lined the far wall. It dripped a dark liquid, dampening a pile of rags below it.

"What do we do now?" the other boy asked.

Deodatus' heart thumped. His mind screamed. He reached—then stopped. "No," he said aloud.

The boys frowned. One said, "Uh?"

Deodatus winced and dropped his candle. "I won't do it. I—I can't. It has to stop!"

The world spun into an indecipherable blur. The boys and surrounding room evaporated like pillars of sand in a wind storm. A deep, dark voice boomed throughout the space. It breathed, "You must," like a heated breeze cutting through Deodatus' soul.

"No! I've changed."

"There's no changing in the Neither."

"No! I won't do it!"

A child's scream pierced his mind.

Deodatus stumbled. Hundreds of tiny fingers tickled across his skin. Deodatus screamed.

In a flash, the world became white again.

Deodatus rubbed his face and recognizable objects took shape. Moldy hay and sounds of complaining goats struck his senses. He was kneeling in a barn, the same barn he'd left before entering The Neither.

"No...don't..." a weak voice whimpered.

Deodatus looked down. In front of him lay Olmo, exposed and vulnerable. "Olmo!"

Olmo scraped his hands against the straw-covered ground. "Please...please don't..." He shook his head, crying.

"Olmo. It's me. It's—" He stopped and felt the sides of his body. He touched his face and felt a beard. His adolescent body had disappeared, replaced by the strong muscles of a grown man. He was no longer fourteen. He wasn't eighteen. Who was he?

"Please don't, Brother Fides." Olmo inched back, the top of his head hitting the barn wall.

"But I'm not Brother Fides."

Olmo quavered. "No. No."

"Olmo, it's me. It's Deodatus."

"No, please. Stop!" Tears streamed down Olmo's face.

Deodatus tugged at Olmo's altar robe, which was bunched up around the boy's chest, and covered his body. He gripped Olmo's shoulders and shook him. "Olmo. It's me. It's me! Your friend."

Olmo stopped whimpering and held his breath. His eyes fixed on Deodatus for a long moment. He stretched out a hand and touched Deodatus' cheek.

Deodatus felt the boy's smooth hand against his skin. He touched his own face and realized he no longer had the beard. He looked over his arms and body. He'd transformed back to himself again.

"Deodatus?" Olmo muttered.

"Yes. I came to get to you and bring you back."

"Bring me back? To where?"

"Back...back home. Away from this horrible place."

Olmo sat upright. "That green creature. He swallowed me." He wrinkled his nose at the sour experience.

"Yes, I know. It told us what happened."

"How do we get back?"

Deodatus sat back and swallowed, looking around the barn that was all an illusion. "I don't know." He turned to Olmo. "But we can pray."

Olmo nodded.

Deodatus took Olmo's hands and cupped them inside his own. Closing his eyes, he said, "Dear Lord, please forgive us for our transgressions. We were forced into this place with lies, deceit, and immorality. Now, we only wish to go back home. We know we're not worthy of such a request, but please have mercy on our souls and send us back to where we truly belong. Please, our merciful Lord. We beseech you. In your name we pray, Amen."

They opened their eyes and stared at each other in silence. Both of them spun their heads. The barn hadn't changed. They hadn't moved. They shared a sad look.

Without warning, a wind kicked up the surrounding straw, battering Deodatus' and Olmo's faces.

A brilliant light materialized at the center of the barn. Starting small at first, it grew into a ball that floated a couple feet above the ground.

Deodatus focused his eyes into the ball. Inside it was a reflected image of the barn. Within it, he saw his father and Samo. Still dressed in furs and a jackal's skull, Samo stood with his hands held out and flames shooting from his fingers. The flames extended to the edges of the circle.

"Leap through the portal!" called out Samo. His speech was strained as he gasped for breath. "I can't hold it open for much longer!"

Deodatus and Olmo leapt to their feet and approached the ball, winds still battering them with flying hay.

"Faster!" Samo yelled.

The closer to the portal they inched, the stronger the winds blew, knocking them to the ground and pushing them away from the opening. They bounded back to their feet, but the winds blasted their faces and bodies again. With every step forward, their feet slipped backwards.

"Hurry!" Samo yelled.

"Deodatus!" Olmo called out. "I can't!"

"Olmo!" Deodatus looked behind him, away from the portal.

The young boy held onto one of the barn's supports for dear life as the winds raged and forced him away from the portal's opening. The surrounding barn walls and loft within The Neither blew away, leaving nothing but the support to which they clung. In their place was blistering tornado-like winds. Dirt battered Deodatus' and Olmo's faces, choking them.

Deodatus reached for the boy, grabbed him from behind, and pushed. "Olmo! Look at me!"

Still clinging to the support, Olmo looked back at Deodatus over his shoulder.

"You've got to try, Olmo." He coughed. "I won't give up on you. Nor should you." He shoved the boy forward at an agonizingly slow pace. "Try!"

Olmo strained with each footstep.

Deodatus kept pushing. Together, they edged closer and closer.

The circle shrank. Samo struggled to keep the portal open. The old man wheezed. "Jump! Now!"

Within the last couple feet, Deodatus gripped Olmo by the hips and threw him through the portal.

Olmo landed on to the other side.

Samo collapsed.

The portal disappeared.

VIII — Aftermath

AUGUSTINE ENTERED the darkness of his empty house.

Olmo stood silently at the center of the main room, an expectant look on his face.

Augustine shook his head sadly.

Olmo wept.

Augustine stepped forward and wrapped his arms around the boy. "Shhhh…"

Olmo looked up. "Are…are you sure?"

Augustine nodded.

Olmo cried even harder. "Why? Why?" He pounded his fists into Augustine's sides.

He hadn't any answers for the boy, beyond what they both already knew.

Upon Olmo's return through the portal, Samo had collapsed—never to awaken. Augustine and Olmo attempted to go back for Deodatus by recreating Samo's séance, but they couldn't remember the strange words he'd chanted nor perform the correct dance. In the end, the pair hung their heads in sorrowful silence, goats laughing at them from the loft above.

After returning Samo's body to Esmerelda, Augustine accompanied Olmo to his home, only to be met by a team of Quaesters—the Milan police.

The moment Augustine and Deodatus had left the bishop's office to seek out Samo, Brother Fides had wasted no time: he'd murdered the good bishop. Fides had then donned the bishop's robes and gone to Olmo's house, where he'd attacked Olmo's parents and three younger sisters.

"Why'd Brother Fides do this to them?" Olmo cried again. "Why?"

Augustine rubbed the boy's back. Why, indeed? Was there any way to explain the wickedness of man to such an innocent youth—especially one who had just lost everyone he loved in this world?

It seemed that in Fides' mind, the only way to clear his name was to remove everyone who knew the truth—the same tactic he'd apparently used in Rome. And even Loffredo's suspicions about Fides' crimes hadn't spared him the fate of his previous victims.

Upon encountering the Quaesters, Augustine had quickly ushered Olmo to his own home and instructed him to wait while he confirmed the fate of Olmo's family.

He'd verified the worst.

"D-do you think they'll have him hung?" Olmo asked shakily.

Augustine shook his head. "They're trying to find him, but I don't think it will come to that."

Olmo stared up at him quizzically.

Augustine had found out more on his trip, as well.

Brother Fides had been sloppier this time, leaving a myriad of clues for the Quaestors: a bloodied fire pick in Loffredo's office, sightings of Fides dashing in and out of Olmo's house swathed in bishop's robes.

Yet, no one could find the man. He seemed to have vanished into thin air.

Augustine explained to Olmo about Fides having deceived the daemon, and how he had no doubt that after Fides' killing spree, said daemon had paid him a final visit to remove him from this earthly realm for good.

Augustine scanned his empty house, once a home where he'd raised Deodatus as a single parent. He pulled away from Olmo.

Dust formed lines on the floor where furniture once sat—the chair he sat on to read stories to Deodatus, the table where they ate meals Augustine made for them, and the footstool on which Deodatus sat while Augustine knelt and bandaged his scraped knee. So many memories. Now, with the furniture sold in preparation for their move to Africa and with Deodatus gone, maybe forever, their meager home was also gone—in its place, this empty dwelling.

"I know this is a lot to ask, but…" Augustine swallowed. "Would you be willing to go to Hippo Regius with me?"

Olmo sniffled and lifted his head. "Where's Hippo Regius?"

"North Africa. Where I was born." Augustine paused. "There's a new church being built there. I've been offered a possible position as bishop. I could use your help."

Olmo hesitated. "I don't want to take care of goats anymore."

Augustine smiled weakly. "I'd give you much more responsibility than that. Without Deodatus, I'll need someone experienced to teach the other boys. And to be a leader."

Olmo turned his head toward the door. "I…I only ever wanted to be like Deodatus."

Augustine's breathing skipped as he held back the urge to cry. "As do I."

Olmo looked up at Augustine. He fell into him.

Augustine laid a soft hand against his back. He'd missed so many opportunities with Deodatus, especially when he was younger, to share such deep moments. Living in a world where such emotions were for women, he struggled to expose this inner shell, even a crack.

After a full minute, Olmo asked, "Do you think we can ever reopen the portal to The Neither?"

Augustine shrugged and gave him a mischievous smirk. "In my youth, I was occasionally forced to steal loaves of bread to survive." He reached his hand into his pocket. "Fortunately, this skill may have served us well." He held out a pair of crusty, browned scrolls.

Olmo's eyes narrowed. "What are those?"

"Samo's research on Enoch. I slipped these out of his old room when we paid our respects to Esmerelda."

"Why didn't you just ask her for them?"

"She loves me to death, but to her, business is business. She would have sold them for more gold than I have. And who knows whose hands they would have ended up in?" He rotated the scrolls. "If we piece together what Samo and Enoch spent their lives researching, there's a chance for Deodatus."

Olmo's eyes brightened.

Augustine dropped the scrolls back into his pocket. "But attempting anything here is dangerous. With the Quaestors still searching for Brother Fides, and the leadership of the Church in shambles, we'd be safer as far away from Milan as possible."

Olmo's smile faded. "The Neither was…it was really bad."

Augustine was loath to think about it. "I know," he replied, being strong for the boy. "But perhaps in time, both you and I will build up the spiritual fortitude that Deodatus forged in his life." He breathed deeply. "As brief as it was."

Olmo nodded thoughtfully. "Before I went through the portal to return here, I sort of gave up. It was too much. But Deodatus wouldn't give up. And he wouldn't let me." Tears formed again in Olmo's eyes. "Now, I don't want to give up on him."

Augustine smiled. And for the first time, a tear trickled down his face. "Never."

Olmo responded with another hug, this one tighter than before.

"No wonder Deodatus wanted to save you," said Augustine. "From The Neither...from Brother Fides." He pulled Olmo just enough away to make eye contact. "You've got the heart of a saint."

Olmo swallowed. "It hurts."

Augustine nodded. "The best and worst things in life do. Though I have a feeling our losses won't be in vain." He smiled again. "Come. Let us go build a church in Hippo Regius."

Olmo sniffled. "And we'll search for Deodatus once we get there?"

"Absolutely." He led the boy to the door.

Together, they set off.

AUTHOR'S NOTES – JOHN HOPE

IN MID-FIFTEENTH CENTURY SALZBURG, Austria, a late Gothic painter and wood-carver named Michael Pacher introduced Austria and parts of Germany to a new age of painting, known as early Renaissance. This form leaned on timeless religious themes and stories shared orally throughout centuries.

Pacher's masterful use of perspective, shadowing, and reflected light brought a stark realism to tales that once lived only in people's imaginations. His evocative work *St. Augustine Confounds the Devil* is no exception. The shocking depiction of a daemon-like creature in all its bizarre detail interacting with a human St. Augustine of Hippo brings an aged tale of the fourth-century bishop to life.

The painting is often mistakenly titled *St. Wolfgang and the Devil* since Pacher was commissioned to paint the scene for the Pilgrimage Church of Sankt Wolfgang in Upper Austria. Pacher based the painting off a fabricated story about how a daemon confronts St. Augustine with a *Book of Vices* and tells him that St. Augustine's name is listed. Augustine demands proof, so the daemon shows him the page. Augustine believes his name is in book that it's because he forgot to say a prayer; so he ducks into the church, quickly says his prayer, returns, and asks the daemon to show him his name again. No longer able find St. Augustine in his *Book of Vices*, the daemon is enraged that he inadvertently tipped off St. Augustine before he could punish the bishop for his sin.

Soul for a Soul posits Augustine meeting up with the daemon bearing the *Book of Vices* in northern Italy during a tumultuous period of the Christian Church. Historically, this era saw the Eastern religion Manichaeism gain popularity among the Romain population, threatening to overtake state-sponsored Christianity. At the peak of this conflict, Augustine opted to move to northern Africa with his son to help grow a new church in the region. Under mysterious circumstances, Augustine reported that his son, still a teenager at the time, had died during their move.

The story *Soul for a Soul* attempts to answer what really happened to Augustine's son, positing that the daemon played a role in his disappearance. This modern tale weaves together historical fact with fantasy, pulling in references to Enoch and his studies of daemonology, along with some political and controversial struggles of the Church that are still in the news today.

~JH

THE EYES OF MONA LISA

BRIA BURTON

A painter should begin every canvas with a wash of black, because all things in nature are dark except where exposed by the light.
~Leonardo da Vinci

I didn't believe it was possible, not until I saw it with my own eyes. Through her eyes. Yes, I truly witnessed the future, vast and complex. In many ways I could not comprehend what I saw, and so shall not reveal all here. In time, everyone will know.

Octavia Yulee's Diary, 1910

A BREEZE NIPPED at Lanea's bare shoulders while she chewed her nails, leafing through a tattered journal that belonged to her great-great-great-grandmother Octavia, whom she referred to as G-G-G. Her skin neither hot nor cold in a tank, jeans, and flip flops, Lanea welcomed the first sign of an autumn chill after the sweltering summer. She waited on a bench outside the nail salon where her best friend Seral worked.

It was the hundredth time Lanea had read every word in the diary cover to cover. Well, the words that were left. The torn-out pages at the end plagued her, deepening the mystery G-G-G had left behind. Inside the journal, unfamiliar words like *perfunctory, ennui, propitious, rancor,* and *blotto* had sent Lanea clicking through an online dictionary. That last one described one of G-G-G's alcoholic uncles who had a temporary residence in the *hoosegow*, a term referring to jail. On the topic of fine art, G-G-G used the term *oeuvre* to encompass the works of Leonardo da Vinci.

Lanea had been saving up from her job as a grocery store cashier to visit the Louvre in Paris. Seral worked extra hours at the nail salon because she wouldn't let Lanea travel to France without her. Only one thing lured Lanea to the City of Light: the world-famous masterpiece that had given her G-G-G a vision of the future.

The *Portrait of Lisa Gherardini, wife of Francesco del Giocondo,* known as the *Mona Lisa.*

The diary's handwriting and style reminded Lanea of an embellished version of her own mother's cursive lettering. Words were scrunched together onto the page to maximize how much could be written, like the way her mom talked, filling in every available space of breathable air. It was why Lanea didn't want to have Seral over for dinner. At twenty, Lanea still lived with her parents. They'd have an easier time planning their Paris trip without Lanea's mom hovering and inserting her opinions.

The wooden bench creaked under the weight of a new body. Lanea glanced up from the journal.

A slender, twenty-something guy with pasty skin in baggy jeans, a black tank, and a tilted baseball cap intruded upon her space. Lanea scooted away, closer to the salon door, until the armrest blocked her. She didn't recognize him from her high school. The college courses she took were online. His Converse-clad feet bounced, rocking the bench.

Lanea counted four empty benches up and down the sidewalk in front of a variety of shops and storefronts. The small downtown area wasn't busy today. Why did this dude have to crowd her?

She said nothing, especially since he hadn't acknowledged her, but made a point to snap the journal shut.

"Whatcha think about the aliens?" said the guy. A squeaky quality marred his masculine voice.

Lanea's eyes moved to look at him, and her head followed. "Excuse me?"

His half-mast gaze aimed across the street. "What if they're out there just waiting to dropkick the planet? You know, annihilate us so they can take over Earth. What do you think?" His gaze shifted skyward.

Of all the things this stranger might've said, Lanea couldn't have predicted aliens as the conversation starter. She'd pegged him as rude, but maybe he was just socially awkward. She thought about a variety of retorts and opted for sincerity. "It's a big universe. Maybe there's alien life out there we haven't found yet."

"They're probably above us in the sky right now, but we can't detect them. They're waiting, you know? For the right moment to strike." He smacked his fist into his other palm.

A *ding* sounded. Seral pushed the glass door open and sauntered out of her workplace. The acrid smells of toluene, acetone, and other chemicals tarnished the air. Her sleek, short black hair framed her face in a pixie cut, and she wore a flowy tank with her skin-tight jeans. "Later, Kiki. I'm leaving work. Can't talk now." She had a cell phone pressed to her ear and let the door swing shut behind her. With a wide, white smile at Lanea, she spoke to her younger sister. "I know. Just. Yes. 'Kay, 'kay. Bye." She hung up and sighed, shoulders dropping, knees bending. "Kiki is driving me—"

"'Sup, Seral, rhymes with Sheryl," said the UFO enthusiast.

Seral's relaxed posture stiffened and she tilted her head. "Oh. Hi." She slipped her phone into her back pocket. "You remembered my name." A glance toward Lanea told her Seral hadn't remembered *his* name.

He pushed out his bottom lip. "It's unique. Like you."

Lanea stared ahead and leaned back to avoid the crossfire of the awkward interlude.

"What's the plan today?" asked Seral, smiling with her mouth, not her eyes.

"Just hittin' the record store." He slapped a rhythm against his thighs. "Keepin' my eyes on the skies, though." He pointed toward the previously mentioned invisible aliens. "Just in case."

Seral squinted. "Cool. My friend and I have to go." She tapped Lanea's shoulder.

"I'm L. Skinny." He raised his chin, peering at Lanea through slits.

She stood and stepped over beside Seral. "I'm Lanea. Have fun at the record store."

Seral gripped Lanea's elbow, kick-starting their brisk pace past the guy.

"Luh-nay-yuh," L. Skinny called after them, sounding out her name. "Rhymes with..."

Lanea tucked the journal under her arm. Her long strides synced with Seral's, whose ankle boots clacked on the cement.

"Rhymes with la-play-ya!"

They turned the corner at the end of the block, breaking apart to avoid crashing into a couple strolling by. Lanea glanced back, feeling a little sorry for him but also relieved he hadn't followed.

Seral groaned, hand gripping her left hip. "All week, he's been hanging around talking about aliens in a cloaked ship. It's annoying, but so far he's harmless." She strode toward an empty bench, pulling out her smartphone. "We'll wait for an Uber over here, though. In case he's not harmless." Her manicured fingers danced on her screen. "Finally, a woman. Four minutes and she'll be here."

As they sat waiting, Lanea stroked the cover of the blue diary. The shredded edges flaked off onto her jeans. She pocketed the pieces, saving them for posterity. Her thoughts shifted back to her longing for answers combined with curiosity about the future as projected from *Mona Lisa's* eyes, culminating in a dull ache in her abdomen. "What do you think will happen when we see her?"

"We'll get in the car and she'll drive us to my apartment."

"No." Lanea shook her head. "The *Mona Lisa*."

"Oh, that." Seral shrugged. "I don't know. Your family has the curse, or whatever. What do you think will happen?"

"It's not a curse. It's a gift." Lanea tossed a lock of long, reddish-brown hair back over her shoulder. "Or something."

G-G-G had been vague about the result of looking into *Mona Lisa*'s eyes except on one point. She claimed to have seen a female American president. Now it had happened over 100 years later. Coincidence? An eventuality others could've predicted? Or a revelation?

Lanea didn't know, but she was hoping to find out for herself.

A sedan with a plate matching Seral's app pulled up along the curb and stopped. The woman inside had a short black Afro haircut like the picture on the app.

Seral compared the photo and the woman. "Yup. We're good."

They both offered "hellos" to the driver and climbed into the backseat where fresh scents of vanilla and pine melded with leather. Vacuum lines marked the clean floor. A hushed voice gave a news report on the radio, too low to hear details. On the dash, a mounted smartphone displayed directions to Seral's apartment.

"How are you ladies today?" asked the driver.

"We're great," said Seral. "Yourself?"

"Gorgeous day. Can't complain." She checked her mirror and pulled onto the street.

Lanea caught the words *"...Mona Lisa as part of a special exhibit..."* from the speakers.

She gasped and fluttered her hand in the radio's direction. "Excuse me. Will you turn that up?"

"Sure." The driver twisted the knob.

"Only once before has da Vinci's Mona Lisa *been on loan to the National Gallery of Art in 1963 at the request of Jacqueline Kennedy,"* said a news-caster. *"Now the request has been made once again on behalf of President Nicole Mills, the first female president in American history. The French govern-ment has agreed to allow the exhibit to mark the historic event."*

Lanea's whole body shivered. "The *Mona Lisa* is coming here?" She met Seral's shocked gaze. "We don't have to go to Paris," Lanea blurted. "D.C. is only an hour away." She searched her best friend for an equal level of excitement.

Seral's expression was unreadable. She faced forward, breaking away from Lanea's gaze.

A sinking feeling in Lanea's gut warned of impending conflict. "We can save all that money?" she tried.

Seral folded her arms. "Don't you want to see the Eiffel Tower?"

Lanea offered a sheepish grin. "Not really. I guess it's why I read so much. Fills my travel needs."

"My sister wants to go to Paris with her boyfriend. That's *not* a trip where I want to tagalong." The edge to Seral's raised voice held a note of sadness.

In the rearview, the driver glanced at them before refocusing on the road.

"I'm sorry, Seral." Lanea touched her friend's arm and held up the journal. "I wanted to see if this wild story was true. Not so much Paris itself." The expense had weighed on Lanea more than she realized. She was hesitant to share the relief washing over her.

Seral raised her chin. "Maybe L. Skinny will go with me. I can ask him to pay for everything."

The idea made Lanea's skin crawl. "He could be a murderer."

"Kidding," Seral whispered, muting any inflection. "I don't want to go with a stranger or my flaky sister. I want to go with my best friend."

Apologizing again felt trivial, so Lanea said, "I know."

Seral blew a puff of air skyward. "I've suspected for a while you were the anonymous donor for my credit card debt. Who else would know I needed the money? I wasn't fundraising."

Breath rushed from Lanea's lungs, making her cough. She bit her lip, unsure what to say.

"I get it." Seral waved away any toxic air left between them. "Money's tight. You helped me, and you're still trying to evac from your parents' house." Seral reached over and hugged Lanea. "Thank you." With a squeeze, Seral let go. "And don't deny being the donor."

"I won't," Lanea said, breaking her oath never to admit what she'd done. She'd been worried about embarrassing Seral, apparently a non-issue. "What are besties for?"

The sedan pulled up along the curb in front of Seral's apartment.

"Thanks," they said in unison.

Out of the car, they strode onto the sidewalk leading to the brick building. As they walked, Seral said, "Maybe I'll get brave and go to Paris by myself."

Lanea's eyes bulged as she imagined Seral alone in a dark French alleyway. "That's almost as bad as going with L. Skinny."

Seral slipped a key into the outer door of the building. "I can look out for myself."

"That's true." An image of Seral dining at a chic French café in broad daylight replaced the sinister alley. She wouldn't put herself into dangerous situations. At least not on purpose. Lanea thumped the journal against her hip. "I won't try to dissuade you."

"'Dissuade' me?" Seral smirked, opening the door wide. She swiped the diary out of Lanea's hands with ease. "You've been begging me to read this thing, and now I will so I can add fancy words to *my* vocabulary."

Grinning, Lanea entered and followed Seral up to her apartment. "Good. Maybe you'll find some clue I missed in there."

FOUR WEEKS LATER, hundreds of people lined up along Seventh Street to gain admittance into the West Building of the National Gallery of Art. A large staircase and a row of pillars marked the entrance to the white marble, Neoclassical structure. Lanea and Seral stood at the end of a mile-long queue along the sidewalk. The guards allowed only a few items inside—no bags, drinks or food. The *Mona Lisa* was one of France's national treasures, and over the years, a variety of individuals had vandalized the painting. She'd been doused with acid, pelted with rocks, spray-painted with red paint, shot at, and even stolen once. Random people were selected for pat downs after passing through the metal detectors. They'd been installed and would remain for the duration of the

Mona Lisa exhibit. One thing they didn't prohibit was an aged diary.

The security guard flipped through the journal, checking for hidden items, Lanea guessed.

"Here you go. Enjoy the museum," he said.

They climbed the stairs and passed through the propped open door. Bright light poured inside from a stories-high dome. Centered below the glass ceiling, a circular fountain trickled, topped with a statue of the god Mercury. In the brochure Lanea had grabbed, she read the rotunda had been modeled after the Pantheon in Rome.

An elderly woman approached wearing a museum badge. "Are you young ladies interested in a tour?" the old woman asked in a shaky voice. "Starts in ten minutes."

"No, thanks." Lanea shivered and was tempted to ask to borrow the woman's sweater. The outside temperature had jumped up to mid-eighties, teasing an extension of summer after the brief cool down a month ago. Inside, however, felt frigid enough for Antarctic penguins. "Where's the *Mona Lisa*?"

The woman pointed to a line of people snaking around a corner. "Only a few at a time are allowed into the room. Line starts there."

Lanea marched ahead and joined the line behind an elderly couple with a strong detergent scent. She read what the brochure had to say about the exhibit.

Seral's painted nails waved over the reading material, gaining Lanea's attention. "This could take hours. We already waited over an hour just to get inside." She hooked a thumb through the air over her shoulder. "Why don't we go on the tour first? Maybe this line will be shorter when we're done."

"Why do you think it will take hours?"

"Because I asked. The lady said a minimum of two and a half hours." Seral stepped out of line and strolled ahead. She peered around the corner and ventured back with a shake of her head. "The line disappears around another corner. I can't tell how many people are ahead of us, but the lady must know."

Lanea leaned, but couldn't see without stepping out of line, too.

"I just—I don't want the tour. I'm here for the *Mona Lisa* and that's it. Everything else is too distracting. I feel like I need to focus if I'm going to have any revelations."

Seral's neat black eyebrows arched above her brown eyes. "You're serious?" She shook her head, blinking. "Look, I'm not trying to be mean, but come on. You don't believe your G-G-G, do you? I read the journal. She sounded like she was in a cult. She might've only guessed that one day a female president would be elected."

Lanea's body shifted and she lowered her voice. "I don't want to say much. Not here."

"Tour starting now," a strong, feminine voice called. "Gather round, folks. You won't see the *Mona Lisa* on this tour, ma'am. You have to stand in the line over there for that exhibit."

Lanea glanced over her shoulder, noting a younger employee across the rotunda serving as the tour guide. She faced Seral. "What if this line is even longer by the time the tour is done?"

Seral's jaw skewered to one side. "I guess I'm not dying to take a tour, either. And you're right. Maybe this is as short as the line gets."

Those ahead shuffled forward. Lanea and Seral progressed by five or six feet. "Who knows?" tried Lanea. "Maybe time will fly. Either way, we're here. We'll get to see *Mona Lisa*, and I'll finally know if G-G-G was a senile cult member or some kind of prophetess."

The old lady, it turned out, had prophetic ability because the line was exactly two hours and thirty minutes. The hallways painted light blue and lined with white crown molding featured a variety of paintings to enjoy along the way. Lanea recognized some of the artists like Monet, Rembrandt, and other works of da Vinci's.

When they waited outside the door of the exhibit, Lanea squeezed Seral's wrist. "I'm sorry this is taking so long. I'm glad you're with me."

"Not a big deal. You waited for three hours with me to get Brendon Urie's autograph after the Panic at the Disco concert." Seral offered a small grin. "You look nervous. But so what if nothing happens? It's still an amazing painting. We're celebrating women and America's first female president, so it's not a waste of time."

That must've been what Seral had told herself for the past two and a half hours. "Thanks."

"What are besties for?" Seral winked.

The employee stationed at the door opened it. "How many?"

"Two," they responded together.

"Go ahead."

The room, colder than the rest of the gallery, sent chills over Lanea afresh, raising goosebumps all over her body. There were no windows, but delicate light flooded the space in a warm glow. In opposite corners of the room, two security guards stood at attention. The walls were cream-colored, and three were bare. On the fourth wall, the top of the gold-framed painting hung about six feet off the ground.

"Don't you want to get closer?" asked Seral.

She did, but Lanea also wanted to savor each moment and explore every angle. With a sidestep, she plowed into a barrel-chested gentleman.

"Sorry." Embarrassment glowed on her cheeks.

"It's okay." He lumbered ahead.

The employee outside the door had admitted about twenty people, most of whom already crowded the painting, blocking the view from Lanea's position in the back of the room. She'd learned that in the Louvre, thousands of people swarmed the *Mona Lisa*. Lanea felt grateful for the National Gallery's high security measures.

Darting forward, she disregarded her former plan to move slowly in search of the magic spot. With *Mona Lisa* gazing off to the left, Lanea moved to the right side of the room. In the space between bodies, she regained a full view of the painting about thirty paces away. A clear, bullet-proof glass case framed the poplar panel. Rather than painting on a canvas, Leonardo da Vinci had transformed a hunk of wood into a masterpiece.

Lanea stared into the brown eyes of the portrait, hoping to discover whatever future revelations her G-G-G hadn't shared—

unless those secrets were in the missing, torn out pages, which Lanea had no hope of recovering.

Seconds passed. Nothing happened.

Lanea moved forward, eyes locked on the woman presumed to be Lisa Gherardini. With each step, Lanea waited for a vision, a voice, something showing or telling her the future.

At fifteen paces, she stopped. The serene woman with a mild smile and clothed in a simple Florentine dress had been brushed into the forefront. The mountainous landscape and a winding stream served as a non-distracting backdrop. Sweeping terrain in grays and blue-greens added warmth, the mood spreading out from the painting.

Lanea felt touched by it. Her nerves fizzled out like a burning matchstick squished between two fingers. Her whole body sighed into relaxation and her mind mellowed with serenity.

Gentle. The word tapped against Lanea's mind. This gentle-woman had kept her composure for centuries. Gentle. Not easily provoked. Lanea couldn't imagine what *Mona Lisa* would've looked like if she were angry. It was as if she wouldn't display anger, even if she felt it. Not suppression, but a strong possession over her emotions.

Lanea wished she were like that.

"Anything?" whispered Seral.

Lanea startled, the hypnosis wearing off. "Yes. No."

"What?"

"Sorry, no," Lanea clarified. "I was kind of taken by her."

"She's one of the most famous paintings in the world. It's only natural. But you're looking for the supernatural part."

"What do you think?"

Seral nodded slowly. "It's beautiful. She's beautiful."

Someone stepped in front of Lanea, blocking her view of *Mona Lisa's* eyes. "I need to figure out where to stand." Inching right and left, forward and backward, Lanea caught glimpses of *Mona Lisa* between shifting people. Unfortunately, there were exponential angles in the room from which to view the portrait. So many angles, so little time.

A velvet rope between two golden stands stretched across the entire room, preventing anyone from getting closer than six feet to the painting. One guard stood inside that rope, staring vaguely at the group as if she'd already evaluated everyone and determined they were harmless.

"Five minutes," announced the guard in the opposite corner closest to the exit door.

"Keep trying," Seral urged. "Get as close as you can."

Lanea stepped up to the rope. Most everyone had already spent time there, and the ones left made way. Fixed on *Mona Lisa's* gaze, Lanea's fingers brushed the velvet as she moved.

In what felt like sixty seconds, the five minutes ended. The steady, painted stare revealed no secrets.

Outside, Lanea descended the stairway. Each downward movement fed the disillusionment ballooning inside her chest until it resembled humiliation. She hadn't meant to believe G-G-G implicitly, not without proof. It seemed there was none to be had. At the bottom, she glanced back, realizing Seral had lingered inside.

When Seral exited the building, she skipped down the steps. "I found out we can come back as many times as we want." She stood beside Lanea. "It's a free museum, so it makes sense."

"You would come back with me?"

"Yeah." Seral's earrings bounced when she bobbed her head. "What if your G-G-G wasn't guessing about the first female president? We should be sure. At least one more visit in case you can find the right spot to stand. If there's a halo that appears above your head, I want to be there to see it."

Lanea laughed, disappointment crushed under the boot of Seral's optimism. "Thanks for being the best friend ever."

"Yep," she said, her good humor infectious.

Still giggling, Lanea said, "But there won't be a halo."

"You don't know that."

"I think G-G-G would've mentioned a halo."

On their mutual day off a week later, Lanea's courage took her right up to the velvet barricade the moment they entered the room. She moved along the rope, gazing without blinking. Each time she took a step back, she stopped long enough to check for people. If they were there, she moved around them.

The second visit yielded nothing different.

"The guards were eyeballing you," Seral said as they climbed down the steps outside. "I was about to tell them you were checking to see if *Mona Lisa's* eyeballs really followed you wherever you went."

"They don't."

"I know, but in case the guards made a move on you, I had a valid explanation ready."

A week after that, Lanea made a W pattern across the room, searching for new angles she hadn't touched. Between every blink, she waited to make sure she didn't miss anything. *Mona Lisa's* stare remained as steadfast as the woman herself.

On the bus ride home, Seral nudged Lanea's foot with her own. "She's not talking, huh?"

Lanea shook her head. "I didn't mean to become obsessive. But I only have six months, and I figure every week I can find different places to stand."

The following week, Seral explored the rest of the museum while Lanea took on *Mona Lisa* alone. The employee who stood outside the room admitted fifteen people, but stopped Lanea. "There's someone who needs to speak to you. Please step out of line."

Lanea's eyes narrowed in confusion, but she obeyed. Five others were admitted inside and the employee shut the exhibit door behind them.

Panic surged. Lanea's chest tightened. Was she about to get thrown out? She texted Seral, asking, *Where are you?*

"This way," said the employee, a guy about her age. He led her down the hall toward the rotunda. Past the fountain, she checked her phone. No reply from Seral.

Beyond an exhibit of Dutch artists, they reached a dead end with a door labeled *Staff Only*. He swiped his badge and Lanea followed him into a hallway with offices. "In here, please."

His bony finger aimed toward the first door on the right, and Lanea noted the room's label: *Security*. Her tongue went thick in her mouth, nearly choking her. She clasped her trembling hands, struggling to make her knocking knees move. Could she be arrested? What had she done wrong?

Inside was a simple office with a desk and computer, short stacks of paperwork, file cabinets, a window, and two chairs facing the desk. The gray-haired man standing behind the desk wore a security uniform. Despite a potbelly spilling over the waistband of his pants, he was otherwise slim and fit. Another table behind the guard and below the window had a row of radios on charging docks. Some of the docks were empty.

The employee who had escorted her in left, shutting the door.

"My team has noticed you and your friend visiting the *Mona Lisa* week after week." The security guard lowered himself into his chair while gesturing for her to sit, which she did while fighting the desire to burst into tears. "Always on Thursday, always around two o'clock in the afternoon."

"That's when we're both off work," Lanea explained. "We asked, and we're allowed to visit the exhibit as often as we want." Like the woman in the portrait, Lanea displayed serenity despite her pulse's attempt at record-breaking speeds.

"As long as you don't pose a threat to anyone, or to the painting, that's true." His tone was low and tinged with suspicion.

Lanea focused on his eyes. They held none of *Mona Lisa*'s gentleness. His piercing gaze searched for a reason to accuse her of something.

"We heard a rumor," she said, seeking a way to offer some actual truth, "that if you look into *Mona Lisa*'s eyes at the right angle, she'll show you the future. Like, if you'll get married, have kids, that sort of thing." A little embellishment wouldn't hurt, right?

The security guard squinted. "You know that's not true, right?" he said, his tone patronizing.

"We came to see for ourselves." She stretched her smile, hoping it looked casual and not forced. "We've moved around the room to try and see her from every angle. So far, we haven't had any luck, but we'll keep trying as long as we're allowed to. No harm in that."

The security guard exhaled through his nostrils, reminding

Lanea of a restless animal. His eyes softened, even relented. "There was a complaint about your movements inside the exhibit."

"Really?" she asked, stunned. "Who complained?"

"A repeat visitor, like yourselves. *Mona Lisa* has been abused in the past. But I see no harm either." He stood. "Except you'll be disappointed. You're better off enjoying the painting for what it is rather than trying to find something that isn't there."

"I do appreciate the painting," Lanea said, her heart still stamping a staccato drumbeat even as her spirits lifted. "And I respect the job you have here. Thank you for understanding."

He grinned, nodding. "I guess it's cheaper than a psychic. Let me know if she gives you the lucky lotto numbers. I've been wanting to retire early."

"Will do." Genuinely smiling, Lanea rose from the chair. "So, can I go to the front of the line? I was next before coming here."

"This way." The guard led her back the same way she'd come.

A text alert beeped from her cell phone. Seral's message said, *Went through the underground walkway to the East Bldg. Modern art. Kinda blah over here. What's up?*

All good, she replied. *I'll text when I'm out.*

The guard bypassed the line and notified the employee manning the door that Lanea was allowed to go into the exhibit alone. "Give her ten minutes, and then you can send in another group."

Lanea's heart throbbed. She wanted to hug him. "Thank you."

He grinned, a warmth that had been missing now alight in his eyes. "I hope you find what you're looking for."

Inside, Lanea edged along the rope. She backed up at an obtuse angle from the corner of the frame, and then moved from right to left. She repeated the process in a weaving pattern, never straying more than thirty feet from the painting. During her many visits, she'd decided it wasn't worth moving farther away than that. She'd already done a lot of the distant angles at their other visits. Without human obstacles in the room, she was free to weave unencumbered.

The steadfast woman in the painting held Lanea's gaze, but gave away no secrets.

When the ten minutes were up, Lanea plodded away from *Mona*

Lisa looking back over her shoulder. She couldn't process her sadness or disappointment because she'd been given this incredible gift and wanted to savor it.

Yet the moment felt like a real goodbye. *Mona Lisa* had nothing to say to Lanea. She fought the urge to cry again.

Back at her parents' house, she and Seral sat outside on the swing set Lanea had played on as a little girl. It was rusting and the hooks creaked while they swung back and forth.

"Next visit," said Seral, "I want to find that security guard and give him a hug. How sweet was he? You got alone time with *Mona Lisa.*"

"After scaring me half to death, he was super sweet." Lanea's smile dropped. "I've read G-G-G's diary over and over. It says, 'When you're positioned correctly, gazing purposefully into *Mona Lisa's* eyes, the visions will begin.'"

"It's not specific enough," lamented Seral. She dug the heels of her boots into the dirt and straightened her legs, pausing her movements. "You need to know how many feet away and in which direction to stand to be 'positioned correctly.'" Again, she put her weight into the seat and pushed off.

A thought struck Lanea like a bolt, jerking her upright in the swing. She planted her shoes on the ground, unmoving. "What if...?" Lanea closed her eyes, willing her next words to be untrue. "What if the bullet-proof glass is somehow blocking the visions?"

Seral blew out a raspberry. "Well, that would suck, wouldn't it?"

"They won't move it for anyone," Lanea said. "Probably not even for the new president. I'll never know if G-G-G was right because I can't look at *Mona Lisa* without the glass being in the way." She bowed her head, kicking her shoe into the ground and spraying dirt. "All because some lunatics have vandalized her over the years."

Seral leaned her head against the linked chains that held up the seat. "Hey, you tried."

All the effort Lanea had made? Ultimately wasted. Her stomach felt hollow and sour. "I don't think I can go anymore. We've covered that room, and if it's not the glass blocking the visions, it means there are no visions to be had anyway."

"Hey, girls." Lanea's mom walked outside with two glasses of iced tea.

"Mrs. McAllister, have you ever read G-G-G's diary?" asked Seral, reaching for the offered glass.

Lanea gave a half-hearted groan and sipped the cold tea. She'd told her mom about visiting the museum with Seral, but not what they were doing. Mom would've said it was a waste of time. And she would've been right.

"When I was younger." Mom's bangles rested on her wrists while her left hand rested on her hip. With her right hand, she smoothed wisps of graying red hair out of her eyes.

Seral drank and then asked, "Do you believe in the visions?"

Mom folded her arms, eyes saddened and sympathy in her voice. "Is that why you girls have been going to the museum? Honey," she said, facing Lanea, "you know it's not true, don't you? Your G-G-G was in some kind of cult."

"That's what *I* said," Seral asserted.

"I know, Mom." Lanea swirled the tea. The ice clinked against the glass. "We tried and it didn't work."

"Sweetie, I'm sorry. That must've been disappointing." A sweat bead trickled down the side of her mom's face. She pinched her billowy top at the neck, shaking in air to cool off. "Whew. Menopause does not agree with me."

"There's no way to get around the bullet-proof glass, anyway." Seral gulped down her drink. "Even if it was true, we don't know the proper place to stand. There weren't instructions from G-G-G."

"It's not that specific." Mom squinted. "Didn't I tell you, Lanea? I did the same thing."

"What now?" asked Seral.

"No," Lanea blurted, wracking her memories. "You didn't tell me that."

Mom's gaze moved to the left, channeling Lisa Gherardini. "My granny, your G-G, took us to Paris when I was six. The safety glass was there for us, too, but Granny didn't believe that was an inhibitor. She had all of us take turns gazing into *Mona Lisa's* eyes. But no one saw anything. She was so disappointed. My brothers and sisters and I knew from that moment on your G-G-G was kind of wacky."

"Back up," Lanea said, releasing her held breath. "What's the correct position?"

"My granny said we had to stand in a place where we could clearly see *Mona Lisa's* eyes with no obstructions."

Seral thrust out one hand in frustration. "There's no X marks the spot?"

"No. My granny never had the visions, either, and she'd been able to look at *Mona Lisa* without any safety glass. But she understood from her mom, your G-G-G, it wasn't where to stand so much as not blinking and really focusing on the eyes."

Defeat punched Lanea in the gut. She hung her head and unlocked her knees, swinging again. The first museum visit had given her the answer and she'd ignored the truth.

A crescendo of chimes rang. Mom pulled her phone out, groaned, "Robot," and plunged it back into her pocket. "Didn't I tell you when I gave you G-G-G's journal?"

That had been over two years ago. "If you did, I guess I forgot." Lanea hadn't taken the journal seriously at first. But as time passed, she'd gotten curious. When President Mills won the election, a spark of belief transformed into conviction that a miracle would happen when Lanea gazed upon the magical *Mona Lisa*. She'd wanted to leave her mom out of it, and that had been to her own detriment. "I feel dumb. Sorry, Seral."

"Hey," said Seral. "I still had fun."

"The diary is the only reason you wanted to go to Paris?" asked her mom.

Lanea nodded. "I'm now convinced. If the gift exists, I don't have it."

EVEN WHEN LANEA could've found other things to do, like study for class, she browsed websites about *Mona Lisa*. But then she'd close the browser halfway into an article. There was no secret to find, no future revelation to be had. One evening, she read *Mona Lisa* would return to Paris in a week. Lanea had a brief urge to see her one last time, but the urge faded. She closed the article.

The next day, Lanea answered a knock on her bedroom door.

Seral slipped inside the room and hugged her. "Your mom let me in. I know you're done with *Mona Lisa*, but you're going to want to hear this."

She and Lanea plopped onto the bed. Lanea pushed aside the textbook she'd been skimming.

"I've been reading," said Seral, "about *Mona Lisa's* theft from the Louvre. Some maintenance guy just walked out with the painting in 1911. Too bad we didn't have that option. Anyway, they had no leads and no one saw it for two years. The *Mona Lisa's* recovery made it a worldwide sensation."

"I read about that, too," Lanea admitted.

"I bet you didn't read about this." Seral held out her smartphone.

Leaning, Lanea skimmed an article. The man who stole the *Mona Lisa* had a great-granddaughter living in the D.C. area named Valentina Krietz. She gave a brief interview about visiting the National Gallery exhibit.

Lanea noted the timeline of the theft with fresh eyes. *1911-1913.* For two years, *La Gioconda*, as *Mona Lisa* was known in Italy, sat in a trunk in the home of Vincenzo Peruggia, the man who had stolen the masterpiece. Lanea pulled out G-G-G's journal. On April 10, 1910, G-G-G wrote about her future revelations, her only given example a female president. The vision happened before the painting was stolen.

It made Lanea pause and consider something crazy. "What if *he* had a vision?"

Seral took her smartphone back, grinning. "Maybe that's why he stole her."

ON AN AFTERNOON IN JANUARY, both Lanea and Seral wore heavy coats, snow boots, and gloves. They climbed a few steps and stood on the porch outside the residence of Mrs. Valentina Krietz.

Lanea held a box full of manicure items. Posing as Seral's assistant meant she had to look the part. Seral held nothing but her purse.

A few days ago, Lanea had tracked down the phone number for the great-granddaughter of Vincenzo Peruggia. Seral called under the guise of offering free manicures to senior citizens, and Mrs. Krietz had accepted.

Their real goal: to find out if the old woman possessed any family diaries with information about her great-grandfather's theft of the *Mona Lisa*. The sparse information on the internet, including the brief interview Mrs. Krietz had given, revealed little about the thief and his motives. Both Lanea and Seral hoped for an inside scoop from his only living descendant.

The woman who opened the door had frizzy white hair, a button-up shirt with one button undone, and a pair of slimming slacks.

"Mrs. Krietz?" asked Seral.

"Come in, come in." She ushered them inside her modest home with sparse decorations—mostly tacky cat-themed décor—and gestured toward the sofa. "You can hang up your coats and leave your boots by the door. Do you like green tea?"

They both nodded, stripping off their gloves, boots, and hanging their coats on the coat rack. The couch was covered in cat fur, but no felines padded through the room.

Mrs. Krietz returned with steaming mugs and placed them on the coffee table. "I hope you don't mind cats. I have eight, but they go into hiding when new people come over."

"We love cats," Seral assured her, sitting to make her point.

Following Seral's example, Lanea placed the box on the coffee table and sat beside her. They both sipped the hot tea. Throat warmed, Lanea set it down, smiling. "Thanks."

"This is such a service you're doing. Thank *you*," said Mrs. Krietz. "I haven't been to a nail salon in a long time. I can't afford many luxuries these days."

Lanea lifted a towel out of the box and laid it over the table. With permission, she filled a bowl with water from the kitchen sink and placed it on top of the towel, adding a few drops of almond oil.

Then she gave Seral what she asked for like a nurse assisting a surgeon.

"Remover and cotton." Seral held out her hands and Lanea placed the items into each of her palms. "Nail clippers?"

Lanea fished them out and set them beside the bowl.

The acetone in the remover filled the room with a sweet alcohol smell. Seral brushed soaked cotton balls over Mrs. Krietz's chipped nail polish.

"What are you girls interested in?" Mrs. Krietz asked. "Are you in school?"

"I'm taking college courses online," said Lanea, brainstorming ways to broach the subject they had come to talk about. "Business classes mostly."

Not looking up from clipping and shaping the nails, Seral said, "I love my job at the salon, but I also have an interest in fine art. Nail file." Seral glanced up at Lanea. "Nail file?" she repeated.

Jerking upright, Lanea picked out a file and slapped it into Seral's palm.

"Did you hear?" asked Seral. "The *Mona Lisa* was loaned to the National Gallery in honor of the first female president." She moved the file over each nail like a violin bow. "We went to see it. Did you get a chance to see it?"

Lanea bit her bottom lip, worried her friend's lack of subtlety might alert the old woman to their intentions prematurely.

"I did, yes," said Mrs. Krietz. She dipped her nails into the bowl at Seral's prompting. "Quite magnificent. Some people say she's plain, but I think she's extraordinary."

"Me, too," said Lanea. "Her eyes especially. They're so gentle and calm."

"Cuticle nippers."

Lanea pulled out an unopened package containing the special-ized clippers and a thin metal utensil with a flat head. She used her nail to separate the plastic from the cardboard back.

"That's the pusher. I'll take both." Seral lifted one of Mrs. Krietz's hands out of the bowl by her slender wrist, placing it on the towel, and then the other. She clipped a few stray cuticles and then set down the nippers. With the flat head utensil, she nudged back the cuticles.

"My family has a history with that painting." Mrs. Krietz grinned slyly. "Did you know it was stolen in the early nineteen hundreds?"

"No!" Seral yelled, pausing her work to gape at the older woman.

Lanea dropped her head into her hands, peeking through her fingers.

"Yes," said Mrs. Krietz.

"Before you tell us more, Mrs. Krietz, please wash your hands and dry them. Then I'll apply the polish."

The older woman rose to her feet, her hands splayed ahead of her as if she already had wet polish on her unpainted nails.

"Base coat."

Lanea handed it over, lips pursed and blinking at her friend.

"Worked, didn't it?" Seral whispered over the sound of water running in the kitchen. She picked up the hot tea and took another drink.

"Yes," conceded Lanea. She never would've had the courage to blurt out questions like Seral had. "You played it smart."

The water stopped. Mrs. Krietz returned with a kitchen towel covered with colorful cats. She dabbed her hands with it. "It's true. A reporter came to interview me while the painting was in town because I'm a direct descendant of the man who stole the *Mona Lisa*. He was my great-grandfather." She sat down and presented her dry hands.

"That's unbelievable." Seral brushed the first coat over each nail. "Can you believe it, Lanea?" She turned and winked.

Lanea shook her head, surrendering to Seral's set-up. "Hard to believe," she agreed.

"Polish."

Lanea placed three bottles beside Seral: the polish, white lacquer for the nail tips, and the top coat.

Seral clasped her hands while the base coat dried. "Tell her about your G-G-G's diary. You'll appreciate this, Mrs. Krietz. Lanea has family history with the painting, too."

The older woman tilted her head, eyes wide in curiosity.

Clearing her throat, Lanea said, "My mom gave me a journal that belonged to my great-great-great-grandmother, and she was in this group. Might've been a cult."

"But the diary is really cool. Tell her about the gift," Seral urged. She shook the polish. Twisting off the lid, she painted Mrs. Krietz's nails a light blush color.

"The diary doesn't say what she saw," Lanea said, "but she claims to have had a vision of the future after looking into *Mona Lisa's* eyes. She also claims my whole family has this gift. Except other family members, including myself, haven't seen anything."

"Golly," said Mrs. Krietz as she leaned over the coffee table. "That's quite a notion."

Seral carefully swiped each nail tip with the white lacquer. Her artistry struck Lanea. The manicure looked lovely.

"Hair dryer after I'm done with this."

While Seral applied the top coat, Lanea found an outlet to plug in the dryer.

"Do you have any family diaries, Mrs. Krietz?" asked Seral, finishing up the final layer.

"I do, but none of them claim anything so exciting."

Lanea drank her tea and Seral blasted warm air over Mrs. Krietz's fingers. Afterward, she gave the dryer back to Lanea to unplug. "I read her G-G-G's diary cover to cover in one night." Seral sipped her tea, cupping the mug in her palms. "Could I possibly read the diaries you have, Mrs. Krietz? This whole thing with *Mona Lisa* fascinates me."

Still examining her nails, Mrs. Krietz flinched and straightened up.

Lanea groaned inwardly. Had they pushed too far?

"I can't say I recall where I put the diaries," Mrs. Krietz finally said.

"No problem. If you happen to find them." Seral stood and drank the rest of her tea.

Lanea replaced the salon items into the box.

"Now, just a minute." Mrs. Krietz glanced around. "I can check a few places before you go. If I find them, you may borrow them. But I would like them back."

"Of course," said Seral. "I can read them right here."

"Oh, it's fine." The old woman grinned, and a streak of red lipstick marked her white front teeth. "I like to hear about young girls being interested in history. That might give us a chance not to repeat the bad things." Mrs. Krietz ushered them into the kitchen. "Just set your empty mugs in the sink. I'll wash them later." She gazed at her polished French manicure. "You have simply made my day."

Lanea carried both cups and placed them in the sink, keeping up appearances.

"I'd like to show you one thing before I look for those diaries." Mrs. Krietz gestured and they walked through a narrow hallway. The older woman unlocked a door, and a pile of cats tore out of the space. "Oh, I wish you kiddos wouldn't do that." She shook her finger at the cats rubbing against Lanea and Seral's legs. "You know I keep this door locked, and still you dart in there whenever I open it. Naughty, naughty." She flipped a switch and stepped down.

The door led into a stairwell. In their socks, Lanea and Seral padded like the cats behind the older woman.

"Once I show you, you might think it's a little silly."

"I'm sure we won't, Mrs. Krietz," Seral called over Lanea's head.

Whatever it was, Lanea felt curious, if not a touch apprehensive. Her breath hitched in the increasingly stale air.

They reached the small basement where boxes sat on mismatched furniture. In one corner, some old skis and poles leaned against the wall. Mrs. Krietz pushed aside a bookcase.

Lanea and Seral stared at her, and then at each other. "Do you need help?" asked Lanea.

"No, no. This thing weighs almost nothing. It's a prop piece." Once the bookcase filled with fake books had moved aside, a hidden door behind it was exposed.

Lanea swallowed. Her skin tingled. Was this a good idea? She wanted to ask Seral, but her friend moved toward Mrs. Krietz.

"You have hidden doors in this place? That's so cool!" said Seral.

"Don't be alarmed," Mrs. Krietz said, raising her palms. "What I'm about to show you is *not* the real thing. Come on in." She opened the door and it croaked like a whining toad. The scent of dust and mothballs permeated the air.

Inside was dark, and Lanea hesitated before going in. Seral went ahead and Lanea waited.

"Now where is that lightbulb?" asked Mrs. Krietz.

Lanea approached, hovering outside.

"Those diaries I'm going to let you borrow will explain this, too, but when my great-grandfather stole the *Mona Lisa*, he knew he couldn't keep it. Eventually, someone would find it and he'd be in big trouble. He found someone who could duplicate the masterpiece so he'd have something to show for his effort."

A light flicked on.

"There!"

Lanea hesitated, not believing her eyes. She stepped into the room beside Seral, jaw hanging open.

Against the back wall of the small space hung the *Mona Lisa*. After studying the painting week after week, Lanea felt she had gained some sense of expertise. Everything about Lisa Gherardini, about the landscape, the textures, the colors, even the frame looked exactly like da Vinci's masterpiece.

Lanea's pulse moved into her temples. Her heartbeat pounded against her skull as if someone knocked, asking to come in. She and Seral exchanged shocked glances.

"An incredible duplication, I know. The diaries I have don't reveal who my great-grandfather found to create this, but it's amazing how much it looks like the real thing."

"Mrs. Krietz, how do you know this isn't the real thing?" asked Seral.

"Oh, it couldn't be." She waved it off. "My great-grandfather knew the Louvre would test the one he brought back to prove it was genuine, so there was no point in him giving them a fake. But it's still a very special family heirloom. One we don't advertise."

The tiny room narrowed in on Lanea. She stopped blinking, stood still, and gazed into *Mona Lisa's* eyes.

Her vision tunneled. A bright light flashed. The room vanished, replaced with new sights. Lanea stood gazing out over the city of Paris, a city she had never visited. At the top of the Eiffel Tower, nearly 1,000 feet above the ground, she gripped a railing to steady her sudden vertigo.

The absence of sound or movement—no wind, no cars, no buses, no people walking or cycling below—left her dazed. She turned around.

The woman standing behind her was familiar because Lanea had seen a black and white photograph of Octavia Yulee. In color, her hair was a bright reddish-orange. She wore the same outfit as the picture, a long-sleeved, ruffled shirt with a skirt that turned out to be a startlingly bright blue. Her buff-colored high-heeled shoes buttoned-up to her mid-calves.

"G-G-G," Lanea breathed.

"My vision was not only the first female American president," said Octavia, her clipped inflection reminiscent of the Mid-Atlantic accent in old films. "But it was breathtaking to know that women would have the right to vote, and would one day be named on the ballots."

"Will I see what you saw?" Lanea asked. "Is this the future?"

"Look again," said Octavia.

When Lanea turned around, she was no longer on the Eiffel Tower, but at the top of the Washington Monument in D.C. She peered out the small window, recognizing the view from within the pyramidion. Beyond, the Reflecting Pool paved a wide, watery line to the Lincoln Memorial.

A shadow covered the white Neoclassical-style temple built to honor the sixteenth American president. Lanea leaned forward into the recessed window.

An aircraft of some kind, huge and unlike anything Lanea had ever seen, hovered over the city. Her body went rigid. Her nails scraped the laminate map at the base of the window's frame. The Unidentified Flying Object resembled a flying saucer's shape, but enormous and stacked three high. Windows covered the vessel, lights flashed all over the ship, and pods speckled the exterior in groups of twenty or so.

A beam of purple light, giant and cylindrical, connected the UFO to the ground. People floated upward within the purple beam toward the spaceship.

Lanea wanted to scream, but there was no noise here, just as there had been no sound at the Eiffel Tower.

As if someone shoved binoculars in front of her face, Lanea's view shifted into an up-close image of the people. Faces she recognized. Her family, her friends, Seral. Finally, she saw herself. She didn't look much older than she was now.

Everyone beaming up, including Lanea, was smiling.

Again, Lanea's vision blacked out. A pinprick of light expanded, exposing *Mona Lisa* once more. She exhaled. "Seral, we need to go."

AT A CAFÉ a few blocks from the salon, Lanea and Seral sat a table near the back across from L. Skinny. He wore a cap, a tank, jeans, and Converse shoes. His heavy coat hung on the back of his chair. They were alone except for the barista whipping up drinks.

Lanea stirred creamer into her coffee while L. Skinny sipped a milkshake. "I thought I came on too strong last time," he said. "But I guess that worked for you, huh?"

Seral choked on her cherry cola.

He licked his lips, round eyes locked on her.

She wiped her mouth with a napkin, eyes narrowing. "Ahem." She cleared her throat, coughing once more into the napkin. "I'll let Lanea do the talking. But to be clear, we're all just friends here. 'Kay?"

"Uh huh." He stared, unfazed, lids lowering to half-mast.

She groaned. "Seriously. This is not a date."

L. Skinny slurped down half of his shake. His right hand slapped against his forehead. "Brain freeze." He shook his head, widening his eyes. "I need to hit the boy's room." He popped up to his feet, scooting his chair back into the wall. His eyes bulged. "Don't leave."

"We'll be here," Lanea promised. When he disappeared down the hall toward the restrooms, Lanea grimaced at Seral. "Maybe this was a bad idea."

Seral folded her arms. "It's fine." She sighed, leaning forward and speaking low. "I can't get over the real *Mona Lisa* being in Mrs. Krietz's basement. We should tell her."

"No." Lanea shook her head. After hustling Seral out of Mrs. Krietz's house with an excuse about a forgotten online exam, she'd explained everything about the vision to Seral on the ride home. "What if that poor old woman gets in trouble?" asked Lanea. "It's not her fault the *Mona Lisa* from the Louvre is the real forgery."

"What's the point of it all, anyway?" Seral asked, swirling her cola with a straw. "You saw aliens beaming us up into their spaceship. What are we supposed to do with that information?"

"I just wonder if L. Skinny might have...insight?" Lanea shrugged, sipping her coffee.

When he returned, he sat and wrapped his hands around the milkshake glass. "So, Luh-nay-yuh." He turned to her as if he lamented any view other than Seral's face. "You're a believer now?"

"Like I said, I saw a vision of a spaceship hovering over D.C. just like you talked about a few months ago."

"And?"

Lanea glanced at Seral, who sipped from her straw. "And I realized you were right about the aliens."

"Thank you." He sat back, slouching in the chair. "That's all I wanted to hear." He pulled out his phone, smirking while he tapped and swiped the screen. Then he placed it face-up on the table.

Both Lanea and Seral leaned over to look.

The photo app had been opened. He'd taken a picture of a pencil drawing on white paper, and it stared up at Lanea like a ghost. The crude sketch resembled the vision of the spaceship she had seen. "That's it," she said to Seral.

"Really?" Seral picked up the phone.

"Did you see this in person?" asked Lanea.

"Not me," said L. Skinny. "I sketched it based on another true believer's description."

"We're going to be beamed up into this ship?" Seral asked, still examining the picture.

"What?" asked L. Skinny.

"In my vision," Lanea explained, "there was this purple beam of light coming from the ship and touching the ground. People I know like Seral and my family were beaming up. I saw myself, too."

"Huh." L. Skinny dropped his elbows onto the table and cupped his hands under his chin. "Seral, you can add your number into my device."

She set the phone down. "No."

"Fine. But since you have information the P.F.S. would value, let's talk initiation."

"P.F.S.? You mean the Peregrinus Falconidae Society," Lanea said, referring to G-G-G's cult.

L. Skinny cleared his throat, lowering his voice. "You know about us?"

"My great-great-great-grandmother was involved. In her diary, she wrote about having a vision of the first female president. I have a feeling she also saw the spaceship, but she doesn't explicitly say that."

He leaned back. "Octavia Yulee was a P.F.S. founder, but no one said anything about a diary. I was sent to recruit you. Good news is," he said, one hand slapping the table, "automatic membership because you're a descendant." His gaze swept toward Seral. "I will personally initiate you."

"That's why you've been lurking around?" snapped Seral. "We don't want to join the cult."

L. Skinny raised his palms. "That's a misconception. We're a group of regular folks who believe the ark has come to rescue the chosen from Earth's demise."

"Ark?" asked Lanea.

"It's what we call the spaceship," he said. "Your vision confirms they're going to beam us up before a meteor hits or nuclear war starts or global warming or whatever causes Earth's downfall."

Lanea tilted her head at him. "But you said the aliens were going to annihilate us."

"That's how I test people. Most humans equate aliens with hostility." He rolled his eyes. "Total speciesists."

Seral raised both of her eyebrows. "That's not a word in the diary."

"The P.F.S. believes these extraterrestrials are benevolent," said Lanea, inclined to their way of thinking. "In my vision, we were all smiling. Maybe it's because they're saving us."

"Yes," L. Skinny whisper-shouted, glancing around. "It's an ark."

The barista ignored them, busy on a phone call.

"Hey, what led to your vision?" he asked.

Lanea considered telling him, but her desire to protect Mrs. Krietz stopped her. "I guess I inherited it." She picked up her coffee, glad it was in a to-go cup, and pushed back her chair. "I appreciate your time, L. Skinny, but I'm not going to join P.F.S. You're welcome to tell them what I told you. We'll see you around, okay?"

"No, wait!" L. Skinny pleaded.

Seral shot to her feet, picking up her soda for one last sip and setting it back down. "Bye."

"If you join, I'll teach you our signals and everything." He posed his hands in a misshapen rectangle.

"Keep it real, L. Skinny," said Seral, flashing him a peace sign.

Outside, Seral insisted they walk somewhere out of sight before summoning a ride. "Why do some guys *not* get it? No means no." Seral sputtered out her exasperation. "It's crazy that he drew the same ship you saw in your vision, though."

"I know." They sat on a bench around the corner from the café. It was Lanea's turn to line up their ride. "Twelve minutes," she said. "Female driver, red SUV."

Silence dominated while Lanea stared at colorful graffiti on the cement wall across the street.

"What do we do now?" asked Seral. "How do we prepare for getting beamed up into a spaceship?"

"I think I know." Lanea grinned, typing in her phone and pulling up a photo from the internet. "You with me?"

Seral's jaw could've hit the concrete. "Girl, yes. Finally."

In the photo, the Eiffel Tower stood like a beacon above Paris, its spire jutting into the sky. Lanea already had a virtual tour, but her best friend deserved the real thing.

AUTHOR'S NOTES - BRIA BURTON

LEONARDO DA VINCI'S *Mona Lisa* could arguably be labeled the most famous and recognizable painting in the world. Without a doubt, the theft of the masterpiece in 1911 contributed to its worldwide acclaim. Stolen art becomes more valuable in the eyes of the public, and the *Mona Lisa* has demonstrated staying power over the centuries.

While the story you've just read is fantastical, supernatural, and very much an invented fiction, historical facts about the *Mona Lisa* are sprinkled throughout the prose which, I hope, enhanced the reader's experience.

Now that you've read *The Eyes of Mona Lisa*, here are some of the noteworthy facts that made an appearance in the story:

The *Mona Lisa* was stolen in 1911 at a time when it wasn't the most famous painting in the Louvre, let alone the world. The thief, a maintenance worker, simply walked out with the painting under his smock with no one the wiser. It wasn't missed for over 24 hours, giving the thief plenty of time to flee without a trace.

An Italian named Vincenzo Peruggia (sometimes spelled Perugia) stole the *Mona Lisa* and hid it in a trunk in his home for two years while the authorities searched with no leads. According to some sources, he incorrectly believed Napoleon had stolen the painting, and Peruggia thought he was doing his patriotic duty by returning it to Italy. He was arrested in Florence when he attempted to sell the *Mona Lisa* to an art dealer.

There is suspicion in the art world that the *Mona Lisa* is not one-of-a-kind. In fact, the *Mona Lisa* in the Louvre could possibly be the second of two very similar paintings by Leonardo da Vinci.

~BB

STOREY'S ORPHANS

VERONICA H. HART

"People like us, who believe in physics, know that the distinction between past, present, and future is only a stubbornly persistent illusion."
—*Albert Einstein*

IN LONDON, at precisely seven forty on a September evening in 1878, as two children were about to head below to a cabin with their parents, the *Bywell Castle*, a coal carrying ship, struck their paddle steamer, the *Princess Alice*. I reached Winifred and Laurance Allen just in time to pluck them from the hands of death and a very nasty watery grave.

My name is Grunsberry Murphy and I live in Guthrie, Oklahoma in a little house on a large piece of land. Though I am thirty-seven years old in 2021, when I travel I can appear to be any age. Let me explain. There are times when I am performing the most ordinary acts, such as sweeping the kitchen, when an aura over-whelms me. It is usually accompanied by a vision. With little warning, this aura sucks me into an event. Sometimes it is in the past, sometimes the future.

In various centuries I am known as a wizard, a witch, a sorcerer, a shaman—you choose. I've even been dubbed a guardian angel, but you have to be dead to be an angel. I drift in and out of times and places, sometimes like a wise little elf, always eager to help. You can see me for yourself, for I was captured quite well by artist George Storey during this particular escapade. I am the little girl on the far left, recognizable by my impish grin in the painting titled *Arrival at the Orphanage*.

It is my nature to know some things in advance, but not all. I'd just finished feeding the chickens and was about to clean their nests when a vision of the *Princess Alice* burst like an explosive cloud of smoke before me. Within the cloud two ships entangled. People screamed. I shuddered and knew I had to move quickly. Could I engage the captain of the *Bywell Castle*? It took but an instant to recognize there was no time. My next thought was of the two young children who had to respond to me immediately and I envisioned, and therefore became, the same age as Miss Winifred Allen.

Just before the *Castle* rammed the *Alice*, I joined Winifred and Laurance, plucking them by their coat collars back from the stairwell. Winn, a tiny thing for twelve years, wriggled out of her coat, which was just as well, and tried to run down the stairs after her parents. With little Laurie firmly in the grip of my right hand, I lunged at the back of Winn's head and managed to grasp a fistful of golden curls poking out from her bonnet.

She screeched but I was relentless in my pursuit to save her and her brother, who now also tried to wriggle free. I'd chosen to represent myself in the image of a child Winn's own age, and, unfortunately, once I commit to a course of action, I'm stuck with it to the end, so it took some doing to physically overcome them and drag them to the railing. I flung them overboard, minus their coats. I followed. The whole maneuver took less than five seconds.

Although I knew about the sewage in the Thames, I was completely unprepared for the stench. The water was so black and foul, it seemed certain the three of us would die within seconds. Oh yes, I can flit through time, but I am not immortal. Even as I considered our next move, the two ships met. The earsplitting screech of metal slicing through metal as the *Alice* was sliced in two drowned out the screams of the passengers. Bodies rained down around us.

I'd read about the River Thames and pollution in high school, but this up close and personal visit was far more revolting and disgusting than anything I could have imagined. Near us, two continuous columns of decomposed fermenting sewage, hissing like soda-water, so black that the water is stained for miles, discharged a corrupt charnel-house odor.

I kept the children's heads up out of the water and towed them toward land, using the powerful strokes I'd learned when I helped train Jennie Fletcher, who went on to win a Bronze Medal in Stockholm in 1912. Though I'd inadvertently chosen this twelve-year-old body, the theory and techniques remained the same. Little Winifred would live to see that day.

The instant we reached the shore, I raced to the nearest house, grabbed a bucket of fresh water hanging by the well and sloshed it over Winn and Laurie. The man and woman who lived there joined me in drenching the children. After several trips, the children both raised their arms in defense, Winnifred declaring if they hadn't drowned in the river, they surely would drown if I drenched them any further.

By then, others had reached shore, gasping for air, struggling to rid themselves of the slime from the river, and crying out for their loved ones. People from nearby houses rushed to the scene and chaos ensued. Everything had happened so fast—from my first perception that the children were in danger, to my appearance on the *Princess Alice*, our descent into the stinking river, and rush to shore—that I hadn't a moment to think things through.

"Where's Mummy?" little Laurance cried.

"I'll go search for her. You two stay here. Look, the nice lady has brought you blankets to keep you warm. Winifred, you're in charge, right?"

"I want Mummy."

I left the two of them huddled together, wrapped in a woolen blanket.

Winifred and Laurance were the only two children of Charles and Eugenie Allen. Six-hundred-fifty-two souls who had gone out for a day trip, died on that fateful night in September of 1878. Roughly one-hundred-thirty-six survived initially, though several later died from ingesting the foul Thames water.

I moved among the moaning survivors who lay stretched out along the shore. The stink was so strong, my stomach rebelled, but I called for Charles and Eugenie, names Winifred provided before I left them. After over an hour of searching, I gave up, certain in my knowledge they were among the dead, and returned to where I thought I left the children.

By dawn, when I couldn't find them, I took myself to the Alexandra Orphanage, which I'd seen in the vision that sent me careening from one era to another without further explanation. They'd most likely be taken there once it became clear their parents had died below decks. A search for other family would come in due course.

When I arrived at the orphanage, I presented myself as a survivor of the *Princess Alice* disaster and so the normal rules for admission were set aside. The nursing sisters cringed at the sight of me. They'd seen so many children already that night. Oddly, they seemed more interested in my name.

"Murphy? You're Irish then?"

"I think my grandparents were from Ireland."

The older sister harrumphed and turned her back, but one who identified herself as Miss Rose took me to bathe and gave me fresh clothing. Once I was dressed the good ladies in charge of the resident children left me to rest. As soon as they were out of sight, I removed myself and set out to find the reason why it was taking so long for Winifred and Laurance to arrive.

I walked several blocks before engaging a hansom cab. Lest anyone wonder how I managed to take care of myself when I transitioned to new surroundings, somehow, whatever legal tender I had on my person automatically converted to that of my new location. I always carried cash in my "real" life which frustrated my sister in Oklahoma, but I never explained my reasons to her.

Now mid-afternoon, pandemonium still raged on the shore of the Thames. Men and women wandered among rows of bodies in search of loved ones. Winifred and Laurance were nowhere. I returned to the orphanage in the wee hours of the morning and crept in via an unsecured window in the rear of the main building. There had been so many new children taken in that night, they never even noticed my absence.

The first few days, I fully expected to see them among the other surviving children from the wreck who arrived, but they were never among them.

I began to suspect that I might have been wrong in my judgement about the Allen family relations. Perhaps a relative had come along after all and taken them in.

The problem was, I couldn't return home until I had resolved the problem that brought me here in the first place.

This was a new one for me. Each day, I made it a point to linger in the small reading group conducted by Miss Rose in the sunny little room that was the "welcoming center" for new arrivals. I liked being there because along with two others, my assignment from Miss Rose was to assist incoming orphans. We were to befriend them, making the administrator's work easier because the new inmates would be more pliable if they felt at home.

Since the rush of orphans following the shipwreck two weeks prior, only three incoming urchins had darkened the doors. Two were four-year-old twin boys who were processed then sent off to the boys' house. The other was a little girl of three. She was content to let Miss Rose take her by the hand and lead her away. Nothing for us to do, but it was pleasant in our little corner and, when we weren't reading or doing numbers, we embroidered.

Today my colleagues were Hortense and Mary, both very nice, diligent in their studies and happy to meet new girls. Me, not so much. I only wanted to see Winifred and Laurance Allen arrive and find out where they'd been these past weeks. If some new crisis came up, I'd have to make a quick decision about leaving them to their own fate or zipping off to offer assistance elsewhere.

I considered visiting with a Spiritualist in order to locate the children, but my rational self reminded me that they only deal with the dead. On the other hand, perhaps one could locate Mr. and Mrs. Allen on the other side and they, in turn, might know what happened to their children. That the children survived, I had no doubt, but where on earth were they?

Since I arrived, I'd been trying to focus on *Under the Lilacs* by Louisa May Alcott, approved reading material for us. Boring for me. I'd rather be reading *Madam Bovary* or anything by Stephen King. One afternoon, a Mr. George Storey showed up and spoke with the director and Miss Rose about creating a painting as part of his series of work about everyday London people. When he left that day, they'd agreed he would paint our little reading room where new children arrived. That had never happened before and so I was anxious to see how it worked, if I would go into a museum one day and see myself in a painting. I didn't even know if the artist was famous or not. I'd never heard of him, but then, I'm not an art connoisseur.

He arrived two days later and was in the process of setting up his equipment in a corner of our little room, when almost like magic, there they were, Winifred and Laurence sitting on the bench in the foyer, dressed in fine clothing, accompanied by a well-dressed lady.

While Mr. Hughes, the orphanage director, and Miss Rose dealt with the lady, who introduced herself as Mrs. Walker, went through the intake process, Mr. Storey sketched quietly in his corner.

How happy I was to see them at last. Mrs. Walker appeared well-off, a woman of comfortable dimensions, her girth enhanced by a sealskin coat, stood and drew a deep breath. The children looked healthy. *Why did she have the children and why did she bring them here?* I wondered.

It became impossible for me to concentrate on my book as I waited to hear the explanation for their arrival at the orphanage so late following the disaster. So far, neither one of them had paid any attention to me. They kept their eyes downcast and looked like they might cry at any moment.

And Mr. Storey, watching them, quietly continued to sketch.

Mr. Hughes, who received all new arrivals, screened for appropriateness, which included whether or not they arrived with funds, clothes, and good health. As a special dispensation, survivors of the disaster who had arrived in a timely way had not had to provide any of the above. Mr. Hughes pondered the meaning of the word 'timely' as he considered accepting them. I had the advantage of knowing he would.

"These children are Winifred and Laurance Allen. They are survivors of the *Princess Alice* disaster," the woman announced when she introduced herself to Mr. Hughes. "I am the widow Mrs. Walker. I have looked after the children since that dreadful day when I found them abandoned among the dead. They tried to assure me that a young woman was helping them, however I believe that was a fantasy conjured up in desperate hope that their parents would yet come find them. But the time has come that I can no longer sustain the expenses involved in their upkeep. Though they provided me the name of an uncle, he has not responded to my query. I have done my best for them, as you can plainly see. I have no funds to provide but you will find them cheerful and they will be an asset to your institution."

Mr. Hughes peered over his glasses at the lady. "That was very kind of you, madam. Why did you not bring them directly here?"

I knew why, but it wasn't my place to say. I would bet she thought she could extract money from the Allens. Though she dressed well enough, her boots were worn down at the heels and the cuffs of the lovely coat showed signs of fraying at the edges.

With her chin raised, Mrs. Walker displayed an imperious demeanor. "These children were as much as dropped on my doorstep by persons unknown immediately following the disaster. Though they'd been *rinsed*, they still reeked of sewage. I made them undress on the doorstep before allowing them in the house. We then had them bathe in the kitchen before providing them with clean, dry clothing. I assure you no one came calling in search of them, nor did their imaginary uncle respond to my letter."

"But once they were settled, did you place an advertisement in the papers? Did you make any further effort to find the family outside of a single letter?"

"Of course, I did. At great expense, I might add. But no one came forward in spite of their assurances that not only had their parents held a certain amount of wealth of their own, but they also had relatives living in considerable comfort." She looked down at the two children who remained mute on the bench, their eyes glued to their boots.

My heart went out to them. I wanted to crawl under the table and rush to their side to hug them, but décorum would not permit such behavior and I wanted to be free to speak with them as soon as the adult business was done.

Mr. Storey sketched, flipping the pages of his drawing book so quickly, I wondered what he was capturing as he drew.

Mr. Hughes raised his eyebrows which shifted his forehead so his hairline moved as if it had a life of its own. "And whose assurances assured you, madame?"

"Why the children themselves, sir. Do you doubt my word?"

"Not in the least." He cleared his throat. "If you are now relinquishing the care of these children to our offices, I will have you sign a paper and you may leave." He pulled a prepared form from a slot on his desk and laid it in front of her, then handed her a pen and pushed the inkpot toward her.

Mrs. Walker harrumphed before bending over the desk and signing the paper.

Miss Rose nudged my hand resting on the book. "It's your turn, Grunsberry. Make Winifred welcome. I'll go upstairs and arrange for her accommodation. Sister Markham is just around the corner in the nurse's office if you need any help. When I come back, we'll take her to the dormitory together."

I nodded obediently. "What about Laurance?"

"Mr. Hughes will take him to the boys' building next door."

Initially, when I was called to rescue them, I somehow thought the process would be totally different. They should have been taken to the orphanage right away along with the other surviving orphans, and then Mr. Allen's brother should have searched for and found them here.

Winifred appeared a lot thinner than the first time I saw her. Dark circles under her crystalline blue eyes contrasted sharply with her pale complexion. I introduced myself to her. Her eyes flashed a brief recognition and I smiled at her, raising my finger to my lips to silence her greeting.

Mr. Hughes took Laurance by the hand and led him back out the front door.

The poor little guy looked like he'd cry any second. "I want to stay wiff my sister."

"You be a man, now, Master Allen. You'll have lots of new friends."

"His clothes are in there," Mrs. Walker said, pointing to the trunk her man had deposited on the floor before her.

"We'll sort it all out later. Thank you for taking care of the children, Mrs. Walker. You may rest assured they are now in good hands."

Seeming unconvinced, the boy kicked Mr. Hughes's ankle. Mr. Hughes hop-stepped back, releasing the boy's hand, which left Laurance free to run across the courtyard toward the carriage that brought him here.

Even from this distance we heard his orders, "Take me to my house! I wanna go home!"

Winifred stepped forward, but I caught her arm. "Hush. He'll be all right."

I'm sure the driver had no intention of driving the boy anywhere but didn't get the chance to prove himself before Mr. Hughes caught up with Laurance and tucked the poor boy under his arm like a package. He bore him, kicking and screaming, to the boys' dormitory.

I dealt my most evil glare at Mr. Hughes's back. Though his policies regarding the orphanage met the city council standards for caring for "friendless and destitute" children, he was hardly a role model of kindness and generosity. Indeed, his bespoke suits suggested an income far exceeding his station. Although the children might be destitute, they did require a sponsor to pay certain fees in order to be accepted into the institution. The surviving orphans from the disaster had been sponsored by a community charitable fund.

I wondered who supervised the supervisor.

"I remember you," Winn whispered to me as we stood watching the drama. "You pushed us overboard."

I put an arm around her waist. "And I'm so happy to finally see you here. I thought at first, you would go to one of your uncles' houses, but then when no one came looking for you, I expected them to bring you here."

"How do you know about our uncle?" Winn continued to whisper.

I nudged her. "Perhaps you ought to bid farewell to the kind lady who took care of you."

Mrs. Walker had stood in preparation of leaving with the manservant.

The girl stepped behind me. "I don't want to."

I pulled her around and gave her a shove forward. "Mrs. Walker," I called out. "Winifred wants to thank you for all you've done for her."

I hissed at Winn's back. "Curtsy and thank her."

Mrs. Walker raised her eyebrows. "Really?" Her demeanor changed and she offered a weak smile. "Such a dear."

Winn dipped a minimum curtsy.

Mrs. Walker then left without saying goodbye, nor did she glance back as she made her way to the carriage.

As soon as Mrs. Walker was out of earshot, Winifred whirled on me. "What's your name? You never told us."

"I'm Grunsberry Murphy. Friends call me Berry."

"Mr. Hughes looks mean."

"He is," I agreed. "But you won't see him often. He stays in his office when he's not out and about trying to impress people with his importance. You don't have to worry about him."

She leaned closer to whisper again. "What about them?" She indicated Hortense and Mary, two girls about twelve years old, the same age I had presented as.

"They're very nice. Mary, on the left, is practicing her letters. She couldn't read at all when she came here. Hortense is working on her arithmetic. She's quite good at it."

"I don't like arithmetic."

"That's all right. Tell me everything that happened after I left you," I said, changing the subject.

I led her slowly through the hallways toward the staircase that went up to the bedrooms.

"A lot of people came and looked at us. I was freezing cold being all wet and all. Then Mrs. Walker came and asked us our names."

"Hm. Did she ask any other survivors their names?"

Winn paused and I turned to see why she stopped. Her eyes were closed as she remembered. "It was dark. There were so many people. So much shouting and crying. Laurie and I huddled together, unsure what to do. He's only six, you know."

I took her hand and encouraged her to continue walking. "I know. So, you don't know whether Mrs. Walker spoke to anyone else?"

"I don't. Not really. Maybe she chose us because we were the cleanest—and closest to her house. Anyway, she said something like we'd do."

"What do you mean?"

Winn shrugged. "I didn't know at the time, but after a few days, it seemed she wanted servants. Laurance was shivering something awful, so I was grateful when she led us to her house and brought us inside. She even had her maid provide us a hot bath that night. When we went to bed on cots in a small room off the kitchen, she said we were welcome to stay as long as necessary. She would find things for us to do around to house to help out."

I considered that for a moment and let a dark thought pass. "Go on."

"In the morning, I let her know that my parents owned a shop where my father was a tailor and Mother was a milliner. She seemed happy to know that and said she would take us home and help us find our parents. I don't think she understood that they had died in the wreck."

"I expect there was quite a bit of confusion."

"In the meantime, while we waited for a letter from Father, she had me working as a scullery maid and Laurance had to clean the fireplaces and bring up the coal every day."

Not exactly the beneficent Mrs. Walker who'd sat in the arrival room.

We reached the staircase, a wide sweep of stairs with hardwood carved railings, left over from when the building was really somebody's home. Very elegant in contrast to the undignified and rough manner with which the children were treated behind the scenes where the public could not see them. How fortunate I was to be free to transmit myself elsewhere once I completed my self-imposed mission to help Winn and Laurie.

IN THE WEE hours of the morning, I tiptoed to Winn's cot and shook her by the shoulder. "Come on," I whispered. "We must hurry. Get dressed."

I had already donned my plain navy-blue day dress but left off the pinafore. I had my hat, boots, and coat on.

She rubbed her eyes. "What's going on?"

"We're going out for a while."

"But, it's still night." She pulled the covers over her head.

"No, Winn, it's nearly five o'clock. Don't you like an adventure?"

She pulled the cover down enough to peer at me with one eye. "An adventure?"

"Shh." I touched her lips.

She pushed the covers all the way down and sat up. "People will know we're gone."

"I've written a note." I *had* written a note, using my adult tone and barely recalled penmanship, to let Miss Rose know what I was up to so she wouldn't sound an alarm.

With just enough moonlight coming through the windows, Winn rummaged around finding her stockings, bloomers and outer clothes, a navy-blue dress similar to mine. Once she stumbled and caused her cot to shift, making a scraping noise. We both held our breath until it was clear the other eight girls in our room weren't disturbed.

Thank heaven for either her spirit of adventure or her curiosity, because she followed me silently through the house and out into the street where the hansom cab I'd hired after dinner the night before waited under the trees at the end of the street. I must say, it took some doing to convince the coachman. Once enough money changed hands, he didn't mind my age so much.

I gave the driver the Allen's home address.

"Why are we going there? Nobody will be there."

"It's only two weeks since the accident, perhaps the servants are still awaiting their orders." I assumed a successful tailor and milliner would manage to have at least a cook and housekeeper if not a full contingent of household help.

"So, if you know so much about me, why is it you don't know everything else?"

"I only have flashes—visions of people who need help. And I go to help. Once I've chosen my course of action, I cannot deviate until the mission is accomplished. I had the idea that you were in trouble, more than the threat of dying in the Thames, so I came."

In the darkness of the carriage, I imagined her shaking her head. "That doesn't make any sense."

"It doesn't, but I'll be here for you until everything is resolved."

"You're not even older than I. What are you, twelve years?"

I shrugged. "About that for the moment, yet I have the experience of centuries before and after in me. The truth is very confusing."

She leaned away from me. "You're very strange, Berry."

I sighed. "I know. It's the way I am."

"Why won't you tell me how you appeared and what do you mean by 'flashes?'"

In the darkness of the interior of the cab, I let my guard down. How could it hurt for her to know the truth? "I'm really thirty-seven-years old and I live on a farm in Guthrie, Oklahoma. That's in the United States. America."

She giggled. "What a wonderful story. Do you ride horses and fight Indians?"

My shoulders dropped in disappointment. I should have known she'd treat it as a fairy tale. "Only when absolutely necessary do I ride horses and Indians don't come around the farm much anymore."

The carriage stopped and the cabbie rapped on the roof. "We're here, miss."

"Come. Let's check your house. If there are any servants still here, they ought to be up and starting the fires." I opened my door and dropped down to the ground, fully expecting Winn to follow. Thankfully, she did.

"Wait here, driver. We won't be a moment." From the lack of light in the windows, I suspected no one would be inside. Nevertheless, I knocked on the door.

Winn pulled on the bell chain and then banged on the door along with me. "Edgar!" She waited a moment then pulled the chain again. "Jenny! Claire!" No one responded.

"Who are they?"

"Edgar's the butler. The others are the cook and housemaid. They live in. Or, they did. Let's go around to the back," she said. "I know a way to get inside."

She led me around the side through a gate. A white gravel path led us through a small garden to the rear of the house where Winn stepped down into a well beside the back door. "It's where Laurie and I used to hide from Nanny."

She dug down into a planter beside the door and withdrew a key. As we crept into a mudroom, she found a candle to light our way into the kitchen, which was completely devoid of life. She held the candle up high, making it clear no pots or pans hung from the hooks, no china lined the shelves of the hutch.

"How odd. Everything is gone."

We found a proper lantern, lit it, and made our way up the stairs to the parlor on the ground floor. This room was also empty. She whispered in awe, "It's all gone. Everything is vanished as if we never lived here."

No curtains hung over the windows. The gaslights flickered off as dawn approached, lighting the room enough to see bits of litter strewn across the bare wooden floorboards. It wasn't even my home and I could feel the heartache of losing everything familiar. There should have been a divan before the fireplace and candelabra on the mantle.

We tiptoed through to the dining room and then to the breakfast room at the back of the house. A broken teacup and a child's high-chair in the kitchen were all that remained, otherwise, nothing.

She choked back tears. "I suppose we ought to go upstairs. What do you think happened to everything?"

I could only imagine. Relatives, believing the entire family had died in the disaster, had cleaned it all out? But Mrs. Walker said she'd notified the family that she had the children. I wondered how many times she really sent letters. With twice daily delivery, someone ought to have been here to collect the mail, at least in the beginning. As we returned to the front of the house and the stair-case, I went back to what I thought was litter and saw that several letters lay on the floor inside the front door. Did Mrs. Walker somehow confiscate all their possessions? I studied the mail and found one letter from Mrs. Walker. The others appeared to be bills and circulars. I opened the sealed envelope and read the note. Winnifred read over my shoulder.

Dear Mr. and Mrs. Allen,

I am most pleased to advise you that your two children, Winifred and Laurance, are at my home awaiting their repatriation with you, their loving family. I look forward to your reply by return mail advising me of when you will arrive to collect them.

I would assume as a courtesy, you will be happy to reimburse me for the considerable expenses involved in their care, which not only includes treatment by our local doctor, but new clothes and the extraordinary amounts of food they eat. To say nothing of the extra labor by my single housekeeper in doing their laundry, feeding them, and cleaning up after them.

Below are the particulars and specific expenses to which I refer.

I remain, yours sincerely,

Mrs. Augustus Walker

"That stupid old cow!" Winn shouted at the end.

I had to agree, especially after seeing the large sum of money she apparently considered fair.

"She made us do all the bloody work!"

"Hush. I don't think you should be using that language, Winifred," I cautioned her.

She scowled. "You're right, Berry, but you read that. She's an out and out liar. And tried to be a thief as well. I don't think I'll ever understand grown-ups."

After calming her, I suggested we head up the stairs to check the rest of the house.

By now we'd stopped whispering. It was obvious there was no one to disturb. We clambered up the stairs to the first floor sitting room. After confirming the empty spaces, we went on to the second-floor bedrooms.

In Laurie's room, Winn picked up a well-worn stuffed rabbit that lay amidst a swept-up pile of debris in the corner. "At least he'll be happy to see Bunny Boy." She placed it in her coat pocket, and we moved on to her bedroom.

She crossed the empty room to the window and looked out on the street below. A light fog shrouded our cab and its horse as they waited for us at the curb. "Did you know all this when you came to save us?" Her voice carried a depth of sadness beyond her years.

"I did not. I only sensed that you needed to get off that boat immediately. I had no time to think." I stood beside her and watched the cloudy puffs of breath coming from the horse's nostrils. Had I had time to consider, I would have arrived as a fully-grown woman, so that my voice would be heard and possibly respected. I thought in that brief moment that the children would more likely respond to a peer rather than an adult stranger. Nothing went the way it should.

"Except you did save us. Did I thank you?"

"Probably. I didn't do it for that reason."

"Then why?" she asked.

"Because I felt the connection and you needed me. It's some-thing that's happened to me since I was probably your age. I promise I'll tell you more later but right now, we have to find out what happened to all your possessions. But first we have to get back to the orphanage before they discover we're missing from our beds."

"So, are you a witch?" she asked as she followed me back to the landing.

"Not a witch, truly."

"Do you know if I'll have to live in the orphanage forever?"

It's against my policy to tell people their future even when I know it. "I can tell you they only keep girls until they're fourteen years of age," I responded.

"Then what?" she asked in a panic.

"Then they find you a position in a household. I think." I hadn't thought that through nor researched it. All I knew is that I would meet her again as an adult at the Olympic games in Stockholm. We climbed the stairs to the servant's quarters, knowing that we'd find nothing. To my surprise, the three rooms contained beds, bureaus, and wardrobes. I supposed the furnishings were of no value to whoever took the family's items.

We went back downstairs and used the front door to exit.

"What do we do next?" she asked once we were settled back in the cab.

"Somehow, we must get out and go to your parents' shop during the day. We may have to ask Miss Rose to accompany us."

We snuggled back into our cots. I don't know about Winn, but the next two hours passed in an instant and the morning bell sounded.

I approached Miss Rose after breakfast and handed her Bunny Boy. I explained about our early excursion and Winifred Allen's distress at not knowing what happened to her parents. After she scolded me, she agreed that we ought to take a trip out to their shop. We arranged to go after lunch while the smaller children napped. I believe she enjoyed an adventure as much as I did.

When we arrived, fortunately, the shop doors stood open, even with a black wreath hooked onto one of them. At least the employees showed that much respect. Not knowing the ins and outs of their business, I let Miss Rose and Winn take the lead.

A robust-looking gentleman approached us. "How can I help you fine ladies today?"

"Mr. Whitely, this is Miss Rose, my guardian. I'm Winifred Grace Allen." She deliberately posed directly in front of him and held her face up.

He peered down at her over the tops of his glasses. "Why, so you are. So you are. I am so sorry about your parents. But what a wonderful surprise that you are here, and you are well. We all thought you and your brother were lost in the disaster as well." He looked around as if expecting to see Laurance behind us. "And your brother *is* well, I trust?"

"He is. Miss Rose has some questions she'd like to ask, if you don't mind. Perhaps we can have tea in the showroom." Winn didn't wait for him to respond but led the way to the back of the shop through a pair of curtains and into a lovely small room with a platform where I presumed ladies, or gentlemen, modeled their clothes.

I suspected her new-found air of authority came from being in familiar surroundings. Mr. Whitely had been an employee of her father's, which, I imagine, gave her the courage to speak that way to him.

"Of course, I'll see to it immediately." Mr. Whitely huffed and puffed behind us.

We took our places on the green velvet cushioned chairs and waited until the tea arrived— tea with biscuits and honey—before

Miss Rose started the conversation. As I had explained our concerns earlier, she went straight to the point. No beating about the bush for Miss Rose.

"Mr. Whitely, can you tell me who is handling the funds for Miss Winifred and Master Laurance?"

Mr. Whitely appeared taken aback. "Why, what do you mean, my dear lady? What funds?"

"As this was their parents' business, it would now belong to the children. Perhaps there is a trustee assigned?"

"My dear, Mr. Charles Allen and I were equal partners in this business. As I understand it, Mr. Andrew Allen is the heir to Mr. Charles' estate. He comes around every Friday to check on the week's work and reviews the books. All funds go into the business accounts which he examines and, together we apportion the week's revenues and salaries. It has been such a short time, you understand." Mr. Whitely appeared a tad nervous to me as he wiped his forehead with his handkerchief.

"I see," said Miss Rose. She hesitated and I feared she forgot what she was meant to ask. "But wasn't there a last will and testament? Has it gone through the proper procedures?"

He leaned toward Winn. "Miss Allen, ought we to be discussing family matters in front of strangers?"

"Need I remind you Miss Rose is my guardian, Mr. Whitely?"

"Had I known you and Master Laurance survived, I most certainly would have demanded to see the papers, I assure you. As it is, perhaps Mr. Allen is securing your future through investing and saving on your behalf…er…in the hopes you had survived." Even he didn't look like he believed what he said.

"You haven't introduced your little friend," he said as he dropped four lumps of sugar into his teacup before adding the tea.

"I need no introductions, sir." I summoned up the most evil, low-throated voice possible from my twelve-year-old body and said, "Rest assured if wrong has been done against either of the Allen children, you shall know me by your worst nightmares."

Both Miss Rose and Winn turned gaping wide eyes on me. I had to suppress a giggle and maintain my stern face.

"Well, really," Mr. Whitely said. "There is no call for that tone of voice, young lady."

I clamped my jaw shut and glared at him. I imagined what I must have looked like to him with Winifred and me dressed in the same schoolgirl costume provided by the orphanage, minus the pinafores.

"Mr. Allen, the junior, came to me following the disaster and informed me that his brother's entire family was lost. I was to continue on as manager of the business. Mr. Charles Allen, your father," he said, looking at Winifred, "trusted me implicitly with his best customers. I am currently in search of a new milliner to replace your mother as her assistant left upon hearing of her passing."

"Back to my original question, sir. About the bookkeeping?" Miss Rose said.

"You will have to discuss that with Mr. Allen. I presume you know where your uncle lives." He stood, dismissing us.

I wanted to object, but Miss Rose insisted we leave.

Once out on the sidewalk, we conferred briefly with Winn. Miss Rose concluded with, "We must travel to Tunbridge Wells and pay your uncle a visit. We'll leave first thing tomorrow morning."

We returned to the orphanage in time for tea. We had Shepherd's pie with very little meat, but the flavor was still delicious. I wished I could ask for more, but that was against the rules. A boring custard arrived for dessert.

WHATEVER MISS ROSE said to Sister Markham, we were excused for the day to travel. Winifred bounced on her seat, her eyes sparkling with happiness as we enjoyed the train ride and perfect autumn weather. The views of the countryside were delightful. She took great interest when we stopped at the smaller stations, listening to birds singing and seeing the riot of autumn colors. It saddened me a bit because I knew how it would all change over the next hundred years. London would expand, swallowing up the passing picturesque villages. Skyscrapers would block out the sun. One good thing would be the Thames being cleaned up.

At the station we hired a carriage to take us to the Allen home. I paid the fare from my diminishing funds. The house turned out to be an ancient Tudor building on the outskirts of the village. A black, wrought iron fence surrounded the property. It appeared that the elder Mr. Allen was a man of means so it struck me as unlikely that he would deliberately deprive the children of their inheritance.

Winn approached the large double oak doors with confidence and pulled the chain to ring the inner bell. After a few minutes, the door creaked open and an elderly butler peered down as us from a great height.

"Yes?" He dragged out the word.

"We are here to see Mr. Allen, if you please," Miss Rose said. She had her reticule clutched in both hands and I could tell she was nervous from the way she gripped it so tightly.

I must confess to not expecting such a grand house and, most certainly didn't imagine a butler.

"It is I, Edgar!" Winn squealed with delight as she pushed past Miss Rose and rushed toward the butler.

The man looked down and gasped. The color drained from his face and he staggered to the degree that Miss Rose reached out to steady him.

"Miss Winifred? How can it be? They said—they said—"

"They said what, Edgar? What did they tell you? What are you doing here?"

He held out an unsteady hand. "May I?"

She grabbed it in her own. "I'm here. Did you think I was a ghost?"

He reached out with his other hand and stroked the side of her face. "I didn't know, Miss Winifred. And little Laurance?"

"He's well. He's at the Alexandra Orphanage. We're staying there at the moment. There was a great deal of confusion after the wreck. Miss Murphy here was instrumental in saving our lives."

I dipped a small curtsy.

"And your parents? Did they also survive?" He looked so hopeful, I fervently wished they had.

Her lower lip trembled as she replied. "No, sir. They didn't."

His eyes watered. "I shall announce your arrival. Shall you wait in the parlor?" His voice quaked as he held out an arm toward an open door to the left. Miss Rose took our hands and we walked into the massive room carpeted with one of the largest Aubusson carpets I'd ever seen. Clusters of overstuffed chairs formed conversation groups and two divans stood perpendicular to the fireplace. A bow-legged mahogany table topped with a huge bouquet of fresh flowers stood between the two sofas.

Winifred gasped and held a hand over her mouth.

"What is it?" I asked.

"That painting." She pointed at a gold framed landscape over the mantel. "That was on the wall at our house. Over *our* mantel-piece in the sitting room."

"Stay calm. There surely will be an explanation." I took her hand. Her fingers trembled as I led her to a divan where we sat. Miss Rose took a seat in a wing-backed chair near the fireplace. She appeared to be studying the painting.

As we waited for what seemed an extraordinary length of time, Winn let her gaze wander about the room.

"These little figures stood on the shelf in the corner of our parlor. I always wanted to grow up and wear a lovely gown like this and be escorted by a handsome gentleman through the park. Those andirons and tools came from our parlor as well." She picked up a crocheted antimacassar from behind me and held it out to us. "Our grandmother made these. I'm sure this is the same as was in our house. Why would Uncle take things from our home? He has so much already."

"Hush, dear. Perhaps your aunt was fond of some things and wished to retain them as a memory of all of you. We shall know soon enough," Miss Rose said.

Winn swung her feet, folded and unfolded her arms, and continued to gaze about the room as we waited for either her aunt or her uncle to make an appearance.

"You're fidgeting," Miss Rose cautioned.

"I can't help it."

After about fifteen minutes, footsteps in the hall indicated the imminent arrival of someone. We all turned toward the door.

Edgar entered first. "Mr. Allen will see you now. Please come with me."

We paraded obediently behind him into the hallway and followed him through to the next door where he tapped and then opened it. "Misses Allen, Rose, and Murphy to see you, sir." He stepped aside so we could enter a library where Mr. Allen sat behind a large desk.

Mr. Andrew Allen stood. A short man, he displayed massive muttonchop whiskers and a small goatee. His face seemed chiseled from stone with sharp protruding cheekbones, a slender sharp nose below fierce black eyes hidden under bushy eyebrows. A countenance to frighten young children.

He looked directly at Miss Rose. "And what is your name?"

"I'm Miss Rose, sir. You know, of course, Miss Winifred—"

"I shall address you as the obvious adult, Miss Rose. The children may wait in the hall."

"The girls, especially Miss Allen, ought to remain with me. It is she with whom I am concerned."

"Bah." He waved his right hand in dismissal. "She is no more my niece than you are, Miss Rose. How dare you bring an imposter to my home and inflict pain on my family."

"What?" Winn and I shrieked in unison.

"You bear a slight resemblance to my niece. Is that why you thought you might get away with presenting her as dear departed Winifred?" He made a great show of removing his handkerchief from his pocket and wiping his eyes. "Explain yourself, Miss Rose."

I stepped forward. "Sir, I am Grunsberry Murphy. It is I who rescued Winifred and her brother Laurance on the night of the *Princess Alice* disaster. A Mrs. Walker claims to have sent you notice of their survival. When she didn't receive a response, she turned them over to the orphanage, where I had already established myself and awaited their arrival."

"You make no sense, young lady. I have asked you to leave."

I backed up and sat on a burgundy leather chair. "No one is

leaving until you recognize your niece and explain what happened to all her family possessions."

"To say nothing of their inheritance," Miss Rose added.

Winn followed my lead and took the matching chair on the other side of Miss Rose. Winn pulled out her own handkerchief and wiped the tears from her face. Poor thing. Neither of us had counted on him disavowing her.

"My brother and his entire family perished that night. I shall have Edgar show you to the door and will not file a complaint about you to the authorities if you assure me you will never make such a foolish attempt again."

I had to hand it to him; he certainly gave a convincing performance. If the old servant hadn't recognized Winn, I might have been tempted to believe we'd come to the wrong home.

"Edgar knows me," Winn said. She turned to me. "He was our butler. He even stole our butler. Uncle never had one before."

At that, Winn seemed to run out of steam, so Miss Rose took over. "There is neither any confusion nor deception going on, sir." She barreled on before Mr. Allen could interrupt. "Here is the question of the children's rightful inheritance. When we went in search of information, we were told that you have taken control of the late Mr. and Mrs. Charles Allen's tailor shop. All the family's possessions have apparently been disposed of from the family home, and it appears that some of them have turned up right here in your home. You have also apparently pilfered the household help. The appropriate adjustments must be made for the children's future. You may either take the children in, or you may fund their education at the orphanage."

"I don't want to live with him," Winn shouted.

The study door opened behind us. I turned to see Edgar waiting to be acknowledged.

"Well, what is it?" Mr. Allen grumbled.

"Mrs. Allen and the children would like to see young Winifred, sir." He bowed slightly at the waist.

Mr. Allen pointed at the butler with a shaking hand. "They are to remain in their rooms until such time as I call them down."

Before Edgar could retreat, three young girls plowed through the door followed by a petite blond woman, most likely Mrs. Allen.

The children paused just long enough to recognize Winn. She jumped up from her seat as they rushed to smother her in hugs. The lady strode across the room and waited her turn to take the girl in her arms.

After a moment, Mr. Allen banged on his desk with a paper-weight. "Enough. Children, you will leave this room. I will deal with you later. And you, Mrs. Allen, what have you to say for yourself? Barging into my private study. Indeed. You are excused. I shall deal with this impudent child and her colleagues."

Mrs. Allen kept her arm around Winn's shoulder. "Charles Allen, how can you be so harsh to our dear niece after she's lost everything?"

She didn't know the half of it—him denying Winn completely.

His face flushed red for a moment before he drew a breath, composed himself, and spoke to Winn as if the earlier conversation never happened. He took a seat. "I asked you to leave us, Mrs. Allen. I have matters to discuss with these—these people."

Mrs. Allen released her hold on Winifred and backed out of the room. As she did, she said, "Please join us for tea before you leave, dear child."

The door closed behind her.

"You may have fooled Mrs. Allen, young woman, however, do not think for a moment that you will steal my poor dear brother's fortune with this fraud. You might enjoy a moment with my children, but trust me, you will not be recognized in any court in this country as Charles's offspring."

"How can you say such a thing?" I asked, unable to keep quiet. "You are, sir, to put it as politely as I can, a slime."

He gasped. "Miss Murphy, what is your concern? This is a family matter."

"You might well ask Miss Rose the same question," I said, again cursing my form. "She will tell you she is now the official guardian of both children. I have befriended them and consider it my duty to ensure their future is secure." I saw Miss Rose gulp at the outright falsehood, but she maintained her calm exterior.

"Then she is the guardian of two imposters. It is time for you to leave."

I continued speaking in my fierce voice. "We have the letter Mrs. Walker sent to the children's home explaining how she cared for them. You had already cleared out the house. But we have the letter and I believe you received a similar letter from her. There are enough people who know the children by sight that there will be no difficulty identifying them as the progeny of Charles and Eugenie Allen. Now, if you'll excuse us, we'll go have tea with Mrs. Allen. I'm sure she will be eager to visit with her niece."

"Stop using that ridiculous tone of voice." He sat upright, rigid, in his otherwise comfortably padded leather chair.

I drew a deep breath and said, "I made a mistake when I chose to arrive as a peer to Miss Allen. In the instant that I sensed she and her brother were in imminent danger, I had to make a snap decision. I chose wrong. A male adult would be far preferable. However, rest assured I have all the knowledge of the centuries at hand and will not rest until you acknowledge your misdeeds, and the Allen children receive their full inheritance, *including* remuneration for all the furnishings of which you disposed. And you can forget about *expenses.*" I paused.

"You are a mad woman—child!" The man's face turned so red, I feared he might have a stroke right there.

"We will return in one week. By then you will have had time to seek the advice of a solicitor and make all the arrangements." I stood.

"Wait a minute!" Mr. Allen shouted. "You can't come to my home and make outrageous statements about—about whatever you were talking about. Being a man? Centuries? Get out of my home, immediately!" He pulled out his handkerchief and wiped his brow, then reached behind him and pulled the bell, summoning Edgar.

I stood and approached his desk and leaned on it, my hands splayed on the rich mahogany. "It appears to me you have overlooked the Law of 1870 which allows a woman to keep her earnings and have complete control over them. *Therefore*, your conversation will not be quite so simple. And you forget yourself when you confiscate Eugenie Allen's dowry, which was hers to dispense with as she saw fit. We can assume she would have entrusted those monies to the care of her children, not the enhancement of her brother-in-law's estate. Besides all that—"

"Enough!" he bellowed, his face as red as the ribbon on my bonnet. "Get out of my house now. All of you. I will not be insulted by a deranged child who does not understand respect of her elders."

Miss Rose and Winn scrambled to their feet. I put out my hand to stop them and turned to Edgar as he entered. "Will you please let Mrs. Allen know we are ready for our tea and will meet her in the front parlor?" I whirled back to Mr. Allen. "Winifred is entitled to visit with them before we leave." My tone dared him to object.

Mr. Allen leapt up and leaned across the desk. I was grateful for the size of the desk as it prevented him from reaching across and strangling me.

Edgar disappeared.

Though my knees felt shaky, I followed Edgar out into the hall with Miss Rose and Winn following. Miss Rose pulled the pocket doors shut behind us.

"Nervy little thing, you are," Miss Rose said. "What was all that nonsense you were spouting in there?"

"Nothing was nonsense. Everything I said was true, including the rights of women to have their own monies. If Mrs. Eugenie Allen ran her millinery business in Mr. Allen's tailor shop, she surely had funds of her own and I doubt she intended them to go to her brother-in-law."

"And what about 'knowledge of the centuries'?"

"I am from the future. Perhaps I ought to introduce you to the works of Jules Vern. He has some fantastic theories that came to fruition even before *my* time."

"I hear the children." And sure enough, they came tumbling down the stairs as we all followed Edgar into the front parlor. I drew a deep breath and settled by myself near a front window while Winn and her cousins chattered to one another. Considering our introduction to Mr. Allen, he might just as easily have pulled a weapon and shot any or all of us, that's how enraged he had appeared.

Eventually, Winn signaled me to come across to her and her cousins. When I did, she introduced them, from oldest to youngest as Penelope, Agatha, and Emily. Penelope informed me that their brother, Maxwell, was away at school.

While Winn fascinated her cousins with the story of her and Laurance's survival of the disaster, I took Mrs. Allen aside. "I brought Winifred here in the hopes of reuniting her with family. As it is, I believe Mr. Allen has no interest in acknowledging his brother's children."

"You misunderstand, Miss Murphy. We believed that the entire family was gone. And why are you speaking instead of Miss Rose?"

"Trust me, I know whereof I speak. You were not in the room with Mr. Allen when he denied his niece. I shall be blunt, Mrs. Allen, your husband shares the same stench as that of the Thames River."

Mrs. Allen's eyes widened. Her pale face blanched whiter than the whitest sheets. She made a strange gurgling sound. For a moment I thought she might expire right there, but she managed to gasp, "You can't, you mustn't..." before she fell back against her chair, limp.

The others hadn't noticed. I reached out and took her hand, then surreptitiously checked her pulse. Though it fluttered somewhat, it remained strong. I leaned close to her ear. "I shall and I will, madam. Your husband has denied his brother's children their birthright. The moment we get back to London, we shall secure the services of a solicitor. You may choose to join us or remain by that villain's side and see what happens to your own children when the time comes." I paused for a moment to make sure she was paying attention. Her eyelids flickered and she glared at me briefly before shutting her eyes again. "Did you come into this marriage with a dowry? And did you turn custody of those funds over to your loving husband?"

"You have to leave," she whimpered. "I will not have such talk in my house."

I was losing patience with her act. I could not believe she would go along with her husband's denial of the children.

"You are welcome to join us with your own children, Mrs. Allen. Leave that cold-hearted monster and live a life free of his tyranny."

"How can you say that? You've only just come into our home. You know nothing, you—you child!"

"That's just the point. I am not a child. I may look like one, but I am not. I knew the moment I laid eyes on him that he was not a nice person."

She once again opened her eyes and glanced toward where the children babbled happily, the littlest one sitting on Miss Rose's lap. "You have no idea," she whispered. "But I cannot leave him. It is not done."

"Bullshit! It's about time you stood up for yourself. What are you teaching your daughters by remaining in such a relationship?"

"Dear God. Watch your language. Who are you to tell me how to behave in front of my own children when you speak like a—like a common street urchin?"

"Guttersnipe, or more degrading, whore, would probably be better words for what you want," I goaded her and didn't even know to what end. I guess I wished she would stand up to her husband and take what she owned and run.

She pulled herself together enough to stand and scold me. "You, young woman, will leave this house immediately. Take that parlor maid with you." She pointed angrily toward the hall.

Miss Rose looked up from where she'd been playing Patty-Cakes with the baby. "Is something wrong?"

I rolled my eyes. "Of course, there's something wrong. We must leave. Come along, Winifred. Kiss your cousins goodbye. You'll see them again soon."

I turned to Mrs. Allen. "I am sorry that you cannot see your husband for what he is, however, rest assured we will not stop until we insure the children's inheritance. And once we establish their housing, Edgar should be prepared to return to his rightful place with them. Now, tell me, are there other relatives that Winifred might be unaware of?"

"I have nothing further to say to you."

Winifred came to my side and took my hand. "Let's leave now, Berry. I'm afraid if we stay any longer, they might call the authorities. It's bad enough we're stuck in that orphanage., I don't think I'd much like a prison cell."

"Especially in this day and age," I added.

"Wait. Please," Mrs. Allen said as we started through the open door. "What about little Laurance?"

"Your nephew is just fine, Mrs. Allen. He is under my care," Miss Rose said.

Mrs. Allen picked up the baby, who now cried and reached out toward Miss Rose. The other two girls remained in the parlor, their eyes wide, looking stunned at the scene playing out before them.

Mr. Allen burst into the hall, startling everyone. When he saw us about to leave, he stopped, placed his hands behind his back, and said, "I have come to a decision regarding your visit, Miss Rose." He slanted his shifty eyes toward his wife. "Take the girls and go into the garden. There is no need for you to be here."

Now what? I thought.

The children curtsied to Miss Rose and slid silently from the room, their heads bowed—even little Emily. It was evident they were well-versed in such a dismissal. Mrs. Allen followed them down the hall carrying the littlest one. She didn't turn around, nor did she say goodbye. How sad.

"After careful consideration, I have come to the conclusion that this has been a very clever ploy on your part, Miss Rose, and be assured that I shall call attention to your larcenous behavior by notifying your superiors at the Alexandra Home. You may leave now."

I felt my jaw drop and my eyes grow large. "But, sir—"

Winn's jaw dropped. "Uncle!"

Mr. Allen turned his attention to Miss Rose. "You should be ashamed of yourself, Miss Rose, for letting yourself be caught up in the scheme to defraud an honest man of his hard-earned money." He folded his arms and looked smug.

I took a step forward, my intuitive gift giving me certainty of knowledge after talking to Mrs. Allen. "First off, sir, your *hard-earned* money came from your wife's inheritance and dowry. I suspect you have never worked a day in your life. And as your children, your wife, and your servant have all recognized Winifred as the daughter of Charles and Eugenie Allen, you won't be able to get away with stealing her and her brother's inheritance as well."

"My wife and children know who is in control of this household. They will obey my instructions. You will never get away with trying to bring an impersonator into my home."

"But, Uncle, you know me. You know I'm not an impersonator. Why would you even say that?"

I knew. *Greed.*

Furious with the man, I took Winn by the shoulders and turned her around. Before Miss Rose could say anything, I smiled my famous impish grin and thanked Mr. Allen for his time and courtesy.

His face reddened. "Edgar!" he shouted. Instead of waiting for the servant to appear, he pushed past us to the front door and pulled it open. Before we could exit, Edgar appeared. He didn't have to say a word. The sadness in his eyes spoke for him.

Mr. Allen relinquished his hold on the door, turned on his heel, and stormed down the hall to his study.

I took Edgar's hand as Winifred and Miss Rose made their way down the steps. "Please don't fret, Edgar. We'll sort this all out and you'll be together again."

He squeezed my hand, stepped back into the hall, and gently closed the door.

MISS ROSE and Winn sat beside me on the train, the two befuddled by the greedy Mr. Allen's response to seeing his niece alive.

The best outcome of the outing would have been to have discovered a loving family who wanted to take the children in and treat them as their own. The worst I imagined was disinterest and perhaps a reluctance to acknowledge the children as heirs to their parents' estate. They might have apologized for jumping the gun.

Well, they wouldn't have used that particular expression, at least not for a few more decades.

Since I'd been there over two weeks already, I knew Friday evening's tea would be fish pie, a gruesome concoction of fish and potatoes in a mushy pie shell. I suggested we stop for tea at a shop in town before taking a hansom cab home.

"We need to find a solicitor who can help the children," Miss Rose said as we ate Cornish pasties in a tearoom. Winn barely ate half of hers and mostly stared out the window at the passersby.

"You won't do yourself any good by not eating, young lady," Miss Rose said to her.

"I know. I'm just not hungry. I was thinking about all those people walking by and wondering if they know how lucky they are."

"Maybe they're not so lucky," I said. "Think about it. If they looked in the window, what would they see? Two girls with perhaps their nanny having tea late on a Friday afternoon. They might be lonely or hungry themselves and think how fortunate we are to be able to afford a meal."

She frowned as she thought about my comment. "Hmm. All right."

"How shall we choose a solicitor?" I asked.

Miss Rose asked, "Winifred, did your father ever make any reference to one?"

She shook her head. "I don't think so. I do remember him saying to Mummy once that everything was in order and she would never have to worry. Do you suppose...?"

"I do suppose," I interrupted. "I think tomorrow we should look for offices near your father's place of business. I would bet he'd go to the nearest one."

"Good idea. Now we have a plan," Miss Rose said.

We could do nothing on Sunday about the children's plight, so we spent the day first at church services, then sitting in the garden, either reading or embroidering until dinner at midday. The day dragged. Even Mr. Storey had taken a day off from his drawing and painting. How I longed for my smartphone where I could search online for all the information we needed.

On Monday and then again on Tuesday, Miss Rose and I went out and inquired at every solicitor's office we could locate within easy walking distance of the Allen Tailor and Milliner's Shop until we came across one who agreed he had written a will for Mr. Charles Allen. We arranged that Winifred and Laurance would meet with him on Friday.

I tagged along, labeled as Miss Winifred's companion. Mr. Willis first went over the arrangements of the family business. That was not part of the personal estate. All the funds Mr. Andrew Allen had taken would be recovered and set aside for the benefit of the children. During the conversation, I reminded her of the painting and other items in Mr. Andrew Allen's house. The solicitor, Mr. Willis, made a list and then later gave it to an investigator who acknowledged the items were all in the Tunbridge Wells residence. He'd had no trouble accessing the house. Edgar had been more than happy to comply, and even offered to testify to Winifred's existence.

To confirm that the items in Mr. Andrew Allen's home were the ones pilfered from Mr. Charles Allen's home, Winifred was sent back to her uncle's house accompanied by an investigator. As she pointed them out, he took notes and made drawings of all the suspect items on display.

Winifred reported back to me after the first day. "You should have seen Uncle's face, Berry! He was so angry, but Roberts kept me by his side so Uncle couldn't touch me. I think he might have strangled me if he could." She giggled with joy, but then her face turned sad. "I wish Mummy could have been there. She would have told him exactly what she thought of him."

"I'm sure she would have," I responded. "What about your aunt?"

"Uncle wouldn't let her or my cousins out of their rooms. I wasn't allowed to see them at all. I wish Uncle could go to jail forever for stealing everything."

"Sadly, dear, his claim that he thought you were all dead cannot be disputed. But he will get his comeuppance, I assure you."

"He told Roberts that he was on a fool's errand because I was not his niece, even though I pointed out so many items he'd taken from our home. And he let Edgar go. Dismissed him without references. Poor Edgar. He was such a sweet man."

That surprised me. I hadn't considered what might become of the butler. "We'll have to see about him. Do you know where he went?"

She shrugged. "Maybe Auntie knows, but we can't talk to her."

"We'll see about that."

I arranged to meet with Mr. Willis and explained the situation regarding the domestic help. He promised to find Edgar and the two ladies who had worked for Winn's family and restore them to their proper places once the children had an established home. In the meantime, Mr. Andrew Allen still denied the survival of Winifred and Laurance. He continued to insist the children were imposters. The case would have to be taken to court.

I REMAINED at the orphanage for several weeks after Mr. Willis took over the children's affairs. Mr. Storey continued sketching and painting. One morning I entered the arrival room early. No one else was there so I took the opportunity to snoop through his sketchbook. His drawings were so lifelike. He'd represented Miss Rose, Mr. Hughes, the girls, Mary and Hortense, and me in various poses before settling on his final composition. I was so caught up in poring over his other drawings of London street scenes, that I didn't hear him enter the room.

He cleared his throat by way of announcement. I jumped and dropped a pile of drawings.

"What do you think, young lady?" he asked, pleasantly enough.

"You capture people's expressions beautifully, Mr. Storey. I'd be proud to hang one of your paintings in my own home." As usual, I forgot I was in a twelve-year-old's body, and spoke from my adult, twenty-first century perspective. "I read about your work ages ago and wondered what became of all your paintings."

He raised his eyebrows. "Ages ago?"

Recognizing my mistake, I said, "I meant an article written ages ago. I read. Anyway, I like your work far better since you turned to realistic subjects. You treat them with poetry and a very sound understanding of color."

He plucked one of the drawings from my hand, studied it a moment and then passed it over to me. "This is yours, Miss..."

"Murphy."

"Miss Murphy. Don't you think it's time for you to expose yourself for who you really are?"

That threw me. "Who I really...?"

"Indeed. Obviously, a mature woman of diminutive size posing as a child. What on earth for?"

"How can you tell?"

"I'm an artist. I observe." He touched a pencil to the side of his nose and winked.

I knew that the bodies in which I periodically found myself were authentic, so I couldn't fathom how he detected my ruse. I resigned myself to his knowing. "What gave me away?"

"Your demeanor, obviously. The physique is appropriate and the disguise well-done. You've fooled everyone else around here. But now that you've been discovered, may I make a suggestion?"

"What's that?" I clutched my prize to my chest and took a step back.

"I see that you have been earnestly working to help Miss Winifred and her brother to reclaim their inheritance. You might be better served showing yourself as you really are, rather than as a child. Remove the disguise. Just because you are a small woman doesn't mean you need run about pretending to be a child."

"But...but...

"Run along now and adorn yourself in clothing more suitable to your age and you might find it far easier to accomplish your goals."

I frowned and considered his words. "But Miss Rose's attire is almost identical to those of the girls here. What might make me appear older?"

"For goodness sake. Doesn't the girl own a tailor's shop and a millinery? You can have them make up something for you forthwith. Before your next appointment with the solicitor and Mr. Andrew Allen."

"I had no idea you took such an interest in our affairs, sir."

The man would have made a good detective in any age.

I TOOK his advice and repaired to Mr. Whitely's shop. It took considerable convincing, but he finally agreed to create a costume for me. As he was more used to tailoring for men, he found a Parisian fashion with few frills and created what he called a traveling suit consisting of a dark green fitted jacket and skirt. As a concession to femininity he added a matching pleated ruffle at the hem. He ordered a paler green blouse with a large bow tied at the neck to complement the suit. We found a hat that Winn's mother had made which suited the outfit perfectly. It perched atop my head with a flourish of wide ribbons cascading down the back.

Thus suitably attired like the adult I was, I headed out early one morning on the train to Tunbridge Wells. I hadn't told anyone of my plan. When I arrived at the estate, a rough looking young man dressed up in an oversized butler's uniform answered the door.

"Mrs. Grace Manchester to see Mrs. Allen." I handed him a calling card I had printed earlier.

He took the card, bowed, and held out a hand to show me into the front parlor. "I shall announce you, madam. Is she expecting you?"

"No, but I know she'll be pleased to see me."

I waited in the chair by the front window.

"Mrs. Manchester?" She spoke as she entered the room.

I rose and crossed the room to greet her. "Mrs. Allen, I am so pleased that you agreed to receive me. I have urgent business to discuss with you. Are we free to speak here?"

"I know you." She backed away from me, a look of fear crossing her face. "You're the little girl with the strange name who came here last month with those children."

"Your niece and nephew. Yes."

"Mr. Allen says they are imposters." She wouldn't look me in the eye.

"You know they aren't. Won't you come with me and support their claim?"

She gasped and held a hand to her mouth. "I couldn't. Such a thing isn't heard of."

"What?" I asked, unsure what she meant.

"A woman can't stand up in public and call her husband a liar. It just isn't done." She turned away and I feared she would leave the room.

I clutched at her sleeve. "Please. The children need you to testify on their behalf. Mr. Whitely is doing right by them, why won't your husband do right by his own brother's children?"

Still looking toward the door and not at me, she said, "Mr. Whitely can do as he pleases. There is no proof..."

"The proof is that you know for a fact who they are, and you can ensure their future by helping them. How can you—"

"Mrs. Manchester?" Andrew Allen barged into the room. He stopped and stared at me for a moment before shouting, "Henry! Immediately!"

I hardly had a chance to move as the butler ran in. "Sir?"

"Escort this girl...woman to the scullery and put her in the pantry. Lock the door."

"You can't do that!" I shouted as I whirled about searching for an escape. But Henry was faster than I. He had me in his clutches and manhandled me down the hall, behind the main staircase to another, more narrow set of stairs. With one arm firmly about my waist, he carried me into the kitchen. Mrs. Allen said not a word.

He shoved me into a small dark space that smelled of earth and onions. Still gripping my arm, he led me down a steep set of narrow stairs before pushing me to the ground. He ran back up and slammed the door shut. Dim light filtered in through a window high on one wall. Once my eyes adjusted, it was easy to see I was indeed trapped in a cellar pantry. Well, at least I wouldn't starve. I leaned against shelves that contained jars of preserves and considered my plight. Surely Mrs. Allen would let me out once Mr. Allen left the house. She had to.

The slime. The Thames stank less than Andrew Allen. The more I thought about my plight, the angrier I became.

I stomped up the stairs and pounded on the door. "Help! Somebody! Let me out of here." I continued until I was frustrated and exhausted. I turned and sat on the top step, my chin in my hands. The bow from my blouse brushed against my hands. I had an idea. I undid the bow and slid the ribbon under the door, pushing it as far as I could to make sure anyone entering the kitchen would see it. I then sat on the other end so that I'd know if someone had tugged on it. That way, should I nod off and fall asleep in the cool darkness of the cellar, I'd be alerted.

As I waited for someone to start dinner, I wondered again what Andrew could have in mind for me. He couldn't kill me, could he? I lived to see Winifred again, right? But I'd already done that in one of my travels, so was it past or future? If he planned to kill me, why didn't he just throw me down the stairs so I'd break my neck?

My head hurt. I leaned back against the door and wished to hear the sound of pots rattling. My stomach told me it should be lunchtime. So much for listening to Mr. Storey's advice.

I awoke when the door opened, and I fell backward onto the floor next to a pair of men's shoes.

"Who are you?"

The voice sounded young. I looked up. A young man reached down to help me to my feet. "I'm...um...who are you?"

"Maxwell Allen, but I asked first. And why are you sitting in our cellar?"

"I...it's good to meet you Maxwell. I'm a friend of your cousins, Winifred and Laurance." I brushed one hand across my forehead and found strands of a cobweb had clung to it.

Maxwell had just put his hand out as if to shake mine, but he withdrew it as soon as I mentioned his cousins. "I'm so sorry. Didn't you hear?"

"Hear what?"

"They died in that terrible crash on the Thames last month. Were you very close?"

"I was there, Maxwell," I growled.

"My God. You survived!" He looked genuinely surprised.

"Of course, I survived, as did your cousins. Haven't your parents explained it all to you?"

"I've just come home for a week's break from school. What do you mean they survived? Father said—"

"He was mistaken. I came here to reason with him. We visited your family two weeks ago and he denied knowing your cousins. Since then they've hired a solicitor to protect their inheritance." As I spoke, I inched my way further into the kitchen and away from the entrance to the cellar. Maxwell could just as easily decide to toss me back in there.

He bristled at that. "You haven't explained what you were doing down there."

"I assure you I did not want to be there. I was placed there by your manservant, Henry—at your father's bidding. If you'll excuse me, I'd like to leave now."

He put out a hand to stop me. "You lie. How can you say that? Henry, I believe is capable of anything, but Father? Never."

"I'm sorry to disillusion you, Max, but your father has managed to pilfer your cousin's inheritance and I'm here to reverse the situation."

I continued edging my way toward the door beyond the center island. It led to the outside, where I could then run around the building and out to the main lane where my cab should be waiting for me. Should be. I'd told him I'd be fifteen minutes.

Max leaned on the counter looking like someone had punched him. "He said they all died...my fees. He paid my fees at the last minute. The school was about to dismiss me..."

"Max, would you be willing to come with me to see the solicitor? You can see your cousins there and attest to their legitimacy. Your father won't permit your mother or sisters to acknowledge them, but you," I closed my eyes and hoped the flattery would work, "you are nearly of age and can make up your own mind about things. Will you come? Please?" I held out my hand to him.

"You're wrong, miss. I'm not nearly of age and need my father's permission."

"Would you know your cousins if you saw them?"

"Of course."

"Then come with me. Your father need not know. We'll go into London. You'll be back by mid-morning. Have you never missed dinner before?"

He looked around the kitchen. "Seems like there is no cook anyway. Mother served up cold meat and cheese for lunch. I came in looking for biscuits." He pushed his long hair from his brow and studied the room as if it would help him make a decision.

"Listen, I'll take you directly to where they're staying and you can see for yourself right away. You won't have to wait. We can all go to dinner together and then first thing in the morning, you can stop by the solicitor's office before coming home. How would that be?"

"Can they take the testimony of a fifteen-year-old boy?"

"Fifteen? Really? I would have guessed closer to eighteen. And in any case, I'm sure your confirmation of their identity will go a long way to helping their case." The longer we stood arguing in the kitchen, the more likely someone would come in and discover us. I reached out and took his hand. "Let's go. I have a cab waiting out by the front gate. We can leave by this back door."

"Are you sure Father ordered Henry to lock you down there?" he asked as I led him to the door.

"Absolutely."

AT THE ORPHANAGE Mr. Storey was packing up his supplies. A fabric draped canvas stood on his easel. Mr. Storey looked surprised but approved of my appearance in spite of my costume being slightly disheveled from my mishandling by Henry. I introduced him to Maxwell.

"Ah, let me show you." He flipped up the fabric to display his painting.

Maxwell studied it for a moment, looking perplexed. His eyes scanned the entire canvas. From left to right it spanned five feet. His eyes lit on the left side. He looked from there to me and back again.

"That looks like you. Except you're in a child's dress. Like one of the orphans." He turned back to the canvas. When his gaze reached the far right his eyes lit up. "By jove, you were right. That's Winnie and Laurie. Good heavens. Are they really here?"

"Wait here." I went in search of Miss Rose, who in turn went to collect the children.

Maxwell and I sat in the arrival room watching Mr. Storey complete his packing.

Little Laurance was the first to arrive. Upon seeing his cousin Maxwell, he launched himself into his arms, squealing with delight. After that, there was no mistaking that Max recognized his cousins.

We all walked four blocks to The Stairs, a well-established restaurant known to serve excellent chops. After agreeing on the lamb chops with parsleyed potatoes and peas as the main course, Winn and Maxwell chattered non-stop. Miss Rose added soup for everyone as a starter.

I felt myself glowing with pleasure at the sight of the happy cousins and feeling a bit wistful knowing that my time here was short. I kind of wished Mr. Storey could be here to capture the moment. Or that I had my cell phone to take a picture.

THOUGH IT TOOK NEARLY A YEAR, the estate was settled. Winifred and Laurance would live back in their old home, which the landlord agreed to hold for them after consulting with Mr. Willis, with Miss Rose as their official guardian. Mr. Andrew Allen, though severely chastised by the court, continued to bully his wife and children until he finally spared them all by dying of a heart attack at age forty-one. Maxwell inherited what little was left of his father's estate and eventually managed it into a successful convalescent facility. After grooming the gardens and pathways surrounding the residence, the property became an attraction for Londoners seeking respite from the city.

Edgar went to work for Miss Rose and the children who continued their educations. Winifred went on to become a physician, and against all odds, succeeded in her profession. Young

Laurance became, of all things, a ship's captain and sailed the world.

Neither of the children ever recognized they were the orphans depicted in Mr. Storey's painting. And years later, once it was purchased and placed in Malcom Forbe's private collection, none of their heirs were privy to that information either.

I had left them once I'd met Maxwell and knew they were in the capable hands of Mr. Willis. At home in Guthrie, Oklahoma, my sister Joan, who didn't have my gift, railed at me for several days before conceding that I had done a good thing. In the end, she even begrudgingly enjoyed my impressions of nasty Andrew Allen and sweet Edgar.

"But now it's your turn to feed the chickens, Grunsberry," she grumped. "Next time you plan to disappear for any length of time, could you give me some notice, please?"

AUTHOR'S NOTES – VERONICA H. HART

THE ALEXANDRA ORPHANAGE, the description of the disaster between the *Bywell Castle* and *Princess Alice*, and George A. Storey's depiction of the orphanage can all be found in Wikipedia. For further information on George A. Storey, I used *The Great Collectors, Masterpieces From Private Collections*, by Véronique Prat, published by Tabard Press in 1990.

~VHH

AMONG THE BLUE HORSES

ELLE ANDREWS PATT

*O*nly today can art be metaphysical, and it will continue to be so. Art will free itself from the needs and desires of men. We will no longer paint a forest as we please or as they seem to us, but as they reall are.

~Franz Marc, 100 Aphorisms 1915

2024, USA

MURIEL STOOD RAPT, absorbing the raw emotion of the painting in front of her. Displayed on a large, high definition screen, it wasn't the actual work, but it was true to size and every brush stroke glowed in the light of a museum across the ocean, in Germany.

Tierschicksale. Fate of the Animals. Painted in 1913. The display told her that it was, in many art curators' opinions, Franz Marc's finest masterwork.

She had originally come to see the popular piece she'd been familiar with since childhood, his *Blaues Pferde I*, *Blue Horse I*. The horse in the painting stood with its head turned slightly away, shy but conscious of its own strength and beauty. Solid legs, bold white blaze on its broad head. Masculine. And blue.

She had never told anyone, but since her teen-age years, she'd become cognizant of dreaming consciously. She wondered often if she was actually awake. An out-of-body experience, the internet told her. Many of the events she witnessed at night—fallen fruit, the death of a cat by coyote, limbs torn from a tree during a storm—proved true come the day.

One of the many things she saw were blue and red horses grazing in the city park.

Horses like Franz Marc's. They weren't there, of course, not really, but in her dream-wanderings, they grazed on the night-wet grass and swished their tails like any real horse might.

It was early. She'd been waiting to enter when the museum opened.

The exhibit was weeks old, the initial excitement at the new installation waning.

She'd returned again and again, able to linger over the displays after the crowds died down.

This exhibit, these artists, not just Franz Marc, but those on display alongside him, spoke to her. Some she'd never heard of, like August Macke, with whom Marc had a bromance for the ages if the narrative was true. Some, like the Russian Wassily Kandinsky, whom she had heard of, were way more famous. They saw what she saw when she slept. When she dreamed.

Now on her fifth visit, she'd looked up *Fate of the Animals* online.

The digital version didn't do it justice. She was certain these animals being sucked into the predatory, duller waking world, like Franz Marc being sucked inexorably into World War I, were what she called spirit animals. Everywhere—in the pieces on display, the augmented reality in play using smart phones, the virtual reality offered in a glassed off alcove that let viewers enter their choice of six different works—she saw her world, the bright night colors, the invisible energy she could feel even in her waking hours.

Although Kandinsky's later paintings were completely abstract, they throbbed with the invisible life that no one else but her seemed to notice. And that Marc and Macke and Kandinsky tried to increasingly disguise from their viewers over time. The horses and cats became bright streaks of color, the wolves and human world the shadows and sharp lines.

Until moments ago, she'd been alone, moving ahead of the few people who came in behind her, letting a couple bypass her so she could stand alone in the branching rooms of the exhibit. The timeline meandered chronologically, from 1909 to 1939, showcasing a mixed display of many artists related to *Der Blaue Reiter* or The Blue Rider, a group Marc, Macke, and Kandinsky, along with their painter wives and other German and Russian artists founded in 1911.

The Blue Rider sought to promote more expressionistic work over both the traditional German realism that held most of the gallery space at the time and a rival group not willing to commit to the birth of modernism to the same extent the members of The Blue Rider were willing to go. Two of the last pieces in the exhibit featured Kandinsky alone, his most complex work, produced 1936 and '39.

After her first visit, knowing very little about any art, Muriel had lain in bed, surfing online sources late into the night, as one tidbit on the Blue Rider artists teased her to the next.

August Macke's realism had devolved earlier than Franz Marc's and Kandinsky left her cold, his more intellectual work too far removed from her own life. But Franz Marc... Marc remained her touchstone, with his brushes firmly grounded in her waking dreams and confusing days. Because, yes. Sometimes her visions walked under the sun.

The man who entered from the future, walking through the exhibit in reverse order, wore a muted grey suit, a museum badge, and appeared to be around her Dad's age. He didn't march directly up to her, but his confident strolling over to her left no doubt he was making a direct approach. Muriel sighed and straightened. At twenty-six, she found herself falling more and more under the gaze of older men who had no younger men hesitation about hitting on her.

"Impressive, no?" His voice was deep and smooth. He settled about three feet to her left, folded his hands together behind his back.

She nodded. "I was enjoying it very much."

"Forgive me for disturbing you." He turned his head, drawing her own around to meet his steady gaze. "I'm Joe Billings, the art director here. I've noticed you're a frequent visitor."

She nodded. Was that a problem? When he said nothing more, she said, "I like the art. Thank you for being innovative and using tech in such a creative way to bring more art to our little town."

He grinned. "I'm not fishing for a compliment, Miss…"

"Muriel. My first name is Muriel."

"Muriel. And I can see you think I might be hitting on you, but I'm not doing that either," he said, his tone self-deprecating, even amused.

"Okay, so is there a problem?"

"I've gone about this the wrong way, obviously. You're only the second person I've ever approached though, and the first woman." As she bowed up, confused and wary, Joe lifted his hands to slow her roll until he could finish. "I'm the same as you. You see what they saw, right?" He swept his right hand out, encompassing the exhibit. "Not all of them, but Franz Marc and August Macke, Kandinsky. There's others, Marc Chagall, if you're familiar with him?"

Muriel shook her head in answer to Chagall, as she bit her tongue in reaction to the first, unsure if he meant what she thought he did.

Joe lowered his voice and leaned towards her as two women drifted into the room from the previous one, following the exhibit through its three-quarter mark. "You've seen the blue horses in town. Maybe the red ones? Have you petted them?"

Her mouth dropped open, her heart jumping in her chest. Joe reached to lay his hand upon her arm but stopped himself. Muriel closed her mouth, but couldn't stop the quick, shallow pant of her breath.

"Will you come with me? We can sit in the conference room.

There's windows out to the office space, you'll be quite safe. I want to tell you a story."

1912, Germany

FRANZ MARC'S white Siberian Shepherd, Russi, leapt to her feet as footsteps pounded up the stairs from the kitchen. Franz paused, brush raised above the canvas in front of him. Not his landlord, who lived on the first floor, and not his wife.

"Franz!" August Macke yelled from halfway up the second flight to the attic.

Franz called back, "Right here, August." And then the man was bursting through the open door and over the threshold. Although slight and lean in build, he filled every space he entered. "When did you arrive?"

"An hour ago. Although the lovely Maria was disappointed Elisabeth isn't with me, she still treated me to coffee." Bypassing the sofa and Maria's workspace, August came to stand next to Franz in front of his easel near the window, hands in his trouser pockets. Russi, never having left Franz's side, sniffed at his shoes. August's gaze roamed over the bold yellow of the new painting.

Franz was trying his hand at heavier lines, interested less and less on realism and more and more on evoking emotion in his growing audience. He remained silent, waiting for his friend's pronouncement.

"Your *Blue Horse One* was creating quite the stir at the gallery in Cologne."

The painting was traveling with The Blue Rider exhibit he, Kandinsky, August, and fellow artist Paul Klee had planned as their first thrust in opposition to the limiting artistic ideals of the fauvist New Artists Association. "In what way?"

"A divisive way. Someday people will see the value in self-expression and innovation versus some art critic deciding what art holds value and which doesn't. A beautiful young woman at the edge of the crowd gathered round was practically incandescent, orgasmic, as she studied it. I think she was like us."

MURIEL COCKED her head at Joe.

"I'll explain. August Macke said this, not me."

"Riiight," Muriel said, but leaned forward anyway, crossing her arms on the conference table between them.

"I THINK SHE WAS LIKE US."

"You couldn't tell?"

"No," August said, finally turning his head to watch Franz's reaction as he spoke. "And I lost sight of her before I could get close enough to find out. When did you see this tiger? In Berlin?"

Franz frequently haunted the zoo in Berlin, but August's tone was doubtful even as he asked, which meant Franz was succeeding in his portrayal. "Crossing the street to the train station last week. In Munich."

"An Ushen? That's ominous."

There were two kinds of walkers. Those like Franz and August with the soul of a human. And those like the tiger, with the soul of an animal. Those like Franz called the others Ushen, though the origin of the name had been lost long ago. Franz didn't know what the Ushen called his kind. He'd never spoken to an Ushen, only seen them from afar. Not many. None of the walkers were many.

Considering the painting, Franz thought again about the way the Ushen prowled the Berlin street, the way his fellow commuters fell into his wake, the way the bankers on their way home half-turned as he passed, absently straightening their ties. They were drawn to the Ushen's predatory energy, as the Ushen, Franz suspected, had been drawn into the city by their corrupt practices, the de-civilizing influence of wealth and power and the materialistic greed the Prussian royals modeled for their citizens to emulate. "I'm beginning to think we need a war to give us a fresh start, purify us."

"Us in particular, or Germany, as a nation?"

"Us," Franz said, waving his paintbrush towards the world beyond his attic window, "as in humanity. I dream of a new Europe. Unified in its goals. Healed in spirit." The mountains remained snow-capped above the choppy lake that defined the municipality of Kochel am See. The fields and farms were greening, inching through March and into a hard-won spring with small bursts of showy colors, buds and blooms poking here and there through the mud and winter worn browns and greys of the dramatic landscape that begged for Franz's brush the moment his stepped foot upon it. There was a lone farmer visible, working along a vine-covered fence line.

Refusing to be distracted, having walked the hills surrounding the house in the tiny village of Sindelsdorf with Franz numerous times, August kept his attention on the half-finished painting. His gaze traced the ragged pencil lines of the sketch that completed the restless menace of the tiger. "I don't know that animals are any better than people."

"Nature is pure in a way man can never be," Franz said. But he laid his brush and palette aside, a particularly deep spot in his belly yawning wide and rolling over. Of late, his thoughts in the dark of night wandered to the same arena it appeared August had been treading. "All animals are better than humanity can ever be."

"And what are we? Where do we fall on the scale of purity?"

This question he could answer with conviction. "We're not on the scale, August. Walkers are merely observers. We only reflect the scale, even the Ushen."

"By forming The Blue Rider, though, we're effecting change, through our words and actions. Just by showing ourselves."

"Our works are merely paintings, August, to the world. Only walkers will see them as more than that and we need them, so we need them to find us." He stepped over to reach his cleaning cloths and poppyseed oil, forcing August over as well.

He began wiping his brushes. August picked up a second cloth and followed suit. They took turns dipping the mostly clean brushes in the open jar of oil before wiping them again on the stained scraps of cloths.

After a few moments, August said, "Why do we need them, if we're only observers?"

August's words thumped against Franz's chest, sunk in to weigh heavy upon his lungs, increasing the seasick wave of his crushing loneliness despite having both August and Kandinsky. August had found him in just this way, from a painting in a gallery, and then tracking Franz to his Munich studio. Now Franz couldn't imagine life without him. August attacked every day with a *joie de vivre* that far eclipsed Franz's abilities to do the same. How would it be, with a whole cadre of walkers forming a family of friends who understood his deepest need?

"Okay, then," Franz admitted. "I need them." He slapped the brushes he held onto the battered table among his scattered jars and tubes of paint. "And I need roasted sausage and potato and some of that bread I can smell baking while you chatter like a little girl."

At the word sausage, Russi bounced up again, her tail banging against both men's legs.

August leaned into Franz, bumping their shoulders together hard, and shoved the paintbrushes in his fist at him to put away before snatching up an open oil tube to cap it. "Okay, brother, I'll shut up. For now."

Dare Franz wish that if war birthed a new form of society into the world, maybe spirit walkers would have a proper place in history, among men, a voice? A way to connect with each other, without being feared as "the shadow men" of legend?

"SHADOW PEOPLE," Muriel breathed. "Am I a shadow person?"

Joe tilted his head with a slight nod, and then continued.

THE MOON LIT a path across the crumpled hills of the quilt. Franz listened to Maria's slow, deep breaths. His own breath stuck in his throat, left him wanting, a suffocating fish lying on the nighttime bank of the river sleep. He eyed the path of light and then he was sliding into it, stripping his nightshirt off and dropping it upon the hardwood floor as he crossed to the second story window to see the moon itself. Russi click-clacked across the floor to flop down at his feet.

As a child, Franz had ventured into the night, in spirit only, a couple of times a month while he slept. At first he'd believed he was only dreaming, but then he'd overheard conversations and seen interactions that briefly made his mother think he had somehow fallen under a gypsy curse and acquired second sight. No one in Bavaria wanted to be associated with the Roma. He learned to shut up.

As a young man, he discovered he could leave his body at will. When his father was gone, he never missed the opportunity to while his afternoon away in near-slumber, watching his neighborhood from above, never daring to stray too high or too far. Months after he turned twenty-four, a few weeks after Annette left him the first time, Franz couldn't escape himself anymore. He lay weighted in his flesh, yearning.

"WAIT," Muriel said, sitting up. "His wife's name is Maria. Who's Annette?"

Joe smiled. "The Board of Directors voted her small display panel out of the exhibit. She both was and wasn't a vital person to Franz Marc's career."

"How do you mean?"

"She was a married antiques dealer who started dealing in art and became very good at it. She introduced Marc to the business and helped him get commissions doing portrait work. Through her, he met other dealers who eventually found clients who could afford to invest in a young, unknown artist. But that was several years into an affair they never quite broke off."

"But he was married, too, right? Twice."

"Yes. He and both his eventual wives, also artists, spent a..." He lifted both hands, grasping at the air as he tried to find the words he wanted. "An interesting summer in Kochel am See. Together. In 1906. Emotionally fraught seems to be the phrase most biographers use to describe it. Marc's depression, his inability to trigger an out-of-body experience, lasted years, from 1904 well into 1907. He was twenty-seven and immediately after marrying his first wife that spring, on their wedding night, in fact, Franz left for Paris. By himself."

IN PARIS, Franz lost himself to the art, spent hours tracing the brushstrokes of the masters.

Wassily Kandinsky found him in the maze of the Louvre one day, as he sat with his head bent over his sketch pad. Kandinsky recognized Franz from the Munich Academy of Art and stood in front of him, hands planted on his gaunt, jutting hips. He was tall, although Franz still had three inches on him, an angular man with a physical energy that pulsed about him.

Franz had sketched his spiritual lines many times since that meeting without yet capturing his essence.

Kandinsky said, "Come with me."

Franz hadn't understood at first. Had no idea why the man took an interest in his work, invited him to gatherings where he met...everyone. All those who changed his life, who gave him hope for his future as a painter, if not a man who was fully sane as he lumbered through life in a body that kept him grounded, when all he wanted was to rise above the landscape and regain the dreamy perspectives of his youth.

The fellow artists, the actors, the patrons, even the hanger-ons, who never minded an argument on the most intricate details of art, helped Franz find new perspectives on the work in front of him, whether in oil or clay or print. As for the ways in which he reached those philosophical highpoints—the heated theoretical arguments while wildly drunk, the cocaine, hashish, morphine, and later, heroin. The angry sex and sober make-ups. Exhilarating love. Ruinous break-ups. Those methods not only destroyed the last of his innocence regarding the desires and spiritual goodness of current civilization, but his belief in his own inherent morality.

Except.

Except the drugs did help when Franz thought all hope lost for traveling out of his body again. Opium in particular. Even now, looking out over the dark, barren dooryard of the Sindelsdorf house, the garden gazebo where he sometimes worked just visible, Franz could smell the sweet smoke, practically taste it on his tongue, although he'd left it all behind in Paris. He sighed, the cold spring air wafting from his mouth, and shifted into the spiritual plane, taking that body he'd once hated with him and relished the color that sprang into the landscape all around him.

A red fox sat upon the blue swirl of a path curling through the field across from him into the distance, the yellow swirl of the distant lake beyond. Spirits flittered across the tall grass. A few floated in the scattered copses, the trees obscuring their forms. The smaller herd of blue horses grazed under the resplendent red and blue moon. All pure spirit.

In Paris that year, soaked to the gills in absinthe and opium, Franz followed Kandinsky through the alleys and backstreets of the Left Bank. Down into the catacombs, up through Croulebarbe, past the Pantheon in one of a hundred different ways, along the narrow, dark streets of a million Parisian homes, out along the damp concrete along the Seine. It was the third trip, maybe the fourth, before he changed bodily for the first time. The loss of weight in mid-stride startled him. He looked down, expecting to see himself face down in the gutter along Rue de Bievre. But he was still walking. He lifted his hand. He had one, a basic difference between his out of body experiences and actual physical spirit walking.

Kandinsky had glanced over his shoulder, shifted in body, and strode straight up the brick wall at the end of the alley. Wrapped in red and blue spirit, he bounced a little at the top, standing horizontal and looking down on Franz where he stood among spilled coffee grinds and citrus pulp and the heap of Kandinsky's dropped clothes. A green cat appeared upon the roof to their right and mewled before leaping down upon Kandinsky's shoulder and rubbing its head along the man's stubbled jaw. Kandinsky petted it.

Franz stood below them, waiting for his thoughts to catch up.

When they did, he said, "How did you know?"

Kandinsky shrugged. "One does, after a while. There aren't many of us, though. I imagine some of us go a lifetime without meeting a fellow walker."

Franz knew three now. Well. Knew August and Kandinsky. Saw the tiger, in Munich. A predatory Ushen. Far from home. The tiger *had* to mean a tipping point in the imperialistic dance between Germany and Russia and France. Franz had meant it when he told August he thought war would be good. He wanted…he didn't know what he wanted. Something different. Change. Acceptance maybe. To be able to declare what he saw to the world in his art and have it be appreciated. For viewers to see the truth in it.

He turned away from the brilliant landscape under the moon and finished stripping. Maria remained at peace, her clear, corn-silk yellow aura lapping along her milky skin in gentle currents. He wondered if he might someday tell her what he was, what he could do, how lovely her spirit. But no, he never would. If he ever broke his silence, Annette remained his greatest temptation.

Nude, only a shadow to all but others of his kind, Franz slipped down the dark stairway into the kitchen, Russi at his heels, paused to listen to the deep snoring of his landlord, and then eased the door open to walk among the blue horses.

STANDING against the wall of a small shop on the east side of the central plaza in Munich, Franz soaked in the early afternoon sun while Maria dawdled over dress fabrics he couldn't afford despite his patron's generous provision. May was coming to a close, bringing with it the first hot breath of summer. Within the hour, he'd be meeting with Reinhard Piper, his publisher, to hold the first print edition of *The Blue Rider Almanac* in his hands. Already, he knew what he wanted to write about for his essay in the second.

Eyes half-closed, Franz let his mind wander, dreaming over the problems of his current canvas. The Ushen didn't register until he'd prowled all the way across the square and froze not ten yards in front of Franz. Before his brain woke up, Franz pushed off the wall and strode for the blonde man bleeding the aura of his tiger soul.

The man, ten years older than Franz, but fitter and twice as wide, held his ground. Franz stopped. He had thought he'd never see the tiger again after that first chance sighting in March.

The bunched muscles of the man's shoulders visibly dropped. As he stood regarding Franz, recognizing him for what he was, Franz walked forward. The man's nostrils flared. Franz drew in a deep breath, but he himself could smell nothing of the tiger in the man, only a bright aftershave and faint whiff of wood smoke. He held out his hand. "Franz."

The man ignored his hand, but nodded. "You're the painter."

Franz inclined his head.

"I saw your work at the Moderne in January. Dortmund wasn't happy."

"Dortmund?"

"The blue horse."

Oh. He'd seen the horse in France. From the train, but its image remained seared into his memory. The field, the horse's confident stance, the contrasting softness in its eye and head. He'd known the moment he saw it, that he would paint it. Had burned from the inside until he'd wrung the last strokes of the its image from his brush. He'd seen any number of blue horses before and since, but none like that one. Now he knew why. None of them except Dortmund, his *Der Blaues Pferde I*, was Ushen in full animal form.

"I didn't know."

"You're playing a dangerous game"—the man lifted his chin at the people parting ways to walk around them and stepping closer, pitched his voice low, for Franz only—"exposing us."

Franz laughed. "As if. I'm just a painter, one not even the critics understand, let alone them. Introduce me to Dortmund."

"He's dead."

A spike of sorrow punctured Franz's heart. He lifted his brows in question.

"I ate him. You're a lot smaller."

Bristling, Franz drew himself up, words forming on his lips, a question about whether the man meant to threaten him.

Before Franz could spill the words into the tension between

them, the man sneered. "Yes, if you pose a danger." He spun on his heel and walked off, letting the coloring of the tiger flare into Franz's sight around him before he disappeared into the crowd.

FOR WEEKS, Franz woke from ill-formed dreams of discovery. Only to be constantly reminded by art critics, dealers, agents, and gallery owners, that the work that most spoke to him was too experimental to be taken seriously by the general public. When August proposed meeting at Kandinsky's for a couple of restorative days of beer, debate, and wandering, Franz accepted immediately. Maria fussed at him, but wrote to her parents, making his excuses for not accompanying her to meet them on holiday in Vienna.

On the second night of his visit, Gabriele dropped a kiss on Kandinsky's lips and then sauntered back into the house from the back porch. The Murnau locals called it the Russian House, scandalized that the independently wealthy Gabriele Münter did nothing but paint landscapes and furniture and live out of wedlock with a socialist Russian who painted colors and nonsense and called it art.

"How she continues to put up with you, I have no idea," August Macke teased the older man.

"She likes my music," Kandinsky offered, pulling his shirt over his head and dropping it on the back steps to retrieve later as he shoved his glasses back into place.

"Someday someone will expect you to actually play a song, rather than wave your hands a lot as you talk about some improvisation you've just slapped paint onto," Franz said, struggling with his button fly. Kandinsky referred to all his art and writing as "improvisations". It was annoying. Kandinsky's balled up socks hit the side of his head. Russi dashed over to retrieve them. Franz looked up, grinning.

"Does she know," August said, stepping out of his pants.

"Does she know what," Kandinsky asked, gathering their clothes, the socks Russi dropped at his feet.

"That we walk."

Franz's breath stuck in his chest, stopping his heart.

But the mild-mannered Kandinsky only shrugged and tugged Franz's pants out of his frozen hand. "I told her years ago, I am a werewolf," he said in his distinctive Russian accent despite years of living in Germany and France.

August slapped the back of his hand across Kandinsky's shoulder.

"It's true," Kandinsky insisted, just as the back door opened. "Gabriele! Hide your eyes."

Gabriele took in the naked men. Franz covered himself with one hand, but it was only Gabriele and he couldn't muster any embarrassment. "You men undress slower than a bride on her wedding night," she said. "He only goes disappearing on the full moon to support his claim."

Kandinsky shook his head. "Some secrets are meant to be kept, my love."

"Your secrets are safe with me, dear man. Now go, so I can worry the neighbors by gathering herbs by the dark of the moon."

"The weeds will wait, Gabriele."

"But sunrise won't and I'm painting on the lake tomorrow. Besides, it's cooler at night."

Kandinsky shoved the armful of clothes at her and Franz was more than a little surprised she took them. "Do what you will, then, woman."

"Always, Mr. Kandinsky."

August saluted Gabriele with the last of his beer, quaffed it, placed his glass stein on the porch rail, planted his hand beside it, winked, and then vaulted over the railing, becoming a dark shadow mid-air.

A small sound escaped Gabriele, but when Franz glanced back at her, her face was composed, the corners of her flattened lips tipped up. Her eyes gave her fascination away though as they met his.

"It's a different world," he said. "I wish you could join us."

"Me, too," she whispered. She stepped back and shut the door again, though, leaving Kandinsky and Franz alone on the stoop,

August already ranging out into the garden. Franz reached for that one particular spot inside, opened himself in spirit, while holding himself physically together. Kandinsky leaped out over the steps, blazed orange and then blue with streaks of yellow, whooped out loud, and charged into the night.

Franz took a deep breath, wondering if Gabriele was still watching. He gathered himself, letting the shift roll through him as he stood completely still, just in case, hoping her eyes were on him, only because he was tired of hiding his nature. If only the common man understood the mystical inner construction that tied them to the spiritual world, they would stop yearning for the material goods that drove the industrial greed that threatened to overwhelm their traditional way of life and destroy places like Kochel am See.

But to directly share what they were with those men? His own energy wavered around him. They'd be persecuted. Like the Roma, like the Jew. Like the Africans. Perhaps enslaved as spies, for as only a shadow in the eyes of others, they could go anywhere. His art could be the only way he revealed himself to most.

With a flick of thought, he covered himself in flickering reds and blues. Then walked down the porch steps and followed Kandinsky once more into the night.

IN SEPTEMBER, August set his coffee down on a table outside a small café near his studio in Bonn. Franz noticed the creases in the skin of his fingers still held dried paint from the mural they were working on together. The brisk wind gusted, sending colored leaves fluttering across the wide, unoccupied sidewalk. He held the second mug out and Franz took it gratefully, wrapping his own work-worn hands around it. Although it wasn't yet cold, he couldn't seem to warm himself.

"Maria's worried," August said after a few moments of sipping and watching the passer-by on the opposite side of the avenue.

Franz shook his head. "Don't, friend. My—" Maria would not be his wife yet for some time. Although they'd had a wedding of sorts in London last year, his defacto father-in-law had made him self-conscious of using the word wife. Although he longed to call her his, he had to wait for his divorce from first wife, Marie, to be finalized. "Maria should not be confiding in you."

"What's going on, Franz? She knows you're gone more nights than not. She's found you missing from your studio when she's brought your mid-day meal. A couple of times a week the past month."

Turning his cup about with his restless fingers, Franz thought about what he could say. He needed—he didn't know what he needed but he couldn't find it here. "Let's go to Paris, August. A few weeks."

August studied him for a long moment over the rim of his coffee mug. "You've been with her, haven't you?"

Franz let his gaze drift past his friend. August knew him too well these days.

"Annette?" August prompted, although they both knew he meant Annette.

As much as he loved Maria, and he did, more than he'd ever envisioned he would when they first met, Annette would always stir him. She'd lit him up at a time when he wasn't sure he could experience physical passion for anything, let alone a person.

He'd still been living at his family home in Pasing, in Munich. In the same way his parents supported his art, they supported his brother's interest in all things Byzantine. The Sanskrit tutor, in truth a well-known Byzantine researcher, turned up at the house one day with his wife, Annette, in tow. Annette and his father talked art at that first meeting. Franz couldn't stop watching the way her mouth moved. His mother made him join her in the kitchen to cut cake while she made coffee. Annette painted and collected. In fact, even then, becoming known in Munich for her astute eye as an art and antiques dealer. Afterward her husband and his brother came down, the conversation moved on to Greece and Rome, and Franz thought nothing more of her.

But then a few weeks later, she'd randomly wandered by him where he lay resting after hiking the fields near Kochel. He'd been twenty-two, Annette thirty-two, and under the tree propping him up, she had opened his eyes to the incandescent art of sex. Even now, he reveled in their occasional dalliance when he came to Munich.

The late afternoon sun slanting across her body still took his breath away, made him that young boy again, experiencing physical pleasure so intense it resonated within and around him, holding him down in his body while simultaneously lifting him above it where he could feel her own bright blue pulsing energy, a state he'd never achieved with another lover. Although that intensity had passed with their first breakup, he still needed her. Even if August didn't approve and cultural constraints kept them apart.

But needing her also meant not too near.

Not too often.

Not sharing his true self.

And that meant he needed to be away from Munich right now.

"Paris, August. We can see Pablo while we're there. Talk to him about loaning something new for the next Blue Rider exhibition."

"I'll speak with Elisabeth. We'll have to impose on someone."

Franz closed his eyes against the surge of relief that swallowed him.

PARIS FLOODED Franz Marc's senses in a way he couldn't explain. Woke parts of his brain that slowly waned every time he returned home, despite his connections in the cities of brotherhood—Berlin, Cologne, Dusseldorf. Despite the rich setting of the Staffelsee and Kochelsee where he roamed with August and Kandinsky. Despite the ferocious, invigorating debates within his Blue Rider clan of artists, the exchanging of thoughts crucial to the development of their work as they strove to reach the common man through his subconscious, drive him to change the world through action and protest and empathy for his fellow man.

The artist colonies of Paris were to Franz as Franz needed his work to be to the Germans who saw it. They couldn't or wouldn't give up their small lives to big concepts. He needed to convey those concepts in a way that transferred them to the viewers' ids, made them restless and wanting until they broke free of their social cages and embraced real change, respected the natural world, lived life in a freer, more natural way without the constraints of politics and economics and structured schooling that made up rules and said life had to be lived a certain way, that there was a right and a wrong way to paint, to consume, to worship, to love.

"They're going about it all wrong," August agreed.

Robert Delaunay sipped from his tipple of absinthe. They sat in mismatched chairs facing the narrow, open windows in Robert's light-filled studio, surrounded by his latest work. "Not wrong, they just don't see the fragmented qualities of life. That we are all pieces of life reflecting light, not meant to be potted together into a single point of view or way of life or concept of right or wrong. What's right for oneself may be wrong for our fellows."

"And vice versa," August said.

"Of course. It's societal constraints, like the constraints of a window frame upon our view of the world, that block the light of individual choices over time."

They meandered on, conversationally, Robert's wife, Sonia facilitating translation, between German and French, but Franz tuned them out. He got up and sorted a couple of the canvases, lining up four to ponder on. When Robert presented his new series, *Windows*, to them earlier, they'd exclaimed over how non-representational the work was, and yet, how imbued it remained with air and light and framing. How each painting captured the essence of a window as if it were an individual being, and after all, it was a fact that every window in the world could claim an exclusive view and position in the world. The Delaunays' were calling the form Orphism, relating it to Cubism.

Franz's thoughts turned to his days in Paris's museums, recreating the masters. How much he had changed in a few short years! Then, Turner's work puzzled him. Sure, *Snow Storm – Hannibal's Army* made sense. It had realism below a fanciful swirl of weather. But *Snow Storm - Steamboat Off A Harbor's Mouth* was formless. He rubbed his chest, remembering how disturbed he'd been as he lingered in front of it. But now, in memory? The raw emotion spilt from the canvas to sweep around him like the fog and snow were reaching from his past to ensnare him. And he hadn't seen that piece in years.

Emotion, light, space. Robert's Windows echoed Turner in its intensity of energy, focused inward, spiraling to the center, but there was also structure here, lines that also reminded Franz of Mondrian's experimental sketches they'd seen days ago at a salon, soft edges from the Fauves, even a bit of Kandinsky's influence, with the brighter squares of color symbolizing the outside.

He wished his friend was here to see these and that Kandinsky could meet Marc Chagall, a young spirit walker to whom Robert had introduced Franz and Maria and August at a gallery party. Chagall had not recognized Franz and August in return. And Robert had not a clue. Oh, that Robert could be one of them! That he could see what he was only guessing at.

Franz turned his head and caught August watching him as Robert continued to elaborate on the concepts that had become his obsession. Conceptual art might be a useful term. Conceptualism? Abstraction, certainly.

He needed his brushes and could see August was on the same page. "This," Franz said loudly. Robert stopped talking mid-sentence. "Is influential work, Robert. I'm inspired. You've inspired me."

Robert's smile broke free. He lifted his glass. "I'm humbled, sir."

SEQUESTERED BACK IN SINDELSDORF, Franz painted and carved wood and wrote daily, with a new appreciation for the golden light that lay over the Kochelsee like nowhere else he'd ever been.

Christmas had come and gone, with long walks through the snow with Maria, Russi leaping in and out of the brush to flush startled birds. They often kept the company of their landlord, Josef, in the evenings. New Year's Eve brought them to Gabriele and Kandinsky's house, in celebration with the other members of the Blue Riders. Franz was especially happy to see Paul Klee again.

1913

MOST OF THE New Year's party departed on the second, with only Maria, Franz, August, and August's wife Elisabeth staying on in Murnau. In the evening, Gabriele nodded at Kandinsky and then proposed an evening of painting with Maria and Elisabeth, and sent the men off to amuse themselves. They wasted no time slipping outside to strip and take themselves spirit walking, before the frigid air chilled them.

Kandinsky's local herd of blue horses, normally only seen from a distance, stood drowsing on the road. One snorted, its head bobbing, as the men bounded into the spiritual plane. The entire herd lifted as one and wheeled to face them, ears pricked. The men froze. Russi, rushing ahead, noticed their absence behind her and stopped short of the herd. The lead horse, a boss mare, eyed them all and then snorted once more and shook her head and neck. The herd relaxed, though a young stallion at the rear remained alert.

Franz wondered once again about the age of souls and if they were created or born. If these spirits would ever be born into physical bodies or if they just were what they were in a world in between the living and the dead. Kandinsky clapped his hands, startling him and the horses both, but the blue horses remained on the road, watching the men with a conscious intelligence real world horses rarely displayed.

"Let's ride them," Kandinsky said.

Franz nearly laughed and August said, "Are you crazy?"

"Why not?"

August frowned at him. "Why?"

Franz considered the idea. "My herd lets me pet them."

August turned his appalled focus on Franz. "You've touched them?"

"Yes, of course, you haven't?"

Kandinsky spread his hands in confusion. "August, you have that little spirit cat that never leaves your studio and sleeps on your feet."

"But these are"—he swung his arm out and the horses shifted as a group, their feet shuffling on the road—"wild horses. They're spirit, not horses. They're—"

"Improvisations," Kandinsky said.

"You and your 'improvisations', Wassily, I'm being serious here."

"As am I. They are like music, these beings, like our pencils and our paints and our words. They flow as needed. And right now, I need to ride."

This was true. When Franz wanted to touch spirit, spirit lay solid under his hand. In spirit, he could walk upon the ground or drift above it. He didn't expand when he shifted in body, he'd tried. And couldn't go faster than he could physically run or fly per se, but he could tread upon the air, like walking up steps or along cobble stones, which is what air felt like, beneath the soles of his feet.

August, arguably the best rider among them, bowed, and as he straightened, said, "By all means then, be my guest, because this I have to see."

Franz suspected they would see Kandinsky on the ground, his spirit bruised, though his body would be safe enough when it hardened around him again. He listened to his own ridiculous thought process and then blurted, "They can't hurt us." Why had riding them never occurred to him before?

Kandinsky walked forward past Russi to stand face to face with the boss mare. He lay a hand upon her neck as Franz passed him, his gaze settling on a stout enough fellow in the middle. The herd parted in a ripple of motion, but the stout stallion stood his ground. The horse met his eye with calm equanimity.

Franz stroked the horse's forehead when he reached him, right between his eyes, and down his nose, trailed his fingers along the arched neck to the solid shoulder. The horse remained still, but brought his head around to nudge Franz's flank. He'd long ago learned it was less disorienting to act as if his body still had weight. He grasped the thick blue mane in his left hand and sprung up, swinging his right leg over the broad back. A shock of connection gallop-trilled across Franz's senses, exploded through his heart and out his limbs.

The horse vibrated under him in response, reshaping his back and sides so that Franz sunk ever so slightly, and very securely, into his curves. A feral sensibility filled Franz's mind. The brilliant colors Franz always saw when walking sharpened. An earthy, lush...fecund scent filled his nose and mouth, the horse's feet on the soft sink of dirt atop the road were his own, his ears pricked to the rustle of the brush nearby, a thin, rich odor threading into his awareness and then the image of a cat rising in his mind's eye. The cold wind blew his tail between his legs, but a pleasant warmth emanated from his belly. Aware of August standing by, tense, he looked to Kandinsky as the man, his hands buried in his horse's mane, turned his head and the boss mare turned in the same direction until she was facing Franz. Kandinsky grinned, his lighter blue teeth brilliant in the dark.

"*Nique ta mère*," August cursed under his breath, but Franz heard him anyway.

They waited for him to choose a mount and get the feel of it. Franz walked his mount in a circle around the curious herd, the young stallion coming close, tucking his nose beside the stout horse's tail and following in their footsteps. Between the turn of his head and hips, tap of his heel, the thought of what he wanted next, he had no problem guiding the horse to his will. In contrast to the soft and willing give of control by the horse, its spirit-hard muscle bunched and stretched with every step, the horse's strength unfathomable in every graceful movement. Like the rest of the horse's senses, that strength became Franz's. He brought the horse/himself to a halt.

Kandinsky stood quiet. August spun his chosen on its haunches, with no apparent cue. He stopped and spun the other way. Stepped sideways and back. Halted. He laughed, breaking the silence. The herd lifted and turned with him when he bumped the horse up into a gallop, Franz feeling the pull of the herd mind before he allowed his horse the motion of joining them. Once he did, the horse plunged into the herd. Franz guided it to the outside left, just behind August, Kandinsky on the other side as they raced down the road away from Murnau, further into the hills.

Leaning low over the bridle-less horse, with nothing to control it save their spiritual bond that made them of one mind, Franz the horse and the horse Franz, they reveled in a soaring exhilaration. Wind rushed through their hair, the roar of it and their own heartbeat filling their ears. Their horse's mane whipped their human face. And then the pound of their hooves lightened, their horses's back bunching and they were galloping on the wind itself, leaving Russi barking from the ground in their wake.

MARIA LIFTED the woodblock from the paper. She turned it in her hands and set it aside to check the print. Franz waited for her reaction. Leaning over the paper she first checked it for defects and smudges, before she straightened to look at the piece critically. She remained expressionless for a long moment before she smiled and clapped her hands together in a loud report that sent the nesting birds exploding from the under the dormer window. He relaxed, not knowing until then how tense he'd been.

"It's lovely," she said. "Really lovely, Franz. Mr. Koehler will find it delightful. Shall we make a baker's dozen for him?"

For this piece, Franz had carved a horse laying on the ground, leaf dappled, placidly watching a hedgehog nestled into the forest floor, nose to the scents only he was privy to on the upper half of the print. On the lower half, embedded perhaps below and within the forest floor, lay the objects that would imply to the viewer what scents the hedgehog might be enjoying. Ripe fruit, grass, a grasshopper. In the distant background, their larger world, the mountains of Kochel, the lake. His patron would indeed appreciate the mix of avant-garde and traditional imagery.

He nodded. "Thank you, Maria," he said, his gratefulness for her rising from his heart to color his tone.

"Always, Franz," she said, already releasing the paper to hang it for drying.

He reached out and grabbed her hand as she turned away and she glanced back at him. He smiled at her. She leaned in to kiss him, just a peck of the lips, but it warmed him. She bustled off and he turned back to his easel. His dabs of paints were drying on his palette as all he'd done for some time was look at the partially finished canvas. Two horses, viewed from behind, stood on the right. A red horse stood broadside to the viewer on left. He could see the horses in his head, but nothing else of their landscape.

He poked his brush into a bit of blue, intending to cut the curve of a tail, but instead of following the shadow of his sketch, he traced the air above the piece, then slashed a line down between the horses. He hesitated, stretching to grasp the unsettled claustrophobia he'd been harboring deep inside himself for months. Maybe since the tiger. Longer, though, if he were honest. Since he and the others had taken a stand with The Blue Rider. In his mind's eye, he once again caught Maria's hand, but when she looked back over her shoulder at him, she was Annette. The memory crashed over him. Annette's hand slipping from his grasp, the white of the bed sheet trailing behind her as she left him that first time.

He'd come here in grief, to Kochel. Painted Marie and Maria sitting together upon the grassy hill above the lake, the mountains beyond. He'd loved them both that summer, the three of them happy together until they weren't.

He dipped the brush again, in white, stroked a line between the two outward facing rumps. Quickly formed a wall between them. The rest of the image sorted itself in his mind's eye. A stable. He scraped his palette and then lay it down. He needed his sketch pad and pencil to re-plan the image, rescue what he'd already accomplished.

Hours later, Maria's hand fell upon his shoulder. "It's late. I've left a cold supper for you, Franz, when you're hungry."

He patted her hand and after she left, stood and stretched. Downstairs, he stood eating buttered bread and sliced sausage in the dark kitchen. Russi sat nearby, watching the transfer of the food from his hand to his mouth with rapt attention. A newspaper lay folded on the table. Franz considered lighting a lamp and sitting down to read, but that feeling he'd managed to dissipate in oil and the quick strokes of his brush came back over him like a cloak.

Anyone could see war on the horizon. The Balkan conflicts were straining alliances and Germany had aligned itself with the

Ottoman Empire. Austria was eyeing Serbia with the same ferocity as Russi sat eyeing his sausage. If they got into it, Russia would have to jump in and Germany, would, of course, side with Austria. These alliances that were supposed to better their lives would end up killing them all. He'd lose his beloved Paris, since there's no way Emperor Wilhelm would leave the French at his back after the dust-up with France in Morocco and threats from the British.

Wilhelm's tactlessness would lose Franz Kandinsky one day, too. Anti-Russian sentiment wasn't limited to the art critics, and Kandinsky would tire of the Germans who spit at him soon, Franz had no doubt. The basis of the worries came down once again to religion and Franz was thankful once again he'd left seminary school behind him. While he remained a Christian, was, in fact, working on an illustrated Bible with Paul Klee, he couldn't deny that the spirit world he walked affected him.

How could he see God as something separate from himself, a higher power, when everything he saw glowed with spirit? Everything was God and God was everything. If only others could see it, there'd be none of this worry over who had the strongest military, the largest Navy, the best territory, and no need to hoard resources. But others didn't see it. Couldn't.

He'd tried to coax Marie into trying it during the single year they'd been married. Said he was researching meditation and out of body experiences. He didn't dare try with Maria. Paul had tried, after Franz and Kandinsky and August decided perhaps only men could spirit walk. August had seen the woman admiring Blue Horse I in Cologne, though, so Gabriele had tried to learn from Kandinsky this past year, after that night she'd come outside to gather their clothes. To no avail. Franz loved her for trying. For loving Kandinsky despite being German. Despite her neighbors. Despite religion and morals and her own culture. If he were God, if God was him, then God loved them, too. The whole messed up bunch of them.

He noticed the bread in his hand and tossed it to Russi along with the last bit of the sausage. There. He'd shared his resources, that didn't seem so hard. Maybe Germany and Russia could learn to as well after the war. Franz blew out his breath and ran his fingers through his hair. A fresh start. That's what they all needed. He should go to bed. But he ached for release. Not the kind Maria could give him. He needed to walk in the natural world, on the spirit plane, not this human construct that hemmed him in both physically and mentally.

Turning on his heel, he opened the kitchen door. The cool spring air wrapped itself around him. Russi crowded his feet and slipped out around him. Two startled does bound away, noiseless on the damp ground.

In the garden gazebo, Franz shifted slowly, taking his body with him, savoring it, letting his clothes fall from him in a heap. A prickle of second sense crawled along the hairs on his neck. He turned to look at the house and could see nothing different, but became certain Maria stood at their bedroom window, watching him. He could rise through the air with just a thought, if he wanted, to hover outside and see her spirit-self radiating from her. Or shift again and steal back up the stairs physically to soak in her loving warmth.

But he couldn't make his feet move.

A cloud crossed the moon, the darkness dousing his hesitation like a gas lamp.

He spun and ran after Russi, visible as a glow of white threading through the underbrush on the bright yellow trail of a dashing red rabbit.

THANK GOD MARIA IS AWAY, Franz thought again. Elbows on his knees, forehead resting on his palms, he sat on a painted wooden stool, a wedding gift from Gabrielle and Kandinsky. The window under the eaves streamed with rain and the attic lay in shadows. The last several days were lost to him. Canvases lay in stacks on the floor, where he'd dug through them for reference. Crumpled pages from his sketchpad and notepaper littered the floor around his desk. Pages of written notes and portions of the essays and stage play he was working on drifted across the surface, his cat Hanni curled up upon them. Wooden dinner boards with scraps of cheese and molding fruit sat on his work bench. A stein half-filled with beer and a jug of water sat on the floor near his easel.

The mostly finished piece sitting on the easel was a nightmare depiction of Tyrol, the beautiful Bavarian land he and Maria had visited weeks ago. Filled with Italians under Austrian rule and threatened by Italy's uneasy alliance with Germany, he could imagine only a bleak future for the people there. His painting featured crosses on the hill of a cemetery, starving horses. A reversion to the literal, fueled by the images he'd seen of the desolation left behind in the wake of the Balkan crisis. Russi lay under the easel, out of the way of the wooden frame Franz had built for a larger oil leaning against the attic wall.

As tall as Franz, and taking up half the length of the studio, that completed work was stark and half-mad with terror. Raw. Franz hated it. Every line was on the diagonal of sunbeams or maybe moonlight through a cathedral of trees, fiery strikes thrown by God from the heavens at the damning nature of man, but in consequence, striking nature itself, destroying the good along with the bad. War like a flood, leveling trees, breaking through the boundary of the spirit plane, leaving behind something different, some new philosophy, some new world order.

He stunk, rank with fear sweat. He scrubbed his fingers into his greasy hair and drew his hands down his bearded jaw. He didn't know the day, but he could feel Maria approaching like a storm gathering. She'd be home soon and he needed to be done with this brooding panic. He stood with resolution. Russi's worried eyes met his, but the dog didn't move, only thumped his tail up and down as Franz continued to look at him. He sat up when Franz bent to pick up a stray brush and came to be petted. Franz rubbed the dog, surveying the mess he'd made in his manic creativity. Hanni stretched and yawned. She leapt from the desk and disappeared down the stairs with her tail held high. Franz thumped Russi's side twice and set about cleaning up.

After a couple of trips to dump his trash in the burn bin and retrieve a bucket and cloth, Franz sat to straighten the table that served as his desk. The letter from Annette, the one that had fueled his terrified outburst, lay on top. He couldn't stop himself from re-reading it yet again. Why her husband would choose to take a posting in Sarajevo now was beyond Franz, but Annette was gone already, without a good-bye. She couldn't bear to see him before they left.

Sarajevo. The Balkans seemed on the very edge of another bloody crisis. Again, Franz's fertile imagination gave him Annette laying torn, grey and dead on a muddy track, trampled in the wake of a retreating army.

Russi whined from his new post by the stairs.

"I know," Franz muttered out loud. "I'm coming." Poor Russi had been the only reason he'd left the attic at all the last few days, but they both needed to be outside despite the rain, to stretch and move.

He folded the letter and then cast around, unsure what to do with it. Stacked on the shelves rising above the desk, his gaze lit upon a beautiful leather-bound book Annette had given him. *Dhammapada of the Pali Canon of Buddha Siddhartha Gautama.* A book of Buddhist verses spoken by Buddha himself to his disciples. He took it down and stroked the cover before flipping the book open to stick the letter inside, landing on a phrase about suffering that seemed particularly apt to his mood. He clapped the book shut and stuck it back on the shelf, then found a sharpened charcoal pencil among the blunts. Tilting the paint frame forward, he scribbled the quote he'd just read on the back the painting. Releasing the dried canvas from the frame, he rolled it and lay it upon a stack of others by the attic door.

After roaming with Russi in the storm, he'd write to August and tell him about his new work while he waited for Maria's return. The inflated titles he'd come up with would amuse August. *The Tower of Blue Horses, The World Cow, The First Animals, Wolves (The Balkans),* and *The Poor Land Tyrol.* And for that big piece he'd been thinking of something involving *Life* or *Fate*, but that seemed too on theme. He stripped in the weak wavering light of the kitchen and folded his clothes before taking them with him as he dashed to the gazebo to stash them there for his return. His landlord didn't care much for the nudists who had moved into the area. And it was easier that he not think Franz wanted to join them. The cold rain woke him, delicious on his bare skin.

He stood looking into the rain and thinking about the big piece long enough for Russi to shake and settle for a snooze, Franz shifted to watch the sizzle and flare of his white and yellow-red glow, his aliveness. His very being. In the large painting, Franz had been going for the parallel of tree rings and animal veins and currents of air and light, all of those carrying the blood of life although each so different from the others. All of them part of...being. And he'd gotten...that freaky mess that screamed pain. Maybe it's rawness and experimental form demanded it be spelled out. *The Trees Show Their Rings, The Animals Their Veins.*

His feeling the need to explain the wolves painting as an allegory of the Balkans would make August out-right laugh, but that was good. Franz liked thinking he would. He'd seen wolves several times in the fields around Sindelsdorf, Kochel, Reid, Murnau. Some corporeal, some not. Russi lifted his head and sniffed the wet breeze. Franz did the same but could smell only the damp and the musty odor of the gazebo's old painted wood. In one smooth motion, the dog rose and bolted into the curtain of rain. He disappeared into the trees, trailing his aura of spirit behind him. Franz rested his shoulder against the solid spirit frame of the gazebo to listen to the drum of the heavy rain on the wooden shakes of the roof and did not follow.

THE SUMMER PASSED in a blur of work and writing and open-air dinners, but Franz couldn't distract himself from the tension in the very air as everyone waited for the moment when the powder keg of rhetoric and political feints across Europe would devolve into a physical fight they could all see coming. Emperor Wilhelm II and his cohorts across nations were like kids poking each other, their citizens the parents who know someone always cries in the end.

In September, having escaped into the woods of Kochel under the full moon, Franz and the blue horse moved as one. His knees skimmed past the trunks of larch, black ash, alder, their half-bare limbs shivering in the stiff breeze. Despite a respite in East Prussia at his sister and brother-in-law's estate, the delight of hours upon hours among their beautifully bred horses, and being presented with the pair of does now living in the garden under his landlord's forbearance, he couldn't shake the dark mood that had shadowed him all year.

He spirit-walked nearly every day now, sometimes twice a day, barely sleeping, losing himself to a glut of work in between. Although Maria worried, the work energized him. He couldn't seem to settle to one project before his thoughts were spilling over into another. He knew artists and writers who struggled to create, had to tear images or words from them one at a time, but he struggled to find the time to capture all his on canvas and paper.

Next week, he and Maria would be back in Paris, maybe for the last time in a long time. He'd go to the salons and galleries and admire the newest works at his friends' studios. He'd drink and walk with August and maybe Kandinsky if he came and they'd try to track Marc Chagall down and introduce him to the life if no other spirit walkers had found him yet. Maybe he'd regain his sense of wonder. Too often this summer, here in the Bavarian countryside, he saw the brutality of the land, rather than the beauty.

A movement in the meadow caught his eye and they, he and the horse, drew to a cautious halt. They stepped back deeper under the shadows at the edge of the tree line. Three wolves crouched over a dead doe. Her spirit stood to one side watching. Unlike the spirit animals he saw every time he opened himself to the spiritual plane, though, she stood filled with pinpoints of light that flashed and blinked and sparkled as if some sun he couldn't see shone through her. She faded as he noticed her and in a second was gone as if she never existed.

Two of wolves were red, but the farthest from Franz flickered red and orange, capturing his attention. It turned its head, snuffling the air, before its gaze seemed to lock on Franz's, despite the dark and the distance.

It stood, elongating into human form, a woman, still clothed in the spirit of the wolf. Franz shivered. They, the horse and he, shifted their feet, tossing their head, wanting to be gone from here. The blood-smeared Ushen raised a hand and the other wolves tore final chunks of flesh from the doe's body, gulping them down, throats working. They moved off, snapping at each other. Their growls carried through night.

The horse part of Franz quieted with the departure. And the human part calculated. They gathered their courage, ready to defend themselves against the Ushen, still fixated on them. But the Ushen only dropped to all fours, giving herself to her wolf form again, and loped after the others. When she caught up, she stopped and threw her head back, a long, undulating howl lifting through her long throat. Her companions joined her, the sound eerie. Their mournful voices seeped into the marrow of Franz's bones, chilling him.

He rode for home, the howl of the Ushen echoing in his ears, certain he'd find tragedy had struck while he'd been walking, but the house was quiet. Everything as always. Maria a steady warmth waiting for his cold return. He had work to do, but instead crawled into bed beside her and for the first time in months, woke there, the sunrise a caress along his cheek

1914

"FRANZ!" Maria called from the kitchen. Her very own kitchen in the house they'd bought in Ried two months ago, in April.

Franz lifted his brush from the delicate work he'd been performing.

"Archduke Ferdinand's been assassinated! In Sarajevo. It's on the radio," she continued as she climbed up to join him. "Austria is saying it was the Serbians."

Franz set his wooden palette aside as she swept into the room and caught her in his arms.

"It's starting," she whispered and burst into tears. The only other time he could remember her crying was the lust-charged summer they spent in the cabin on Kochel Lake with Marie when he had wavered between them, torn between love and friendship.

MURIEL HELD UP HER HAND.

Joe obliged her, without another word.

"Where's Ried?"

"Still in Kochel am See, not far from Sindelsdorf."

"And didn't Annette move to Sarajevo?"

Joe nodded. Muriel was starting to appreciate his efficiency.

"I wasn't the best history student, but Archduke Ferdinand's assassination is the start of World War One, correct?"

"Yes."

Muriel stared down at her hands, sorting her feelings. Noticing her numb butt, she drew her legs up to sit cross-legged in the board room chair. In the center of the table, condensation sat on the surface of a water pitcher, like the dew on the moonlit grass outside Franz Marc's bedroom window. Apparently still watching her closely, Joe didn't need to be asked. He poured water into two glasses, and then rose halfway up to reach across the table and place hers in front of her. He sat back down.

"I want to say I feel sorry for Franz," Muriel said. "But it's what he wanted. The war. Did he really hate the world that much?"

Joe's gaze wandered the room as he thought. Muriel was glad he didn't have a pat answer. He studied her face, her hands, before finally speaking. "He hated the rapid changes he saw happening around him. The Austrian-Hungarian, Russian, German, and British empires all wanted more territory and resources, fighting over Africa and parts of Asia to get it. Development was beginning to affect natural spaces like Kochel am See. Railways, and electricity, and telephone lines were invading the countryside. People wanted more in their lives, more comfort, more ease in the chores of daily life, and manufacturing answered. Greater materialism drove up the cost of living."

"And he was living at the whim of a patron," Muriel said. "And family money, I guess? His parents and Maria's?"

"And making ends meet with commissions and portraits, not the work he wanted to devote himself to. He was of the bourgeois class, but hated most everything associated with it. The move to Ried was an attempt to control his surroundings. To preserve a rural space around himself."

"Even though there's wolves waiting to pluck off the animal spirits in *Fate of the Animals*."

"He'd learned nature wasn't any purer than people, but he also couldn't deny the blue horses still grazing on spirit grass in the fields."

There were lots of things Muriel could think of that Marc couldn't deny. "He was lonely, he'd been rejected by Annette, the critics hated his art, but he had friends, and a wife who loved him enough to buck society and live with him before marriage and after what, a love triangle? A threesome? And privilege! Travel and painting and living by a lake at the foot at the Alps. So much white boy privilege. Though, I know, he wasn't aware of that. That's a now thing."

"Marc was idealistic to a fault. And you're right, as a man of his times, it's not like he was cognizant of his privilege, but he was defi- nitely torn. He wanted black and white in the world and was forced to see the grey."

"Did he still want it? Did he think he could just sit back and watch, with Annette in Sarajevo and war on the way?"

"Wars then were several pitched battles over time and a lot of negotiation. No one knew what was coming." He looked away, through the glass at her back, his face drawn as if he'd seen the coming brutality himself. "No one knew."

"I CAN'T PAINT with you, old man," August said two weeks later, in mid-July. He was standing in Franz's new studio space at the house. He'd come with Elisabeth and his two little boys to visit for few days, after their move back to Bonn from Switzerland and eight months of an artist's residency at Lake Thune. He waved a hand at Franz's latest canvases. "Robert got into your head, didn't he?"

"Like you can't say the same," Franz laughed. It felt good. It was true, their Paris visit last October, and especially their time with Robert Delaunay, had released whatever in Franz still clung to the waking world and the desire for praise from the critics. Now he painted only his emotional truth and at this moment, that meant the circle of life and the tangle of the trinity and the things he saw in the way he saw them. All of life was cruel. Maybe he'd find innocence again in the natural world after this war destroyed the blight upon it.

"Franz," August said, snapping his fingers, and Franz swung his head around from his contemplation of the piece he'd been working on. "You need beer."

"I do."

August held up a print from the stack on Franz's work bench. "Is this one of the pieces for the Genesis project?"

Franz nodded. He spent a good part of the past year, when not writing or painting, carving wood blocks and writing to the Blue Riders and other artists in France, soliciting their work for an illustrated Bible. All to no avail. Artists were hard to pin down in normal times and the news had been too distracting of late.

"Is it dead?"

"For now."

"You were working on writing a new version of The Tempest for that producer, too, weren't you?"

Franz shrugged.

"The second Blue Rider Almanac?"

"That may still have a chance, if we don't go to war too soon."

August clapped a hand on Franz's shoulder. "Beer, brother."

Franz slung his arm across August's narrow shoulders in return. "Much beer. While we can. Paul Klee said you were enlightened in Tunisia, Mister Color. Tell me what you saw."

TIME SEEMED to be collapsing in on itself. Days after August returned to Bonn, Germany declared war on Russia. The next morning, Kandinsky stood waiting in the yard, the does, Hanni and Ruth, nosing at his pockets for apple slices.

Franz walked out to meet him, Maria coming to stand on the steps behind him.

The sun was just brightening the yard.

Dew sparkled on the grass.

"You're leaving," Franz said.

The Russian spread his hands. "I have no choice."

"Gabriele is staying?"

"No, we're going to Switzerland tomorrow. She's closing the house now. I don't know how long I'll be able to stay there, but we'll try. I won't subject her to more hatred because of me."

"Stay here then. Her neighbors already hate you."

"This is true, but it will only get worse, and you know it."

Franz couldn't argue the point. He waved Maria forward to say her goodbyes and then walked with Kandinsky to where he'd tied a borrowed horse at the front gate.

"Will you fight, then?" Kandinsky asked.

"Only if I'm called up. Will you?"

"Not at my age, unless Mother Russia gets desperate." At nearly fifty, with bad eyes, Kandinsky was probably safe from action, but other duties might be required of him. "It's not my war. I love Germany and Austria and France. I'm only leaving because I'm the enemy. I won't burden my friends like that."

"My friend," Franz said, stopping to clasp the smaller Kandinsky to him.

The Russian bear hugged him and then pushed him away with both hands on Franz's biceps and held him there. "Use your skills if you end up in the fight. You're a big man, they won't care that you aren't twenty anymore."

"How will an artist's skills help?"

Kandinsky raised his brows as if Franz were a slow student.

"You mean my skills as a spirit walker."

"Go in as a cavalryman if you can."

"Yes, sir," Franz said and Kandinsky let go of him. "Is this goodbye?"

"I'll send my letters here, to Maria. Don't forget the horses, right? You'll figure out how to make it work."

AUGUST MACKE. Dead already. At September's end. Not two months after they'd been drafted. In the trenches of Champagne. Bile rose in Franz's throat. Why had August gone infantry? Had he not received Franz's letter offering Kandinsky's advice to go cavalry before he left Bonn? Had he been denied?

Franz stuffed Maria's letter into the front pocket of his coat. He'd seen too much already. He could imagine August's death in excruciating detail. His sons would not remember him, they were too young. Poor Elisabeth, joining the ranks of the war widows so young. And August, not yet twenty-seven years old, his brilliance yet unknown to the greater art world. Franz swallowed again, losing his fight against the hot brand smoldering in his chest.

"Marc! We're moving!"

Marc raised a hand in acknowledgement. Wiped the falling tears from his face. Slung his rifle back over his chest and levered himself up from the sloping mud wall of the trench. Gaze wandering over the collecting men, he once again acknowledged the syrupy surrealism of his surroundings. He couldn't seem to shake it. As he'd written to Maria weeks ago, the noise deafened him, left him listening for the voice of God in the seashore hiss and tinny ring of faraway church bells that filled his ears. What he didn't tell her about was how he'd been cracked open somehow by this awful, bloody horror. Sleeping or awake, on the spirit plane or not, the glorious, swirling light show of spirit overlay every battle, lit the trail of every bullet, rose from every man and beast that fell.

He'd take back every wish he'd ever made for change wrought by war for one more happy day in Joseph's house in Sindelsdorf, no war on the horizon, Maria roasting sausages, August pounding up the stairs into the attic.

1915

THE RAIN SHIFTED, blowing into the face of the French line. "Now," Franz bellowed. The blue horses charged forward, three of fifteen mounted with fellow spirit walkers Franz found in the trenches.

A howl rose above the French forces. An Ushen wolf scrambled across the mud, injured and frenzied, tearing out the throats of dying men between the trenches. Franz ignored him. Ignored the slog of the troops below him, the bullets, the explosive mortars throwing mud and blood and feet and arms thirty feet into the air.

It did not affect him and his.

He couldn't allow it to.

He and his men and his herd galloped the sky, thundering hooves louder in Franz's heart and soul than the boom of the heavy artillery, their shadows falling over the battle, shifting across the rising dead.

Their mission was reconnaissance.

The troops they ate and bathed and shit beside were depending on them.

What his superiors didn't know about how he surveyed the lay of the land so accurately and in so much secrecy that the troops called him Djinn behind his back, they didn't want to know.

What he pretended the troops didn't know when his shadow slid over them as they rose to fight gave him the only hope he still held that one day he'd have a voice and a people to turn to when he needed them.

SWEATING in his bunk in the relative safety of an underground bunker, Franz propped the little notebook sideways on his knee.

 # 82 — I saw what the moorhen sees as it dives: the thousand rings that encircle each little life, the blue of the whispering sky swallowed by the lake, the enraptured moment of surfacing in another place. Know, my friends, what images are: the experience of surfacing in another place.

. . .

"HERE'S the paint you requested, Franz." The private, one of his walkers, could have been Franz's son, he was so young. Franz wanted to protect them all. No man should see again the things they'd all seen this year. "What is this one for?"

When command had discovered he was a painter of minor renown in Bavaria, they'd set Franz up in the loft of a massive barn to paint tarps for artillery camouflage. While he had zero desire to paint anything artistic, he'd been surprised at the contentment he found behind the lines painting nothing but camouflage. He'd decided on a pointillist style and taken Kandinsky's splotchier work as inspiration, which amused himself to no end.

He'd taught his boys to both travel out of body and to shift their bodies into the spiritual plane at will. He lifted his chin as he accepted the buckets of black and yellow to add to the green he was working with. "I laid three tarps on the north side of the barn. Go high, plane high, and see if it conceals the farm equipment and chicken coops."

He had, of course, requested a plane and a photographer for testing, but he wasn't planning to waste his time waiting for those requests to be granted while painting unusable cover. His little troop had a reputation to maintain based on their reconnaissance and the more valuable they made themselves, the more important keeping them alive would be to command.

At least that's what he told his men. In truth, it got them a lot of dangerous missions, but ones the walkers could use their skills for to mitigate the dangers of the non-walkers in their small re-con company. In turn the more observant non-walkers covered for them and the battalion benefitted greatly in less fatalities.

1916

A STAMPEDING band of red and yellow horses galloped straight at them, glowing in the night, a spirit walker riding low over the neck of the lead horse. Franz's walkers froze on their bellies three-quarters through the no-man's ground between the trenches of Verdun.

Unaware, the troops around them kept moving.

As if the phantom herd were dragging a veil behind it, snowflakes fell in lazy spirals from the darkness, gathering on helmets and backs, adding the sheen of ice to rifles.

Eons of men before him depicted war as soldiers huddled around campfires, battalions of cavalry on horseback, blazing villages, but those were not this misery. This is what Franz would paint when got home: men like snakes, inching forward in the dark over frozen corpses, sheltering in craters, the sheen of moonlight bouncing from snow and metal.

"MY DEAREST,

Kohler wrote me today on a Sturm postcard of my Fate of Animals. *On looking at it, I was completely disconcerted and agitated. It is like a premonition of the war; horrible; and gripping. I can hardly imagine that I painted that! In any case, in the blurred photograph it was so incomprehensively convincing, that I felt quite uneasy."*

Tapping his pencil stub upon the letter to Maria, Franz wondered if she had seen the inscription he'd made on the back of the canvas that terrible day. Although he barely recalled painting it, his fingers recalled the softness of Annette's leather-bound book of Buddhist lessons.

All being is flaming suffering. It seemed so apt then and remained apt now.

Would Maria ever know his regret, not just for his unquenchable thirst for Annette, but for her suffering when he had first chosen Marie? Would she ever know the depth of his sorrow that she loved him so well who did not deserve it?

Perhaps this hell surrounding him, the lonely song that even now floated through the darkness of the freezing trench over the huddled men, this hell he so wished he'd never longed for now, but which he could still only remain hopeful would change men for the better, was his penance.

Pray God that he could make it home to her when this interminable war ended.

· · ·

JOE CLOSED HIS MOUTH. Silence filled the holes his words had punched into the air. Muriel became aware that at some point she'd drawn her legs up under her. That she was resting more than half her weight on the conference room table, leaning forward as if to bathe in the unfolding story. She cleared her throat and eased back. Worked her legs free and sat back down properly. Sipped from the glass of melted ice water in front of her as if she'd done all the talking herself.

"And then?"

Joe studied her.

"What?"

He slid his hand into the inner pocket of his grey suit jacket and withdrew a plastic bag with the word "Archival" stamped upon it, over and over in repeated rows. Laid it down and used his fingertips to slide it across the table. His hands were more workmanlike than you'd think an art director's hands might be. Rugged but not rough. The nails blunt and clean, but not polished. His knuckles worn, a diagonal scar bisecting his ring finger.

She glanced up and saw he'd noticed her noticing. He smiled but kept his silence.

He lifted his fingers from the bag only after she laid her own upon it.

A small card lay inside it. A faded array of colored shapes she couldn't quite make out. On the other side, dark, fluid print.

Muriel opened the bag and tipped the postcard inside onto the table. It was old, tea colored and filled side to side in handwritten German. Crammed into the bottom left-hand corner, Franz Marc had penned his name. She stopped herself just before her fingers hit the ink. Glanced up again. Joe lifted his chin in an encouraging nod.

Muriel caressed the signature. And then she picked up the card.

The blue horses stood waiting in the trench, steam rising like ghosts from their nostrils and rumps. Troops scurried through them, unaware of their pres-

ence, ducking as the howitzers boomed. Franz took his assignment from the General's lieutenant.

He signaled his men to meet him at their dug-in alcove off the main line and they peeled off the wall, tapping others as they passed, the horses waiting until Franz caught up, ambling along behind him.

When the shell hit, Franz ducked, covering his head, yelling at the man ahead of him. He ran forward through the shower of earth, ten feet down the trench before he ran straight through a screaming soldier facing him.

He stopped, looking at his sparkling hands. When had he shifted?

He turned.

His torn body lay behind him, along with several of his men, two of them walkers, but he stood alone in spirit.

The horses faded.

The frantic soldiers shooting and reloading around him faded.

The trench faded.

A bird called over the noise of the artillery.

It was as if his hearing had been restored to him.

Another answered.

Grass rose beneath his feet.

He turned in wonder, seeing again his beloved blue land of Kochel.

The snow-covered mountains. The ripple of the lake.

Russi, dead weeks ago, came bounding to meet him.

And there, in the distance, raising his hand in greeting, August.

Breathing hard, having lived a lifetime in seconds, Muriel stared at the blue horses stacked one upon the other on the postcard, stars and moons on their chests and torsos. In their chests, she knew now. Part of them. These were the spirits of horses that died. She waited, but nothing more came to her. Whatever heaven Franz Marc occupied now, his life and thoughts were now his own.

"I wondered," she said. "As you spoke, how you knew such details."

"There's still not many of us," Joe said. "And like Kandinsky said, probably some of us never meet another."

Muriel's heart hurt with Marc's loneliness, his pain at living a secret life, his regret for wishing any kind of war on anyone while still hating the society he lived in, the horror of the war a burning brand that couldn't ever be healed completely. "Who did you meet?

"A welder. He learned about absorbing another walker's memories from certain items through his own mentor. It only works after the owner's passed. He doesn't believe in looking for more walkers, in communing together, as he put it."

Muriel covered her face with her hands, bowed her body over her crossed legs, and nearly let go the keen building in her throat, but in that moment, her body rocked back upright, a different sound working its way free as Marc's whole lifetime of deep and abiding love for others and desire for connection filled her with unwavering joy. She threw her arms out, tilted her head to the heavens above and laughed.

The moment passed. Although the intensity left her gasping for air. "But you've touched Franz Marc."

"And after three tries, August Macke. And, last year, Marc Chagall."

The calm of a weighted blanket settled over Muriel. It wasn't heavy, this calm. Or suffocating. The experience of a lived life and a death survived grounded her in a way she'd never experienced before. Made her surer of herself than she'd ever been. "Kandinsky?"

"Not yet. Security. Gloves. Items not imbued with the needed energy. It takes strategy in the case of well-known walkers. Pure luck in the case of others."

She didn't have to ask how Joe lived with lifetimes inside him. It was as if she'd been missing part of herself her whole life and now she'd found it. "God," she said. "Franz Marc never got to have this. You gave me me. How could I not want to do that for others? How many do you know?"

"Eight. There are eight of us."

AUTHOR'S NOTES - ELLE ANDREWS PATT

THE PHYSICAL EVENTS in Franz Marc's journey through this story are based on recorded fact. The philosophy drawn from Marc's own writings. The imaginative addition of spirit-walking and Marc's encounters with it, of course, are fictional elements. Out of body experiences (OBE) are a subjective reality. I do, in fact, know someone who gave actionable intel to his military unit through active OBE, but there's no evidence of Marc having ever experienced an OBE. I took inspiration from his *100 Aphorisms* (1915) #82, which is quoted in the story. And the letter towards the end is also a direct quote from a letter to Maria during the war.

Not all the common knowledge cited on various art sites regarding Franz Marc is accurate. Much is cut and pasted and so carried onward in internet perpetuity. I found Jean Marie Carey's obsession with Marc very useful as she has run down documentation of many facts about Marc's life and work as well as visiting the places Marc lived. GermanModernism.org. and Sabine Magnet's tour of the Franz Marc Museum and Franz Marc's Kochel am See was also invaluable. www.Munich.travel

Images of the paintings are included in the single e-book version of Among The Blue Horses at my website, elleandrewspatt.com.

~EAP

ABOUT THE AUTHORS

JADE KERRION
CHARLES A. CORNELL
KEN PELHAM
KRISTIN DURFEE
JOHN HOPE
BRIA BURTON
VERONICA H. HART
ELLE ANDREWS PATT

JADE KERRION

"…This is the kind of series you'd expect to see with a movie deal"
—Full Time Reader, *Amazon Reviewer*

USA Today bestselling author Jade Kerrion defied (or leveraged, depending on your point of view) her undergraduate degrees in Biology and Philosophy, as well as her MBA, to embark on her second (and concurrent) career as an award-winning science fiction, fantasy, and contemporary romance author.

Her debut novel, *Perfection Unleashed*, published in 2012, won six literary awards and launched her best-selling futuristic thriller series, *Double Helix*, which blends cutting-edge genetic engineering and high-octane action with an unforgettable romance between an alpha empath and an assassin.

Earth-Sim and *Eternal Night* won first place Royal Palm Literary Awards in the Young Adult and Fantasy categories respectively. *Life Shocks Romances*, Jade's sweet and sexy contemporary romance series, features unlikely romances you will root for and happy endings you can believe in. They prove that, at the very least, she knows how to alphabetize books.

Jade's latest completed series involve mer-folk with Daughters of Air and Lord of the Ocean available as box sets. Visit her website to subscribe to her ongoing Confessions of the Underworld Boater featuring the immortal Charon, Ferryman of the River Styx.

If she sounds busy, it's because she is. Jade writes at 3:00 am when her husband and three sons are asleep, and aspires to make her readers as sleep-deprived as she is.

www.jadekerrion.com

CHARLES A. CORNELL

Charles A Cornell writes speculative fiction ranging from the mysterious to the macabre; blending science fiction, fantasy, alternative history and horror. He is a regular contributor to podcasts, seminars and conferences, and conducts webinars and workshops on his specialty, retro-punk fiction (Steampunk, Dieselpunk).

Charles lives in a rural English village in Lincolnshire with his wife and ginger tabby. His first published novel, *Tiger Paw*, won the 2012 Royal Palm Literary Award for Best Thriller from the Florida Writers Association.

His dieselpunk work, *DragonFly* is a retro-futuristic collision of science fiction and fantasy with a generous dash of alternative history. *DragonFly* won a 2014 Royal Palm Literary Award Bronze Medal in Science Fiction, received two prestigious Reader's Favorite Five Star Reviews, and won the 2018 Reader's Favorite Silver Medal in the Young Adult - Action category.

Charles's short stories and novellas have appeared in the anthologies, *The Prometheus Saga*, *Return To Earth*, and *In Shadows Written*. His Prometheus Saga science fiction stories "Crystal Night" and "The Orchid Man" have both won FWA Royal Palm Literary Award Gold Medals (2016, 2018). Visit him at CharlesACornell.com for news on his latest publications, writing projects, author signings, promotions, and giveaways; and for musings on dieselpunk and retrofuturism. Also check out his world of Steampunk at SteampunkNovels.com and the DragonFly series at DragonFly-Novels.com featuring galleries of retrofuturistic aircraft and other illustrations from DragonFly.

www.CharlesACornell.Com
www.SteampunkNovels.com
www.DragonFly-Novels.com

KEN PELHAM

Ken Pelham's debut novel, *Brigands Key*, winner of the 2009 Royal Palm Literary Award, was published in hardcover in 2012, in softcover in 2014, and in audiobook in 2015. The prequel, *Place of Fear*, a 2012 first-place winner of the Royal Palm, was released in 2013. A short story, "The Wreck of the Edinburgh Kate," garnered a second-place award in 2014. Another, "When the Hurly Burly's Done," won a Silver award in 2019.

His book on the craft of writing, *Out of Sight, Out of Mind: A Writer's Guide to Mastering Viewpoint*, won the Florida Writers Association's highest award—2015 Published Book of the Year—and has been translated into Italian, Spanish, and Portuguese.

Ken grew up in the small South Florida town of Immokalee, and lives with his wife, Laura, in Maitland, Florida. A member of International Thriller Writers and the Florida Writers Association, he's sometimes spotted cycling, fishing, or scuba diving, seldom simultaneously.

NOVELS
Brigands Key
Place of Fear

NONFICTION BOOKS
Out of Sight, Out of Mind: A Writer's Guide to Mastering Viewpoint
Great Danger: A Writer's Guide to Building Suspense
Gumshoes, Fangs, Rockets, and Spies: How Literary Genres Evolve and Change Our World

SHORT STORY COLLECTIONS
Treacherous Bastards: Stories of Suspense, Deceit, and Skullduggery
A Double Shot of Fright: Two Tales of Terror
Tales of Old Brigands Key
Borderlands: Tales of Mystery and Imagination

www.kenpelham.com

KRISTIN DURFEE

Kristin Durfee grew up outside of Philadelphia where an initial struggle with reading blossomed into a love and passion for the written word. She currently resides outside of Orlando, Florida, and when not enjoying the theme parks or Florida sun, she spends most of her time with her husband, son, and their two quirky dogs.

NOVELETTES

Revenge From Within (The Hunt 2 Suspense Anthology)
Project Bright Star (Return to Earth Anthology)
The Lottery (The Masters Reimagined Anthology)
Highball (The Prometheus Saga 2 Anthology)
Revenge From Within (The Hunted Anthology)

NOVELS

Four Corners — Four Corners Trilogy Book 1
Two Worlds — Four Corners Trilogy Book 2
One Earth — Four Corners Trilogy Book 3
Mass

SHORT STORIES

Baking Cookies for the End of the World (The Light Fantastic Anthology)
Briar Rose (Sleeping Beauty) (Fairy Tales the Sequel Anthology)

www.kristindurfee.com

JOHN HOPE

John Hope is an award-winning short story, children's, middle grade, young adult, and nonfiction history writer, including authoring the Amazon best seller *Silencing Sharks*. An active member of the Florida Writers Association and winner of the 2018 Kaye Coppersmith Award for exemplifying FWA's mission of writers helping writers, he conducts workshops/school visits on a regular basis, providing entertaining and educational presentations to inspire writers of all ages.

CHILDREN'S PICTURE BOOKS
*Frozen Floppies** — Story of Unlikely Friendships
Floppyopolis—Story of Taking Pride in the Community
Watch the Butterfly—Story of Learning Patience
The Band Aid—Story of Understanding/Dealing with Grief
MIDDLE GRADE / YOUNG ADULT
Father's Violin—Historical Fiction Story of Heroism and Survival
*Fairy Tales, the Sequel**—Fantasy Stories that Expand Classic Fairy Tales
*Silencing Sharks**—Fantasy/Adventure Story of Heroism
*No Good**—Historical Fiction Story of Acceptance
*Secret Adventures of Foxfire**—Story of Friendship and Loss
*Pankyland**—Adventure Story of Friendship
Pankyland 2: The Movie—Adventure Story of Sibling Rivalry
Pankyland 3: Be Little World—Adventure Story of Friendship
BOOKS FOR ADULTS
*Colby in the Crosshairs**—*Poignant Story of Child Abuse*
John's Shorts Vol 1 & 2**—Collections of Short Stories
Lake Mary, Images of America—History of a Small Town
Everybody Dies—Humorous Farce Picture Book About Death
Everybody's Offensive—Humorous Farce Picture Book About Political Correctness
* Indicates winner of one or more awards

www.johnhopewriting.com

BRIA BURTON

Bria Burton's short fiction has appeared in over twenty anthologies and magazines, including Royal Palm Literary Award winners. She's married with one son and two pets. At St. Pete Running Company, she writes blogs and web content.

NOVELS
The Running Girls
Little Angel Helper
Lance & Ringo Tails

SHORT STORY PUBLICATIONS

"The Bloodiest Sword is King" – *Havok Magazine*
"Journey Into the Dying Light of Stars" – *Journey Into podcast*
"Her Midnight Ride" – *The Prometheus Saga Vol. 2*
"The Count of the Alician Apocalypse" – *The Masters Reimagined*
"AOB" – *Return to Earth*
"Empty Girl" – *Revisions: Stories of Starting Over (FWA Collection)*
"A Dream Within A Dream" – *In Shadows Written*
"The Mute Girl" – *Youth Imagination*
"Maribel's Day of Death" – *About Time*
"Tight Pants" – *Page & Spine*
"Ticket to Heaven" – *Faith, Hope, & Fiction*
"The Price of Integrity" – *It's a Crime (FWA Collection)*
"The Wheels Must Turn" – *Broken Worlds*
"On Both Sides" – *The Prometheus Saga*
"In Line at the DMYV" – *Welcome to the Future*
"The Darkness Below" – *The Colored Lens*
"Switching" – *The Dunesteef Audio Fiction Magazine*
"Ligeia" – *Journey Into podcast*
"Ma Says" – *Let's Talk (FWA Collection)*
"This is Hollywood" – *FICTION on the WEB*

www.briaburton.com

VERONICA H. HART

Veronica lives with her retired veterinarian/author husband, Robert, in Ormond Beach, Florida. They settled there after spending the major part of their lives traveling, living, and working in various areas of the world. Between them, they have six daughters and eleven grandchildren who keep their minds active trying to remember birthdays and anniversaries.

NOVELS
The Prince of Keegan Bay *– Blenders Book I
The Swimming Corpse – Blenders Book II
Safari Stew – Blenders Book III
Midnight in Mongolia – Blenders Book IV
A Wedding at Keegan Bay – Blenders Book V
The Knife
Boy Comes Home
Silent Autumn *
Escape from Iran *
Elena – the Girl with the Piano *
The Reluctant Daughters

SHORT STORY PUBLICATIONS
All of the following are in the Florida Writers Association Collections:
"Larry and the Cat" – *From Our Family to Yours,* 2009
"Standoff in the Alborz Mountains" – Slices of Life, 2010
"The Anniversary Dinner" – *It's a Crime* , 2013
"The Suitcase" – *The First Step,* 2014
"Poisonberry Wine" – *Revisions,* 2015
"Margaret Barnes" – *Hide and Seek,* 2016
* Winner of one or more awards

www.veronicahhart.com

ELLE ANDREWS PATT

Elle Andrews Patt writes speculative fiction. She's received recognition for her work from Writers of The Future, the National Indie Excellence Awards, the Silver Falchion Award, and the Royal Palm Literary Awards. When she's not writing, Elle can be found mucking stalls and working her day job in telecommunications and digital marketing.

NOVELS
Ghost – Andrea Kelley Mystery I
Spirit – Andrea Kelley Mystery II
Wraith – Andrea Kelley Mystery III

NOVELETTES
Manteo — *The Prometheus Saga* Anthology
Someday Loyal — *Return To Earth* Anthology
Regarding Mr. Bulkington — *The Masters Reimagined*
Remuda — *The Prometheus Saga 2*
Missing: Prelude To A Murder Conviction (Dark Fuse Magazine)
Among The Blue Horses — *The Masters Reimagined 2*

SHORT STORY PUBLICATIONS
"Karl's Last Night – *The Rag Literary Magazine*
"Becky's Story" – *Saw Palm: Florida Literature*
"The Legend of Johnny Bell" –*Solarcide Anthology*
"Coming of Age" – FWA Collection #6- *First Steps*
"Skinned" - *Summer of Sci-fi and Fantasy I*

www.elleandrewspatt.com

THE ALVARIUM EXPERIMENT
ANTHOLOGIES

THE LIGHT FANTASTIC

RETURN TO EARTH

THE MASTERS REIMAGINED

THE MASTERS REIMAGINED 2

THE PROMETHEUS SAGA

THE PROMETHEUS SAGA 2

www.ingramcontent.com/pod-product-compliance
Lightning Source LLC
Chambersburg PA
CBHW020231260626
47156CB00002B/626